Praise for Rebecca Chance

'A bright new star in blockbusters, Rebecca Chance's
Divas sizzles with glamour, romance and revenge.
Unputdownable. A glittering page-turner, this debut
had me hooked from the first page'
LOUISE BAGSHAWE

'I laughed, I cried, I very nearly choked. Just brilliant!
This has to be the holiday read of the year. Rebecca
Chance's debut will bring colour to your cheeks even
if the credit crunch means you're reading it in
Bognor rather than the Balearics'
OLIVIA DARLING

'Glitzy, hedonistic and scandalous, this compelling
read is a real page-turner'
CLOSER

'A fun, frivolous read'
SUN

Also by Rebecca Chance

Divas
Bad Girls

BAD SISTERS

Rebecca
CHANCE

SIMON &
SCHUSTER

London · New York · Sydney · Toronto

A CBS COMPANY

First published in Great Britain by Simon and Schuster, 2011
A CBS Company

3 5 7 9 10 8 6 4 2

Simon & Schuster UK Ltd
1st Floor
222 Gray's Inn Road
London
WC1X 8HB

www.simonandschuster.co.uk

Simon & Schuster Australia
Sydney

A CIP catalogue record for this book is available from the British Library

ISBN 978-0-85720-483-7

Typeset by Hewer Text UK Ltd, Edinburgh
Printed and bound in Great Britain by Cox & Wyman,
Reading, Berkshire RG1 8EX

For all the good sisters out there (and some of the bad ones)

Acknowledgements

Big, big heartfelt thanks to:

— Maxine, Libby, and everyone at Simon and Schuster who are working so hard to make these books raving successes, to design covers that pop off the shelves, and to market the living daylights out of them. I couldn't be in better hands and am hugely grateful. And to Anthony, my agent, and everyone at David Higham, who work just as hard on my behalf, and always make me feel like the only client they have;

— the real Matt Bates, who's been Rebecca Chance's greatest supporter ever since the first book, and is just as gorgeous as his namesake (though more in the Will Young than Danny Cipriani style of good looks);

— Katharine Walsh, gorgeous pouting blond PR girl supreme, raccoon-fur coat and all, who's enough of a Rebecca Chance heroine to deserve a whole book of her own – one day!

— everyone at the Grand Jersey Hotel, who took such good care of us while we were visiting for research purposes;

— Jason Phillips and Bethany Russell at Franco's, who looked after us wonderfully at our research dinner. It's completely our fault that we were heavy-headed the next day from the double grappas and moscati . . .

Prologue
Riseholme, UK

1993

*T*he three girls huddled together, looking down at the body of an unconscious man. He was slumped on the ugly, threadbare brown carpet tiles in an awkward heap, his face to the ground. And he wasn't moving.

'Is he dead?' breathed 9-year-old Deeley McKenna, her dark eyes huge with shock. She bent down as if to touch him, then flinched at the last moment, pulling her hand back.

'He isn't supposed to be dead!' Devon exclaimed in panic. She was thirteen and trying valiantly to seem poised, as befitted a new teenager, but it was the flimsiest of facades: she was as horrified as Deeley at what they had just done.

'He deserves whatever he gets,' Maxie, the oldest of the three, said grimly, her jaw set hard.

'How do we tell if he's dead?' Devon asked, pushing her hair back from her face.

It was immediately obvious that the three of them were sisters. They had the same heart-shaped faces, the same thick dark hair growing back from widow's peaks, the same big dark eyes and full, pink lips, the same smooth, creamy skin. Devon, the middle sister, was already a beauty, with her curvy figure and wide, photogenic cheekbones.

'I read in a book you can hold a hand mirror to someone's mouth to see if they're still breathing,' suggested Maxie, always practical.

But none of the girls moved to follow up this suggestion. Instead, Deeley's small hand slipped into Maxie's, reaching for comfort from her beloved big sister. Maxie had always been like a mother to her younger siblings who looked up to her with absolute trust and love. Now Deeley's pretty, round baby face was pinched with fear, and she clung to Maxie, her one rock of certainty in a terrifyingly unstable world.

'I'm scared, Maxie,' she said in a tiny voice. 'I'm really scared. We didn't mean him to be dead, did we?'

'Don't worry, Deels,' Maxie said, squeezing her little sister's hand tight. 'It'll be all right. I've thought of everything.'

With stronger features than her sisters, Maxie was striking rather than beautiful. And at seventeen, she already looked like a woman, tall and confident. It was no wonder Deeley and Devon followed wherever she led.

'Shall I get a mirror, then?' Devon asked eventually. 'To, you know, check if he's . . .'

She trailed off, unable to finish the sentence. Maxie shivered despite herself.

'I suppose it'd be better than checking his pulse,' she said.

'He was so nice!' Deeley blurted out, tears beginning to well up in her huge brown eyes. 'He always read me a bedtime story . . . and he bought me the bike for my birthday, the one I'd wanted for ages and ages, from the Argos catalogue, brand new, with the basket and everything . . . and he was teaching me how to ride it . . .'

'Deeley!' Maxie snapped. 'You know what he did!'

'I'm sorry, Maxie . . .' Deeley was sobbing now. 'Don't be cross, please don't be cross . . .'

She threw herself against her big sister, wrapping her arms tightly around Maxie's waist, clinging to her like a limpet.

'Don't snap at her, Max,' Devon said quickly. 'She didn't mean anything by it.'

'I know,' Maxie said, stroking her little sister's glossy dark hair from the crown to the two thick plaits she had carefully done herself that morning. Deeley was still clinging to her as desperately as ivy twined round a tree, unable to stand up on its own.

Maxie reached out her other hand to Devon, who took two quick steps around the prone body on the floor to wind her fingers through Maxie's.

'We're in this together,' Maxie said firmly, her voice strong. 'All for one and one for all. Like we agreed. OK?'

'Yes, Maxie,' Deeley mumbled into her sister's cheap acrylic sweater, which was now damp with her tears.

'Yes, Maxie,' Devon said, swallowing hard.

'We'll do whatever we need to do to keep ourselves safe,' Maxie said. 'That's the most important thing. We're sisters. We stick together. That's what sisters do.'

Deeley loosened her grip and pulled back to look up at her big sisters, her round cheeks pink and tear-stained, but her face still deliciously pretty.

'We do stick together,' she said fervently. 'Always. Promise?' She darted her stare urgently back and forth between Maxie and Devon, her expression serious. 'Promise!' she insisted.

'Promise,' Devon said, smiling, despite the desperate crisis, at her baby sister's childish plea.

'Promise,' Maxie echoed. 'And you both have to promise never to tell anyone about what we did today. Whatever happens.'

Deeley held up two fingers and drew them over her throat, her eyes wide with resolve as she said, 'Cross my heart and hope to die, Maxie. I promise.'

Devon nodded as Maxie continued, staring now at the body lying on the floor.

'Whatever happens.'

Part One
Eighteen years later

Deeley

This is the life, Deeley thought, stretching out her long, long legs on the lounger till her toes were dangling off the end. She was pleasantly tired from her Pilates session that morning, a dynamic workout on the Reformer followed by roll-downs on the Tower that had left her back feeling almost as great as it had from the hot stone massage the day before. Carefully, she turned over, making sure her toes didn't touch the lounger; she'd just had her nails done, and not only did she want to avoid smudging them, but Nicky would throw a fit if she got hot pink nail polish on the white towelling fabric that covered the lounger. He was ridiculously fussy that way.

Warm sunlight licked along her back; deliciously relaxing, it was like being bathed in liquid gold. Deeley was careful not to sunbathe at the height of the day, and to always use factor 30 sunblock. You couldn't live in LA without having a dermatologist, and you couldn't have a dermatologist in LA without being lectured constantly about the damage the sun did to your skin, especially when you were as naturally pale as Deeley. But it felt so lovely to a girl who'd spent the first twenty-two years of her life in cold, rainy Britain that Deeley couldn't resist slipping out after four in the afternoon, when the sun was lower in the sky, to soak up some rays and zone out, completely de-stressing.

Because my life is so stressful, of course! she thought, self-aware enough to tease herself. *No one knows how hard I have it!*

Squinting through the dark lenses of her YSL sunglasses, she looked across the glittering blue water of the infinity pool to the glass-walled house beyond, its low structure wrapped around two sides of the swimming pool. Juan, the pool boy, was desultorily fishing a few floating leaves out of the water. Through the open sliding glass door, Deeley could make out the lean figure of her boyfriend Nicky. Wearing a snug white t-shirt and HOM briefs, he was sprawled in a leather armchair, fingers splayed on the armrests, as the manicurist who had just painted Deeley's nails sat on a footstool below him, painstakingly working almond oil into his cuticles.

Big night tonight, Deeley reflected happily. *We both need to look perfect.*

'Deeley, hon?'

Randie, Nicky's assistant, pushed open the door a little further, stepping out onto the terrace. Like most women who worked as assistants to celebrities, Randie was a little overweight by LA standards, and frumpily dressed: the first rule of her job was never to upstage her employer – or his girlfriend. Her loose chinos and baggy Gap t-shirt indicated that she was much too busy organizing all the myriad details of Nicky and Deeley's hugely important lives to take any trouble with her own appearance.

'Hey,' Deeley said, raising her head a little and smiling at Randie.

Randie flashed her a bright smile, showing no hint of resentment that Deeley was sunbathing blissfully, a tiny pink Hello Kitty bikini bottom the only item of clothing on her perfect, lightly tanned body, while Randie was hard at work, a BlackBerry in one hand, another phone wedged between her shoulder and her ear, her slightly sweaty forehead furrowed in concentration.

'Just FYI,' Randie said, clicking away at the BlackBerry, 'Serita'll be here in an hour or so to finalize Nicky's outfit for tonight, OK? And then she'll come over and dress you. Plus, I managed to snag Hervé to come do your hair and make-up – how cool is that!'

Hervé was one of LA's top make-up artists, always in demand.

'He's booked solid, so he won't have much time, but it's huge that he's coming at all, right?' Randie was beaming with her success.

'Fab!' Deeley sat up, not bothering to cover her high, firm breasts with her hands. 'Hervé always makes me look amazing!'

Deeley pictured the silver-sequinned vintage Cardin sheath that Serita, their stylist, had picked out for her. Wrist-length sleeves and a stratospherically short hem, putting her long, gloriously slim legs on display. Serita had chosen Marc Jacobs gold platform slingbacks to go with the dress; she loved to mix up her metals. Just imagining how great she'd look in the photos, Deeley beamed complacently.

'Great! So everyone's in the loop!' Randie pivoted with a rubber squeak of her practical Converse trainers and darted back inside the house again, another item ticked off her long list.

Deeley heaved a deep sigh of contentment, swinging her legs, contemplating the perfect shine on her toenails and the flex of lean muscle in her calves. She was at her peak, she knew: old enough to work a red carpet with total confidence, dressed to the nines, and young enough to be able to wear even the craziest, most fashion-forward outfit a stylist chose for her. And that was crucial, because as the girlfriend of Nicky Shore, the latest, hottest male TV star, it was Deeley's job to make it into the weekly fashion round-ups in the gossip magazines. If at least one photo of Deeley smiling gloriously at the cameras on Nicky's arm didn't make it into *InTouch*, *US Weekly* or *Star* on a weekly basis, Carmen, Nicky's publicist, would rip Deeley a new one.

Juan, the pool boy, had put down his leaf-catching net and was squatting by the side of the pool, dipping in the thermometer to test that the water was at the perfect temperature. His white trousers pulled over his buttocks, showing off their round, firm contours, and making it very clear that he wasn't wearing any underwear. His bicep, swelling the sleeve of his tight white t-shirt, flexed as he lifted the thermometer from the water, turning it to take a reading. Sensing her eyes on him, he swivelled slightly, turning to glance over his shoulder, his dark slanting eyes meeting hers for a brief moment before he looked back at the thermometer again.

Deeley watched from the lounger as Juan stood up, stretching out his solid, muscled back, walking over to the shed where the pool equipment was kept. Juan was built like a fireplug: square, every inch of him stocky, solid muscle. And Deeley had a big thing about muscles.

She made just enough noise standing up from the lounger, slipping on her Hawaiiana flip-flops, so that out of the corner of her eye she saw Juan pause, turn, and watch her as she picked up her towel, slinging it over her shoulder, walking bare-breasted round the pool, flicking her fingers in a wave at Nicky through the glass doors as she went. He lifted the hand the manicurist wasn't working on, flashing her his adorably sweet smile even as he said something to his trainer, Sean, who was busy at the marble kitchen counter, loading carrots and spinach into the big white juicer.

'Want one?' Nicky called, nodding at the juicer.

'No thanks,' Deeley called back, smiling at Sean as she passed, heading for the far side of the pool and the long sprawling extension to the house, separate but equally luxurious. She paused as she reached the sliding glass door, her hand on the latch, making eye contact, making sure that her message was clearly received and understood, then she pushed the door open and stepped over the threshold, kicking off her flip-flops, throwing her towel on the slate floor, and heading for the Italian-mosaic bathroom, a riot of tiny pink-and-gold glittering tiles and gilt-framed mirrors.

It had been almost five years living in the height of luxury in LA, and Deeley still couldn't get over how amazing American water pressure was. The huge rainforest shower poured down like a tropical storm and she was drenched within a couple of seconds of stepping under it. She took a bottle of Pucci bath oil from the glass shelf, uncapped the stopper and poured some over her shoulders, the green floral scent perfect for her mood, for a golden LA afternoon. Deeley closed her eyes, the water cooling her sun-warmed skin, breathing in the perfumed oil, smiling to herself.

And when she opened them again, Juan was standing in the doorway.

The bedroom was thickly carpeted, and he was in deck shoes – even without the shower beating down on her, Deeley wouldn't have heard his approach. Blinking the water out of her eyes, she took a step forward, letting the full force of the drops pound like a massage on her shoulders. She raised her hands and pushed back her heavy hair, the weight of it settling down her bare spine. And then she met Juan's stare full on.

His dark eyes were slitted as he looked her up and down. Juan's face might have been hacked roughly out of sandstone. His features were as blunt and solid as his body, entirely expressionless. Deeley's gaze dropped below his waist and she noticed with approval that at least his body was showing its appreciation; through the tight white trousers, his cock was fully erect, pointing at her as best it could, fighting with the thin layer of fabric.

She took one more step forward, and that was all it took. Raising her eyebrows, she hooked her thumbs into her bikini bottoms and lowered them a half-inch, her eyes fixed on Juan's, challenging him now. With one quick movement, Juan dropped to his knees in front of her, his hands reaching for the ties of her bikini and flicking them undone, his mouth hot between her legs as the bikini bottom fell to the floor. He had been out in the sun all day, and was warm to the core. His hands came up to grip her buttocks, to pull them further towards him, tilt her to his mouth, equally hot against her skin, and Deeley moaned out loud as his tongue started to flick against her, tracing around her, closing in slowly but surely exactly where she wanted it. Her moans rose in volume as he closed his jaw, never stopping the constant motion of his tongue.

She flung her arms above her head as if she were reaching for something, but there was nothing for her fingers to grasp; the walk-in shower was huge, and there was no way she could touch the tiled walls. Instead, her uplifted hands met the full force of the shower, water cascading from the tips of her fingers down her arms, over her breasts, onto her flat stomach as she bucked and heaved against Juan's mouth, his tongue, fighting to get where she wanted, where he was inevitably taking her, the shower so loud that its steady downpour drowned out the ever increasing noise she was making, the screams that reached their climax as she did, coming again and again. Juan's thickly muscled arms were more than strong enough to hold her, stop her slipping on the tiled floor as the orgasms hit her in swift succession, rippling her body into an arched bow. She drove her pelvis into Juan's mouth in quick frenzied beats, determined to wrench every last moment of pleasure, until her legs gave way completely and, gasping, she collapsed against him.

Deeley's eyes were closed, her body throbbing with the aftermath of her orgasms, and as Juan pushed himself to stand up, she was hanging over his shoulder. He didn't bother to switch off the shower; he carried her into the bedroom, threw her down on the bed, where she landed starfished out, her eyes still shut. Deftly he rummaged in the drawer of the bedside table and pulled out a condom. Deeley heard his zipper being dragged down, his trousers being kicked off along with his shoes, the condom wrapper being torn open, and she braced herself. What had just happened had been all about her.

What was about to happen would be all about Juan.

She was so wet from his mouth and from her multiple orgasms that Juan's hard cock slid right into her in one stroke, provoking the first sound she'd heard him make that afternoon: a deep grunt of primitive male satisfaction. And then he was pounding away at her in a fast, frantic rhythm. Deeley opened her eyes; he was above her, arms braced on either side of her, the dark curls low on his bull-like forehead dampening with sweat as he worked away, his lips drawing back from his teeth in a grimace, his thick stocky torso thudding into her as he worked himself to his own orgasm. No variation of stroke or speed, no sophisticated techniques, just a machine-like piston stroke, slamming into Deeley again and again and again as she lay there, spread wide for him, knowing that nothing was expected from her. No participation, no moans of encouragement, though she was gasping deep in her throat with every stroke.

He was almost there, Deeley could tell; his strokes weren't speeding up, but his grunts were growing louder, his cock swelling as he worked away at her. His upper lip curled into a sneer as he finally froze for a split second, juddered against her, and let out a long groan of satisfaction as he spilled himself. Deeley felt his cock jerking inside her and closed her eyes to let the full delicious final rush of sensations flood through her, her own body throbbing in response to his.

It was through a haze that she felt Juan kneeling back, carefully pulling himself, plus condom, out of her, and padding into the bathroom to dispose of it. Still in a haze, she felt the creak of the mattress as he sat down heavily on the side of the bed to pull on his trousers and shoes.

He didn't even bother to take his socks off, she thought, smiling to herself. *Pretty much the definition of a quickie.*

Juan stood up, looking down at her. She opened her eyes fully, still smiling, and fluttered her fingers at him as a goodbye; he nodded at her in return, one swift acknowledgement of what they had just done, his face once again impassive. This was the most communication she and Juan ever had during one of their encounters; from the first time onwards, they'd barely exchanged a word during or after, being much too busy concentrating on the act itself. Smoothing down his t-shirt, he walked briskly from the bedroom. She heard him slide the glass door shut, considerate of her nakedness.

Dreamily, Deeley rolled over on her front, savouring the aftermath, her nerve endings still shimmering with pleasure.

That was such a good call – the best beauty treatment is really great sex. I'm going to look amazing in the photographs tonight . . .

'You got laid, didn't you?' Hervé challenged her, his eyebrows shooting up as he swivelled her chair till her face was fully in the light. 'You little slut! You totally got laid today! Don't lie to me, sugar. I can always tell.'

Deeley smirked as Hervé plonked his huge make-up travel case on her dressing table and plugged in his heated rollers.

'It does half your work for you,' she pointed out. 'You shouldn't complain.'

'Oh, I'm not complaining,' Hervé said. 'I'm just *jealous*. You're glowing like a nuclear reactor.'

He looked over his shoulder at Serita, who was bustling in with a garment bag over her arm and a Samsonite pull-case containing the shoes and jewellery she'd picked out for Deeley.

'Serita, angel? Hair thoughts?'

'Down, down, down,' Serita said in her breathy baby voice. '*Cascading* down the back, super-simple but with lots of body. Like she did a hair commercial and then fucked the director.'

'Don't say another word,' Hervé said happily. 'I *totally* get it.'

Serita was extracting the silver Cardin dress from the garment bag as worshipfully as if it were a just-discovered Old Master painting. She laid it on the bed and stood back to survey it, clasping her heavily ringed hands at her bony ribcage.

'To *die* for!' she sighed. 'I mean, *completely*!'

'Oh, that's *gorgeous*,' Hervé agreed, patting base carefully onto Deeley's face.

'She's got such a lovely figure,' Serita said, looking over at Deeley in her silk kimono wrap. 'I mean, she's not exactly skinny – forget sample sizes for this one! But she's *perfectly* in proportion. The tiny waist! And those boobs! I love dressing those boobs! I mean, I'd hate to have to do it all the time, but every so often, it's so much fun!' Serita concluded happily. 'It's like picking out clothes for a gigantic Barbie!'

'*Tits and ass can change your life. They sure . . . changed . . . mine!*' Hervé warbled playfully.

'*A Chorus Line*,' Serita said, setting a gigantic bangle and a pair of diamond earrings on the dressing table. 'I love that movie.'

During her first months in LA, Deeley had been totally thrown by the way stylists, make-up artists and personal trainers talked about their clients as if they weren't even present. Now she was so accustomed to it that she didn't blink an eye. Which was useful, because Hervé was presently employed in gluing individual lashes to her lids to transform her already naturally thick eyelashes into a miracle of nature.

To hear Serita and Hervé talk, Deeley reflected, you'd think that she was a plus-size model, instead of five foot eight and an English size 10. Though mind you, nowadays that probably *would* make her a plus-size model, she thought, amused. By contrast, Serita was so skinny that her chest, shown off by the low V of her neckline, looked like a slatted window blind.

'But you know, this is what straight men like,' Hervé said, finishing his eyelash application and standing back, squinting, to make sure they were even. He gestured at Deeley's body. 'Tits and ass. All the married guys in LA cheat on their skinny wives with pole dancers with some meat on them. And she's perfect for Nicky!' Hervé added cheerfully, starting to wind Deeley's hair around the rollers. 'How hetero does a man look with this on his arm? I mean, she's like some life-size blow-up doll!'

Serita, kneeling in front of Deeley, strapping on the gold platform slingbacks, giggled madly.

Though Deeley might not particularly relish being compared to a blow-up doll, when she was finally allowed to see herself in the full-length mirror, she had to admit that Serita and Hervé had done her up in a way that belied their words. The silver dress, fitted to hug every curve, clung to her like a lover; Serita's styling genius meant that the dress, though sexy, managed to avoid being vulgar. The sequins slid over Deeley with a dull sheen echoed in the soft gold of the high heels and the antique bangle; diamond studs glittered in the thick waves of Deeley's hair, which an artful colourist had lightened to a rich deep caramel. Her dark eyes looked huge, and, to tone down too much overt sexiness, Hervé had cleverly painted her lips a subtle shade of golden coral.

'Wow,' Nicky said from the doorway. 'You look brilliant, Deels!'

Deeley pivoted elegantly on her heel, flicking her hair back, one hand on her hip, facing her boyfriend. In a light grey Tom Ford suit, so snug at the waist that only a lean gym obsessive could wear it, buttoned over a white silk shirt, Nicky was handsome enough to take anyone's breath away. His tan set off his tight gold curls and bright blue eyes, and his smile was heart-melting. The icing on the cake was that the smile was genuine; he really was as nice, sweet and gentle as he appeared. Deeley beamed back at him in utter contentment at her good luck.

'Love you, Nicky,' she said happily.

'You too, babe,' he said fondly.

'Oh my *God*,' Sean, Nicky's trainer, exclaimed, appearing behind Nicky. He slung one arm around Nicky's shoulder, looking Deeley up and down. 'Deeley! You're sex on a stick!'

'Well, got to bustle!' Serita said, nipping out of Deeley's bedroom, pausing to kiss Nicky on the lips as she went. '*Too* fabulous, both of you. I could kill myself now and die happy.'

'Remember to touch up the lippy in the limo,' Hervé reminded Deeley, as he packed up the last of his equipment. He winked at Sean and Nicky on the way out, his heavy make-up case bumping over the metal of the door frame.

'And you two – stay pretty, OK?' he added appreciatively.

'Aww,' Sean cooed, planting a big kiss on his lover's full pink lips. 'He will if I have anything to do with it!'

'He's a sodding slave-driver,' Nicky sighed. 'I was running up and down the stairs at the Hollywood Bowl all morning! And the bastard made me do all sorts of things this afternoon—'

'Oh, I just bet he did,' Hervé tossed over his shoulder as he trundled his case around the swimming pool. 'Careful, hon! That stuff's *packed* with calories, you know . . .'

Deeley, Sean and Nicky cracked up at this perfect exit line.

'Hervé's a trip,' Sean said, grinning widely.

'And he's not completely wrong, is he?' Nicky said flirtatiously, sliding his hand down to squeeze Sean's bottom.

'Oh, please! No kissing and telling!' Sean squealed as Nicky pinched him.

'*Hello*.' Nicky rolled his eyes. 'What do you think Juan was doing in Deeley's place this afternoon? Taking the temperature of her bathwater?'

'God, Deeley, you lucky thing,' Sean said enviously. 'Dirty pool boy sex. Yum yum.'

'I have to get it somewhere,' Deeley pointed out, turning to check herself out in the mirror again. 'I mean, it's not like my boyfriend's going to give me one any time soon, is it?'

'I hope not!' Sean giggled.

'Oh, darling, I think you're safe there,' Nicky said, wrapping his arm round Sean's waist. 'I mean, if I've had Deeley across the way for five years and haven't laid a finger on her yet, I'm not exactly going to be consumed with mad passion for her now, am I?'

Sean grinned at Deeley, his perfect teeth white against his warm brown skin. 'Nah,' he said cheerfully. 'If you're not getting a hard-on looking at her all dressed up like that, I'd say you're 100 per cent homo.'

'Ssh!' Nicky lifted a finger to his lips. 'Stop it! We're off to the Dyslexic Teen Aids benefit in an hour, and I have to put my best hetero face on! Let's go have a glass of champagne. It always helps me lose my inhibitions and grope Deeley on the red carpet.'

'Vodka and diet soda,' Sean said sternly. 'Champagne has too many carbs.'

'Ah, *fuck*,' Nicky sighed, as a voluptuous raven-haired woman in a red silk sheath and four-inch spike heels stalked into the room.

'Lovely way to say hi, Nicky,' she said.

'Carmen, you know I wasn't . . .' Nicky started nervously. Everyone in Hollywood was intimidated by Carmen Delgado, publicist to the stars and iron hand in the most elegant of iron gloves.

'I was joking, pretty boy,' Carmen said, raising her perfectly plucked eyebrows at him. 'When I'm cross with you, believe me, you'll know.'

Carmen took in Deeley in her silver-and-gold glory and her red-lipsticked mouth pursed into a whistle of approval.

'Very hot,' she commented. 'Serita and Hervé do earn their money.'

'*Really*,' Sean gushed, only to have Carmen swivel and fix him with a steely stare, making it more than clear, without speaking a word, that the opinion of a personal trainer weighed with her about as much as that of a tabloid journalist.

'I need a moment here, OK?' Carmen said.

'With me?' Deeley said, taken aback.

She barely had any dealings with Carmen now, apart from the odd briefing session where Deeley was summoned to hear Carmen's feedback on how she was coming across in the press. In the beginning, when Deeley and Nicky had first moved to LA, Nicky, as the star of a much-hyped new series, had hired Carmen to manage his image, and Carmen had been at the house all the time. Coaching Nicky on how to handle the press. Restyling him into something less 'English poof', as she charmingly put it, and more US-friendly. And working out a whole backstory for him and Deeley – how they met, how long they'd been together, what their plans for the future were.

It had been a fairy story for Deeley. She'd met Nicky in London a year before they came to LA, that much was true. But, contrary to their meet-cute version of events (Nicky had seen her walking in a London park, picked some flowers and given them to her in tribute to her beauty, then begged her for a date) they'd actually bumped into each other on the dance floor at GAY. They'd happily bumped and ground for the rest of the night, swapped numbers and been friends and fellow clubbers ever since. Nicky was a struggling actor, with some decent stage and TV work on his CV, but desperate for his big break. He'd been over to LA for pilot season the year before, acquired an agent, even shot a pilot, but nothing had seemed to come of it, and he'd returned to London, dispirited.

And then the miracle happened: Nicky's pilot had killed with the focus groups. He played a sexy chef-cum-private detective, who had a different gorgeous love interest each episode, but whose real passion was for his Siamese cat Mitzi. Originally turned down by straight male studio execs, the pilot had been picked up by a female one who had immediately seen Nicky's appeal. And now, five years later, *Cooking up Murder* was a smash hit; it was going into syndication, which meant untold riches for everyone associated with it.

Nicky couldn't have known, of course, how big *Cooking up Murder* was going to be. But he had panicked at the thought of hiding his sexuality all alone in LA, knowing there was no way the public would accept an unknown gay actor as the latest TV heart-throb. So he had turned to his friend Deeley, who photographed like a dream, and as Serita and Hervé had just said, with her killer curves, would make any man by her side look like the most red-blooded of heterosexuals.

Carmen, all business, had promptly applauded Nicky's good sense and drawn up a contract for Deeley to sign. An initial bonus, bed and board, her own car, and a yearly allowance index-linked to Nicky's salary; Deeley had signed it without even reading it through. No way could she be worse off than she had been back in London, living in a crappy shared flat in Acton, waitressing and working as a hostess at trade shows to scrape a living, constantly having to fend off the grop-ing hands of male employers. Well, that was one hazard she certainly wouldn't have in her role as Nicky's devoted girlfriend.

It had been utter bliss. Carmen had told Deeley she needed to lose some weight, and she'd freaked, but Pilates, plus the low-carb eating plan Nicky was on, had melted off some pounds without her even trying, and comments on the online gossip columns were so positive about Nicky's girlfriend having 'real curves' that Carmen had backed off. In interviews, Nicky was usually asked about what he liked in a woman, to which he would blushingly confess that maybe he was old-fashioned, but he loved that Deeley wasn't a stick insect. In fact, he would add – to the delight of the entire female readership – he'd be even happier if she put on a few more pounds.

It was all going absolutely perfectly. And when Nicky had fallen for Sean and moved him into the house, it had been the easiest thing in the world; the success of the Nicky/Deeley love fest had meant that no fan would ever believe that Sean was anything but Nicky's trainer and nutritionist.

So why was Carmen looking at Deeley now as if she were about to fire a bolt pistol into her skull?

Deeley sat down slowly on the chair in front of her dressing table, her legs suddenly feeling weak. Carmen's piercing stare had that effect on people. Strange, because Carmen was a stunningly good-looking woman. But you didn't notice the attractive pattern of a cobra's scales when it reared up in front of you and fixed you with a beady stare.

'So! Five years!' Carmen said, smiling.

The smile's even worse than the stare, Deeley thought nervously.

'Congrats! Job very well done!' Long black earrings glittered in the dark mass of Carmen's curly hair as she paced the room, pulling out a cigarette packet from her diamanté-encrusted Judith Leiber clutch. 'Nicky's straight as a ruler,' she lit her cigarette, '*Cooking up Murder* is still killing in the ratings,' she shoved the packet back into the clutch and took a long drag on her cigarette, '*plus* Nicky's first two features are doing fantastic box office!'

In the summer hiatuses from *Cooking up Murder*, Nicky had taken second lead in an action movie and played the love interest in a Kate Hudson romcom that had had rave reviews. His movie career was well on the way.

'*So . . .*' Carmen pointed her cigarette at Deeley, who flinched back from the glowing point being waved in her face. 'Time to upgrade his personal life. You two have been an item for five years. More than long enough.'

Every muscle in Deeley's body froze.

'Do you mean you want us to get married?' she managed to get out, though she could barely move her lips.

Nicky and she had talked about this in the past. California had a community property divorce law that split everything down the middle, which would be so disadvantageous to Nicky he wouldn't consider it. But they wouldn't have to get married in California; they could elope to Hawaii, say, and make sure that Deeley had signed a cast-iron pre-nup. Deeley had fantasized about it; the dress, the photos, the glamour of it all. They could have IVF kids down the line. She'd thought she would be with Nicky forever; why would he want to swap her for another girl when he, she and Sean all got along so well? Nothing in Deeley's messed-up childhood had given her any belief in true love or lasting relationships. Being settled with her lovely Nicky, cocooned in luxury, her only job to look beautiful at premieres and parties, was a far better life than she had ever thought she could achieve.

And Deeley knew that Nicky wouldn't come out, not as long as he had any kind of viable acting career. Other actors might be doing it, but not Nicky. Being a star was more important to him, and you wouldn't make it to the A-list as an out gay man. Not yet, anyway.

Carmen's expression changed. To Deeley's absolute horror, Carmen looked . . . *pitying.*

'Oh, sweetie, no,' Carmen said, rolling her eyes. 'No, no, no. Look, you have a killer face and body – I suppose you don't need brains as well, do you?'

Deeley bridled furiously, but Carmen was already continuing.

'*Up*grade, sweetie. That means someone of a higher status. Get it?' She gestured to the ceiling with her cigarette to emphasize her point. 'Nicky definitely needs to be with a woman – officially. We've sold him as one of the good guys. Lovely girlfriend by his side. Needs to be in a relationship to be happy.' She took a long drag. 'Works very well – he plays a Casanova on TV, but off screen, he's a devoted boyfriend. The women eat it up with a spoon.'

He is a devoted boyfriend, Deeley thought ironically. *Just not to me.*

'So this is what's going to happen,' Carmen said, sitting down on the love seat and crossing her superb legs. Her stiletto heels, reaching halfway up her calves with a complicated arrangement of buckles and straps, looked like a cross between fetishwear and deadly weapons. 'Nicky, regretfully, decides that you're not The One.' She raised her manicured hands and put quotation marks around the last two words. 'It's been five years – make or break. Does he propose, or does he regretfully move on? Beep! He picks Door B. Very sad, but these things happen. He has to be honest about his feelings.'

She looked around for an ashtray, didn't find one, and tapped her ash into a half-full water glass instead.

'So,' she continued, 'a natural period of grieving takes place. Various starlets try to console him. He goes on some dates, but it never pans out. Until!' She smiled like a crocodile. 'Until he and

Jennifer Downs star in an action thriller at the end of the year! Jennifer will be heartbroken too. Her engagement to Joe Jeffreys hasn't worked out, and they've called it quits. Again, the right thing to do, but not easy. Nicky and Jennifer console each other, bond over their break-ups. Next thing you know – bing! They're an item. They're engaged. And this time, it goes all the way – they get married. Jennifer's The One. Happily ever after, with a big shiny red ribbon around the package.'

It was common knowledge among the small inner circle of actors and movie-makers in Hollywood that Jennifer Downs, beautiful, Oscar-winning Jennifer Downs, was not only gay, but in a long-term relationship with Carmen herself. Deeley knew this perfectly well. She also knew, through the gossip mill, that Carmen had set Jennifer up with Joe Jeffreys, A-list movie star, to counter any speculation about Jennifer's sexuality. You didn't get more macho than Joe. He was like the male Deeley.

'What about Joe?' Deeley asked; she couldn't help being curious.

'Get this!' Carmen grinned. 'He's in love! For real! Whole big redemption story – she had quite a past. We're making her into an actress now – it'll play really well. They're already engaged. Secretly, of course.'

She tipped her cigarette into the water glass, where it hissed out.

'It's all planned out,' she said. 'You get your five-year bonus – it's in the contract – and Nicky'll kick in a nice little resettlement sum for you as well.'

'Resettlement?' Deeley whispered.

'You're going back to the UK, sweetie. That's the story. You were in LA to be with your man, and it hasn't worked out. So you need a fresh start. It wouldn't look good to have you kicking round LA at a loose end. God knows what you'd get up to. We can't have you falling in and out of clubs on the Strip. Nicky's got a classy rep to maintain.'

Deeley sat up straight, her eyes burning with indignation. 'How *dare*—' she started furiously, but Carmen cut her off.

'Please,' she said, standing up, flicking her hand at Deeley in dismissal. 'I roll over three girls like you before my morning espresso, OK? You've done a great job, and you'll get paid for it. But let's face it, you're – what, twenty-eight now?'

'Twenty-seven,' Deeley muttered angrily.

'*Way* over the hill in starlet years. Time to take your earnings, go on home and snag yourself a rich husband who lets you decorate the place like Barbie's love nest,' Carmen said snarkily, glancing around her at the pink decor. 'Oh, and fuck pool boys. I hear that's your type.'

'I didn't exactly have much choice who I had sex with, did I?' Deeley snapped, jumping to her feet in fury. 'I had to be discreet for Nicky!'

'Whatever,' Carmen said over her shoulder, already on her way to the door. 'Just remember, that contract you signed is ironclad. Breathe a word about what really happened with you and Nicky and you'll have to pay back every cent of what you got over the last five years. Plus I'll have you arrested. Keep your mouth shut and you'll be well taken care of.'

She turned in the doorway, spearing Deeley with a last terrifying black stare.

'And don't go crying to Nicky. It won't change anything and it'll just make him uncomfortable. Believe me, he's 100 per cent on board with all this. You know how ambitious he is. Who do you think he's going to listen to – you or me?'

And with a toss of her black curls, Carmen strode away past the pool to the main house, her spike heels tapping out a metallic tattoo on the stone paving.

Deeley sank back into her chair, her heart racing like an express train. In the space of a few minutes, her life had been turned completely upside down. Everything she had taken for granted had been picked up by Carmen and thrown into the dustbin.

She looked around at her beautiful suite of rooms, decorated to her exact specifications; it was a bower fit for a fairy princess, all pink and gold and lavender. How dare Carmen call it a Barbie love nest? It was really sophisticated! Deeley glanced lovingly at the fuschia velvet love seat, piled high with sequinned and beaded throw pillows; at her canopied bed, taffeta curtains tumbling down from a central rose in the ceiling and held back with silk tasselled ties. Her Italian pink-and-gold mosaic-tiled bathroom with its claw-footed bath was like something out of a film. So was the dressing table she was sitting at – every little girl's dream, mirrored glass with a silver chair in front of it, laden with expensive perfumes.

But all this was no longer hers. She had just been a temporary tenant, and now she was being evicted.

Tears sprang to her eyes, but she had to blink them back to avoid ruining her make-up. No matter how upset she was, she knew that she was expected to leave with Nicky tonight, walk the red carpet, put on a perfect front, until Carmen instructed her otherwise. Carmen was holding that extra end-of-contract money over her head, and she'd be watching to make sure Deeley earned it.

What am I going to do? Deeley thought frantically. *Where am I going to go?* She didn't have any ties in London any more; she'd left everyone and everything behind to start a new glamorous life in LA with Nicky. The people she'd known in London had just been club friends, girls who shared the run-down flat in Acton with her, fellow hostesses at trade shows trying to climb the greasy pole of success, all of them elbowing each other out of the way for a shot at an opportunity. No one she cared about or had bonded with enough to keep in touch with them when she moved half a world away.

She turned slowly in her chair, staring at herself in the dressing table mirror. In the full view, and the two smaller wings on either side, she looked as stunning as ever. Her genetic inheritance was excellent. Her mother had been a complete disaster as far as her maternal responsibilities went, but she had passed on her stunning features to all three of her daughters. Deeley had the big dark McKenna eyes, the smooth creamy McKenna skin, now gently gilded by the LA sun, and the thick dark McKenna hair, which she had lightened to shades of toffee and caramel. Deeley leaned into the mirror, looking for crow's feet, lifting her hair to see if there were any lines on her forehead. She couldn't see any. And even though she was wearing smoothly blended base and foundation, courtesy of Hervé, when she squinted up her eyes, she still couldn't spot any lines. But Carmen's words had sunk into her like heavy lead bullets. *Twenty-seven, twenty-eight . . . way over the hill in starlet years.*

Not being able to stay in LA was the killer. She loved it here. Everything was so easy. She wafted along on an invisible cushion of money and fame, every door opening to her without her even having to lift a hand.

But it won't be so easy when you're not dating Nicky, a little voice inside her head told her. *You can kiss goodbye to the automatic tables at Nobu and Katsuya and the Ivy. And you won't get the gold-star treatment in Fred Siegel if you don't have a no-limits platinum Amex to flash around. If you stayed on here, you'd be last week's news as soon as you broke up with Nicky. You'd be lucky to get offered a place on one of those shitty VH1 'Celebreality' shows.*

The thought of doing something like that made her shiver; how she and Sean and Nicky had loved to watch those shows, all curled up on Nicky's huge wraparound beige suede sofa, laughing at the fame-hungry contestants. What a slide down the ladder it would be to humble herself by stooping to them now.

Forget it, Deeley, the voice snapped. *Carmen would never let you do a show like that; it'd make Nicky look like shit. That contract you signed must have been thirty pages thick. I bet it's got more sub-clauses than the Bible.*

She kept staring at herself, trying to assess her worth, because that was how she'd always calculated her value. Looks were all she'd ever had; her older sisters had got all the brains in the family. *Snag a rich husband,* Carmen had said, but Deeley couldn't help seeing that as prostitution. Having sex with someone you didn't fancy because he had tons of money – what else was that? She shivered again at the thought. It felt as if the world was closing in around her, squeezing her down to nothing. No options at all. Whatever money Nicky gave her wouldn't last long, she knew; she was terrible with money, always had been.

And then she thought of her older sisters. *Maxie. Devon. They're both back in London, and doing so well. They've really made something of themselves.*

Deeley hadn't seen either of them for years. Longer than the time she'd been in LA. What had happened that day in the front room of Bill's council house in Riseholme – that day she tried never to think about – should have brought them closer together than anything, bonded them for life. But for her, at least, that hadn't happened. Never the brainy one, Deeley had dropped out of school at sixteen and headed to London, where Maxie and Devon were already living by then; but they'd been too busy establishing their careers, building their glamorous lives, to have much room for a younger sister with no greater ambition than to go out dancing every night. When Nicky had whisked her off to LA, Deeley knew that both her sisters had thought it was just the right place for her. And since then they'd barely been in touch.

It was Deeley's fault as much as theirs. She'd been swept away by Nicky's amazing lifestyle and had never looked back. She hadn't even gone back to London for Devon's wedding to Matt Bates, the England rugby star.

Well, it's time to build some bridges. I need Maxie and Devon now. Maxie always looked after me . . . she'll help me till I get on my feet in London, I'm sure she will.

After all, we promised to stick together – whatever happened . . . didn't we?

Devon

$\mathcal{D}$evon felt really, really fat. Hugely, grotesquely, enormously fat.

She reached down and put both hands round her stomach. She was lying in bed, so it was at its flattest, but she could still make her tummy bulge into a solid roll, thumbs digging in on one side, fingers into the other, like a big doughnut round her waist that easily filled her palms. She couldn't think why she was feeling this bloated when she'd had such a virtuous dinner last night: she'd made pasta carbonara for Matt, but only had a few forkfuls herself, filling up on carrot sticks and beetroot slices. No cream in the carbonara, the fat trimmed off the bacon, and barely any cheese on hers; besides, it had been rice pasta. Matt wasn't as keen on the rice pasta, but sod him, it was much more digestible than the wheat version and it didn't make her retain water . . .

Oh. Shit. A memory of the last part of the evening flooded back to her. Matt had gone to sleep early, as he always did when he was training. One beer with dinner, then his favourite TV programme, *Escape to the Country*, a kiss on Devon's lips, and then off to bed by nine thirty with the latest issue of *XBox* magazine. *The glamour of married life*, Devon thought sourly. *If the people who read OK and Hello! and gawk at the spreads of me and Matt 'enjoying a cocktail*

*while relaxing in our gorgeous living room' could see the reality, they'd
be a lot less jealous of our lifestyle. Honestly, most of the time I'm bored
out of my mind.*

Matt never wanted to go out any more. Devon grimaced. To be
fair, Matt had never wanted to go out. The longer they were
together, the clearer it was how different their lifestyles were. In the
first exciting flush of dating, Matt had accompanied her everywhere, but she had made the fatal mistake of assuming that this was
because he loved parties as much as she did. Actually, the reason
was simpler: he just wanted to be with her. Now that they were
settled down, Matt still wanted to be with Devon as much as ever,
but for him that meant cosy evenings in at home, dinner and a TV
programme, and then bed. He'd given up asking her to come to bed
with him, to curl up and read a novel while he paged through his
gaming magazine; he'd resigned himself to the knowledge that he
and his wife had very different body clocks. And very different
ideas of what constituted a fun evening.

And Devon, still wide awake, had roamed the house, a big glass
of red wine in her hand. She'd Twittered, logged on to her Facebook
page and checked out what her friends were up to, envious of the
ones who were out at gallery openings and cocktail parties and
launches, dying to be out with them, all dressed up, laughing and
gossiping and sinking martinis.

But I was supposed to be having a quiet night in, she'd thought
gloomily, shutting her MacBook and watching as the apple glowed
brightly and then faded to grey. *I've been going out too much. And
when I go out, I drink too much, and eat canapés, which are really
fattening, and then I get home drunk, and Matt's fast asleep, so I raid
the kitchen and stuff down cheese and biscuits and bread and butter
and ice cream . . .*

She'd curled up in one of the corners of the huge leather
U-shaped sofa, swaddling herself in her favourite cable-knit plum
Mongolian cashmere throw, and watched some crappy TV, refilling
her glass a couple of times till the bottle was empty. If she turned
her head, she could see herself in the huge antique mirror hanging

above the wrought-iron fireplace to her left, tilted down at a slight angle so it reflected the room. Thick dark hair piled up on top of her head, secured with a big tortoiseshell clip, creamy skin against the purple of her silk lounging pyjamas, her body flatteringly concealed by the soft knitted throw; she looked stunning, like one of those shots from a magazine: *'Devon McKenna, culinary goddess, relaxing at home with a glass of Pinot Noir after a long day whipping up delicious recipes!'*

Only, when she unwound the throw and stood up, glancing at herself in the mirror, the image wasn't quite so picture-perfect. She could see the curve of her bum distorting the smooth line of the silk pyjama jacket, which ought to hang down straight, but instead stuck out like a pelmet over her bottom. And her boobs, lifted and supported by a bra (she never, ever went bra-less unless she was in bed or in the bath, it was too uncomfortable) were doing exactly the same on the front of her body, straining the buttons of the jacket. The silk was pulled tight at the buttons, gaping open on either side of them; anyone looking at her would have said the pyjamas were too small.

And they were a size Large.

Devon shuddered, turning away from the mirror. She knew she should go to bed; it was nearly midnight. Yes, she'd had a couple of glasses of wine too many – more than a couple, if she were being honest, because their Riedel crystal Burgundy wine glasses were enormous, and she'd been pouring very generously. And the calories in wine were . . . well, she wasn't going to think about that now. It was too depressing.

A little voice was telling her to put the wine glass on the mantelpiece, turn off the lights and head upstairs to the master bedroom, where her husband was already, doubtless, fast asleep, making those little snuffling noises that she'd used to think cute, years ago, and now just made her want to hold a pillow over his face. But instead – because she really ought to put the wine glass in the dishwasher, not just leave it like litter around the house – she found herself walking into the hallway, its stained-glass skylight overhead dark now, and into the huge, stunning, perfect kitchen where her TV cooking show was filmed.

A great deal of money had been spent on making this kitchen camera-ready, probably fifty thousand pounds. But it had been essential. An ex-model turned TV cook had made her debut last year, and been slated for letting the viewers believe that the lovely white-painted kitchen where the series had been filmed was her own. The whole point of these series was not, really, for the viewers to learn how to cook. It was for them to bask in the reflected glow of the perfect life they saw on screen: to imagine, for the forty-five minutes of the programme, that they were part of it. Acting as if she had been in her own house, when she wasn't, the ex-model had invited catty criticism.

Devon hadn't been stupid enough to make that mistake. Her kitchen took up the entire back of her Georgian house, and had been extended out into the hundred-foot garden with hyper-modern glass walls and a sloping glass roof that provided all the natural light that any TV crew could need. Black granite Corian topped the cherrywood cabinets and kitchen island, all the fittings were stainless steel, and though the walls were white, for filming purposes, the ceramic floor tiles and all the appliances were deep purple, Devon's signature colour.

It was a dream kitchen, kept shiny and polished by the clean-ing lady who came in every day, working baby oil into the Corian surfaces to keep them glossy. Like a showroom from a catalogue, it was unreal in its perfection. But a few minutes after Devon had come in, that perfection was a distant memory. The Tupperware container of leftover pasta carbonara was out on the countertop next to the open Sub-Zero fridge, a folding chopping board with a heap of grated Parmesan beside it, which Devon was scattering so thickly over the pasta that it disappeared under the heavy coating. She pulled open the larder and extracted a bottle of extra-virgin olive oil, uncapping it and drizzling a bright green stream of rich, peppery oil over the layer of cheese. Mixing it all up with a fork, she added the rest of the Parmesan and some more oil for good measure before starting to fork up mouthfuls, barely taking time to chew one big bite before adding the next.

It was delicious. Crunchy little bites of pancetta contrasted with the eggy sauce coating each strand of spaghetti; the freshly grated cheese was sharp and tangy, the olive oil giving it an extra spicy kick. Of course, it would have been even better if she'd taken the time to reheat the pasta, melting the cheese into it, maybe scattering a few red chilli flakes into the mix; but she was binging, not cooking, and this wasn't about anything but stuffing food into her mouth as fast as she could.

Devon didn't sit down, because that would have meant acknowledging what she was doing. Standing up at the counter, she could stay in the moment, pretend it wasn't really happening, that she was in some sort of suspended, parallel world where calories didn't count and it wasn't her, sophisticated, grown-up, envied and celebrated Devon McKenna, celebrity TV cook, gorging on leftovers like a fat greedy pig.

She didn't stop till the container was finished. If someone had walked in while she was stuffing herself, she'd have shoved everything into the fridge as fast as she could, pretended that nothing was happening; but she'd have sneaked back in later to demolish what was left in the container. Once she'd started, nothing on earth could have stopped her till it was empty. And afterwards, she cleaned up everything till there was no evidence left: Tupperware, chopping board and fork loaded into the Miele dishwasher, oil and cheese back where they'd come from. Matt would never notice that the leftovers had vanished from the fridge; though he ate a lot, he wasn't greedy.

Unlike Devon.

And then she did what she always did after a binge. She went into her office, sat down at her modular desk, opened up her MacBook once again, and went onto the *Daily Mail* website. It specialized in photos of female celebrities, their bodies displayed for judgement by the *Mail* and its online readers. Devon, in the

Vivienne Westwood, Donna Karan and Karen Millen dresses that flattered her hourglass figure, was by no means thin, and the occasional snarky comment emphasized that cruelly:

'Voluptuous? More like obese!'

'Looks like the hourglass is expanding dangerously at both ends!'

'Come on – any of you who don't think she's fat must be porkers yourselves!'

But every single nasty post about Devon's weight had been red-arrowed by the rest of the commenters. And the positive posts outnumbered the negatives by at least ten to one.

'Leave her alone, she's stunning! I wish I had her curves, LOL!'

'All those skinny-minny Kate Moss types could do with looking more like Devon – this is how men like their women – someone to squeeze!'

'What do you mean fat? Devon can't be over a size 14, that's still fine in my book! She loves food, you can see that on her programmes, if she was thin she'd be bulimic wouldn't she? It's amazing she's not much bigger, good for her.'

It *was* amazing she wasn't bigger, Devon thought gloomily, closing the laptop. Usually the comments section cheered her up, but it was always a risk. The negative remarks affected her much more than the positive ones, naturally, but the sheer number of people who bothered to post was always a tribute to how many fans she had. Devon was a poster girl for women with curves, women who loved to eat; if she lost a few stone, she'd lose her devoted following as well. But if she lost a stone – well, twenty pounds, who was she kidding — if she lost twenty pounds, got back to the weight she'd been when she first got her TV series, the weight she'd been on her wedding day . . .

For a moment, Devon allowed herself the bliss of imagining it. Imagining herself able to fit into a size 12 – even to fit her boobs into a size 12, if the top were generously cut. God, how happy she'd be! She thought miserably of all the clothes in her huge closet that she couldn't fit into any longer. Jeans that had been her normal, everyday wear. Dresses that had made her feel like a film star. Even shoes she wouldn't put on any longer; she wasn't comfortable wearing ankle straps any more, because she thought they cut her legs off and made them look stumpy.

If I'd only been happy with my weight then! The trouble was that you never enjoyed what you had. You always wanted to be thinner. If you were a size 12, you wanted to be a size 10. Women were never happy with their bodies, in Devon's experience.

If I could only somehow manage to get back to the size I was . . . if I went on one of those bikini boot camps, or did a cabbage soup diet, or just stopped binging after dinner . . .

I will. I will stop binging after dinner. That'll do it. I must have eaten a thousand calories just now with that pasta. Much more if I count the wine as well . . . Oh God . . .

Depression had fully settled in, waves of exhaustion and gloom sweeping over her. Which meant she was ready to go to bed. Padding up the staircase that wrapped around the open hall, her cashmere White Company slippers making no sound on the polished floor, she pushed open the door that led to the master bedroom suite. Matt was fast asleep, making those snuffling noises, damn him. She slipped under the white velvet coverlet and closed her eyes, hoping to fall asleep straight away – before she got so annoyed with Matt's bloody snuffling that she pushed him right off the mattress . . .

'Dev? You awake? Oi! Dev!'

Devon snapped out of her memories of the night before, very grateful for the distraction. *No more late-night snacking*, she told herself firmly now, a resolution that she had made many, many times already.

'Dev!'

Someone was knocking on the bedroom door. It couldn't be Matt – he was long gone, always up just after dawn to have breakfast before heading off to training. Devon pushed the pillows behind her and sat up.

'Gary?' she called. 'Is that you?'

'Of course it's bloody me,' Gary Jordan, her make-up artist, said impatiently, opening the door and coming in, carrying a tray with two cups of coffee and a plate of pastries. 'Who were you expecting, the Easter bunny?'

He set down the tray on the bedside table and crossed the room to draw the light silk curtains. Spring morning light flooded into the bedroom. With his back to the window, Gary surveyed Devon, who had reached gratefully for her coffee and was sipping it, her head clearing as the caffeine hit her system. The morning light illuminated her face all too clearly; beautiful as she was, the regular binging and drinking was making her eyes a little puffy and her skin dull.

'Ooh *dear*,' he said, clicking his tongue. 'I've got my work cut out for me today, haven't I?'

'Shut up. The Easter bunny would be nicer to me,' Devon said, sticking her tongue out at Gary. '*And* he'd bring me chocolate.'

'*You* shut up,' Gary said. 'Chocolate's the last thing you need.'

Taking the second cup of coffee and a croissant, he perched comfortably on the bed. In his grey waistcoat, tight black jeans and jaunty grey tweed cap over his carefully tonged hair, Gary resembled a modern version of the Artful Dodger.

'Mmn, nice,' he said appreciatively, stroking the mauve silk coverlet. 'So what are we doing today? Bit early for you to book me in when you're not working! You usually like to sleep till noon, don't you, love? Going out for a posh lunch?'

Devon shook her head. 'Interview,' she said through a mouthful of Danish pastry. '*Women's Life* magazine.'

'Photos?' Gary asked, narrowing his eyes.

'No, did them last week, remember,' she said. 'In their test kitchen.'

'Oh, so it's just nice and natural, cover up the spots and don't scare the horses,' Gary said, relaxing.

Devon had been working with Gary since she first started in TV; he'd been doing the make-up on the breakfast show on which she'd started out as a lowly runner. They'd both come a long way since then. Gary was in high demand, working on major TV series and feature films, but Devon booked him whenever she could. Gary knew exactly what she needed, how to shade her jaw so it looked slimmer, how to make her lips look fuller and more lush than anyone else could; she never had to tell him anything.

And Gary's total lack of respect for her fame and fortune, the way he teased her just as if she were still a runner on a breakfast TV show, not a famous icon and sex symbol, was exactly what she needed. A born-and-bred Londoner with an acid tongue, Gary wouldn't have dreamed of sucking up to anyone. Which was ideal, as Devon had always responded best to people who made fun of her. Growing up, she'd missed out on the banter and jokes that would be expected between three sisters relatively close in age. She, Maxie and Deeley had been too traumatized, too fearful, to ever relax and mess around with each other like more normal sisters did. Nor had they been able to have close friends at school; their family problems were too intense, their secrets too profound, for them to be able to form bonds outside their little threesome.

Devon still didn't have any close girlfriends. She'd never learned how. She and Maxie were very close – though, to be honest, Devon didn't much like Maxie, and had the feeling that the sentiments were returned. But what they had been through when they were young, culminating in that awful night in the autumn of 1993, had locked them together forever, as tightly as if they each had a wrist in a pair of handcuffs.

Deeley, somehow, had escaped. Perhaps by being so young, that night, too young to have been as involved in what they had done as her two older sisters had been. And she had disappeared, literally, off to LA, living a golden existence with her gorgeous gay boyfriend, with nothing to do but look pretty and smile and dress up like a beautiful doll. No responsibilities, no career to manage, no marriage problems, no weight issues.

Lucky Deeley. Lucky, lucky Deeley.

Devon pushed back the wave of resentment that tended to flood up whenever she thought about her younger sister's charmed, easy life, and turned back to the present.

'What spots?' she said, drinking more coffee. 'Fuck off, Gary. I've never had spots.'

Gary snorted. 'Of course you haven't, darling,' he said. 'Just like you've never had an STD.'

'I've *never* . . .' Devon started indignantly, then stopped, realizing he was joking. 'Shut up,' she said, taking another bite of Danish. 'Just for that, you'd better make me look absolutely gorgeous.'

'Wow, Devon, you're so lucky!' the interviewer from the women's magazine gushed. 'You have *such* a great life – this kitchen's even more amazing in real life than on TV!'

Devon flashed her biggest, most charming smile, tossing back her shiny dark hair. Gary had done a fantastic job with her hair and make-up; she looked flawless, but natural. She was in Earl jeans and a black Ghost crêpe shirt that flowed over her curves rather than clinging to them, amethyst earrings dangling in her ears. Simple, relatable clothes. Devon's image wasn't exactly the girl next door, but it was crucial that she seemed approachable. Friendly. Normal. I.e., not so groomed and perfect that she intimidated the interviewer and caused her to write a catty article in revenge.

'Oh, I spent hours tidying up this morning!' Devon lied cheerfully. 'It's usually an awful mess.'

'And the sofa's even comfier than it looks,' the interviewer said, patting the arm of the huge cranberry velvet sofa that sprawled along the back wall of the kitchen. 'I love that bit on your shows when you've finished cooking, and you take a portion of what you've just made and sit down here to eat it . . .'

That was how Devon's programmes usually ended; with her announcing that she'd worked hard to feed everyone else and she was going to take a special, indulgent moment to treat herself.

'Or a drink,' Devon said, smiling. 'Sometimes I take a lovely big glass of wine and sit down here to put my feet up.'

'Oh yes! Everyone loves that too!' The interviewer giggled girl-ishly. 'What do you call it?'

'My little bit extra,' Devon said, winking at her. 'I have to have my little bit extra. I think we all do, don't we?'

She had this line down pat. And though it was a routine, it wasn't hypocritical; Devon genuinely meant it. That was the secret of her appeal; the persona she projected on TV was her own – exagger-ated, as everything is on TV, but definitely her own. She wasn't playing a part.

The interviewer giggled harder. 'That's what the next show's going to be called, right?' she said. 'It's such a great title!'

Across the room, perched on a chrome and white-leather bar stool, Devon's publicist, who was fiddling with her BlackBerry but mainly listening hard to the interview, nodded approvingly. Five minutes into the conversation and the title of the next series had already been namechecked; *nice work*, the nod said.

'I've been saying it for years,' Devon said, curling up in the corner of the sofa, tucking her bare feet sideways. 'Ever since I first started out on *Wake up UK*. So finally Rory – that's the producer I work with at the TV company that makes the show for the Beeb – he said, "You know, this is the perfect title for the new series – *Devon's Little Bit Extra*." I think it's hilarious.'

'Oh yes!' The interviewer beamed, sliding her digital recorder a little closer along the coffee table to Devon till it butted against the one Devon's publicist had placed there. This was standard practice now for celebrities; you always kept your own copy of the interview, to ensure no quotes got exaggerated, embellished or just simply made up. 'Can you talk a bit about how you got started on *Wake up UK*? I mean, you didn't actually train as a cook, right?'

Devon had to be careful not to stiffen up at this question. It was one of her two main weak points, and no matter how nice an inter-viewer seemed, how much they were telling you that they loved you and your house and your life, if you showed weakness, they'd sense it and use it to dig away at you.

So she smiled as easily as ever, and tossed her hair back casually as she said, 'Yes, that's right! I think that a lot of women identify with me because of that. I mean, I'm just like them. I didn't go to cooking school, and I didn't apprentice in restaurants. I taught myself to cook and I never put on airs and graces about it – I mean, I'd never call myself a chef.' She looked self-deprecating. 'But what I really love is to help people learn to cook. You know, nothing pretentious. Just nice comfort food, the kind you want to eat every day. And that's how I got started. I was working as a runner on TV – very lowly, just racing around getting people coffee.'

'Did you always want to be on TV?' the interviewer asked, tilting her head to one side.

'I didn't know *what* I wanted to do,' Devon lied. 'I got the job through a temp agency and just sort of stayed on.'

Of course I wanted to be on TV! she thought. *Everyone wants to be on TV!* But you couldn't say that. It made you sound stuck-up and ambitious, and there was still a lot of hostility towards ambitious women. And *of course* she hadn't got the job through a temp agency; she'd written letters and pestered producers and got Maxie's then fiancé, Olly, to pull some strings to get her into an interview that had led to her being taken on as a runner – not even a researcher. But it had got her foot that tiny crack in the door, even if it was a lowly job where she was paid practically nothing to get up at 3 a.m. every day for the breakfast show and to get screamed at by everyone for not getting their coffee fast enough.

'And you ended up doing a cooking slot on the show,' the interviewer prompted.

'It was so funny!' Devon said cheerfully. 'There was this guest,' she named a famous footballer, 'who mentioned in an interview that he'd never cooked anything in his life. So they said they'd book him in the week after to give him a cooking lesson, but the chef who was supposed to do it pulled out at the last minute.'

Too hungover to be in the studio by 7 a.m., she remembered. *Bloody celebrity chefs think the world shines out of their bum.*

'And the producer asked me to do it,' she continued.

'You must have been terrified!'

Well, not really. What really happened was that I begged the producer, practically on my knees. I pleaded, I swore I could do it, and when he said yes, I could do the cooking segment, I was so excited I could barely breathe. I wanted to be on TV so badly I'd have done anything. Anything at all.

But she didn't mention any of that when she answered, smiling, 'I thought I was going to throw up, I was so scared!' She leaned back, crossing her legs. 'But I loved it. It was really fun. We laughed and laughed. I tried to show him how to cook an egg, and he barely even knew how to tell when water was boiling. We got swamped with phone calls and texts – all the viewers loved it – so the producer said that I should do it regularly. I mean, at first it was really basic. You wouldn't believe the amount of famous guys who didn't even know how to make toast.'

'Wasn't the joke that they were too busy looking at your – um . . .' the interviewer looked knowing as she nodded in the direction of Devon's bosom, 'to, um, concentrate on cooking anything?'

Devon rolled her eyes. '*Men*,' she sighed. 'I had to slap them so many times! I hit Robbie Williams with a frying pan once when he was trying to pinch my bum. But I did get him to stuff a baked potato, in the end. And, you know, it was all in good fun.'

'You were an overnight sensation,' the interviewer said. 'I mean, I remember it really well. The male viewing figures for *Wake up UK* went up by,' she glanced at her notes, 'over 25 per cent in a month.'

Devon's publicist shifted on the bar stool, enough to get Devon's attention, to remind her to be careful.

'It's really women that I connect with,' Devon said, leaning forward and looking sincere. 'That's who I write for. That's my real audience. I mean, I do have male fans—'

'But that's because of the way you look,' the interviewer interrupted. 'I mean, my boyfriend thinks you're totally gorgeous – he's watching because you make cooking look so sexy. He's not going to go out and buy the book.' She rolled her eyes. 'Or actually cook a recipe from it, God knows.'

Devon had to tread carefully. 'I'm disappointed to hear that,' she said, widening her big brown eyes, dark and rich as the chocolate she licked off her fingers whenever she made cupcakes. 'I spent so much time on TV teaching guys to cook – you'd hope they'd have learned something, wouldn't you!'

'Do you feel that sometimes you maybe go a bit over the top with the sexy part?' the interviewer asked. 'I mean, you've obviously got a great figure, but – well, some people have said that if you covered up a bit more and didn't lick your fingers quite so much, you'd be taken more seriously as a cook . . .'

And here it is – the question I get every single time. Every single interview.

'First of all,' Devon said, sitting back to make herself look more relaxed, very aware of her publicist listening like a hawk, 'I have big boobs, naturally. Believe me, I would never choose to be this size.' She flashed a look at the interviewer, who luckily was quite well-endowed herself. 'Because they're really hard to dress. If I cover them up too much, I just look fat. You know? If I wear a polo neck sweater, I look the size of a house.' She pulled a face. 'There are *so* many things I can't wear, and I'd love to. I can only wear a few designers, because most of them cut too small for me. I'm no skinny-minny. I celebrate my curves. I mean, most women in the UK are curvy!'

Devon was on a roll now. The interviewer was smiling and nodding, and so was her publicist.

'I get a lot of nasty people telling me I weigh a bit too much,' she continued, 'but you know what? I'm just a normal woman. Yes, I'd love to lose a few pounds – who wouldn't? But I can't help the way I look. I hate to hear the comments about me being fat. It's really hurtful.'

'Oh, you're not *fat*!' the interviewer protested.

'Well, thank you,' Devon said, biting her full lower lip and looking poignantly grateful. 'I keep telling myself that. I like to think that I represent normal women. Ones who don't look like film stars or actresses, who aren't just skin and bones. I don't want to starve myself just to fit into some idea of how women should look, and I don't think I should have to! None of us should have to.'

'That's so inspiring,' the interviewer breathed.

And I'm such a liar, Devon thought miserably. *I'd love to be a sample size. I'd love to fit into every single one of the clothes on a shoot, not pose in dresses that are open at the back because I can't zip them up.*

Because that was exactly what had happened on the photo shoot for pictures to accompany this article – they'd had to hold the dresses together at the back with gigantic safety pins bridging the gap.

I'm a liar and a hypocrite.

Devon bit her lip harder and reminded herself that everything she had, she'd made for herself. She looked round the amazing, magazine-spread kitchen, with its amethyst floor tiles, its black Corian surfaces, the sunlight pouring in through the glass roof making everything shine entrancingly – even the chrome and stainless steel, which took so much work to polish. Her eyes lingered on the KitchenAid mixer, a rich purple the manufacturers called boysenberry, which alone had cost hundreds of pounds.

Ten years ago I had nothing. Less than nothing, if I count the over-draft and credit card debts. And look at me now. I wasn't born with a silver spoon in my mouth – I earned all this through sheer hard work and determination. Like Maxie earned her own success.

Ugh, why do I always come back to Maxie? It's like I can never get away from her!

Lost in her thoughts, she'd tuned out for a few moments, and when she came back to earth, she realized that the interviewer's expression had changed. Her head was ducked so she wouldn't meet Devon's eyes. Never a good sign.

Devon had a nasty sense of what was coming next.

'So, my editor wants me to ask this,' the interviewer said apologetically, fiddling with her fingers, 'but . . . um . . . anyway . . . if we could just briefly cover the comments that were made about your first book – mostly about your first book – um, that some of the recipes don't actually work? I know there was an issue with your signature chocolate cake . . . a lot of people apparently couldn't get it to rise . . .'

Devon took a deep breath. This was the other of her two weak areas in interviews: both of them revolved around her lack of any training as a cook. *I should have got people to check those recipes more,* she thought, as she'd done a thousand times already. *But the publishers were rushing me and I was so excited to have the TV deal and the book coming out, I couldn't tell them to slow down.*

She opened her mouth, hating this moment, very aware of her publicist's eyes boring into the side of her head like twin gimlets, willing her to give a good answer.

And then salvation appeared, all six foot four of him, wide-shouldered, curly haired, a classic rugby player's build, with arms as large as Devon's thighs and thighs as wide as Devon's waist. Salvation was so enormous and manly that the interviewer turned, took one look at him and went as red as the cranberry velvet sofa, any awkward questions thoroughly wiped from her mind by the sight of him.

'Hi Matt,' said the publicist flirtatiously. Used as she was to the sight of Devon's husband, jaded as she was by meeting endless celebrities, even she wasn't immune to the 250 pounds of solid muscle that was Matt Bates.

And to Devon, he was an answer to a prayer. Her irritation at the way Matt could eat anything he wanted without putting on weight, at his early nights which left her up roaming the house bored, drinking and snacking, at their totally incompatible lifestyles, all faded immediately as she grabbed the escape route that his appearance had given her.

'Darling!' she cried, jumping up from the sofa and running towards him. 'I didn't expect you back so early!'

Initially taken aback at his wife's unusual enthusiasm to see him, Matt broke into a beaming smile as Devon hurtled into his arms. A weaker man might have staggered back at five foot eight, size fourteen Devon thudding into him, but it was Matt's job to have men much larger and heavier than Devon tackling him all day long, and he took the impact of Devon crashing into him as if he were catching a bouquet, rather than a woman who weighed a hundred and sixty pounds.

'Well, what a nice way to say hello!' he said, kissing the top of Devon's head. 'Mmn. You smell good, love.'

'*Ohhhhh . . .*' sighed the interviewer wistfully at the sight of Matt lovingly enfolding his wife in his enormous arms, the fabric of his cotton shirt straining over his biceps.

'I'm doing an interview for *Women's Life,*' Devon said, pulling back and looking up at Matt. In her bare feet, Matt was so much taller than her that she needed to crane her head back, her thick hair tumbling down over her shoulders. She gestured at the interviewer, who was wriggling on the sofa, pink-faced and flustered as an excited 5-year-old girl who's just seen a life-size Disney character walk into the room.

'Oh, hi!' Matt raised a plate-sized hand in a greeting to the interviewer. 'Sorry to interrupt.'

'Oh no – it's fine – it's great to meet you.' The interviewer swallowed audibly. 'Could you, um, tell me how you feel about Devon's show? Do you watch it? How do you feel about your wife being a sex symbol for a lot of men?'

Matt grinned, a wide, lazy smile. He was no stranger to interviews either, although he didn't much like them; but a professional rugby player couldn't help but have to speak to the press on a regular basis.

'I'm so proud of her,' he said, still holding Devon by the waist. 'Devon's a real live wire – she's always got something on the go. TV, or books, or crockery, or something. I can't keep up.'

'*Crockery?*' Devon said incredulously.

'Yeah!' Matt frowned, looking embarrassed. 'Am I wrong? I

could've sworn you do crockery, love, don't you? Jars and plates and things?'

Devon rolled her eyes at him. Having grown up poor and working class, she was paranoid about being caught out using the wrong words, or talking with the wrong accent; she and Maxie had worked really hard to polish their rough, uneducated tones into much posher, smoother, more educated-sounding pronunciation. Maxie, as in everything, had led the way: gone to study at Oxford, realized on the first day that she didn't sound right, and kept her mouth shut until she could copy successfully the way the children of privilege spoke. God knew, Maxie had assimilated perfectly. And Devon, just as ambitious, had followed in Maxie's footsteps. Deeley was the only sister of the three who had never cared so much about getting on and fitting in.

Everything always came easy to Deeley, Devon thought jealously for a moment, before she remembered what she was supposed to be focussing on. Pulling herself back to the present, she flashed a charming, seductive smile to the interviewer.

'He means my ceramics line,' she explained. 'China and stoneware. That's how you say it, darling,' she added to Matt over her shoulder.

'Sorry!' Matt looked abashed. 'My gran always called it all crockery. But it doesn't really matter what I call a plate, as long as I make sure to put it in the dishwasher when I'm finished, right?'

'Awww,' the interviewer sighed, relapsing into 5-year-old behaviour again.

'Sweetie?' Devon prompted Matt. 'She was asking you how you feel about me being a sort of sex symbol?'

'Oh, yeah,' Matt said cheerfully. 'I don't care one way or the other. I mean, the lads'll have a laugh in training, sometimes, if they watch Dev's show and she's licking a spoon or something, but I reckon they're all just jealous of me. And you've got to have a thick skin in my job, don't you?' He raised one hand to his face. 'I mean, I've had my nose mashed in twice, and this ear's all wonky.' He pulled at one lobe, which looked as if a fellow rugby player had taken a bite out of it. 'I've got enough to worry about on the field without blokes fancying my wife.'

He looked wistfully at Devon, who had walked over to the central island and was leaning against it.

'As long as we're happy, who cares what anyone else thinks?' he concluded a little sadly. 'I mean, that's the only thing that matters.'

Matt had been handsome before he started playing rugby. His once classically straight nose, as he'd said, was bumpy after a couple of bad breaks, and one cheekbone was a little dented. But what he had lost in handsomeness, he had gained in sex appeal. The bumps and dents gave his even, regular features a touch of raffishness, a contrast to the very youthful clear blue eyes and tight brown curls. He was tanned from all the outdoor training, and the deep crinkles round his eyes and slight chapping to his lips gave his boyish good looks a manliness that no woman, and few men, could help responding to.

But even if Matt had had a face like the back of a bus, his body would still have been a work of art: sculpted by Michelangelo, photographed by Bruce Weber. The word 'strapping' could have been invented for Matt. He was built on a massive scale. A Hollywood producer would have taken one look at him and cast him as a Roman gladiator or a Greek god. Devon, instead, made him pose for aftershave ads, which he loathed with every fibre of his being.

Seeing the way the interviewer was undressing Matt with her eyes, Devon made a quick decision. She glanced across at her publicist, who was, she could tell, in full agreement with her.

'Well, this has been a great interview!' the publicist said brightly, adjusting her hemline so she could step down from the barstool without flashing her knickers. 'But Devon and Matt have a really busy schedule, so I'm afraid I'm going to have to call an end to this now.'

'We *do*?' Matt, a bit slow on the uptake, mouthed at Devon, his wide forehead scrunching in concern. She knew perfectly well that, once back from training, all he wanted to do was play Xbox, do some gardening, and talk about what they were having for dinner; that was as busy a schedule as Matt could handle.

'Yes!' Devon said, ignoring her husband's look of panic. 'It's been *so* great talking to you.' She crossed the wide expanse of kitchen floor to the sofa, where the interviewer was reluctantly rising to her feet. 'I hope you got everything you needed.'

'Well, there still are a couple of things . . .' the interviewer started.

'Great! Fantastic! Do email me with any follow-ups,' the publicist said, leading her firmly out of the kitchen. 'Look forward to reading the article!'

'She seemed nice,' Matt said, nodding at the retreating back of the interviewer.

'Oh, *Matt*. You think everyone's nice,' Devon said impatiently. 'You even think Maxie's nice.'

'Well, she's never been nasty to me,' Matt pointed out reasonably.

He stretched his arms above his head, easing out his back and shoulders, one hand locked around the other wrist to pull both arms straight. Anyone else would have goggled at this sheer display of brawn; Matt's arms, biceps and triceps bulging looked as big as sides of beef. Devon's fingers couldn't possibly encircle Matt's wrist, and she was built on a fairly substantial scale herself.

'Maxie's tough as old boots,' Devon said. 'That's why she's done so well for herself. But she isn't nice.'

'You've done well for yourself too, love,' her husband said, taking a couple of strides across the floor to reach her, wrapping his arms around her. 'I can't even come into my own kitchen for a cuppa without finding you talking to someone from a magazine, can I? I'm dead proud of you, you know. I should've said that to that lady journalist. I mean, none of the other lads've got wives who've made something of themselves, you know? Look at you – on TV all the time, front page of the papers when you go to one of your parties!'

'You don't care about that, really,' Devon said petulantly and unfairly. 'You'd rather I was home at night cooking your dinner.'

'I can cook my own dinner,' Matt said. 'Well, I can bung some fish fingers in the oven.' He looked down at her, his blue eyes serious. 'I'd like you to be home more, there's no secret about that. I like a quiet life. But I am dead proud of you, Dev. You know I am.'

He leaned down for a kiss, but only managed to plant one briefly on Devon's full red lips before she pushed him away. It was a token push; she could no more have shifted Matt physically than she could have uprooted an oak tree. But he pulled back immediately, looking hurt.

'Give us a proper kiss, eh?' he said.

'Matt . . . there's people here . . .' Devon twisted away from him.

'We're married, Dev!' Matt pointed out. 'We can kiss in our own kitchen as much as we want to. That's probably in the vows some-where, don't you remember? Love, honour and snog in your own kitchen . . .'

But just then the publicist whisked back into the kitchen with a whir of keys as she tapped on her BlackBerry without missing a step.

'That went *very* well!' she said happily. 'God, I wish I could arrange for Matt to come in halfway through every single inter-view! He melts the women and the gay men – plus the straight men just want to talk to him about sport; it's the *best* distraction.'

'Distraction?' Matt's brow furrowed. 'Why'd you need a distraction?'

'Never mind,' Devon said impatiently. 'Look, shall I make you a cup of tea or something? Isn't that what you wanted?'

Matt looked even more hurt. 'It can wait,' he said. 'I'll go and check my email or something. See if one of the lads is home by now and wants to play Xbox online.'

'It's all games with them, isn't it?' the publicist said rather patronizingly. 'Men and their balls!'

'We play quiz shows as well,' Matt said crossly. 'General knowl-edge. We're not all complete thickos, you know, even if some of us haven't got a lot of formal education.'

This was a weak spot for Matt, and Devon, suddenly remembering that she needed him in a good mood, hurried to soften him up. Leaning into him, stroking his arm, she reached up to kiss him, feeling him immediately bend towards her, his irritation all forgotten. Matt was like a huge dog, never happier than when he was curled up in a pack, loving physical contact; it made total sense that he was a rugby player. No one could have been more suited to the game: shoving his opponents in a scrum, tackling a forward to the muddy ground, or piling on top of each other, was all in a day's work for Matt, and once the game was over he was the first to be hugging his opponents and teammates, slapping them on the back, or throwing his arm affectionately round a fellow player's shoulders.

'Love you, sweetie,' Devon said against his mouth. 'Sorry I was a bitch just now. That interviewer wound me up the wrong way.'

'No prob,' Matt said fondly, kissing her back. 'I don't even know how you do it. I mean, I don't mind the post-game wrap-up interviews and all that, but selling things all the time – I couldn't do that. No way.'

Whoops, Devon thought quickly. *Maybe I should back away from it right now* . . .

But unfortunately, the publicist didn't read Matt as well as Devon did.

'Ooh! And talking about selling, Matt, I have some amazing news!' she said breezily. 'You know that aftershave ad you shot last year?'

Matt cringed. 'Don't remind me,' he muttered.

Confident with his body as Matt was, being stripped naked, greased up and shot in very revealing black-and-white photos with a bottle posed strategically between his legs had been a step too far even for him. *Though it got him into all the gay mags*, Devon reflected. *Which is exactly where you want to be to sell yourself as an icon.*

'*Well*! Guess who came calling?' the publicist sang out. 'This is *amazing*!'

'I'm not going to like this, am I?' Matt said, pulling a clownishly comic face of distress.

'*Calvin Klein!*' the publicist carolled joyously. 'They want you for *Calvin Klein*! Underpants! It's huge!'

'Oh, I don't know about that,' Matt said, blushing. 'I mean, I'm OK with it, but you see some blokes in the showers who—'

'Matt! She doesn't mean your willy!' Devon cracked up. 'She means it's huge that they asked you!'

'Oh.' Matt went as red as a turkey-comb and rubbed his springy curls so roughly that he looked as if he were trying to exfoliate his scalp. 'Um. Sorry.'

'They'll totally photoshop you if they feel they need to,' the publicist said helpfully.

'Aaahhh!' Matt clamped his hands over his ears, looking even more comic than before. 'I can't listen to this! You're talking about putting my willy on display!'

'Matt, sweetie . . .' Devon reached up and unclamped one of her husband's enormous hands from his equally large ear. 'Tons of footballers have done it! David Beckham, Ronaldo, Freddie Ljungberg . . .'

'That's why it's such a compliment!' the publicist said eagerly. 'It's a really big deal – there'd be gigantic posters everywhere!'

Not helping, Devon thought, watching Matt cringe at the thought.

'It would *really* build the brand,' the publicist added, her eyes wide with anticipation. '*Totally* take you and Devon to the next level.'

'We're not a brand!' Matt protested, his jaw setting. 'We're a couple – we're *married*. Husband and wife. That's not a *brand*.'

'Tell that to Victoria and David Beckham,' Devon couldn't help saying. 'Look at all their perfume ads.'

'All right for them, I suppose,' Matt said, looking miserable. 'Seems bloody weird to me, but it's not my business, is it? It's not for me, though. And I didn't think it was for Dev, either.'

He looked over at Devon, his blue eyes pleading.

'Is that what you want, Dev? My bollocks up on a billboard six feet wide, for everyone to gawp at? Just to make a ton of dosh that we don't even need anyway?'

'You posed for that rugby calendar last year,' Devon protested. 'All of you guys naked, holding rugby balls in front of you. I didn't think you'd mind that much.'

'That was for charity,' Matt said, his voice rising. 'For flipping Great Ormond Street children's hospital! Of course we all got our kit off for that! Can't you see the difference between that and posing in a pair of tightie whities with my willy flopping over my leg? I'd feel like such a twat, Dev!'

'It would be really super-tasteful,' the publicist said in an attempt to reassure him.

It didn't work. Matt shot her a look of seething resentment.

'I don't mean to be rude,' he said with the air of a man trying very hard to cling to the last remnants of his self-control, 'but this is really between me and my wife. I mean, it's my privates we're talking about here.'

'I'll leave you two alone, shall I?' the publicist said, slipping past them adroitly. In silence, husband and wife heard her footsteps click across the marble hallway and the front door open and close behind her.

When Devon looked up at Matt again, she was expecting him still to be angry, resentful that she didn't understand him well enough to have turned down the Calvin Klein offer without even suggesting it to him. Anger she could have dealt with, expertly redirected down a different path to – hopefully – reach the outcome she wanted; anger was a strong, powerful emotion that a woman who knew how to manage men could often use, like a blowtorch, to burn through to where she wanted to go.

But instead, Matt looked sad. Which was much harder to deal with.

It was the easiest thing in the world to read Matt. He had no filters, no wall that he put up: sad, happy, elated, angry, whatever he was feeling showed clearly on his face. He was completely sincere.

Devon reached up, stroking his arm, feeling how taut and tense his big muscles were.

'Matt,' she started carefully, 'I don't want you to do anything you don't want to do. Please believe me.'

Matt shrugged, a gesture that for him spoke volumes. 'Dev,' he said gently, 'you sort of do. You want me to do this ad. And now you're going to try to talk me into it.'

'I . . .'

Devon, who had got her start on live TV, who was brilliant at ad-libbing and banter, who had competed on celebrity quiz shows and was never lost for words in an interview, found herself grinding to a halt now, unable to go on. Because Matt was absolutely right. He'd caught her in a lie. And she had no idea how to get out of it.

'Dev,' Matt said, even more gently. 'Come here.'

He folded her in his arms. It had always been so wonderful to be held by Matt; he made her feel small, delicate, feminine – he could pick her up as if she weighed nothing at all. Even though she'd weighed considerably less when they first met, Devon had never – as she'd said to the interviewer – been skinny.

But now, all she could feel was how repulsed Matt must be at how fat she was. His arms, wrapping round her back, couldn't avoid touching the roll directly below the constriction of her bra strap; though Matt had always loved her breasts, he must be aware of how much bigger they'd grown in the last few years. He'd loved to watch her walk round naked after a bath or shower; now, she never let him see her naked if she could possibly help it. Her stomach, pressing against him, stuck out like a shelf. Surely he must secretly be revolted by her.

'I know you're always worried about money,' he said into her thick, glossy hair. 'But we've got enough to last us the rest of our lives, even if we retired now. We couldn't go on living like this, of course,' one hand left her back briefly to gesture round the lavish kitchen, 'but we don't even use half of the rooms in this house, do we? We could – what do they call it? – downsize tomorrow and not even notice.'

Despite her resolution to win Matt round to seeing things her way, Devon stiffened in her husband's embrace at the idea of giving up anything they had; she couldn't help it.

He laughed ruefully. 'Don't worry, Dev,' he said. 'I'm just making the point that we're not going to starve, whatever happens. If I ripped my Achilles tomorrow and couldn't play again, we'd still be all right. I know nothing'll stop you from building your empire, and I respect that. You're going to have your TV shows and your books and your – what did I say that was so wrong? *Crockery!* – and make barrowloads of dosh for both of us. And I'd find some other way to earn a living. Coach, or something. I'm not the idle type. What I'm saying is, there's no need to pressure me into showing my photoshopped willy in a pair of boxer shorts, just so we can have enough to buy another posh sofa, or go on holiday again.'

'It'd be a lot more than a sofa,' Devon muttered against his chest.

But it's not about the money, she admitted to herself. Matt was right; they had plenty of money. More than she'd ever imagined in her wildest dreams. Matt's salary and endorsement deals aside, her books sold in Germany, the US, Australia, Japan, wherever her TV show was on. Her ceramics line was doing really well. And she was about to launch a whole collection of glassware; the signature piece would be extra-large wine glasses, for *Devon's Little Bit Extra.*

No, it wasn't the money. It was the attention. Devon had always loved attention, lapped it up as greedily as a cat with cream, been unable to pass a mirror without looking into it and posing. She'd tried to be an actress, but it hadn't worked; she was so photogenic you couldn't take a bad shot of her, but she had no talent whatsoever, and she'd been sensible enough to realize that soon enough, and stop flogging a dead horse. Devon's talent was in being herself, writ large. Smiling, chatting, using her own words, her own charm, being a person that viewers wanted to watch on the screen, have in their living rooms at the end of the day. She adored being on TV; she adored it when people stopped her in the street, asked her to sign their copies of her books, wrote about her in papers and on the internet.

It's the attention. That's what I love. And that's what I can't tell Matt. He understands about the money; he understands about growing up poor and hungry. But he doesn't understand about my need for attention. And he never will.

If Matt did a Calvin Klein ad, we'd really be in the big time. Devon McKenna and Matt Bates – we're already famous, but this would be huge. It'd shoot us right up into the top ten celebrity couples in the UK.

And maybe I'm shallow for wanting to be famous, for wanting attention. But if wanting to be on TV means you're shallow, tons of other people are too! Really, what's so wrong with it?

'I'd be really proud,' she attempted finally. 'Married to a Calvin Klein model. That'd be amazing.'

'Love . . .' Matt took her by the shoulders and looked down into her big brown eyes. 'Be proud of me when I score a try that wins us the World Cup, or I get my hundredth cap for England. Or when the London Tigers win at Twickenham, with me as captain. That'd be something to be proud of. Maybe I'll get an MBE some day, go to the palace and have the Queen pin it on me, or whatever she does. With you by my side, looking like a total stunner in a fantastic hat.'

This prospect was so appealing to Devon that her eyes widened automatically, her lips parting slightly, moist and inviting. Matt couldn't help but laugh.

'God, you look so sexy when you're excited about something!' he said fondly. 'Is it meeting the Queen?'

More the fact that we'd be bound to get on the front pages for an MBE, Devon thought. *A big, lovely photo of Matt looking hunky and me staring up at him lovingly. And not in a hat. My hair pinned up really high, like Sophia Loren, with a Philip Treacy feather clip in it.*

Her expression turned so soft and dreamy at this ideal picture that Matt's arms tightened around her. Bending down, he kissed her, and as always, Devon responded to him, reaching up to wrap her arms around his neck – which took some doing, as Matt's neck was as thick as an oak beam. His hand came up to cradle her head, his tongue, warm and insistent, slid through her parted lips, and she felt that familiar wet hot stir of excitement deep inside her, her body instantly opening up to him.

She'd fancied Matt from the moment she first met him on the rickety set of *Wake up UK*; he'd loomed over everyone else like a colossus. They'd all assumed that because he was a sportsman, he'd be a bit slow on the uptake, and Devon had been hugely relieved when she realized that not only was he gorgeous, he had more than a few brain cells knocking around in that enormous cranium. Their chemistry had been blindingly obvious to everyone who'd seen them bantering live on TV as Devon helped him make pasta sauce; he'd asked her out to dinner that night, and she'd barely even played hard to get.

The lovely thing about big muscly men was that they generally liked girls with curves. If Devon's taste had been more inclined to posh, Sloaney boys, she'd have been in trouble, as they tended to prefer their women blonde, skinny, and flat-chested. She'd had the opportunity to observe that over and over again at the parties Maxie threw with her super-posh husband; both the men and the women treated Devon as if she were common because she was voluptuous; though they were impressed that she was on TV. It was bizarre: in Devon's experience, if posh women weren't stick figures, they tended to be pear-shaped, with no boobs to speak of and big flat bums as wide as the Grand Canyon, which they'd often emphasize by wearing tartan skirts, for goodness' sake! And yet they looked down on her for having all her curves in the right places.

Oh well, that's Maxie's problem, Devon thought, kissing her husband. *If she wants to starve herself to skin and bones just to fit in with Olly and his posh boys, rather her than me.*

And then, it happened. Just as Matt's other hand, caressing her bottom, lifted and nudged her into the space between his legs, letting her feel how hard he was just from kissing her; just as her own body melted against him, reaching up to him, rubbing herself against him in a way that made it more than clear how much she wanted him too; just as Matt swung her round, half-pulling, half-carrying her towards the door, heading for the bedroom, where they could shut the door firmly against the cleaning lady and Devon's assistant, both of whom might come into the kitchen at any time – just then, Devon caught sight of her reflection in the big mirror over the sofa.

She froze.

Oh God! I'm the size of a house!

It was a bright, sunny day, and the kitchen, with its glass extension, had been specially designed to let in as much light as possible for the TV cameras. Which meant that there was nowhere for Devon to hide from the sight of herself. She'd thought the outfit she'd so carefully put on that morning was very flattering – and when she'd been posing in it in front of her walk-in closet mirrors, before breakfast, it had been. Slim-fitting jeans, with a tummy-control panel for extra help, so that when she adjusted the waistband to sit just below her belly button, they sucked her in and lifted her bottom to where it ought to be. The black Ghost crêpe shirt, with a deep cleavage to show off her best assets, a nipped-in waist, and long tails that swept over her tummy and bottom, giving her extra coverage where she needed it most. And big amethyst Zoppini earrings, the stones set in stainless steel, the purple setting off her dark hair and eyes perfectly. Purple was the best colour for brunettes.

But now the waistband of her jeans had ridden down, and not even the heavy, forgiving crêpe fabric of the shirt could hide the muffin-top roll that bulged over the top of the denim. The way Matt was holding her, she could clearly see the roll below her bra strap, too. She'd always been proud of her legs, but her thighs, at this angle, looked chunky in the tight jeans. And a soft little bulge of fat under her jaw was almost a double chin at this angle.

Her face was still beautiful; she had strong enough features to carry the extra plumpness. Her hair was dark and glossy, her skin smooth and creamy. But those were the only positives. The rest was unbearable to look at.

Almost violently, she pushed away from her surprised husband. The thought of going to bed with him – of taking off her clothes in front of him, of him seeing the red marks on her skin where her bra and jeans and knickers had cut into her – was too much for her to handle. On the few occasions they'd had sex recently, she'd staged it very carefully; in the evening, by the soft light of candles or a bedside lamp, with Devon wearing a baby-doll negligee that served up her bosoms like two succulent white peaches in snug chiffon – the frillier the better, for Matt's tastes – and flowed in lavish pleats over the rest of her torso.

By daylight, it would be too much. Matt would see how big she'd really become. Tears pricked at her eyes, tears of humiliation and self-hate.

'What is it, Dev?' Matt was asking, coming towards her, trying to take her hands.

She turned away. But she could see him in the mirror, his craggy face now all concern for her, his hard-on momentarily forgotten as he tried, and failed, to work out what on earth could have just gone so badly wrong.

Matt's so bloody nice! she thought almost resentfully. *Why doesn't he get angry for a change – tell me I'm messing him around?* Perversely, she would have welcomed that much more than tender concern. A nice squabble, to let off steam – a good row, shouting at each other, throwing some plates (or crockery, as Matt would put it) – that was exactly what the built-up tension inside her needed in order to find release.

But Matt was never going to give her that. He just wasn't the quarrelling type.

'I don't feel like it,' she said. The hot rush of excitement had ebbed away as quickly as it had come, leaving her feeling like a beached whale, washed up on a rocky, uncomfortable shore. The only thing she wanted to do was stuff her face, so she could shove down these horrible emotions, make them disappear under the sheer weight of the food.

Long-term, it was a disastrous idea. But short-term, she knew it would work. It always had before. And now, all she wanted, with a passion almost as strong as she'd had for Matt just moments ago, was to somehow get him out of the kitchen so she could raid the fridge.

'Dev, I know something's wrong,' Matt said with such fervour in his voice that she flinched away, even more guilty now. 'Tell me! Whatever it is, we can fix it – I know we can.'

His blue eyes were filled with nothing but worry for her: no frustration, no reproach for having got him hard and then left him hanging. Matt was so bloody nice that it made her feel even worse. *Why can't he yell or sulk? Call me names? Or even storm out to jerk off in the bathroom?* Again, she realized she was longing for a fight, something her gentle husband would never give her.

I'm more comfortable with Gary, she thought suddenly. *Because he bickers with me all the time. It actually suits me better, somehow.*

'I don't know if we *can* fix it,' she blurted out, and Matt flinched back at her words.

The phone rang, but neither of them went to answer it; Devon's secretary Marcy fielded all the calls on the landline number. But a few seconds later, the extension in the kitchen buzzed. Marcy had vetted and put through the phone call. She had a sixth sense for knowing where her employers were in the house at any given time.

'Don't take it, Dev,' Matt pleaded. 'We need to talk about what's going on.'

His soft West Country burr was more pronounced now, as it always was when he was passionate or emotional. Devon usually loved it, the gentle blurring of the syllables, the slow, soft speech of a man who liked to take his time. But hearing it now was the last straw. Knowing that she had hurt him, made him vulnerable, ratcheted up her guilt and self-loathing even more.

So she did the only logical thing in the situation. She hurt him still more. Striding across the kitchen, raising his hopes for a second or two before dashing them by sliding by him without even touching him as she went, she picked the phone off the handset and said, 'Yes? Oh, hi Maxie! What's up?' into the mouthpiece.

Behind her, Matt's huge, stocky shoulders slumped. Whenever Maxie rang, Devon jumped to attention; he knew he had no chance of recapturing his wife's focus now. Devon heard his heavy tread leaving the kitchen as Maxie's high, clipped tones said urgently, 'Devon? It's me. Look, Deeley just rang me. Dev, she's coming back to London. For good!' Maxie's voice rose even higher. 'Dev. This could be a disaster. What are we going to *do*?'

Maxie

*M*axie paced furiously up and down her living room in stock-inged feet, thinking hard. Plotting, planning; that was what Maxie did best. Ever since they'd been little girls, three young sisters, their mother either in prison or off with some man, Maxie had had to scheme and strategize to keep them all safe. No one else would do it but her. Only Maxie had the brains and the cunning necessary to deal with the social workers who came sniffing around; to make sure the sisters didn't get taken into care and split up; to keep the three of them fed and clothed and going to school and safe from the kind of predators who were all too ready to exploit underage girls.

And I did a pretty good job, she told herself now. *Look at us, how far we've come! We'd never have managed that without me pushing us all!*

Maxie was the strategist, the long-term thinker. She had an academic brain that had got her into Oxford, and the quick instincts that had taught her to spot the most privileged, richest, best-connected social circle, and manage to fit in with them. Devon was ambitious too, but she didn't have Maxie's drive and sharpness.

Probably because Devon's so beautiful, Maxie thought. *She didn't have to work so hard to succeed.* It was impossible not to be jealous of a younger sister who'd been so lusciously gorgeous that from the age of fourteen grown men had turned to gape at her in the street with open desire. Devon had been destined to end up as a TV presenter; she had the kind of looks that made people want to stare at her for hours. What Devon actually did on TV, Maxie suspected, was pretty much irrelevant. She could have been a weathergirl or a daytime talk-show host or a gossip journalist to exactly the same effect. The thought of Devon as a cook still made Maxie smile with amusement; Devon had barely cooked at home beyond the most standard basics. Her sister might have deluded herself by now into believing her own myth, but Maxie knew perfectly well that all Devon's recipes were concocted for her by a team of researchers.

Still, Maxie could trust Devon implicitly. Devon owed Maxie for so much – all the care Maxie had taken of her over the years, as well as the influence that Olly had exerted to get Devon into her first job in TV. Devon would never open her mouth about what had happened all those years ago, back in that grubby little council house. Devon valued everything she'd achieved much too much to ever breathe a word about how Bill had died. *Particularly since she'd be implicating herself, too*, Maxie thought grimly. *She was in it up to her neck.*

But Deeley . . . Deeley was the weak link. Deeley was the classic youngest sister, spoiled and cosseted and protected by her older siblings. Deeley had always relied on them for everything. When Deeley had finished school at sixteen, she'd promptly moved down to London, to be close to Maxie and Devon; but Maxie's life as a 24-year-old career woman, married to Olly, who was just taking over his father's seat in Parliament, was so grown-up, so mature, that she and Deeley had found they had nothing in common. Sixteen-year-olds didn't want to accompany their older sister and her husband to dinner parties and corporate entertaining boxes at the opera. Deeley had quickly found a series of temporary jobs and a house-share with some girls her own age with whom she could go out partying. Devon had already been working on *Wake up UK*. Getting to the set at three every morning meant that Devon had to go to bed very early; she was on a completely different schedule from her younger sisters. Devon and Deeley had hardly crossed paths in London at all.

It had been Maxie who Deeley rang with all her problems, Maxie from whom Deeley borrowed small sums of money when she was late with her rent. But Maxie hadn't actually seen that much of Deeley, and when Deeley went off to LA with Nicky, they lost touch almost completely. Deeley hadn't even managed to come back to the UK for Devon's wedding.

And the distance that had opened up between them, Maxie and Devon on one side of the Atlantic, and Deeley on the other, had been absolutely fine as far as the older sisters were concerned. Deeley, Maxie knew, had been very affected by the events of that night in Riseholme. She had wanted to talk about it, many times, but Maxie had never allowed that. *Least said, soonest mended*. Maxie had put it all behind her, and she was confident that Devon had too. She held Devon close, kept an eye on her, to make sure that she didn't do anything to embarrass her, and to reassure herself that Devon showed no signs of ever spilling the beans about what had happened to Bill.

Devon had too much to lose by doing that. Devon was safe. But Deeley, running back from LA, deeply upset at her perfect life falling to pieces all around her, Deeley, who'd never been comfortable keeping their shared secret, Deeley, who'd always been a little blabbermouth – Deeley was a loose cannon. Panicking at the thought of being on her own once again, Deeley's voice on the phone had been lost, hopeless, wanting Maxie to snap back into her old role, and take care of her.

Typical. As soon as Nicky dumps her, she comes running back to me. The weight of responsibility for her sisters descended onto Maxie's narrow shoulders, heavy and oppressive, an all-too-familiar sensation.

Maxie came to a decided halt. *Well, I won't do it,* she told herself firmly. *Deeley's a grown woman now. She can stand on her own two feet.*

But what if she can't keep her mouth shut?

Maxie had stopped in the centre of the living room, on the Aubusson rug that had been in her husband's family for at least a century. Practically all the furniture had been in Olly's family for that amount of time. The middle classes were often dismissed by snobbish aristocrats as 'having to buy their own furniture'; well Olly Stangroom, MP for Brampton-on-Sea, would never be vulnerable to that kind of attack. The Stangrooms were an old, rich, well-established county family. Olly, the oldest son, would inherit the baronetcy when his father died.

Which will make me Lady Stangroom, Maxie reflected, feeling her mood improve tremendously as she regarded herself with satisfaction in the ornate, nineteenth-century Venetian glass mirror that hung over the fireplace. Her appearance testified to how hard she'd worked to get to where she was. Naturally, Maxie was neither slim nor blonde, but she'd made herself into both of those precious commodities by exercising like a maniac, living on cucumber slices and carrot sticks, and having a standing appointment at Nicky Clarke in Mount Street every three weeks to have her dark McKenna hair lightened to a pale gold that made her look much less like an Irish colleen (which would *not* have gone down well in their social circle) and much more like a perfect Sloane wife. The blonde tint actually made Maxie more striking; it was a contrast to her dark brows and eyes, giving an interest to her appearance that made people look at her twice.

Maxie wasn't beautiful like Devon, or stunningly pretty like Deeley, though she was striking in her own way. But she had made her peace with that a long time ago. *I didn't get the looks in the family,* she thought, adjusting the silk Hermès scarf tied elegantly at her neck. *But I certainly got the brains.*

And now I have to work out what on earth to do about Deeley coming back to London.

'Darling? Is everything all right?'

Maxie swivelled on her heels as her husband came into the room. Pink-cheeked, fair-haired, cherub-faced, Olly Stangroom was the archetypal posh boy, with the comfortable plumpness of someone who'd never quite lost his baby fat. He was tugging disconsolately at his jacket, trying to get it to hang right.

'I hate this bloody Marks and Spencer suit!' he complained bitterly. 'It feels revoltingly cheap. I wouldn't be surprised if there's *polyester* in this.'

Maxie was temporarily distracted from her own concerns; Olly never wore a suit that hadn't been handmade for him on Savile Row.

'You're in a Marks and Spencer suit?' she exclaimed, staring at him in surprise. It didn't actually look terrible, she had to admit. Still, Olly's tailor cut his suits to cleverly widen his client's shoulders and conceal the slight podge of his tummy; by contrast the off-the-peg M & S suit was not quite as flattering.

Olly pulled a face, which made him look charmingly like a 6-year-old boy.

'Didn't I tell you?' he said, grimacing. 'Diktat from the chief whip. We've all got to look "relatable", of all the ghastly American words. No more "conspicuous consumption". We're banned from drinking champagne in public, and we've all got to bicycle everywhere, and if some bloody pinko commie journalist from the *Guardian* asks us where our suit's from, we look surprised and say "M & S, of course!" so we can come across as Men of the People.'

'Oh, poor darling!' Maxie commiserated, walking over to straighten his tie. 'Listen, you may have to buy suits from M & S, but there's no reason you can't take them to Trevor to have them tailored, is there?'

Olly's forehead furrows disappeared as if by magic at the mention of Trevor, his man in Savile Row.

'Oh Max, you're a gem,' he said gratefully. 'That's sheer genius. You always have an answer for everything. Gosh, I wonder if I have time to pop in to see Trevor before I have to be at the House . . .'

He pondered this, before realizing that Maxie wasn't helping him with his timetable, as she usually would. This definitely meant that something was off. He looked more closely at his wife.

'Everything all right, old girl?' he asked cautiously. Maxie was like a superbly functioning machine, and she ran their lives with maximum efficiency: but no machine was perfect, and if she got any grit in her workings, Olly needed to oil it out pronto to avoid meltdowns.

'Oh God, Olly.' Maxie slumped into the closest armchair. Like all their period furniture, it was hideously uncomfortable, upholstered in silk caught with little buttons that cut into anyone who, like Maxie, had very little excess flesh to pad her out. She grabbed a cushion and shoved it behind her, but it didn't help much. 'It's Deeley,' she said, looking up at her husband. 'Things haven't worked out for her in Los Angeles. She's broken up with her boyfriend.'

'I thought he was gay,' Olly said, confused.

'Well, yes, he is. But that hasn't stopped him from chucking her for someone more famous. Now she doesn't have an income or anywhere to live, and they're making her come back to the UK.'

To Maxie's intense annoyance, her husband perked up at this news.

'Well, not to worry!' he said cheerfully. 'She can stay here! We have plenty of room, don't we?'

He waved his arms expansively, indicating the size of their five-storey Holland Park mansion.

'I mean, I haven't been up to the top floor in yonks!' he said. 'God knows what's even up there! Surely we can fit her in somewhere . . .'

Maxie narrowed her eyes at him. She knew exactly what was going through his mind; he was picturing Deeley wandering around the house in a bathrobe. Olly had always had an eye for the pretty girls. He'd been sensible enough to marry Maxie, knowing that, even though she had no family background, she'd make the perfect wife for an aspiring Tory politician. Even Olly's cold-as-ice, fearsomely snobbish mother, after putting Maxie under searing observation one terrifying weekend at the Stangroom country house, had pretty much instructed her son to propose to Maxie forthwith. It had been abundantly clear to Lady Stangroom that Maxie had all the brains, organizational abilities and backbone that Olly lacked. Which compensated for her lack of pedigree – or inheritance.

But Maxie had always been aware that though Olly had been sensible enough to marry her, it hadn't been because he thought she was the prettiest thing he'd ever seen in his life.

'You can drool over Deeley all you want,' she snapped. 'She won't look twice at you – she doesn't exactly go for podgy middle-aged Tory MPs.'

It was very hard to offend upper-class, privileged white men, and indeed, Olly just smiled complacently at his wife's words.

'Oh, we'll find her a rich husband easily enough,' he said cheerfully. 'Some banker chappie who's on the lookout for a trophy wife'll snap her up – a girl as pretty as your sister. You know how it works with City boys – first wife to help you make the money, second wife to help you spend it.' He winked at his wife. 'Don't worry, darling,' he added. 'That doesn't apply to politicians.'

No, Maxie thought with a surge of hostility that took her by surprise. And it wasn't at Olly's comment; she knew that her marriage was 100 per cent secure. She gave Olly not only what he needed, but what he wanted. He wasn't going anywhere.

No, her objection was a very different one. *I'm not having Deeley marry someone in our social circle – we'd have to invite her round all the time, maybe even holiday together. I'd either be watching all the men drooling over my prettier, younger sister, or have her ringing me up non-stop asking me to organize things for her.*

It's bad enough with Devon, but at least Devon's a social asset – everyone wants to meet her. Devon actually does something, or pretends to. All Deeley does is look glamorous and wear short skirts.

It's time for her to get her own life. Stop running back to me as soon as her LA set-up crashes. I can't be Deeley's safety blanket any more.

'Oh, there won't be room here, darling,' she said, tilting her head to the side and trying her best to look regretful. 'Remember, the baby comes next week. The entire top floor's a nursery now. Plus rooms for the day and night nannies.'

'Oh God, the baby!' Olly pulled a long face. 'Maxie, you know I've never been keen on this whole baby thing. Don't suppose there's any chance we could pull the plug, is there?'

Maxie shook her head firmly. '*Much* too late for that,' she said. 'Trust me, Olly, it's a brilliant idea. We can't have children, so we adopt. It looks odd if we don't. So we get extra points by picking a black one. No one's done Rwanda yet, so that'll be even more press coverage. And I made sure it's a girl, so she won't be inheriting the title – no worries there.'

'Well, that's the one bright spot in all of this,' Olly said gloomily. 'Mummy's *not* happy, I can tell you. She's not madly keen on adoption anyway, but the whole African thing . . .' He grimaced, his rounded cheeks contorting. 'At least I could reassure her that it was a girl.'

Maxie smiled, the special small smile with her lips pressed tightly together which meant that she had pulled off an especially successful scheme.

'Wait till your mother sees all the articles in the press,' she advised her husband. 'Wait till we're on the front of all those magazines. Not just Sunday supplements, the housewives' mags too. It's *just* the demographic the party needs to win round. Women with families. All the online sites, too – Mumsnet's champing at the bit to do a live chat with us. And it'll be the publicity gift that keeps on giving! This won't be a one-off. Any time you need a boost, we can pick her up from school, or take her to the park. The tabloids'll love it. We're so blonde and she'll be dark – the photos will be sensational. Besides, think of all the great charity work opportunities. Anything to do with Africa, we'll have first dibs on! It'll look fantastic.'

Olly's brow was clearing slightly; any mention of guaranteed press coverage could always be relied upon to make an MP interested in an idea.

'What if it backfires?' he asked, duly cautious, as befitted a politician. 'You know, if people think we're just doing it for PR?'

Maxie waved a dismissive hand. 'We're not film stars or pop stars who trot their kids out for publicity and then complain about paparazzi invading their privacy,' she assured her husband. 'This kind of thing only backfires if you overplay your hand, and you can rely on me not to do that, darling. I'll pace it carefully and make sure that doesn't happen. You trust me, don't you?'

'You *know* I trust you,' Olly said fondly. 'You're a PR whizz, my sweet. Only . . . isn't it quite a high price to pay? I mean, she'll be here all the time. We won't be able to get rid of her. It's not like getting a pet or something.'

'Oh, the nannies will do all the work,' Maxie said, shrugging off this concern. 'Madonna, Brad Pitt and Angelina Jolie – do you really think they spend as much time with their children as they say? They're bound to have an army of nannies in the background. They're just careful to keep them out of the press photos. Besides, she'll be off at boarding school before you know it. We'll say it's to help her assimilate fully. You know – we'll miss her terribly but we want her to have all the benefits you did.'

She leaned forward, crossing her slim legs, her feet shod in impeccable Ferragamo heels.

'And the most important thing of all, Olly – do remember – you'll have instant name recognition. More than any other MP, on either side of the House. I mean, "Gordon Brown's got only one eye", "Louise Bagshawe writes bestsellers" – all of that *pales* next to "Olly Stangroom adopted a Rwandan baby"! Every single person in the UK will know your name. I mean, right now, what are you? "Olly Stangroom, Under-Secretary for Used Cars", or something. Who knows? Who cares?'

'Under-Secretary for Social Justice actually, darling,' Olly said crossly.

'Well, exactly! "Social Justice" – what does that even mean? From now on *everyone* will know who you are! And no one else in the House will be able to go the African baby adoption route, because they'll look like total copycats!'

Olly was smiling now. 'You really are awfully clever, aren't you, darling?' he said fondly. 'Mummy was absolutely right when she told me to snap you up.'

'It's a new world,' Maxie said briskly. 'New values. And most importantly, new ways of getting publicity. You have to think big nowadays to get the big pay-offs. Look at what I've done with Bilberry!'

Maxie was referring to the high-end leather goods company of which she was commercial director. She had taken it from a staid, old-fashioned brand whose clientele was aging fast, to a modern, cutting-edge firm whose handbags were named after supermodels and It girls. Bilberry's mobile phone covers and crocodile skin Kindle reader sleeves were highly expensive and much sought after. Maxie's stroke of genius – apart from getting the celebrity endorsements – had been to hike the prices and introduce waiting lists for practically every single item, thus ensuring that every rich wannabe in London society clamoured to spend their money on Bilberry products. At a recent launch of the latest shoulder bag – named after Helena Bonham Carter, who had not only a posh surname, but A-list status as an eccentric English fashion icon – socialites, trophy wives, titled nobodies and MTV presenters had practically trampled each other to snap up freebies and place orders for the bag.

Times had changed for the English upper classes. Not only was there no shame in being in trade, it was positively admired. Look at Samantha Cameron, wife of the current Tory prime minister – not only had she been creative director of Smythson, which pushed stationery at £200 a box of personalized notecards, but her mother, Lady Astor, ran a hugely successful home furnishings company which sold silk napkin tassels for £49 and rattan dog beds for £265. If you could make that much money pushing a version of upper-class taste to the aspiring middle classes, the aristocrats, rather than looking down on you, would not only applaud you, but try to marry into your family.

'And I'm not going to give it up,' Maxie continued firmly. 'Not only would I go out of my mind being a stay-at-home mother, but it would look awful in the press. Really old-fashioned. The modern woman works – she has to. She juggles everything, she's got tons of balls in the air. Most mothers can't afford to stay at home, and they don't sympathize with the ones who do. And the women without children would hate it even more than the mums if I stopped working.'

Olly winced. 'Darling, don't say "mum",' he said sotto voce. 'It's awfully common.'

'I know *exactly* what I'm doing,' Maxie concluded, making a mental note of her husband's correction. 'Trust me, Olly.'

'I know you do,' her husband said, coming over to pull her to her feet and press his lips briefly against hers. 'You always do, Max. You should have been the MP.'

Maxie laughed. 'Darling, I could have been the MP in two seconds!' she said cheerfully. 'But then what would you have done? You couldn't have worked in the City – you're no good with numbers.'

'Oh God, I know!' Olly said just as cheerfully. 'I'm such a thickie! I do hope they don't send me to the Treasury. That would be terribly awkward.'

Maxie waved her hand. 'Oh, the civil servants do all the work and tell you what to say,' she said, shrugging. 'You'd be fine, darling. After all, that's how it'll be when you're prime minister.'

Olly's blue eyes gleamed with excitement at the mention of the magic words. It was every politician's dream, whether they'd admit it to themselves or not, whether they had the abilities or not. There wasn't an MP who had ever lived who hadn't pictured themselves standing on the doorstep of 10 Downing Street, camera shutters clicking. Going to Buckingham Palace to officially tell the Queen that they were forming a government. Standing at the despatch box, defeating the leader of the opposition in debate. Jetting round the globe as a head of state, being treated almost like a sovereign by world leaders . . .

Maxie saw the glazed look of ambition in her husband's eyes, and smiled to herself.

'I picked the prettiest baby girl,' she said, patting his cheek. 'Don't worry about that. I know you wouldn't have liked an ugly little thing running round the house. She's passed every health check, and if we take her to a specialist paediatrician here, she'll be fine. No nasty contagious diseases in the house.'

'Oh, phew,' Olly said, his cheeks puffing out as he exhaled heavily in relief. 'I don't like sick people, you know that, darling.'

'Of course I do!' Maxie patted his cheek again. 'I know you better than you know yourself! That's my job!'

'Talking of which,' Olly said hopefully, shuffling his feet and going a little pink in the cheeks, 'I've been awfully good about this whole African baby thing, Max.'

'*Rwandan* baby,' she corrected quickly.

'Rwandan baby,' he repeated dutifully. 'Sorry! But you must admit—'

'Yes,' Maxie agreed, nodding tolerantly. 'You have been really good.'

'So I deserve a treat?' he said hopefully, his cheeks going pinker. 'It's been ages!'

'You *do* deserve a treat,' she said. It was an old routine between them, but one of which Olly never tired.

'Tonight?' he said, so excited now that his voice was a little breathy. 'Really? Really, Max?'

She leaned in towards him and whispered in his ear, as one hand slid down to briefly stroke his now hard penis through the fabric of his trousers. 'Tonight, you naughty boy, I'm going to give you a jolly good spanking. Is that what you want?'

Olly, beyond words now, bobbed his head frantically up and down in assent.

'Maybe,' she said, drawing it out until he gasped in anticipation, her palm cupping the firm head of his penis, 'maybe, if I'm feeling really randy, I'll paddle you so hard you'll have to sleep facedown . . .'

Olly's penis surged so violently into her hand that she withdrew it, worried he'd come in his trousers.

'Oh God,' he panted. 'Oh God, Maxie . . .'

He's right, Maxie thought, as her husband staggered out of the room, clutching himself in gleeful anticipation. *That suit is definitely part-polyester.*

Deeley

*T*hey didn't want her.

Neither of her sisters wanted her back in London.

If Deeley had let herself admit it, she'd been aware of the state of things since the first phone call she'd made to Maxie, a couple of weeks ago. It had been all too clear that Maxie had assumed that Deeley would be staying on in LA after her break-up with Nicky. When Deeley had explained that part of the settlement included the condition that she leave the States – and Carmen had later been kind enough to clarify in an email that she'd make sure that Deeley's US visa would not be renewed, thus ensuring that Deeley would have no option to stay on – Maxie's shock had been audible.

'But what are you going to *do* back here?' Maxie had asked incredulously. 'I mean, you don't know anyone, you don't have a job . . .'

'Well, I know you! And Devon!' Deeley had said, hearing her own voice falter. 'I thought it would be a great opportunity for us to spend some time together, just hanging out and reconnecting . . .'

'Hanging out and reconnecting? God, you sound awfully LA,' Maxie had drawled, in her own artificially posh accent.

'Well, I've been here for five years,' Deeley had said defensively.

'And it's a *much* better fit for you than London,' Maxie had said. 'Isn't it?'

Probably, Deeley thought now, looking out of the window at the grey sky, which seemed to hang so low that she was almost surprised it didn't brush against the heads of the people scurrying, wrapped up tight in warm coats against the wind and the rain. It had been glorious spring in Los Angeles when she'd left, doing her best not to cry. She'd been crowded by the paparazzi at LAX, who were gleefully snapping candid shots of Nicky Shore's now ex-girlfriend escaping LA in dejection because he'd dumped her. Stacks of suitcases piled up on a trolley, pushed by a porter, Deeley, in huge YSL sunglasses and a silk sweater under a fake fur gilet, a big Hayden-Harnett pony skin tote slung over her shoulder, holding up a hand to signal that she wouldn't be stopping to pose.

It had been a suitably dramatic end to the last five years of her life. *The end of a movie,* she thought. *Deeley gets on a plane and flies away. Maybe the last time in my life I turn left when I get on an aeroplane – from now on, it'll be right. Into cattle class.*

Neither Devon nor Maxie had invited her to stay. Maxie had specified that she didn't have room in their vast Holland Park mansion, as she was adopting a Rwandan baby. Maxie had been very keen to specify that the baby was Rwandan, which presumably meant that it was the latest trendy location for sourcing foreign babies. *Trust Maxie to be ahead of the curve,* Deeley thought with appreciation. Maxie had always known exactly how things should be done: which university to attend, which group to hang out with, which son of privilege to target and marry, which career to follow that would ensure she placed herself exactly at the centre of the world she wanted to inhabit. Which African country was the hot place of the moment to source a baby.

Deeley had always unquestioningly admired this skill of her eldest sister's. Maxie was able to manoeuvre through her own life, steering it precisely how she wanted it, while Deeley was the polar opposite – Deeley was blown around by any prevailing wind. Nicky had suggested that she be his fake girlfriend, and she'd gone along with it because it seemed like a good idea at the time; but then Nicky's people had decided that Deeley's stint was over, and Deeley was out. In other words, everyone else had made decisions for her.

I don't have any control over my life, Deeley reflected miserably. *I was hoping Maxie would help me get sorted out, but I can tell she doesn't have any time for me.*

And Devon hadn't been much better. Devon didn't have room for Deeley either, though she hadn't given an excuse as to why there wasn't a spare room in her Mayfair house. She'd suggested the boutique hotel in Fitzrovia where Deeley was staying now, and said that Deeley must come to the party to celebrate Devon's new TV series. But, initially, that had been the entire extent of her welcome to her younger sister as Deeley started her new life in London. Deeley had had to repeatedly ring – almost harass – both her sisters enough for them to finally, grudgingly, get their secretaries to organize a dinner date for all of them to meet and catch up.

She'd been here for a whole week, and she hadn't seen either Devon or Maxie – in the flesh, at least. Devon's face had been all over the TV, with endless promos for *Devon's Little Bit Extra*. *Just her face*, Deeley couldn't help noticing. *Not much of her body*. Devon had clearly put on weight in the last few years, and wasn't as keen to be filmed in full-body shots as she had been back in the heyday of *Wake up UK*, when the camera had literally followed her around like a little dog, charting her every move; but she was as beautiful as ever, her skin pale and smooth, her red lips pouting and full, her hair cascading around her face in a thick rich mass of dark curls.

Devon was always the beautiful one, Deeley thought without a hint of envy. *Maxie's the clever one.*

But who am I? Just the youngest.

She sighed.

No wonder I haven't done anything with my life. I can't even manage one positive adjective to define myself against my sisters. Look how successful they are! How much they've achieved! And me? I've got a wardrobe of clothes that aren't suitable for London weather, and a rapidly dwindling bank account. Plus, I'm mainly famous for being dumped by a guy who no one knows is gay.

Wow, Deeley. Slow handclap. Congratulations. You're a real achiever.

Deeley was late for dinner with her sisters; she'd got lost coming from Fitzrovia, where her hotel was located, to Jermyn Street, below Piccadilly. *Five years away and I don't remember London as well as I thought I did*, she reflected ruefully, finally entering Franco's restaurant, her high heels already hurting. *I should have taken a black cab.* She stopped just inside the doors, getting her bearings. It was a weekday, but the bar was bustling, and as she entered, people looked up from their tables as if expecting to see someone they knew, always a sign of a restaurant with plenty of regulars or celebrity customers.

It was warm and inviting, with soft lamps glowing on the bar tables and huge black rectangular vases of orchids and sakura blossom on the reception desk and bar. A classic Italian restaurant, Franco's was located in St James's, an ideal location for the auctioneers, hedge funders, oil and mining executives, and headhunters who had their offices close by in the elegant and discreet little streets around St James's Square, above Pall Mall. And Franco's was a perfect reflection of the small, private section of SW1 in which it was located; it was equally elegant and discreet, one of wealthy London's best-kept secrets. Rich and famous people dined at Franco's because it served some of the best Italian food in London, and because its staff could be trusted, absolutely, never to call the paparazzi, or gossip to the press about the celebrities who had eaten there.

Lunchtime here was frenetic. Deals were being brokered, pictures were being sold to affluent ladies by suave art dealers; the atmosphere was buzzy, punchy, fizzing with energy. But in the evening, Franco's was even more like the cosy private club it very much resembled; you felt at home as soon as you walked through the door. A waiter setting cocktails on a bar table smiled a welcome at Deeley. She was slipping off her fake fur Dolce & Gabbana jacket, looking for the cloakroom, when a man coming out of the restaurant area sidestepped to avoid the waiter, bumped into her extended elbow, and knocked her off balance.

'Oh God, I'm sorry!' he exclaimed, grabbing her upper arms to steady her as she tripped and nearly fell, her heels sliding away from her on the polished parquet floor.

He wasn't holding her hard, just enough to stop her falling, but as soon as he touched her, everything went into slow motion. She could see herself from a distance, arms bent like chicken wings, scrabbling to get her Gina heels under her again, straighten her knees, find her balance, her head ducked for stability. It was like a comedy sequence in a film, the clumsy heroine who keeps falling over and needs to get rescued.

But it wasn't funny at all.

Because his hands, somehow, were having a magnetic effect on her. Instantly reassuring, incredibly physical, out of any proportion to the comparative lightness of his touch. She momentarily resisted looking up to see his face, in case he was old, or ugly, or leering down at her cleavage – anything that would ruin the sudden, completely unexpected magic of this moment. But when she did, it was such a shock she stumbled again, and he had to close his hands even tighter on her.

He was absolutely gorgeous. Phenomenally sexy. And, as her eyes met his, she could tell his expression mirrored hers, that they were each as dazed as each other, trying to deal with the immediate impact of their physical contact.

'I'm sorry,' he mumbled again, at the same time as she said, 'Thanks – I'm OK . . .'

But he didn't let go of her for a few seconds more. It was ridiculous, because her jacket was still halfway down her straightening arms, sliding down to her wrists, and only when she realized it was about to hit the ground did she move to catch it, which made him jerk his hands away from her, going red and mumbling his third 'sorry' of their encounter. She grabbed the jacket, bundling it up in front of her in a careless ball as if it were some cheap H & M knock-off, and looked up once more to meet his eyes.

Not an actor, she thought instantly. *Thank God. He's much too tall to be an actor.* Deeley had met every male star in Hollywood, and barely any of them were over six foot. *Besides, he doesn't have the actor vibe. He's not behaving as if I should know who he is.*

In LA, his build and physical competence would have meant she'd take him for a bodyguard. *But his suit's too good – it fits him too well. Security don't wear £2,000 suits tailored to their bodies like that.*

And I recognize him from somewhere. There's something very familiar about his face. I know I've seen him – on TV, I think . . .

The thought of his body made her heat up inside. She could still feel his hands on her arms, huge and warm and secure, so strong that it had felt as though he could pick her up and swing her around as if she weighed nothing at all. For one crazy moment she actually thought of tripping, falling against him, to feel his arms come around her as she pressed herself up against his solid, muscular body. The impulse was insanely strong, and she knew she was going red too as she deliberately took a step back to resist the temptation.

What colour are his eyes? Blue, or grey? A little short-sighted, she stared up, trying to make out the precise shade, wondering where she might have seen him before. And he wasn't moving either; he was simply standing there, looking down at her. Neither of them spoke, because neither of them could come up with a word to say.

They both jumped when a woman's voice cut between them, saying, 'I'm so sorry to keep you waiting, madam. Let me take your coat now.'

It was a slim redhead in a black jacket over a black miniskirt, her hair pulled back smoothly from her pretty face. Deeley handed over her balled-up jacket without even taking her eyes from the man in front of her, as if they'd hypnotized each other; but then the redhead gave her a cloakroom ticket, and Deeley had to take that and slip it in her bag, and the connection was broken.

'Thanks again,' she managed to say to him. He looked dazed still, as if someone had hit him over the head. And that was what made her think, *Oh, he's a boxer! That's where I've seen him, on some TV promo – or a poster for a fight in Vegas.* She had a flash of memory: blood running down his face, a bandage round his scalp, his expression grim.

'Are you joining a party?' the redhead asked Deeley, who nodded mutely, stalling for time. Waiting for the man to ask her for her name, her phone number.

But instead he shook his head like a dog emerging from water. His jaw tightened, his lips drew together, and he turned away, pulling his mobile phone out of his pocket, heading for the door. Dumbly she watched him go, admiring his long, muscled legs, the high firm buttocks whose movement wasn't completely hidden by the back flap of his jacket.

He'll come back in, get the waiter to slip me a note, she told herself firmly as she got hold of herself and said to the pretty hostess that she was meeting Maxie Stangroom and Devon McKenna. *He'll come and find me.* Used to naming celebrities she was dining with, Deeley watched the flicker in the woman's eyes at her sisters' names, and was impressed with the reaction. Clearly, her sisters were London A-list. Smiling in acknowledgement, the redhead led Deeley through the bar and into the restaurant, to where Maxie and Devon were seated at one of the prime tables, by the far windows.

Franco's didn't have piped music; the only noise in the restaurant was the happy babble of its diners. Maxie and Devon were chattering away and only noticed Deeley when she was standing right next to them. They rose a little on sight of her, their faces breaking into practised smiles. But that was all.

Oh, Deeley thought, her heart sinking a little. *I only get the 'come to a half-squat behind the table' greeting, not the 'wriggle out from my seat and actually hug you' one. This isn't good.*

'Hi!' she said over-brightly, over-loudly, as if to compensate for her sisters' lack of enthusiasm. 'Wow, it's so great to see you guys! I can't believe how good you both look!'

Awkwardly, she leaned over the table to plant a kiss on Maxie's cheek, and then shuffled in to tuck into the seat next to Devon, kissing her too. And, glancing past Devon at Maxie, the sister to whom Deeley had always looked for approval, Deeley realized with dawning fear that Maxie's eyebrows had shot up almost to her hairline, and she was staring down her nose at her youngest sister. It was the expression Maxie had always used when Deeley did something wrong, didn't snap into line when reminded, or in any way failed to follow the clear-as-crystal plan for the McKenna girls which Maxie had laid out ever since she was a steely-eyed, barely teenaged girl, planning and plotting to get them out of the hellhole in which they lived.

'What?' Deeley said nervously, feeling, as she so often did with Maxie, like a child being reprimanded by her mother. 'What is it?'

'You look *very* LA,' Maxie said, her voice layered with that particular, upper-class tone that disapproves of anything it considers remotely vulgar.

Deeley might be out of touch with London mores, but she recognized the attitude; she'd heard it from New Yorkers visiting LA, who were usually wearing black, out-of-shape and pasty, but who looked down on the denizens of Los Angeles who took a lot better care of themselves, worked out, watched what they ate and wore clothes that showed themselves off.

She glanced down at herself quickly. She was in the simple, elegant black Alessandro Dell'Acqua dress that she had specially chosen as being perfect for tonight. It was a simple stretch jersey tube, falling to her knees – no miniskirt, nothing tarty – with a loose cowl neckline that showed off her tanned shoulders, and bracelet-length sleeves. Her only jewellery were her diamond stud earrings and a diamond tennis bracelet, both presents from Nicky. Her hair was pushed back from her face, falling down her back, and she had spent ages doing the discreet, freshly glowing make-up style that Hervé had taught her. Nothing obvious, all beiges and pinks and corals. By LA standards, she was really dressed down. It was the outfit and look of a woman going out to dinner with girlfriends whom she didn't want to upstage.

So it should have been exactly right. But, as Deeley looked at both of her sisters, she realized that it wasn't.

English women were very different from LA ones. They did both less and more, simultaneously. Both Devon and Maxie were dramatically made-up, Devon with her huge, stunning dark eyes strongly outlined, her eyelashes thick and lush, her lips red and shiny. Maxie's features were carefully contoured, shading, liner, blusher, layers of pink gloss to make her lips look wider, highlighter along her cheekbones to make them more noticeable. Shiny pieced blonde streaks at her hairline framed her face; one brief glance at Maxie told you that this was a woman who took great care with every aspect of her appearance. Devon wore a Vivienne Westwood red-and-grey tartan dress which dipped deep to show off her magnificent cleavage, while Maxie's sleek silk printed top was accessorized with a big, heavy gold necklace and matching earrings.

In a way, Deeley's carefully studied, understated look was a slap in the face to her sisters. Because no one wants to look as if they're trying too hard.

'You look like an LA trophy wife,' Maxie added.

'Well, that's what I was,' Deeley said simply.

'You're so *thin*,' Devon said unguardedly, staring at her younger sister. 'You've lost so much weight!'

'A bit,' Deeley said. 'But not that much, really. I mean, I do a lot of Pilates, and that helps. But honestly, by LA standards, I'm practically a fattie. The stylists used to complain all the time about having to fit my boobs.'

Devon's eyebrows shot up. 'Wow, how completely horrible for you,' she said, reaching for her glass of Prosecco.

'I didn't mean it like that!' Deeley said quickly. 'I just meant, I'm not a sample size over there, that's all.'

'Well, you look fine to me,' Devon said sourly. 'I'd kill to be as much of a fattie as you.' She put the word 'fattie' between inverted commas that were almost audible. 'Did they put you on a diet?'

'At first,' Deeley said cautiously. 'But after I lost a few pounds, they decided it was better if I stayed the way I was. It looked good for Nicky to have a girlfriend who wasn't a stick insect.'

Maxie nodded, understanding the thinking behind the decision, but Devon lifted one white smooth shoulder.

'If you're a fattie, God knows what that makes me,' she muttered, tipping her glass to her mouth.

'Dev, I didn't mean . . .' Deeley said hastily. 'You look stunning, really gorgeous.'

'Prosecco, *signora*?' the waiter murmured beside her, and she nodded automatically as he tilted the bottle into her glass. Gratefully, she took the cool, condensation-beaded flute and took a long sip. Devon wasn't looking at her, and Deeley knew she was offended. To Deeley, Devon looked as lovely as ever. Devon had always been Deeley's idea of beauty; her features were perfect, her skin flawlessly pale, her hair thicker and more lush than either of her sisters'. *OK, she's put on a few pounds, but she still looks amazing,* Deeley thought. *Everyone's staring at her! And she's so successful – she has a new TV series coming out – so I'm a bit thinner than her at the moment, who cares?*

The trouble was, she had a feeling that Devon cared. Quite a lot.

'So what are your plans, Deeley?' Maxie asked, taking a carefully judged sip of Prosecco from her nearly full glass and replacing it in the precise place on the linen tablecloth from where she had taken it. 'Do you have to stay in the UK? Isn't that one of the conditions of getting your settlement?'

'Technically, I just had to get out of the States,' Deeley said, leaning forward, her caramel-coloured hair falling over one smooth shoulder. 'I mean, I suppose I could go anywhere, but I wouldn't have the faintest idea where else to go. London's home to me.'

Maxie's lips tightened. Devon, meanwhile, was smiling at the waiter, who was refilling her Prosecco glass. Despite the sophistication of Franco's and its staff, the waiter couldn't help being dazzled by Devon, whose charisma was as glittering as a fully illuminated glass chandelier.

'Maybe you should travel for a while?' Devon suggested, playing with a thick shiny ringlet of her black hair, her nails as fire red as her lips. 'See the world. You've got the money, and you can't have holidayed that much with Nicky – he was always working, right?'

Deeley nodded. 'We did Cannes a couple of times, and promotional trips,' she agreed. 'But that was all crazy. I mean, you just see a lot of suites in five-star hotels and a lot of red carpets. Mostly I had to sit watching him do press conferences. I'm not complaining,' she hastened to add, as Maxie had glanced sideways at Devon in sardonic amusement when Deeley spoke disparagingly about red carpets. 'It's just not really seeing the world. Like Devon said.' She smiled at her middle sister. 'You're right, I haven't done much of that. Not properly.'

'So you should go!' Devon said brightly, flashing a stunning smile at Deeley. 'Buy a first-class round-trip ticket and set off! Have adventures, meet people . . .'

'I'm not very good at being alone,' Deeley confessed in a small voice. Her glass was somehow empty now; she must be even more nervous than she realized. 'I always lived with someone. First with you, then the girls in my house-share in London, then Nicky. I mean, I was in the pool house, but he was always there. It feels really weird to be in the hotel by myself.'

'You have to be OK with yourself before you can be with someone else,' Maxie said in the pious tones of an agony aunt.

'Why don't you want me around?' Deeley said plaintively, as the attentive waiter topped up her glass. 'I don't understand!'

Maxie shot her a dagger-like glare; not so much at what she'd said, as that it had been in earshot of the waiter.

'I don't care!' Deeley said resentfully, hunching her shoulders as the waiter slipped away. 'If you're being mean to me, I'll say it and I don't care who hears it.'

'God, you're such a child, Deeley,' Devon said. 'It's like you haven't grown up at all.'

'You may not have a reputation to maintain, but we do,' Maxie snapped. 'Pull yourself together!'

And here we are again, Deeley realized miserably. *Back in our old roles. Maxie tells me what to do, Devon goes along with whatever Maxie says and patronizes me into the bargain – and I act like I'm five years old. It took barely ten minutes for us to fall back into the way we were when we were young. Nothing's changed.*

'I say – look at the McKenna sisters – what a bevy of beauties! Like three lovely angels!'

It was the plummy voice of a posh boy, oozing status and privilege. All three heads tilted up to see the butter yellow hair and pink-and-white face of Olly Stangroom MP, smiling complacently down at his wife and sisters-in-law.

'He looks like a Battenberg cake,' Devon muttered naughtily to Deeley, who smothered a giggle – not only at Devon's comment, but at her pleasure that they'd slipped back into another of their old roles; being mischievous behind the back of their older sister and maternal figure.

'Every man in the restaurant's wishing he was in my place right now,' he added smugly, hands in his pockets, rocking back on his heels. 'Do shove up, darling! I'm dying for a drink!'

Maxie worked her chair a few inches sideways to make room for her husband to pull out his own. He squeezed his plump bottom in beside her and beamed lasciviously at Deeley.

'Excellent! This must be the best view in town, eh? Devon, my dear, you look as luscious as ever. A bevy of beauties!' he repeated, as proudly as if he'd just invented the phrase himself.

Olly grabbed a glass of Prosecco from the waiter, and downed it in one long swallow, promptly holding it out for a refill.

'Good stuff!' he said. 'Franco's always does us proud!' He looked complacently at his wife. 'She found this place years ago. Clever girl. Maxie knows what I like,' he said to Deeley. 'Secret of a happy marriage: a wife who knows what you like. Doesn't mean I can't appreciate top totty, though. And you, my dear, are *definitely* top totty!'

Deeley had been dealing with men like her brother-in-law for what felt like her whole life, but was really only about ten years. In her experience there were two types of men who leered at girls and she had categorized him on first sight as the second harmless kind. The first was a real menace, the kind you never wanted to be alone in a room with, all grabbing hands and hot stinky breath on your face, the kind of man who assumed that because he fancied you, you were therefore fair game for his advances. From the men at trade shows where she'd been a hostess, right through to top Hollywood producers, she'd had plenty of practice with fending them off; you got really good at turning sideways, slipping away before they could corner you, plastering a friendly polite smile to your face as your body simultaneously twisted from their groping hands.

While the second type was all talk and no action. This was the category that commented very loudly on your assets, as if you were a cow at a cattle market, but, mercifully, didn't do anything about it.

Whatever his tastes were, Deeley didn't fit. There was no heat behind his eyes as he stared at her, no lust there at all. Deeley glanced over at Devon, and she could tell that her sister was just as aware of this as she was. Devon was smiling tolerantly at Olly as he leered at her glorious bosoms as if he were a pet Jack Russell terrier; a bit jumpy and licky, but no harm in him at all.

Really, I'm not Olly's type at all. And he's certainly not mine.

And that thought jolted back the image of the man who'd bumped into her in the foyer. Deeley felt a rush of warmth inside her that was nothing to do with the fact that she was well into her second glass of Prosecco. Surely he would come to find her, or get the waiter to slip her his number? If not, she'd make a trip to the ladies' soon, to give him a chance to see her and get up his nerve. The connection between them had been so strong, so powerful, there was no way he'd be able to ignore it. Deeley was utterly sure of that.

'Deeley! Honestly, are you drunk already? She can't be jetlagged, she's been here a week,' Maxie said sharply, waking Deeley from her reverie.

'Sorry, no,' she said quickly. 'What were you saying?'

'*Olly* was saying, actually,' Maxie corrected, making that 'actually' sound as sharp as a slap around the face, 'that it was a shame you couldn't come to Devon and Matt's wedding.'

Deeley turned to look at Devon, her face crinkling up in embarrassment.

'I'm sorry,' she apologized. 'I really am. It's just – LA's like a total bubble, you know? Once you're inside it, it's hard to even connect with the outside world. And my time really wasn't my own.' She lowered her voice a little, conscious of the ironclad confidentiality clause in her contract. 'I was totally at their beck and call. Nicky's team, I mean. When they said "Jump", I wouldn't even need to ask "How high?" 'cause they'd already have told me.'

'Oh, don't worry about it,' Devon said kindly, leaning over the empty chair between them to pat Deeley's hand. 'It was completely rammed. I'd have loved you to be one of my bridesmaids, but we did understand. And honestly, I was so distracted with everything that was going on – *Hello!* was photographing it, and they shoved us from pillar to post all day. I don't remember half of it.'

She smiled at Deeley.

'You'd have loved Matt's groomsmen, though,' she added. 'Total hunks of muscle. The *Hello!* journalist was drooling all over them.'

Tears pricked at Deeley's eyes at Devon being so nice to her. 'I *totally* wish I could have come,' she said in a heartfelt voice.

'You've *got* to get rid of that American accent you've picked up, Deeley!' Maxie drawled disapprovingly. 'It's vile!'

'Oh, I quite like it!' Olly said, beaming at Deeley. 'It's rather exotic, don't you think?'

'I've still got my copy of the *Hello!* you sent,' Deeley said to Devon, squeezing her hand back. 'You looked stunning.'

'I did, didn't I?' Devon said almost sadly. As if she were on auto-pilot, she reached for her bread plate and started to eat a thick piece of ciabatta.

Deeley was taken aback by the sudden darkness in her sister's eyes. 'Dev?' she started tentatively, but she was interrupted by her brother-in-law bellowing.

'Jason! Yes, I *am* bloody ready to order, dammit! I'm starving! Truffle risotto and rib-eye for me. What about you, Maxie?'

Jason, Franco's affable and charming maître d', had come over to take their order; Maxie looked up at him, pulling a face of apology.

'I'm so sorry, Jason,' she said. 'We're not quite ready. Matt's wandered off somewhere.'

'Yes, Jason – have you seen Matt?' Devon asked. 'He went off to ring his coach – he got some garbled message about training tomorrow – but he's been ages.'

'I saw him in the bar just now,' Jason said, grinning. 'Shall I go and hurry him along?'

'Yes! Good chap!' Olly said loudly.

But just then a man loomed up at their table.

'Honestly, Matt,' Devon said crossly, 'where *have* you been? We're all starving! Jason, darling, I don't even need to see the menu – you know what I want.'

'Black crab tagliolini and veal Milanese,' Jason said, exchanging a smile with her as he wrote it down. 'As always.'

'Yummy!' Devon said happily, almost masking the apology her errant husband was mumbling as he took his seat.

And since 'sorry' was all Deeley had heard her boxer say, she recognized his voice immediately. Her whole body froze in horror. It was like a curse in a fairy tale; she was instantly turned to ice. All she could manage to move was her eyes, and even those very slowly, because she was praying that when she did look up, she wouldn't see him standing there.

But she did. That once handsome, now adorably battered face, with its broken nose and dented left cheekbone. The height, the bulk of him, the wide, wide shoulders and narrow hips. The eyes – she could see now in the lighting over the table that they were hyacinth blue, a ridiculously pretty colour for so butch a man.

It was him. Her 'boxer'. And he was looking straight at her, the colour fading from his face; under his tan, he had gone as white as a sheet.

Deeley did too. Because, of course, she knew now all too well where she had seen him before. On TV, yes, because he was a sportsman of some sort. Memory flooded back: he was a rugby player. And though Deeley might have seen him, briefly, as she changed channels, standing nobly on the pitch, blood trickling from a graze on his forehead, that wasn't where she had really seen him. It was in the *Hello!* spread that Devon had sent her: Devon had married a rugby player.

Her 'boxer' was her sister's husband.

'Matt darling, what on earth have you been *doing*?' Devon said lightly. 'You look like you've seen a ghost!'

After his encounter with her, Matt had headed to the bar for a stiff drink. Whisky, probably a double. Deeley knew this, because she could smell the fumes. And the reason she could smell the fumes was because he was sitting next to her. They were both stiff as boards, trying to avoid touching in any way, jumping nervously when the other one had to move for any reason.

She wasn't looking to her left at all, couldn't risk making eye contact with Matt. Still, she couldn't help smelling the whisky on his breath as he spoke, the rich scent of his aftershave; and beneath that, his own body. *Oh God*. She was trying not to inhale too much, in case she got too intoxicated and leaned into him, wanting to smell more.

And end up nuzzling my sister's husband.

Deeley hadn't even looked for a ring on his hand before. She'd been out of the dating game for so long, in her five-year stint as Nicky's 'girlfriend', that she'd forgotten all the strategies and tricks. It hadn't even occurred to her that a man as good-looking as Matt was bound to have a girlfriend or, God help her, a wife; no, she'd acted like a naïve teenager addicted to romance novels, falling head over heels for how someone looked and felt without using her brain at all.

Devon was trilling away, telling a story and dropping a string of famous names, and Deeley dared to glance sideways at Matt for the first time, since his head was turned away from her, towards his wife. A muscle was pumping in his lower jaw, probably with the effort of keeping it set as if it had been carved from stone. His skin was very smooth; either he'd shaved just before coming out, or he wasn't very hairy, because he had no regrowth from that morning.

Oh, no no no. This is a mistake.

Because now she was picturing his naked body. Wondering exactly where he was hairy, and where he was smooth. Imagining his bare chest, with just a little curly brown hair between his pectorals; his flat abs, ridged with muscle, and a faint line of brown hair running down towards his . . .

'Deeley!' Maxie exclaimed. 'For God's sake!'

Deeley snapped back to reality. She had been trying to eat her main course – sea bass with artichokes, olives and cherry tomatoes. It was utterly delicious, light and fresh, but sitting next to Matt was ruining her appetite; she had been clinging onto her cutlery for minutes without taking a bite, and now her mental images of Matt had distracted her so much that she'd loosened her grip, her knife and fork clattering noisily onto the plate.

'Sorry,' she said hopelessly. 'I was thinking of – um, something.'

'Really!' Olly said cheerfully. 'We can't take you anywhere!'

Everyone was staring at her now: Devon and Maxie with open disapproval, Olly, already half-cut, red-faced and grinning. Everyone but Matt. It seemed so blatant to Deeley, the fact that Matt was grimly refusing to turn his head towards her, as if he had a half-paralysis which meant he was incapable of looking to the right. *I can't believe no one else is noticing this,* she thought, riven with panic.

'Are you on drugs?' Maxie persisted. 'Prescription drugs – that's very LA, isn't it? Everyone's on uppers or downers there, according to the papers.'

'No, I'm not. Honestly,' Deeley said hopelessly. 'I'm just . . . nervous.'

'Well, of course she's nervous!' Olly said jovially, forking up a roast garlic potato. 'She hasn't seen you two for yonks, and, face it, you're both rather famous now! It must be awfully intimidating, mustn't it?'

Deeley nodded vigorously. It was easier than talking.

'You need to be taken under our wing,' Olly said, flushed with rich Amarone red wine. 'Introduced to the important people in London. Such a shame you can't stay with us for a while, but you know, Maxie's got this whole African—'

His wife elbowed him vigorously.

'*Rwandan* baby thing going on,' he corrected himself. 'Sorry, m'dear. So the house is apparently going to be bursting at the seams in a couple of days. But what about you two?' He looked at Devon and Matt. 'You must have plenty of room for a little slip of a thing like Deeley, eh? Till she gets on her feet in London?' He winked at Deeley. 'Somebody'll snap her up in a month, won't he! I mean, just look at her! If I were single . . . whoops! Sorry, darling!'

He lurched, pretending that Maxie had elbowed him again, though she hadn't bothered; Maxie's assessment of her husband was exactly the same as Deeley's.

'You must have a spare room in Mayfair, eh, chaps?' Olly was continuing. He finished his glass of Amarone and snapped his fingers for the waiter, who was already approaching the table to refill it. 'Where are you staying, Deeley? Some awful digs?'

'The Charlotte Street Hotel,' Deeley said.

'I don't know it. Must be a ghastly dump, if I don't know it, eh?' Olly was braying by now, his eyes glassy. 'Not one of the good places!'

'You're drunk,' Maxie snapped, her lips tight.

'You know what Winston Churchill said!' Olly crowed. 'Tomorrow I'll be sober, but you'll still be . . .' His voice trailed off, as he realized that the punchline of his joke would be calling his wife ugly. 'Ooops! Silly me!' He looked guiltily at Maxie. 'Didn't mean it, darling! But, you know! Little sister all alone – awful shame! Shouldn't happen!'

If he were sitting next to me, he'd be patting my hand by now, Deeley thought.

'Devon! Matt! Haven't you got any room for your lil' sis? Just till she gets on her feet? Poor lil' thing, all alone in some grotty hotel . . .' Olly stuffed another crunchy roast potato into his mouth. 'Shouldn't be allowed,' he added indistinctly. 'Besides, it looks bad. Doesn't it?' He turned to his wife, who reached up with her napkin and rubbed a stray fragment of potato off his chin. 'Lil' Deeley, dumped by her big Hollywood boyfriend, comes back to London all dejected, tail between her legs, and neither of her sisters takes her in and gives her a roof over her head on a temp'ry basis? Looks bloody awful, frankly. People're going to start to ask why. Don't you think?'

Maxie paused, the linen napkin still in her hands, as the import of her husband's words sank in. 'Ah,' she said slowly.

'Right? See what I mean?' Olly thumped his fist enthusiastically on the table. 'Bloody poor show! Surprised it hasn't been in the gossip columns already!'

Maxie looked at Devon.

'I just *can't* take her in,' she said. 'Not with the baby coming the day after tomorrow. But Olly's absolutely right. Someone should. It looks bad if we don't.'

Oh, I remember this, too. Deeley had a flash of déjà vu that went right back to her childhood. *The way the two of them would go on and on about 'what shall we do with Deeley?' in front of me. Like I was their dolly.*

God, she realized. *I was my sisters' doll, and then I was Nicky and Carmen's. I can't believe I only just made that connection.*

'No, you're right,' Devon agreed, nodding. 'We should definitely help Deels out. Deeley, you can stay for a while, OK? Until you get your feet under you. We've got a granny flat in the basement. We meant to make it into a gym for Matt, but we never got round to it. And it's got a separate entrance.' She glanced at Matt. 'You don't mind if Deeley stays downstairs for a bit, do you?'

Matt didn't say a word. His hands, knotted together on the table-cloth, wound even more tightly together. Deeley saw blood draining from his knuckles with the tension.

'OK, well, that's settled, then!' Devon said, shrugging. 'Matt obviously doesn't care one way or the other.'

'Wait!'

Deeley finally caught up with the full import of what her sisters had been discussing; Matt's physical closeness was as distracting to her as if she really had been on prescription medication, as Maxie had speculated. *Or ecstasy*, she thought. *I'm practically sitting on my hands to stop myself reaching out and touching him. If we were alone, I'd be climbing into his lap so he could stroke me like a kitten.*

No, I wouldn't! Of course I wouldn't! He's my sister's husband, for God's sake!

Deeley sank her nails into her thighs to force herself to concentrate on the immediate crisis before her, as the waiter started clearing the plates.

'I don't think I should stay with you,' she said to Devon. 'Because, um . . .' She racked her brains for a plausible reason. 'Wouldn't it be too much? Like, we'd be practically on top of each other the whole time?'

Matt's knuckles were as white as the tablecloth now. *'On top of each other the whole time' probably wasn't the best choice of words*, Deeley thought helplessly.

Devon's strongly defined dark eyebrows raised elegantly in pantomimed surprise.

'Deels, I just *said* we have a granny flat!' she said. 'There's a kitchenette down there, I think. And a bathroom. We don't even have to see each other if we don't want to. I'm doing tons of stuff to promote the new show, anyway. I'll hardly be in. Matt will,' she added, with a casual flip of her hand towards her catatonic husband. 'But he just trains and plays video games. And spends hours gardening. You can always join him on the sofa for Xbox if you want, I suppose. It'd be nice for him to have someone to play with.'

Convulsively, Matt jerked back in his seat, unlocking his hands to grab the edge of the table.

'Sorry,' he muttered, still not looking at Deeley, but jerking his head in her direction. 'Need to get out – not feeling brilliant . . .'

Deeley scooched her chair away, scrambling to her feet. She thought she'd left enough room for Matt to pass her, but she'd underestimated his sheer size; as he swung his long legs out from under the table and stood up, he brushed against her, and she trembled involuntarily, a ripple passing through her from head to toe. She was hot and cold simultaneously, icy heat shivering out from her bones, desire mingled with something that was almost like a premonition – *Like when they say someone's walking on your grave*, she thought. The sheer strength of the chemistry between her and Matt was actually frightening.

And when she risked a quick glance up into his eyes, in the

moment before he turned away and she ducked to slide into her seat again, she was sure he felt the same way.

'Well! That's settled!' Maxie said gaily, sitting back with the complacent expression on her face that was very familiar to Devon and Deeley, the expression that said that, yet again, things had been organized exactly the way that suited Maxie best. 'Deeley's going to come to you for a while, Dev. That'll give us time to work out what to do with her next. Maybe we should have a little party for her, to officially welcome her to London,' she added thoughtfully, as Olly nodded in approval, the exaggerated nods of a man now well into his cups.

'What on *earth* is wrong with Matt tonight?' Devon said crossly. 'First he takes ages at the bar, then he sits here like he's been embalmed – not even saying a word to Deeley – then he rushes out again. God.'

'Trouble in paradise?' Maxie asked.

Devon heaved up a sigh that sounded as if it started at her toes and finished with a vibration of the exposed white curves of her upper breasts. This was so utterly hypnotic that Olly not only gawped at her, mouth dropping open, but remained staring at her bosom for a whole minute after.

She may be a bit overweight now, but you still can't take your eyes off her, Deeley thought, looking at her ridiculously beautiful sister. *Matt'll go home with her tonight, and they'll shag like bunnies, and this weird infatuation thing between us will fizzle out in a few days. I mean, look at Devon! She's like sex on legs! As soon as he's alone with her, he won't be able to think of anyone else.*

'I don't know,' Devon said eventually. 'We're sort of going past each other a lot at the moment . . .'

'Would you like to see the dessert menu?' Jason, tactful as always, had waited for a break in the conversation before approaching their table. 'There's a ginger panna cotta with caramel sauce you might like, Devon. And we have that dessert wine you loved last time – the *passito di vermentino di Sardegna . . .*'

'Ooh, Jason, you do know what a girl likes!' Devon said,

cheering up, and shaking back her heavy dark ringlets as she reached for the dessert menu.

Maxie, always on a diet, waved hers aside, but Olly reached greedily for his.

'I'll definitely have a glass of the dessert wine. Mmm, lemon and pistachio crème brûlée!' Devon said happily. 'I shouldn't, but I know I will . . . Look, maybe you should keep away from Matt at the moment,' she added to Deeley, who almost jumped out of her skin at the shock of these words; did Devon somehow know what was going on?

'He barely said a word to you,' Devon observed, still scanning the dessert menu. 'He doesn't seem that keen on the idea of you staying in the granny flat – God knows why. But it might be a good idea to steer clear of him for a bit. He's a bit like a bear with a sore head at the moment. Sorry about that.'

She pulled a sympathetic face at her sister. 'Don't let it make you feel that you're not welcome.'

Deeley nodded devoutly. 'I'll definitely stay away from him,' she said, and never was a truer word spoken.

She had no intention, if she could possibly avoid it, of coming within ten feet of her sister's husband ever again.

Maxie

'Um, Mrs Stangroom?'

The Bilberry receptionist was new and very nervous indeed, so nervous that she was stuttering. Maxie looked up from the designs she was studying, annoyed at the unscheduled interruption.

'I assume this is something *very* important, Sally,' Maxie said coldly, 'for you to step away from your desk and come to bother me without even ringing my extension beforehand to warn me . . .'

Still hovering in the doorway to Maxie's office, her expression now indicating that she fully expected to be fired, the receptionist fumbled with the big stiff-backed envelope she was carrying. She was a pretty girl, and fashionably dressed – to maintain the Bilberry image, Maxie would never have dreamed of hiring anyone who wasn't both those things – but, confronted with her boss's iron stare, Sally was sagging visibly, resembling nothing so much as a limp dishcloth.

'Um, Reed Miller PR sent this just now?' Sally said, holding the envelope up in front of her as if it were a shield, nerves making her voice rise higher at the end of every sentence, as if she were asking a question. 'It's marked Extremely Urgent and For Your Eyes Only, so I thought I'd better bring it to you straight away? I mean, I know they send over the media round-up every week, but this is marked Extremely Urgent? So I thought—'

'Oh, for God's sake, just bring it over here and stop talking!' Maxie said impatiently, holding out her hand for the envelope, her heavy gold bracelet falling down her arm to her wrist, glinting expensively. Sally almost tripped over her own feet rushing across the polished floorboards to the big glass table that Maxie used as a desk. With its silver Mac desktop computer, two brushed-steel in and out trays, lined up perfectly, one on each side of the table, and a huge bottle-green crocodile-skin Bilberry day planner open in front of her, Maxie's workspace was kept with such immaculate precision that her staff were intimidated simply by entering her office.

Which was exactly the effect she intended.

She took the envelope from Sally, nodding as she did so: a wordless dismissal. Sally was all too grateful to leave Maxie's office, nearly turning her ankle on her suede stack heels as she tumbled out as fast as she could go.

Probably going to cry in the loos, Maxie thought, as she reached for her paperknife – Bilberry, of course – its green crocodile handle matching her day planner. She silently congratulated herself on her instinctive use of the word 'loo', which she had painstakingly taught herself to use: it had seemed really rude to her when she was young. The McKennas had said 'toilet', which sounded posher. And then she'd got to Oxford and realized that posh people swore like troopers and used the most basic words for everything, because saying 'toilet', to them, was middle class and bourgeois. Older ones said 'WC' or 'lavatory', younger ones said 'loo', or sometimes even 'bog'. It had been a steep learning curve.

Maxie slit open the envelope and pulled out the contents: a copy of *Yes!* magazine, a glossy, upmarket weekly gossip and fashion bible in which Bilberry advertised extensively. There was a Post-it note on the cover, on which her PR had scrawled: *Pages 22-25. Did you know about this??*

This wasn't good. Anything that had taken Maxie's very efficient PR firm by surprise was definitely bad. Maxie turned to page 22, bracing herself, but what she saw as she opened the magazine to the double-page spread was even worse than she'd imagined.

Deeley McKenna – Her Tragic Childhood! blared the headline. *'I'll bounce back from Nicky's dumping me,' says beautiful Deeley. 'My sisters and I grew up in total poverty – I know I can survive this heartbreak!'*

Maxie froze, staring at the photograph over which these words were superimposed; a full-page shot of Deeley, wearing an ankle-length chartreuse sequin dress, stretched out on a sofa in a luxurious hotel suite, doing her best to look serious, heartbroken, but also radiantly beautiful. On the facing page were further shots of Deeley, posed in the hotel lobby, and sitting at a restaurant table, dressed in a pearl grey silk sheath, diamond pendants dangling from her earlobes. The table bore a single glass of wine; that photo was captioned: *Table for One – after years of living with handsome TV star Nicky Shore, Deeley is single once more. 'It's really hard,' says Deeley. 'But I'll be OK – the McKenna sisters are all strong women. We've come through so much to get to where we are today. No one has any idea how hard we've had to struggle.'*

Maxie was actually frightened to let out the air she was holding in her lungs, in case she found herself screaming loudly enough to shatter the glass table on which the magazine lay. When her phone rang, the noise was almost a relief, because something else, rather than her, was making the sound.

It was Alison Reed, the head of the PR firm Maxie employed. She wasted no time in getting down to brass tacks.

'Have you seen it?' Alison demanded. 'I just biked it over. It hits the shelves tomorrow. Thank God I got a twenty-four hour head start, at least – I can work on damage control.'

'I'm looking at it now,' Maxie said, her teeth gritted as she skimmed the text of the article, reading:

'With their mum in prison or in a drug den, and a series of unreliable 'stepdads', the beautiful McKenna sisters had a truly deprived childhood. 'More often than not, we didn't know where our next meal was coming from,' Deeley reveals. 'Maxie held us together, stopped us being taken into care. She was always like a mother to me and Devon. We'd often cry ourselves to sleep at night because we were so hungry,

and we never had a real home – just this series of creepy stepdads. It was incredibly scary.'

'Did you know she was going to do this?' Alison Reed was asking tensely. 'Because this is *so* not what we've been working to push as an image! It's just not Bilberry. And I can't imagine Devon's people will be over the moon about it either.'

'They won't be,' Maxie snapped. 'And no, of course I didn't bloody know she was doing this! Are you insane? I'd have locked her in and put guards on the door before I'd have let her out to do something this . . . this *shitty*!'

She felt as if smoke were coming out of her ears. Two of her designers came down the corridor, clearly visible through the glass walls of her office; they had obviously been planning to drop in on Maxie for a discussion, but one look at her rigid face and posture, and they barely broke stride, continuing on past the office door with the smoothness of long practice in reading their boss's moods, their heads tactfully turned away.

That's how I want to be seen! Maxie thought savagely. *Intimidating! Tough! Not some pathetic, dirt-poor victim!*

'The whole tragic childhood thing – we really never wanted to focus on that,' Alison was saying. 'It just really pulls down the whole glamorous image, you know? Unless it's useful for Olly when he's campaigning—'

'It isn't,' Maxie said curtly. 'He has a safe seat in a very rich constituency.'

'So what on earth is Deeley doing?' Alison demanded. 'She's *completely* off-message! And who set this up? Why didn't she come to me? We could have placed a really nice piece about her break-up and being single, without all this deprived childhood stuff.'

'Believe me, Alison, I'm as much in the dark as you are,' Maxie said, her tone so sharp it could have cut glass. 'But I'm going to get to the bottom of it right now. Deeley has no idea how much trouble she's in.'

Hanging up, Maxie got to her feet. She realized she was shaking with fury. The magazine lay on the table in front of her; her youngest sister's lovely face, framed by cascades of caramel-streaked hair, stared up at her, wide-eyed, lips slightly parted.

Bloody, bloody Deeley! I knew her coming back to London would be nothing but trouble!

Alison thinks it's just about our image, Devon's and mine. That we want to be seen as chic and sophisticated career women, not helpless little victims.

She has no idea what the real danger is here. If people start snooping into our past, the three of us could be in terrible trouble. The scandal would ruin us all – and God knows, that's not even the worst that could happen . . . not by a long shot . . .

She even mentioned 'creepy stepdads'. Has she gone insane?

Shivering in fear and anger, Maxie picked up the magazine, rolled it up, and threw it like a dart at the wall. It hit, splattered open, and fell with a weak flutter of thin, shiny pages; not nearly enough to relieve Maxie's built-up rage. She strode over and kicked the magazine viciously across the floor, getting the toe of her boot underneath it and pelting it high into the air; it fanned out as it flew, landing on her desk again. Maxie's PA, coming along the corridor with her boss's mid-morning skinny latte, took one quick look into the office, skidded to a halt, and turned on her heel, shooting back down the corridor as if fleeing a serial killer with a screaming chainsaw.

I'm going to ram this down Deeley's throat till she chokes on it, Maxie thought fiercely, grabbing the copy of *Yes!* off the desk with one hand, snatching her Bilberry tote with the other, and storming out of the office, yelling to her PA, 'Get me a cab, *now!*'

Maxie had rung Devon from the cab and as it ticked to a halt in front of Devon's Mayfair house, Devon was already standing in the doorway, waiting for her. Maxie wrenched the cab door open with so much force it thudded against the side of the vehicle, and she stormed out without bothering to shut it again. Muttering to himself, the cab driver climbed out to close the door; it was an account booking, which meant there was no tip, just a very bad attitude.

God, Devon's definitely put on weight, Maxie thought as she climbed the stairs that led up to the elevated ground floor. Her sister was dressed in a black crêpe top which gathered under the bust and then flowed out in a series of folds designed to conceal lurking rolls of fat; it showcased her breasts, which were undeniably good, but there was no question that Devon had piled on the pounds.

And TV puts on an extra ten, Maxie reflected, smoothing down the silk wrap dress that was belted tightly around her own slim frame as she stepped onto the black-and-white checked tiles of the hallway. *She'll have to take a good pull at herself. Nothing comes easy. You have to work for everything you have – work, scheme, and starve yourself to the bone for it. Devon's getting too comfortable, that's her problem.*

Getting comfortable was a luxury Maxie had never allowed herself.

'Is Deeley in?' Maxie asked, gesturing down to the floor with her thumb.

'Of course she's bloody in. It's the morning,' Devon snapped, striding across the hall and into the living room so fast Maxie worried she might split her trousers. 'She doesn't get up till noon. Then she goes to Pilates, or runs round the park. God, Americans annoy me with their fitness crap! She's always banging on about it. I can't stand to *hear* about people's exercise, let alone do it. Matt's just the same.'

It wouldn't kill you to go for a run with her every now and then, Maxie thought, watching how Devon carefully arranged the voluminous folds of her top over her lap to hide any bulges as she sank into a velvet-upholstered armchair. *Deeley's probably trying to give you a tactful hint.*

'You'd think Matt would have done enough at training!' Devon was continuing crossly. 'But no, he comes home now and nags me to go for walks with him! I hate bloody walking!'

'Maybe he should run with Deeley,' Maxie said, sitting down on the sofa opposite her sister, wondering sardonically if the suggestion might make Devon a little keener to exercise with her husband.

But Devon just rolled her eyes to the lavishly moulded ceiling, with its elaborate white-painted central rosette and decorative plaster swags.

'God, *that's* never going to happen,' she said. 'He's really taken against her. Doesn't want her in the house – you know, up here.' She gestured around her. 'Can barely hear her name mentioned. It's weird; he never takes an instant dislike to people normally.'

Maxie could not have cared less about Matt taking a dislike to Deeley; she ignored this completely, instead slapping down the copy of *Yes!* onto the coffee table, open already to the article featuring their younger sister.

'Read that,' she said tersely. 'We have a crisis on our hands.'

Devon did as Maxie said, a series of horrified little gasps issuing from her pursed lips as she took in Deeley's indiscreet comments. It gave Maxie some satisfaction: as always, Devon saw things as she did, was obediently toeing the line. Devon set the magazine down on the table, and the two sisters looked at each other, Devon's big, kohl-pencilled eyes meeting Maxie's narrowed ones. For a few seconds the family resemblance was unmistakeable.

'She never could keep her mouth shut,' Devon said unhappily, reading her sister's thoughts. 'When she went off to LA, it felt a lot safer. I mean, I missed her, but when she was here I was always worried she might let something slip. In LA – well, it sounds awful, but no one was interested in what she said.'

'Well, no point crying over spilled milk!' Maxie said briskly, an expression she'd picked up from her very formidable mother-in-law. 'I say we go downstairs and scare the living daylights out of her.'

Devon's mouth twisted. 'It was always easy to scare Deeley,' she commented wryly.

Maxie couldn't help smiling. 'Do you remember how we used to terrorize her with the vacuum cleaner?' she asked.

'Oh my God, of course!' Devon was laughing now. 'She'd do anything as long as we didn't turn on the vacuum and say we were going to suck her up with the hose!'

And for a moment, both their expressions softened, as memories of their childhood flooded back.

'She looked up to you so much,' Devon said. 'She followed you around like a little duckling.'

'Yes, but she was always trying to do her hair like yours – remember?' Maxie said. 'You'd get so cross! You'd do yourself up so carefully and then Deeley would turn herself into a little version of you, only really messy, and you'd get absolutely furious with her.'

'I thought she was doing it to make me look stupid,' Devon confessed. 'I hated her copying me.'

'Oh God, no! I did try to tell you! It was heroine worship,' Maxie said, smiling. 'I was like her mum – telling her off all the time. And you were the one she wanted to be.'

Devon grimaced. 'I could have been nicer to her, I suppose,' she said reluctantly.

'Please, no dwelling,' Maxie said, waving away any regrets with a brisk snap of her wrist.

This was another phrase of Lady Stangroom's. Lady Stangroom never dwelled on the past, and never used five words where two could do. One of the great attractions of Olly for Maxie – apart, of course, from his money and title – was how redoubtable his mother was. If Devon had been Deeley's role model, Lady Stangroom was Maxie's: tough as old boots, sharp as a whip, effortlessly in command of her empire. Maxie had very deliberately modelled herself on her mother-in-law, with the latter's full approval.

'We need to deal with the present,' she continued firmly. 'Deeley isn't a little girl any more. She's a grown woman who has to take responsibility for her own actions. If she keeps doing interviews like this, we'll all be in danger. Journalists will start asking us questions about our childhood – Mum – tracing things back. Someone might even decide that an unauthorized biography of the three McKenna sisters might make very good reading.'

Devon paled visibly, the blusher on her cheeks and the natural red of her lips standing out in vivid contrast to her sheet-white face.

'Oh *God*,' she whispered. 'I hadn't even *thought* of that.'

'You never do, Devon,' Maxie snapped. 'That's my job.'

She stood up from the sofa, coming to her feet in one swift, efficient movement.

'If a journalist or a writer starts digging around in our past . . .' Devon's carefully manicured, fuschia-tipped hands flew up to her mouth, as if she were trying to silence herself.

'Exactly,' Maxie said grimly. 'I used that very same word to myself twenty minutes ago. Terrifying, isn't it?'

Devon could only nod dumbly, hands still over her lips.

'Now let's go and find Deeley,' Maxie said, swivelling on her heels. 'How do we get down to your granny flat?'

She didn't even look back to see if Devon were following her; she knew she would, because she always had.

'We're going to put the fear of God into that girl,' she said, her jaw set hard.

Deeley

*D*eeley was brushing her hair, still bleary-eyed from sleep, when she heard footsteps coming down the back stairs. In the old days, the basement had been the kitchen and servants' quarters, and so the staircase that led up to the main house was narrow and cramped by comparison with the sweeping main staircase that wrapped around the central hall, designed for the ladies of the house to be able to navigate in their big, flowing skirts and wide-brimmed hats. She heard Devon curse, as usual, as she negotiated the shallow treads, placing her heels slowly and carefully so she didn't trip.

Deeley wrapped her dressing gown around her, belting it tightly, and secured her hair in a messy bun on top of her head with an elastic band. It looked bad enough that she was barely out of bed by noon; she could at least pull her hair off her face.

The trouble was, she was finding it harder and harder to get up in the morning. Her life had absolutely no purpose, which meant that there was nothing to get up *for*. In London, previously, there had been jobs, waitressing or hostessing; in LA, she had gone shopping with her stylist, or to a raft of daytime charity events (*Deeley McKenna, Nicky Shore's gorgeous girlfriend, shares a joke with January Jones of* Mad Men *as they bid at the Homeless Aids charity auction brunch!*).

Now she was bereft. She'd hoped to be hanging out with Devon, but that hadn't happened; Devon seemed much too busy with her interview schedule and pre-show meetings to have time for her younger sister. Deeley knew that one of the signs of depression was being unable to get up in the morning. She was working out every day in an attempt to pump endorphins through her system, make herself feel better, but the high you got after a run, or a Pilates workout, never lasted more than a few hours. And then there she was, back in her sister's basement, with no prospects, no real talent, and no future.

Trying very hard not to think about her sister's husband.

I'm lucky to have a roof over my head, she reminded herself firmly. *And some money in the bank. If you'd told me when I was little that I'd have both those things and still be unhappy, I'd have thought you were lying through your teeth.*

But as much as she tried to fight self-pity and hopelessness, they kept slipping back in when she let down her guard. The contrast between her sisters' lives and her own was too marked for her to feel anything but utterly inferior. Look at everything they had! Great lives, great homes, great careers, great husbands! *Well, maybe Olly isn't exactly a young girl's dream,* she thought. *But for Maxie, he's perfect. He's an MP with a title, and he pretty much does whatever she says, and thinks she's amazing – that's the ideal man for her.*

And Matt . . . No. I'm not thinking about Matt.

Devon was opening the connecting door at the bottom of the staircase now, which stuck a little, as the basement had damp issues and the wood was warped. Devon cursed even harder, and Deeley braced herself. Devon sounded like she was in a bad mood; was she coming to tell Deeley she needed to move out? Deeley had absolutely no idea where she would go after this brief respite at her sister's house. Suddenly, life in the basement didn't seem so bad after all. Swiftly, Deeley dashed to the open-plan kitchen, grabbed as many dirty plates and glasses as she could from where they were strewn on the counter, and put them in the sink, turning on the tap; it couldn't hurt for Devon to think she was doing the washing-up.

'Ugh! Bloody narrow stairs, bloody door!' Devon complained, falling through the latter in a tumble of jangling earrings. 'It's like this whole basement was built for skinny midgets!'

'It's the servants' quarters,' Maxie said crisply, following hard on her heels. 'What do you expect?'

Deeley wheeled round, washing-up forgotten. Maxie was here too. That couldn't be good. Maxie, in the daytime, when she would normally be at work, running her luxury goods empire like Caligula did Rome . . .

'Turn that tap off, Deeley, you'll flood the place,' her oldest sister ordered her. 'And next time you pretend to do the washing-up, make sure you've got the detergent out of the cupboard first, eh?'

Deeley obeyed, her heart sinking. She'd never been able to fool Maxie about anything. She wished now that she hadn't put her hair up; if she hadn't, she'd be able to hang her head and hide, at least partially, behind her thick curtain of hair, the way she'd always done when Maxie started to tell her off.

Maxie stalked over to the breakfast bar which separated the kitchenette from the main living space, and slapped a glossy magazine down on it with enough force to make Deeley flinch back.

'Explain *this*, why don't you?' she said so icily both her sisters shivered in fear.

'I don't know what . . .' Deeley began, as Maxie clicked her tongue impatiently and practically tore the magazine open to the spread of Deeley lying on the sofa, looking wan and beautiful. 'Ooh!' Deeley exclaimed, momentarily perking up at the sight of a good photo of herself. 'I didn't know it was out yet! They really didn't tell me much,' she explained, looking up at her sisters, and then realizing, from the steely fury in their eyes, that something about the article had made them very angry indeed.

'What is it?' she said, furrowing her pretty brow. 'I thought you'd be pleased! I made some money off it, got some publicity . . . there's quite a good living in doing these magazine things . . . Oh!'

Thinking that she'd solved the mystery of why her sisters were so worked up, she beamed at both of them with an ingenuous smile.

'Don't worry – this won't affect my deal with Nicky!' she reassured them. 'Carmen never banned me from doing interviews. I just have to tell them that he realized I wasn't The One, and dumped me, and that I'm moving forward bravely. And honestly, that's all I said!'

She looked from Devon to Maxie, completely failing to understand why they weren't relaxing at the news that Deeley's financial settlement from Nicky was safe. And then Maxie's French-manicured finger stabbed at one of the paragraphs printed in bold type. Deeley scanned it as her sister read bitingly: '"Deprived childhood"? "Creepy stepdads"?'

'How could you even *mention* stepdads, Deeley!' Devon wailed. 'Are you *insane*?'

'I didn't realize I'd said all that!' Deeley said feebly. 'I didn't do much press in the States. I mean, no one really wanted to talk to me,' she admitted frankly. 'Why would they? Sometimes, people would be profiling Nicky, and Carmen would tell me to wander in and do girlfriend-type things – you know, tease him about how many hair products he has, talk about a holiday we were planning. To make us sound like a real couple. But that was all sort of worked out in advance.'

'She told you what to say,' Maxie snapped. 'And the rest of the time, she told you to *keep your fucking mouth shut and look pretty*, right?'

'Well, yes . . .'

'Because she knew she couldn't trust you as far as she could throw you!' Maxie yelled. 'You're an idiot! A total fucking idiot! What the *hell* made you think you could start blurting out stuff about our childhood?'

Deeley was hanging her head now, even though she didn't have the hair to cover her face. At least this way she didn't have to meet Maxie's eyes.

'I don't even remember saying that,' she mumbled; and it was true, she didn't. She and the very nice journalist had just had a cosy chat over tea in the hotel, between set-ups for the various shots.

Yes! was very well known as a publication that never said anything rude about anyone, happy to go along with whatever story celebrities were selling that week, as long as it thought their readers would be interested. Deeley had felt perfectly safe; the journalist had treated her relationship with Nicky as if it had been 100 per cent real, which was all she'd been worried about.

'We just, you know, talked,' she added even more feebly. 'I mean, is it so bad? None of us ever pretended we were born with silver spoons in our mouths, did we? I thought the whole "worked our way up from nothing" made you both look even better ... you know, like you worked for everything you had, it wasn't just handed to you ...'

'It was OK in the beginning, but it's humiliating now,' Devon said angrily. 'I don't want to be having to answer lots of questions about our *deprived childhood* when I'm trying to promote a happy, fun, sexy TV show about being indulgent!' She glared magnificently at Deeley, her nostrils flaring. 'How on earth did this interview happen anyway?' she demanded. 'I didn't think you'd made any contacts in London!'

'Well, you've done your best to make sure I didn't!' Deeley retorted, determined not to let Devon have it all her own way. 'It was actually sort of through Carmen, if you must know. *Yes!* did a cover story on Nicky a couple of months ago, and the journalist rang up Carmen last week to get my UK cell phone numb— *mobile* number,' she corrected herself. 'And they were very nice, and said they'd pay me and I'd get some good publicity and nice photos out of it. Which I did.' She was getting cross now, rather than feeling guilty. 'And it's more than either of you have done for me, the whole time I've been here. Neither of you gives a shit about what's going to happen to me! You can't blame me for trying to get some sort of career started, can you?'

'Your "career",' Maxie said, putting the word in audible, contemptuous quotes that made Deeley cringe and wish she'd never used that word. 'Please! But that's by no means the main issue here.' She folded her arms across her chest. 'You're such a *child*, Deeley,' she continued. 'Devon and I spoiled you, I suppose. You bounced around London doing God knows what, and then you fell into a cushy little set-up with Nicky. You never grew up. You never learned to think before you speak. Whatever brains you have in that pretty little head of yours never got any use at all. But even having said all of that . . .' Maxie fixed her younger sister with a terrifying stare. 'Even having said *all* of that, I would have thought that *even you*, Deeley, would realize that talking about our past could be incredibly dangerous for all of us! Have you really forgotten what happened in Thompson Road? Don't you realize that people might get curious about our past and—'

'*Dig stuff up!*' Devon broke in, unable to control herself any longer. She pounded across the room and grabbed Deeley's shoulders, shaking her until the elastic band holding back Deeley's messy bun came loose, hair tumbling over her face. '*Dig stuff up!* Literally? Do you not *get* that? How bloody thick *are* you, for fuck's sake?'

Deeley wanted to stay strong, to act like a grown-up, not crumble like the pathetic stupid little girl her sisters were accusing her of being. But under their onslaught, as Devon yelled right into her face, as Maxie, with a furious gesture, knocked the magazine off the breakfast bar and sent it flying halfway across the room, Deeley did what she was trying so hard not to, what she'd always done when her sisters rounded on her.

She burst into hysterical tears.

1993

'What do we do now?' Devon asked, looking at Maxie.

'It's not dark enough yet,' Maxie said, glancing out of the grimy window to the long narrow strip of garden beyond. 'We'll have to wait a bit.'

'It worked really well,' Devon said respectfully. 'Just like you said it would.'

Maxie couldn't help flushing with pride; ever since she'd been small, there was nothing she'd liked better than a compliment to her organizational skills.

'What were those pills of Mum's that you gave him?' Deeley asked, wiping the tears off her face with the sleeve of her school uniform shirt, trying to sound as grown-up as possible.

'Methadone,' Maxie said. 'A whole pack of them.'

'I thought she went to the clinic to get that every day,' Deeley said, puzzled. 'And they gave it to her to drink, in a little plastic cup. Isn't that what happened? I didn't know they gave her pills too.'

She looked at Devon for corroboration, but Devon just shrugged. It was Maxie who answered: 'No, you're right, Deels. They wouldn't give her pills. They don't trust addicts – that's why they make them go to the clinic every day to get their dose. Mum got these off someone. Bought them, or something . . .'

Over Deeley's head, she met Devon's eyes: both Maxie and Devon had a very good idea of what their mother had done in return for a whole pack of methadone pills, but there was no point upsetting Deeley further by telling her. She wasn't even ten yet.

'I found them,' Maxie continued. 'You know I always used to go through her stuff.'

Both her younger sisters nodded. Maxie's bravery in pillaging their mother's possessions for spare cash had often meant the difference between eating that night and going hungry.

'And when I found them, I took them,' Maxie said. 'I didn't have any choice. She could have overdosed on them really easily.'

Again, Deeley and Devon nodded. They'd seen their mother passed out on drugs more times than they could count; she'd had a couple of near overdoses already. Generally, it was a combination of whatever she could get her hands on, but opiates were her drug of choice, and a whole pack of methadone pills could easily have been lethal.

'She tore the place apart looking for them,' Maxie said. 'Remember? When we were staying in that tower block, at Steve's?'

'She thought Steve took them,' Devon remembered. 'That's why we left there, wasn't it? They had that huge fight, and she hit him with a bottle and told us to grab our stuff and go.'

'I didn't like it at Steve's anyway,' Deeley said softly. 'It smelled of wee.'

'Ugh, those dogs!' Devon pulled a face.

Steve had had two mutts he barely let out of the flat, being too lazy to walk them; they went on the balcony when they could, but it hadn't made much difference. The place stank like the urinal it effectively was.

'Well, I kept the pills,' Maxie said. 'You know, just in case. And then, when Bill started to come into my room at night, I got them out.'

Both Devon and Deeley swallowed hard. Bill's council semi had three bedrooms, and though Devon, at thirteen, had resented being lumped in with her younger sister – as if she had anything in common with a 9-year-old! – there was no question that Maxie, being seventeen, had the privilege of a room of her own. When their mother had been sent away for receiving stolen goods, Bill had acted like he took it for

*granted the girls would go on staying with him. They'd been patheti-
cally grateful. The worst part of all of this – apart, of course, from what
he'd done to Maxie – was how nice he had been to them. Almost like a
real dad. Making sure they had a cooked breakfast in the morning
before school, that their clothes were washed, treating them to a KFC
now and then. He'd even said they might go on holiday that summer,
to Magaluf. He was saving up. They'd been so excited about it.*

'We won't get to go on holiday now, will we?' Deeley said, tears well-
ing up in her eyes again. 'We were going to go on a plane! I really
wanted to go on a plane!'

'Deeley!' Devon snapped. 'You're so selfish! Think about what he
did to Maxie!'

But Deeley couldn't, not really. Maxie had spared them the details
of what had happened when Bill had come into her room, what he'd
made her do; she'd just hinted at it, and told them that he'd made her
stay really quiet so her sisters wouldn't hear anything.

'We should've gone to the police,' Deeley said in a small voice.
'Because he did those bad things to Maxie. We should've told them.'

Maxie sighed deeply. 'Deels,' she said, repressing an urge to shake
her little sister till her teeth rattled, 'we've been over this, OK? The
police probably wouldn't believe me, not with Mum's record. And even
if they did, they'd take us away from here. They'd separate us and put
us into care. We've told you about all the bad things that happen to kids
in care, haven't we? Besides, Bill said he wouldn't let us go. That he'd
come after us. I only did this because he said he was going to start with
Devon too.' She sighed deeply. 'I had to do it – this,' she jerked her head
down at Bill's body, 'to protect all of us. That's my job. And your job is
to help me, and not talk about it any more once we've done it.'

Deeley nodded obediently, big eyes wide, swayed, as always, by her
older sister's authority. 'I was good at crushing up all the pills, wasn't
I?' she said, hoping for approval.

'You were,' Maxie said, softening. 'You did a really good job. It was
so lucky he drank stout,' she added, looking over at Bill's empty pint
glass on the kitchen table. 'That stuff's so bitter he didn't even notice
there was a whole ton of methadone in it.' She took a long breath. 'I

should wash that glass up straight away,' she said, crossing the room and picking it up. 'That's what they do on telly, to get rid of the evidence. And I should burn the pill packet.'

'So now do we—' Devon started, then screamed. Deeley did too.

Because Bill's arm had moved.

He was trying to bend it, to put his palm flat on the floor and push himself up; it was a weak, feeble attempt, the fingers trembling, the movement painfully slow. Still the two girls were watching it as if hypnotized, his hand scrabbling across the cheap carpet tiles, dragging his arm, the elbow bending upwards, the fingers trying desperately to flatten out, to take some of his body's weight.

But that wasn't the scariest part. Instinctively, Devon and Deeley clung to each other, terrified, as Bill, still face down on the floor, started to make a horrible moaning noise. His back heaved, his head jerked, his forehead banged on the floor repeatedly, making Deeley whimper in fear. And then the moans turned into a guttural, painful-sounding croaking, as if each breath was being ripped out of his throat by sharp invisible claws.

Standing by the sink, still holding the glass stained with beer foam and – just visible now – tiny white particles of ground-up pills, Maxie watched, barely daring to breathe, frozen in place. Racing through her mind was everything that she had done to get them to this place; the plotting, the planning, the terrible risks she had run, the secrets she was still hiding from her sisters.

The croaks rose in volume, the spasms in Bill's back were even more pronounced; his head was trying to lift off the floor, both his hands pushing feebly at the carpet, to no avail. He was retching now, trying to bring up the bellyful of pills and stout, his dinner of fish fingers and oven chips.

And if he did, he would survive. The methadone wouldn't have killed him.

Maxie couldn't let that happen. 'Devon!' she yelled. 'Hit him over the head with something!'

The fireplace, with its wonky gas heater and tiled surround, was directly to Devon's right. On the mantelpiece were Bill's precious dart trophies, neatly arranged and painstakingly dusted, tributes to his steady hand and excellent aim. Without thinking – because if she thought about it for even one second, she couldn't do it – Devon grabbed the closest one, a heavy engraved acrylic rectangle, bent over, and whacked it into Bill's skull in one long continuous stroke. The crack of acrylic against bone was audible right across the room.

The trophy fell from Devon's hands, thudding onto the carpet. Deeley started to whimper like a desperate puppy. And those small, pathetic gulps of misery were the only sound in the room. Bill's groans and retches had stopped dead; his fingers were no longer scrabbling at the floor.

Taking a deep breath, commanding herself to take control, Maxie set down the glass in the sink, her hands shaking. Then she walked slowly back across the lounge, looking down at the body of their 'stepdad'.

'Well, if he wasn't dead before, he is now,' she said, feeling her heart pound in her chest as she saw the unmistakeable angle at which Bill's head was lying. 'Dev just broke his neck.'

Part Two

Devon

*F*or a crisis meeting, everyone round the table was very silent. The trouble was, there was very little to be said. The clippings lying on the conference table – some from newspapers and magazines, others printouts from online news and gossip sites – spoke for themselves. British journalists prided themselves on their headline-writing skills, and from the selection of articles present, there might have been a nationwide competition to find the most creative way to inform the country not only that Devon's latest cookery show was a failure, but that its hostess seemed to have been spending much more time stuffing her face than she had on concocting recipes.

DEVON HELP HER! blared the *Sun*, over a very unflattering picture of Devon in a loose-flowing black dress and flip-flops.

NO MORE PIES, FOR DEVON'S SAKE! contributed the *Express*, in much the same vein.

LITTLE BIT EXTRA? PULL THE OTHER ONE! said the *Mirror.*

And *WHEN DOES INDULGENCE TURN TO GLUTTONY?* the *Guardian* asked – more polite, but just as pointed.

'It's not a complete disaster,' Bettany, the producer of *Devon's Little Bit Extra*, said finally, in a voice doing its best to sound confident. But she didn't have the nerve to lift her head and look anyone in the eye. 'I mean, the ratings are quite strong.'

'Book sales aren't,' snapped the publisher of the tie-in-book, shoving a copy forward petulantly. 'They've fallen off a bloody cliff.'

Everyone looked at the cover of the book, a lavishly produced hardback. Devon's face in the cover photo was as beautiful as ever, her lush dark hair cascading onto her shoulders, a snug red velvet top lifting her bosoms to a perfect amount of white cleavage, just enough to attract without being so overtly sexual that it would put off the mums who bought Devon's book in droves. Her lipstick matched the velvet top, her cheeks were glowing with blusher, her eyes wide and perfectly made-up; she was smiling seductively while holding out a plate of strawberry shortcake. Luscious red berries, white cream spilling out from the glowing golden split biscuit, curls of dark chocolate decorating the white plate; the crimson, white and deep brown shades cleverly echoing Devon's own colouring, the whole image evoking celebration, summer, rich indulgent sweetness.

A perfect shot. Only no one looking at it could avoid seeing what wasn't in the photograph: the rest of Devon's body. The photo had been originally intended as at least waist-length. And previous book covers of Devon's had shown her entire body in pretty little printed tea dresses that finished just on the knee, and suede sandals that fastened around her elegant ankles.

This one, however, had been ruthlessly cropped just below her breasts, to display her remaining assets: her face and her bosoms. Unfortunately, on a TV show it wasn't so easy to conceal the rest of your presenter. There had been one ill-judged shot of Devon bending over to put a tray of biscuits in the oven that had made her look positively huge. One of the online sites had freeze-framed that, blown it up and posted it with the caption: *NEEDED: BIGGER OVEN FOR XMAS TURKEY!*

'It wasn't *supposed* to be a show about food you eat every day,' Devon mumbled eventually, looking down at the articles from *The Times* and the *Guardian* which were focussed, negatively, on the nutritional value of such suggested treats as Brie and redcurrant toasties and Baileys-and-cream cocktails. The *Guardian* journalist had even totted up the calorie count of some of the recipes, to staggering results.

'No, absolutely not,' Bettany agreed quickly. 'They're really misunderstanding the point of it.'

'I mean, it wasn't called *Devon's Daily Diet*,' Devon said, warming to her theme now she had Bettany's support. 'You don't eat pasta carbonara with bacon and cream every day!'

'No, of course you don't,' Bettany echoed, not that she was Devon's most unbiased supporter; her neck was on the line if the series was considered a disaster.

Rory Shipman, the head of the independent TV company that produced Devon's shows for the BBC, banged his fist down on the table, making everyone jump. He was a large, square-built Yorkshireman, pragmatic and blunt, and the clippings nearest to him scattered away with the impact of his blow. Devon and Bettany looked over at him apprehensively.

'Right,' he said bluntly. 'If no one else will say it, I will. Devon, you look like you *do* eat sodding pasta carbonara every day! You've piled on the pounds since the last series! When you showed up for filming, there were a lot of comments, OK? I didn't have a go at you at the time, because I thought the audience might like it. You know, woman on TV who looks like woman on the street, that kind of thing. Average woman in the UK's what, a size 16?'

One of his researchers bobbed her head in swift confirmation.

'So here we go, lots of birds with one stone, show we're not sizeist, bung on one of our stars who happens to have porked up a bit, get a bit of relief from all the overweight women out there who keep complaining that we're not representing them on TV . . .' He rolled his eyes. 'As if TV's there to represent people! Stupid arses!'

All the researchers tittered dutifully at this.

'But you know what?' Rory banged his fist down on the table again. 'It hasn't – bloody – *worked*! It's a sodding disaster! All those fat heifers out there say they want to see themselves on TV, and when they do, they don't – bloody – *like it*!' He looked around the table at his audience, none of whom would have dared to say a word to interrupt him. 'They might keep watching the show to poke fun at you, Devon, but no one's buying the damn book! What does that tell you?'

Devon opened her mouth to answer him, but no words would come out.

'They'll watch you to have a laugh,' Rory continued, 'but they won't shell out their hard-earned dosh to buy a book with recipes that are going to make them as fat as you! *That's* the elephant in the room!'

Devon and Bettany gasped in horror; even the researchers cringed, wide-eyed, at the spectacle of Rory pointing at Devon and using the word 'elephant'.

'Rory!' Bettany said feebly, torn between sucking up to him and defending her star.

'What?' he snapped. 'It's no more than the truth!'

'I'm not fat!' Devon said in a very small voice.

Rory rounded on her like a tiger who had been just toying with its prey up till now. 'On TV, you are,' he said straightforwardly. 'And you're not supposed to be fat. You're supposed to be sexy, for fuck's sake. This isn't *Two Fat Ladies*, or that porky bloke on *Masterchef*. You're supposed to be the girl men want to fuck and women want to be! That's what we've sold you as! It's not like you're even a proper *cook*!'

If Devon's weight had been the first elephant in the room, this was the second. It was perfectly well known at the production company and Devon's publishers that most of the recipes didn't originate from her, but from the team of researchers sitting around the table. Devon was a truly gifted presenter, not just a pretty face that they put in front of the cameras and told what to say; she had a real knack for taking a basic concept and putting her own spin on it, lacing a creamy Brie sandwich with fresh sharp redcurrants, adding mint chocolate swirls to a Baileys cocktail, ideas that made a viewer genuinely excited to try them out. In her most creative moments, she'd been responsible for supermarkets selling out of ingredients the day after she'd been on TV, talking through a recipe, selling it with the charm and charisma that had made her a star almost overnight.

'I *am* a cook!' Devon said, outraged. 'I cook all the time!'

'Devon . . .' Rory started.

'No!' she said furiously. 'OK, I may not have been much of a cook when I started out, but I've been doing this for years now! I'm not saying I could walk into a restaurant and do a dinner service, but I *do* cook, and I come up with tons of good ideas!'

'Icing on the cake,' Rory said. 'You don't bake the bloody cake.'

'I *can*!'

'You fucking *eat* the bloody cake, by the looks of you!' he said. 'And if you don't lose the weight you've put on, we won't be commissioning you again, Devon. No one will. You're getting like the before picture in a weight-loss ad!'

It was like being slapped across the face – in front of a group of people who, before this awful meeting, had done nothing but crawl to Devon, telling her how wonderful she was. Total humiliation. And the worst part was that, years ago, Devon had actually had a brief affair with Rory. He'd been the producer who spotted her on *Wake up UK* and decided to give her a cooking show. It hadn't been a casting-couch situation – Rory hadn't made it a condition that she sleep with him – but, dazzled with excitement, Devon had done it anyway. The sex hadn't been anything memorable, and nor had Rory's pink, freckled, slightly podgy body, which looked a lot less impressive out of his smart business suits.

He'd talked dirty, she remembered bitterly. Told her how beautiful she was. Said he couldn't believe he was getting to do it with her, to be exactly where so many men wanted to be. He hadn't even lasted that long, too carried away with excitement at getting to see Devon McKenna naked. It had fizzled out quite soon – *just like him in bed*, she thought meanly – after the initial buzz had worn off. When the sex wasn't that great, that was what happened. There hadn't been any bad aftertaste. Rory was all business, and it had been a mutual, unspoken decision to let things tail off.

But now, looking at him, Devon felt her blood boil. *He's put on weight, too,* she thought savagely, *and he wasn't exactly skinny to begin with. All those expense account lunches and dinners – I can tell he's got a paunch under that posh suit he's wearing. Bastard! How dare he call me fat!*

She stood up, pushing back her chair, all eyes in the room riveted to her. 'I know I need to lose some weight,' she said bravely. 'I'll go on a diet.'

Every single person there sagged visibly with relief. Devon was a high-earning brand, and their careers were all closely tied to hers; if she could pull herself out of this downward spiral, diet herself back into the size 12 Devon the nation loved . . .

'*And,*' she said, a martial light in her eyes, 'I'm going to go on *1-2-3 Cook*. They've been asking me for years, and I never did it, because all you lot told me not to! Well, I *can* bloody cook, and I'll show you I can!'

It would have been comical, the way her audience's faces gaped in horror – from happiness to tragedy in a few seconds – if their expressions hadn't demonstrated all too clearly how little faith they had in her cooking skills.

'Devon!' blurted out the previously loyal Bettany. 'The reason we didn't want you to do it is . . . well . . .'

She glanced swiftly round the table, hoping someone else would step in. No one did, not even Rory; but he gave her a sharp nod of assent, almost a command to continue.

'*1-2-3 Cook* is *live,*' Bettany went on, her voice wavering. 'In *real time.* You only have half an hour to make a dish. *And* it's in front of a studio audience. There are cameras *everywhere.* It's really only for professional chefs – I mean, people who've worked in kitchens a lot, who do cooking demonstrations – you know we've always steered you away from those big live shows at Birmingham and Earl's Court, it's not the best use of your talents—'

'This is exactly what I need to do!' Devon interrupted imperiously. 'I'm going to go on one of those crash protein-shake diets, and in a month I'll have lost pounds and pounds, and then I'll go on *1-2-3 Cook* and everyone will see that I've lost weight *and* that I can cook!'

She drew herself up to her full height, looking majestic and imposing.

'It'll turn everything around,' she proclaimed. 'So fuck you, Rory!' She tossed her hair back dramatically and turned on her heels.

'Oh no, wait,' she said, looking over her shoulder with perfect dramatic timing. 'I already did.'

She stormed out of the conference room, bosoms heaving, her hair bouncing dramatically on her shoulders, the people seated on her side of the table squeezing in frantically to let her pass. The door slammed shut behind her, and an even deeper silence fell than the one that had hung like a pall at the start of the meeting; the researchers hardly even dared to breathe, for fear of calling attention to themselves.

'Oh, *bugger*,' Rory eventually said, summing up perfectly what everyone was thinking. 'We're totally and utterly fucked.'

Devon fumed all the way home in the taxi. Shepherd's Bush to Mayfair was a long ride in bad traffic, but the forty minutes it took to chug along the side of Hyde Park didn't calm her down at all; her mobile kept ringing, Bettany desperately trying to get in touch with her.

I'm not answering her, Devon thought furiously, sitting there as the phone rang and rang, letting the calls go to voicemail, one after the other. *She's just going to be totally unsupportive, like she was in the meeting.* The cabbie glanced in the rear-view mirror the first few times, wondering why she wasn't answering her phone, but at the sight of Devon's furious face, he sensibly avoided making a comment, choosing to slide shut the Plexiglass panel between them and turn up his radio instead.

Every time the phone rang, Devon looked at the little screen, hoping it was Rory calling her to apologize, tell her he was sorry for the awful insults he'd thrown at her. If Rory rang, that would mean he'd had second thoughts; that he valued her as talent he still wanted to work with. The fact that he was remaining resolutely silent after her diva-esque exit from the meeting spoke volumes. He was washing his hands of her. He wouldn't commission any more Devon McKenna cookery series.

Her career was going down the toilet – unless she managed to turn it around on her own.

All they did was criticize me! Devon thought, sizzling with anger. *No one offered one constructive suggestion about how we could sort this out! I was the one who said I'd do a crash diet! I was the one who offered to go on* 1-2-3 Cook. *They shot down my ideas, but did they bloody come up with anything else that would work? No, they bloody didn't! Useless bastards – they've made a shitload of money out of me, and now they're just sitting back and watching me drown without even chucking me a lifejacket!*

She knew she still had a great deal of goodwill from the public. For everyone who mocked her weight, there'd be plenty of supporters, women who sympathized because they were struggling hard to keep slim themselves and knew how difficult it was. If she could lose the extra pounds, get back to where she'd been before, it would be a triumph. Devon had never been thin: no one would expect her to put out an exercise video, like soap opera stars or reality TV would-be celebrities clinging to their last few seconds of fame. She wouldn't have to be photographed working out in a public park with her trainer, or standing on her doorstep taking delivery of a PowerPlate machine, dressed in workout gear to show how keen she was to get herself into shape.

No, she'd just have to slim back to a voluptuous size 12, diet the muffin top down from the waistband of her jeans, and the Devon McKenna brand would be stronger than ever.

Look at the singers and actors who go into rehab and make amazing comebacks afterwards! Devon told herself. *And no publicity is bad publicity, surely . . .*

The cab was pulling to a stop outside the Green Street house. Devon glanced down past the area steps, to the safety-barred windows of the basement flat in which Deeley was ensconced. She sighed. Having Deeley downstairs was stirring up such a confusing mixture of feelings in Devon. She was realizing how much she had missed her little sister. They'd shared a room for their whole childhood: squabbled, made up, shared confidences and crushes, helped each other stay brave through all the turbulence of their mother's drug abuse, and crawled into bed with each other many nights, especially after Bill's death, when both of them had had awful nightmares for years afterwards.

And then I finished school and shot off to London, and I was so busy working I barely even had time to talk to Deeley on the phone. And when she came down to London too, we didn't see much of each other. Maxie said to let her go her own way, that she needed to grow up and find her feet.

When Nicky had whisked Deeley off to LA, Maxie had said that it was the best thing that could possibly happen; she had even discouraged Devon from visiting Deeley. Maxie had assumed that Deeley would stay in LA forever, because why would anyone leave California for rainy old London? *She'll meet some rich man over there and marry him,* Maxie had said. *She'll never come back. And it's better that way. Deeley needs to forget all about us. All about Bill. Because Deeley had that stupid little girl crush on him; she always felt bad about what happened. And the one thing that could bring us down is if Deeley starts talking about it to someone.*

Sadly, Devon had agreed with Maxie. *Though when don't I?* Devon thought now. *When do I ever do anything Maxie disapproves of?*

She sighed again. *But Maxie's always right. She warned me that Deeley can't keep her mouth shut, and look what happened with that magazine article!*

Anger rose up in Devon, anger and an even more powerful sense of betrayal. Deeley had been unforgivably careless, had chattered away to a journalist and skimmed the edges of the McKenna sisters' deadly secret. Maxie and Devon had tried so hard for all those years to take care of little, sweet-faced, vulnerable Deeley, and look how she'd rewarded them: by proving that Maxie was right, that Deeley was a total loose cannon, not safe anywhere near the UK press.

Oh, Deeley . . . Devon felt horribly torn. Between Maxie and Deeley. Between her memories of curling up on a narrow single bed with her little sister, both of them crying quietly, overwhelmed by the mess and insecurity of their lives, clinging to each other, drawing comfort from the warmth of another body, from the familiar smell and feel of their sister; and the knowledge that, so recently, Deeley had totally messed up. She hadn't been in the UK for a week before she'd started talking to journalists and putting everything her older sisters had worked so hard for into terrible jeopardy.

Part of Devon wanted to go down the area steps right now, to find Deeley and hug her hard, to sit down on the sofa, holding each other's hands, and catch up on everything that had been going on in their lives for the years that they hadn't been in contact. To confide in Deeley about what had just happened with her awful meeting, about her need to diet, about the way that she and Matt just seemed to keep going past each other, about her underlying fear that Matt and she weren't actually that compatible . . .

And part of her was afraid that Maxie, as usual, was absolutely right. That Deeley wasn't a safe confidante, that she simply couldn't be trusted, and that it would have been much better for both of them if she'd stayed permanently in LA.

'Um – miss?' The cabbie was looking at her in the rear-view mirror. 'The meter's still running. You getting out or what?'

'Oh! Yes!' Devon gathered her coat and bag and stepped out, settling up the fare. She hesitated for a moment, still wondering whether she should see if Deeley was in. And just then, the front door swung open. Matt was standing on the doorstep, having seen the cab draw up outside the house.

'Everything OK?' Matt bounded down the short flight of stairs. 'I didn't expect you back this early . . .'

He trailed off as he saw the expression on Devon's face: if she'd been in a comic, the graphic artist would have drawn thunderclouds clustering round her head. Without saying a word, she strode past him, heading up the stairs and into the house.

Where she stopped dead at the sight in front of her. A waist-high silver champagne cooler stood in the centre of the black-and-white tiled hall, two lead-crystal champagne flutes on a small circular table beside it.

I didn't even know we had a cooler like that, she thought, dazed, as she took in the rest of the new decorations: a trail of red roses leading up the wide circular staircase, the bright crimson blooms standing out beautifully against the cream of the stair carpet, like big drops of blood. Two-thirds of the way up the stairs lay a huge bunch of roses, next to a basket which was spilling over with scarlet, velvety rose petals.

'I thought I had a good hour or so at least,' Matt said apologetically, closing the front door behind him. 'I saw you coming from up there,' he gestured to the long window set into the stair wall, which gave onto Green Street, 'and shot down to welcome you – but maybe I should've kept going and finished the job – I was going to do a whole line of red roses, all the way upstairs and into the bedroom, and scatter the petals all over the bed – you know, like in a film . . .'

He looked anxiously at his wife.

'Is everything OK?' he asked nervously.

'No,' Devon snapped, all the frustration and humiliation from her abortive meeting, and the tangle of confusion that surrounded her relationship with her younger sister, spilling out on her poor husband. 'No, it isn't.'

She grabbed the bottle of champagne out of the cooler, sending cubes of ice clattering to the tiled floor like rough chunks of glass, scattering to the far corners of the hallway. The foil covering the cork had already, thoughtfully, been removed by Matt; she twisted off the wire in one swift, practised movement, throwing it to the floor, and eased the cork out with her thumbs with a quiet pop. It followed the wire, as she leaned over to the table and filled one of the glasses so impatiently with Veuve Cliquot that bubbles spilled all down the side, flooding onto the steel top of the table.

'I bought the champagne thingy yesterday,' Matt mumbled. 'I thought it'd be really nice to make a bit of a special moment for us when you got back from your big commissioning meeting – we haven't really spent much time together for the last month or two, have we? So . . . um . . .'

He came up behind her, putting his two big hands on her shoulders. It was meant to be a comforting gesture, but Devon twisted away from him. Angrily, she raised the glass to her mouth and drank half of it in one go, coughing on the bubbles.

'I wish you wouldn't drink so much,' Matt said unwisely, his handsome, chunky face frowning now. 'Sometimes I get down in the morning and see what's in the recycling. I mean, the whole bottle from the night before'll be in there, and I just had one glass.'

Devon refused to meet his eyes. Defiantly, she finished the glass and refilled it, not even offering her husband any.

'I don't need a lecture, OK?' she snapped. 'I've just had the most totally shitty meeting of my entire life!'

'Oh no! Babe! What happened?' Matt's blue eyes clouded with worry. Devon had once told him, jokingly, that he'd be perfect for panto, and he'd laughed and said that all the lads'd troop along to watch him playing Widow Twanky in a dress, wig and lots of lipstick.

But now his transparency annoyed her. It was like talking to a child. Children got upset by your news, and then you ended up looking after them, instead of being allowed to be upset on your own account. Vivid memories of Deeley as a little girl rushed back to Devon as she started on her second glass of Veuve; how Deeley's big brown eyes had welled up with tears at every bit of bad news, every time their mum had been arrested or banged up, every time they'd had to move from one shithole to the next. And she, Devon, had had to comfort her little sister, to stop her kicking off, when all the time she'd been desperate to burst into tears herself.

That was who Matt reminded her of, she realized suddenly. Deeley. Matt and Deeley had had things comparatively easy: looked after, practically cosseted, sheltered from the worst of life's problems by a loving family. Matt was the youngest of three boys, with an adoring mum and a firm-but-fair dad who were still together – no divorce in the Bates family. He'd grown up in a leafy part of Hertfordshire, in a nice detached house; he'd been given a decent education, and his parents had been willing to drive him all over for his rugby practice – junior club side matches, county squad events, often ferrying around other team members, muddied and bloodied, never complaining.

He doesn't know he's born, Devon thought viciously, looking at her big, sturdy husband and feeling horribly resentful of all the privileges he'd enjoyed.

'The show's doing really badly. And the book sales are falling off a cliff,' she snapped, using the publisher's vivid metaphor.

'Ah, bugger!' Matt said, pulling a long face. 'Still, it's just one show, isn't it? And just one book?'

He still hadn't gauged the full extent of the dark mood that was surrounding Devon; he knew enough now not to approach her, but he opened his arms wide for her to walk into and have a big, comforting hug. Six foot four of Matt was huge enough, but with his arms open, he looked to Devon like a bear rearing up in front of her, like something off an Alaskan nature show, enormous and overwhelming.

Grabbing the bottle of champagne, Devon turned away from him, heading into the living room. She bypassed the wraparound chocolate leather sofas – American-import, big enough for Matt and his rugby mates to spread out on and watch the playback of a game, slinging back beers and yelling cheerfully at their successes and mess-ups. If she sat there, it would be all too easy for Matt to sink down next to her, throw a big arm round her shoulders, try to comfort her. And right then, Devon didn't even want her husband to touch her.

I'm behaving like a complete and utter bitch, she thought miserably, self-aware enough to know that she was taking out all her humiliation and frustration on poor Matt. More, that he was being the perfect, sympathetic, supportive husband, the kind any woman would dream of having. *But I just feel so awful about myself right now! I hate myself! I'm a failure, a big fat porky failure!*

And how can I respect a man who loves a big fat porky failure?

Devon sank down onto the padded purple velvet cushions that were scattered across the seat beneath the big bay window over-looking the garden beyond, standing the Veuve bottle next to her, making sure there was no room for Matt to sit beside her. She was shocked by the realization that had just hit her: that the reason she had been pushing Matt away for these last months wasn't just because she felt fat and undesirable.

If I hate myself so much, there must be something really wrong with anyone who wants to be with me! Mustn't there?

I mean, how could he possibly fancy this?

Deliberately goading herself to even higher levels of self-revulsion, Devon reached down and squeezed a roll of fat just below her bosoms, her fingers sinking in easily all around it. She could hold it firmly and wobble it up and down, making her breasts wobble too.

I'm revolting. No wonder everyone's laughing at me on TV, and all the papers are making fun of me. I'm a big fat greedy pig.

Matt's heavy tread was crossing the hall now, coming into the living room, thudding on the polished dark boards of the floor. Catching sight of Devon curled up on the window seat, he came to a halt directly underneath the enormous black-painted chandelier, heavy with ornamental black glass droplets and beading. The ceiling was so high on the ground floor of this Regency house that it could accommodate a four-foot chandelier and still give clearance for Matt and his rugby player friends to walk beneath it without whacking their heads on the dangling pendants.

Matt had realized immediately why Devon had chosen the window seat, rather than the sofa. Standing there, he still looked like the bear to which Devon had compared him, but now a wounded one, as if his mate had given him a huge, unprovoked whack round the head with her claws out, drawing blood.

'I'm going to go on *1-2-3 Cook,*' Devon announced, finishing her second glass of champagne. She was beginning to feel a little dizzy now: drinking during the day definitely went to your head faster than in the evening. Challengingly, she stared at her husband, daring him to try to tell her not to go ahead with it.

But his reaction was not at all what she'd expected.

'That's brilliant!' Matt exclaimed with a big, beaming smile. 'You mean that afternoon TV show, right? You'd be perfect on that!'

Devon's jaw dropped; she almost dropped her glass too.

'Are you serious?' she blurted out, dumbfounded. 'Everyone else thinks it's a totally mad idea.'

'Well, they're all mad then, aren't they?' Matt said, folding his arms, which made his muscular body and bulging arms look like Mr Clean. 'You'll be a star on it! I remember you teaching me how to make pasta sauce on live TV at seven in the morning, the first time we met – you were brilliant, you had the whole camera crew laughing. I mean, I was totally cack-handed, and I wasn't even listening to a word you said, 'cos I was too busy goggling at how pretty you were, so you really had your work cut out for you! Why shouldn't you be able to do something like that cooking show, eh? You've done live TV loads of times before.'

'Because the cooking I did on live TV before was all planned out in advance,' Devon said, realizing, to her extreme annoyance, that now she was being her own devil's advocate. 'But *1-2-3 Cook* isn't. They just bung you some ingredients, and you have to make a proper dish out of them, in thirty minutes start to finish, *and* describe what you're doing to the camera, *and* coach some idiot audience member at the same time. You can really end up looking like a moron if you don't manage to pull it off.'

'Oh, you'll be fine!' Matt said with happy confidence. 'You cook lovely meals for us, don't you?'

'Yes, but those are all planned out in advance too,' Devon said, her voice rising, swinging her legs off the window seat and onto the floor as she faced him, determined to make him understand. 'Like the things I used to make on *Wake up UK*. And that was just beans on toast, or a baked potato. I mean, the whole joke was that they were really simple, it was just that the blokes didn't know how to make them . . .'

She looked helplessly at her husband, who was shaking his head.

'You'll be fine,' he repeated, his faith in her abilities unshaken by her words.

Oh God, Devon thought, panicky now. *The only person who thinks I can do this is Matt, and he knows fuck all about it. Maybe I shouldn't go on* 1-2-3 *Cook after all – I mean, if he's the only one who's pushing me to do it, what does that say about the idea?*

But she didn't have time to process this thought. With the surprising swiftness that had made Matt a star of the rugby pitch, he crossed the space between them and sank into a squat in front of his wife.

'Babe,' he said, laying both hands on her knees, and looking directly into her eyes. 'I love you, OK? And I think you're gorgeous. You know I always think you're gorgeous.'

More fool you, Devon thought bitterly.

'Even if you don't believe it, I do,' Matt said, acutely picking up on her reaction. 'Now look, this afternoon hasn't exactly gone as I planned, but it's not too late to turn things around, is it? There's no reason that one shitty meeting should mess us up. It's nothing to do with you and me.'

He reached for her hands, planting a kiss on each one of them in turn.

'Tell you what,' he continued, 'you stay here for five minutes while I pop upstairs and finish what I started, OK? I'm going to cover the bed in rose petals, come back, carry you upstairs, and make sure we have such a lovely time rolling around on 'em that you completely forget that you had a horrible afternoon with a bunch of wankers who don't appreciate you like they should.' He kissed her hands again. 'Sound like a plan?'

'Oh, Matt . . .' Devon heaved a deep, deep sigh. She didn't pull her hands away, but they just lay in his much larger ones like two limp fish.

'Don't say no, Dev,' Matt said urgently, squeezing her hands, refusing to be put off by her lack of response. 'We need this. You know we need this. We haven't had sex for ages. Months, if I'm being honest. And it's not just about me getting my rocks off – you know it isn't. We need to be connected again. We need to get back to where we were when we first got together – remember? We couldn't keep our hands off each other!'

'Things change,' Devon said feebly, unable to meet his pleading gaze. 'We've been married for years, Matt. No one keeps up that pace. They'd never get anything done.'

Matt heaved a sigh of his own. 'I'm not saying we should be shagging like rabbits every hour of the day and night, Dev,' he said patiently. 'But we need to be connected again. We've really lost our way. If I feel that, I know you must too.'

'Funny how you think that a good shag'll make everything all right,' Devon said, knowing that she was being nasty, but unable to help herself. 'That's such a male solution, isn't it? Get your end away, and everything will just fall into place, right? You're totally ignoring my problems, the way I feel . . .'

She achieved her goal with those unpleasant words. Matt dropped her hands and stood up, his brow furrowed with pain.

'Dev,' he said hopelessly, 'I'm doing everything I can think of to make you happy, and you're just throwing it back in my face!' He looked agonized now, his jaw set. 'You don't know what I'm going through – you're not even putting yourself in my place for one second! Here's my wife slipping away from me, either ignoring me or pushing me away, and it's been going on for months now! How am I supposed to feel? What am I supposed to do? The only time you want to be near me is when we're going out somewhere to have photos taken of us looking like a happy couple for the tabloids or the gossip mags! This is so messed up!'

Every word he's saying is true, Devon knew. She hung her head, unable to look at him. She felt horribly guilty, an evil, vile bitch. *But I can't make love with him right now. I can't have him seeing me naked. I just can't . . . it would be too humiliating . . .*

It didn't help either that Matt was in such amazing shape. That was the awful irony of the situation. She'd fancied him instantly, as soon as she'd laid eyes on him, because he was such a stunning specimen of male perfection, fifteen stone of bone and muscle in optimal physical condition. Naked, he was a sculptor's dream model, every muscle defined, not an ounce of visible fat on his entire breathtaking body.

The trouble was that his physical flawlessness made it even worse for Devon. *Because what on earth will I look like, next to him? Like a big, fat, white, sagging whale!*

'You're my *wife*, Dev! That means everything to me!' Matt was pleading now. 'I said "for better, for worse" and "till death do us part", and I meant every word! There's never been a divorce in my family, and I don't want us to be the first! I want to work at this. But I need you to help me, Dev. I can't put this back together on my own.'

He covered his face with his hands for a long moment, and when he took them away, it looked as if he were fighting valiantly to suppress tears.

'I need you,' he said hoarsely. 'I need you really badly, Dev. I've been . . . things have sort of . . .' Matt rubbed his face furiously with one big hand. 'Things have got really weird for me lately, and I don't want them to. I want to be with my wife! That's what I signed up for, and that's what I want!'

'Oh God, Matt,' Devon said wearily, reaching for the bottle of champagne, slowly filling her glass again, moving at a snail's pace; she was aching, her bones sore, so weary she could have passed out then and there. 'You're so nice. Maybe you shouldn't be so nice with me. Did you ever think that? Maybe the nicer you are to me, the nastier and bitchier I get. Like some awful chain reaction. We're bouncing back and forth off each other, and making things worse and worse – the nicer you get, the more it drives me crazy. Because I don't deserve you being good to me! I'm a total fucking bitch to you! You should get angry with me, not keep going on about your marriage vows!'

Matt stood there, his fists clenching by his sides in frustration, his blue eyes flashing with a mixture of emotions too complex and confused for him to easily articulate. He opened his mouth, but no words came out. The truth was, he had said everything there was to say: he'd pleaded with Devon, done his best to show her his desperation, his need for her to reconnect with him, his vulnerability. He'd made a big romantic gesture – he'd been on the net all the previous day finding a florist who could take an order for two hundred red roses and a basket of petals, and spent an arm and a leg just on the delivery charge to get them to Green Street in time for Devon's return.

And it had all been for nothing. He'd shot his bolt, he had nothing left.

Slowly, head hanging, he turned and left the living room.

Devon didn't watch him go. Sunk in a swamp of misery and guilt that she knew was entirely of her own making, she curled up in a ball and stared, unseeingly, out of the big bay window beside her. Wishing herself very, very far away from her seemingly perfect life.

Deeley

*F*rom the moment she stepped off the train, Deeley's stomach had been doing somersaults.

You can't turn back now, she told herself firmly, even as she realized she was looking up longingly at the Departures board in the station to see what time the next train left for London. *That would be completely pathetic.*

Riseholme Station, half an hour out of Leeds, had had a major makeover: where previously the facing platforms had been bare wastelands of old shuttered offices whose doors were locked and bolted, their paint crumbling, they were now bright and inviting little café outlets called Pumpkin or Dee-Vine, serving coffees and calorie-counted chicken wraps. Deeley bought a cappuccino, even though the chubby, pink-cheeked girl behind the counter admitted to her, embarrassed, that they only had half-fat milk.

'We don't get much call for skim,' she mumbled, taking in Deeley's appearance with a mixture of admiration and envy. 'You're not from round here, are you?'

'I used to be,' Deeley said, taking the coffee and dropping a pound in the tip jar; the girl's eyes opened wide with appreciation.

'Well, you're not any more,' she said bluntly. 'I can tell you that for nothing.'

No, I'm definitely not, Deeley thought, as she left the station, her footsteps automatically turning right, down the parade. A couple of minicab drivers, waiting outside their small office, swivelled to stare at her blatantly. She'd tried to dress down, but as she caught her reflection in the window of a WH Smith and compared herself to the locals bustling past, she had the perfect visual image of how far she'd come since her days here. Deeley's idea of dressing down was a slim pair of jeans tucked into soft suede boots, a feather-light black merino wool sweater under a belted leather jacket. Hair pulled back into a smooth ponytail, sunglasses propped on her head, diamond studs in her ears her only jewellery. Simple, discreet, what a woman in LA or New York would wear when going out to do errands.

And the girls on the street, who had bought the magazines with photos of celebrities out during the day, had tried to copy their clothes as much as possible. They looked like cheaper versions of Deeley – they might even have modelled themselves on a photo of Deeley herself, shopping on Rodeo Drive. Plenty of girls here had cheap copies of Deeley's Fendi bag, made from vinyl rather than patent leather, the buckles over-shiny and already tarnishing, bought from Primark or Asda for a tiny fraction of the $650 Deeley had paid for hers. Their boots were microfibre rather than butter-soft suede, their jeans thin Dorothy Perkins imitations of her Seven for All Mankind skinnies, their highlights skunk stripes rather than her hand-painted, delicately blended ones: but their look was unmistakeably Deeley's.

And their glances, as they noticed her, were distinctly unfriendly.

Realizing that the grey day wasn't remotely bright enough to warrant her wearing sunglasses, and getting a little nervous that someone might mug her for her YSLs, Deeley pulled hers off the crown of her head and slipped them into her bag. She was walking now past a line of chippies and takeaways, which gave her a first blast of familiarity. The tarted-up parade, with its brave efforts to prettify the grotty little town, its hanging baskets with sprays of flowers, and its low-grade chain stores, hadn't rung any bells; all these regeneration efforts had happened years after the McKenna sisters had left. But the kebab shops, the smell of stale frying oil and curry powder and malt vinegar sharp in her nostrils, the way the litter bins were already brimming with discarded chip boxes and drinks cans – that Deeley remembered all too well. She found herself trying to recall which their favourite chippy had been, the one where the owner scooped up extra crunchy bits to drizzle over their newspaper cones full of the chips that had often been the only dinner they had.

Mum thought ketchup really was a vegetable, Deeley thought, her mouth twisting. She tried not to remember her mother, who had overdosed when Deeley was twelve, three years after Bill's death. Maureen McKenna had come out of prison, and headed straight for her old druggie friends. They'd found Maureen's body a week later, in the squat where she'd holed up with her fellow addicts. Neighbours had begun to complain about the smell.

Bill's old house on Thompson Road wasn't far from the station, only two more streets away. Deeley's footsteps were slowing down, she realized, as she approached the turn.

This is where I thought I was safest. Where we thought we finally had a home, with someone who wanted to be our dad.

Bill hadn't been a drinker or a druggie; his worst vice was a couple of Dunhills and a pint or so of stout when he got home from work. He'd met their mother in a pub, drunk, high, a ruin of her former self, but still undeniably attractive, and, like a lot of men before him, had thought he could help her. Get her back on the straight and narrow. And look after her three kids into the bargain.

Well, no one managed to help Mum. Not that she'd have let them. It was hard even now for Deeley to remember that Maureen McKenna hadn't even come to find her daughters when she'd finished her last stretch in prison; choosing instead a binge of Tennent's Extra and a cocktail of speed, methadone and Valium that had finally done for her. Maxie, Devon and Deeley had been gone from Bill's by then; Maxie had managed to persuade Maureen's estranged sister, Sandra, to take them in after Bill 'went missing', on the understanding that they'd do jobs after school to help pay their way, and that their mother would never be informed of their whereabouts.

Aunt Sandra had done her duty and taken Maureen's daughters to her funeral. But after that, Maureen was never mentioned again, which was fine with the girls. Their mother had been nothing but a source of misery to them, and they barely remembered their father, a soldier who'd been shot serving in Northern Ireland shortly after Deeley was born; he'd hardly been around even when he was on leave. Maureen had blamed her spiral downwards into drug addiction and alcoholism on the shock of Patrick McKenna's death, and the girls had believed her for years, until Maxie slowly put the pieces together and realized that their mother had been up to all sorts of mischief all the time her husband was on active duty.

Oh God, Mum, Deeley thought sadly. *You should never have had kids. Or you should have given them away to someone who wanted them. Aunt Sandra did her best, I suppose, but she didn't want kids either.*

Aunt Sandra had died of a stroke when Deeley was nineteen and living in London. The sisters had no family left; they'd never known their father's relatives. All they had was each other.

And that's not going so well at the moment, is it? Deeley thought sadly, feeling suddenly very alone.

Deeley shoved her hands in her pockets and stared down at her feet. She'd needed to make this pilgrimage to Bill's for all sorts of reasons, but the main one was the weirdest.

I feel like I want to thank him for everything he did for us.

It was wrong, irrational, completely illogical. Bill had abused Maxie; he'd told her he was going to start on Devon next. He'd cynically taken them in, not to help out their mum after all, but for the sake of having her three attractive and underage daughters in his house, under his control.

I'm so messed up about this, Deeley thought helplessly. *How can I possibly remember Bill and not feel like I want to throw up, after everything he did? Maybe this is why I've never had a proper relationship, why I agreed to date Nicky and put any real chance of romance on hold for years and years. Because I didn't trust myself to pick someone nice. I'm too confused by the fact that the only memories I have of our awful, abusive sort-of-stepdad are ones where he was amazing to me, like the dad I never had and always longed for so much. He really made me feel loved and wanted . . .*

She knew she was in front of the house now. Her feet had stopped, her brain telling her that it had recognized the familiar chipped old wall in front of it. The low gate had been broken then, needing a new latch: Bill had always said he'd get round to repairing it, but never found the time. Now it was hanging completely off its hinges, rusted and fallen against the battered brown recycling bin that was contemptuously overflowing with plastic bags out of which were spilling polystyrene takeaway containers, half-gnawed chicken bones, general household detritus. Nothing that could possibly be recycled. Just like the contents of the recycling bins on every other house on the street that Deeley had passed. The inhabitants of this area obviously didn't think much of the local council's effort to go green.

Hasn't exactly come up in the world, Thompson Road, she thought, taking in the pebble-dashed semi with a shock of recognition. It was much smaller than she remembered, but that was only to be expected. Things always seem bigger from a child's perspective. What took her aback most was how much the house had deteriorated. She recalled Bill as having been very house-proud. The narrow patio outside had been sprayed down and weeded in his time, the windows washed with vinegar and newspaper, the plants on the sills watered, the curtains taken to the cleaners every so often. Now the flagstones were cracked almost to splinters in places, straggled dandelions forcing their way through the gaps. The glass of the windows was smeared and dirty, and in place of a curtain, the front lounge had what looked like a tablecloth half-pinned up over the bay window.

Bill would hate this, she thought instinctively. She craned her head sideways to look into the long thin stretch of back garden; the wall that separated his semi from the house next door was in worse repair than ever, and it was easy to see into the garden. Unsurprisingly, considering the state of the house, it looked as if no one had touched the garden since Bill's time in residence. The grass was so long you could have plaited it, waving in the wind like a green sea, weeds growing high through it now there was no Bill to pop out every Saturday with his Argos strimmer and keep it in order.

And the sycamore tree was still there. Its roots had already been tearing up the wall of their back garden when they'd lived there; Bill had reported it to the council, but no one had cared then, and clearly nothing had changed in the eighteen years since Bill's death. The tree was much taller now, and, by the crumbling brickwork she could see in the garden next door its roots had clearly reached further, undermining the neighbours' walls too.

Bill's death. A shiver ran right through Deeley, rippling up her spine, chilling her blood. *It's not just Mum*, she thought, feeling suddenly panicky now she was so close to what had happened eighteen years ago. *There are so many things the McKenna sisters don't want to remember . . .*

'You lost?'

A voice beside her made her jump almost out of her skin. She turned, nearly tripping, to see a woman standing right next to her. *How did she get that close to me without my noticing?* Deeley wondered. *I must have been in a complete daze . . .*

'You're not from round here,' the woman said. A statement, not a question, made in the strong local accent that, even after all these years, Deeley had no difficulty in understanding.

'No,' Deeley admitted. 'I'm not.'

The woman's hair was scraped back into a tight high ponytail, like a poor person's attempt at a facelift. It hadn't helped much, particularly as the style was too young for her, just like the big gold hoop earrings she was wearing. Deeley felt a rush of familiarity looking at her, even though she didn't recognize her; but she was so archetypically like the women from this town, this area. The grey-ish skin, lined and leathered prematurely by smoking before she was even in her teens; the tight, pinched mouth and perpetual frown; the scrawny frame in t-shirt and denim jacket; the slight smell of beer on her breath. So many women round here looked just like her. The only difference in the last eighteen years was that instead of jeans, the woman wore velour tracksuit trousers in a bright shade of pink, tucked into flopping Ugg-style boots.

All probably bought from the local market, Deeley thought, remembering what a huge deal the thrice-weekly market had been. How she and her sisters had craved and saved up for the cheap make-up, the knock-off L'Oréal eyeshadow palettes labelled in Chinese that caked as soon as they applied them, the 'fashion tights' that had no lycra in them and bagged around their ankles halfway through the first wear.

'I know you,' the woman said, the crow's feet around her eyes deepening even further as she squinted at Deeley. She took a long drag on the cigarette she was holding in a nicotine-stained hand, its fingers tipped with long elaborate acrylic nails. 'You used to live round here. I never forget a face.'

Her narrow gaze took in Deeley from head to toe. It wasn't pleasant; Deeley found herself taking a step back.

'And what're you doing back here?' the woman mused to herself. 'Rich lady like you? Look at that handbag. Cost a bloody fortune, didn't it?'

Deeley tried not to tighten her grip on the Fendi bag.

A chilly wind rippled down the street. The woman nipped in the collar of her denim jacket with a claw-like hand, the cigarette still in the other, her head now tipped to one side.

'You're one of those sisters, aren't you?' she said eventually. 'I was thinking about who's been in number forty-two over the years. There's some nasty scum there now, I can tell you. If you were thinking about ringing the bell, don't. You'd be lucky to get out with the clothes on your back.'

Deeley started to say something about needing to get back to catch a train, but the woman rode right over her as if she were deaf.

'One of those sisters,' she mused. 'The three pretty ones. Too pretty for round here, we all thought. Kept yourselves to yourselves, didn't you? You were living with Bill Duncan. Oh, I remember Bill Duncan all right. One day he was here, the next he wasn't. No one ever knew where he went.'

She fixed her eyes on Deeley. They were heavily lined with dark blue pencil, the only make-up she was wearing, and it had bled a little into her crow's feet. She was by far the smaller of the two women, so skinny she could almost have been considered frail; but Deeley knew women like this, remembered them vividly. Very often they were the ones that ran things. The ones who sat in the pub, at the bar, who everyone looked to for decisions; an infinitesimal nod or shake of the head from a scrawny little chain-smoking woman like this could decide someone's fate.

'He tried to keep his hands clean, best he could, Bill Duncan,' the woman said reflectively, lighting one cigarette from the stub of the previous one, throwing the still-lit butt into the middle of the road without looking to see if it might hit anyone, or anything. 'But that's not so easy round here, is it?'

Now she did seem to expect a response. Deeley gulped, not knowing what to say.

'I was really small then,' she said. 'I'm the youngest sister. I don't remember much of anything.'

'But you came back, didn't you?' the woman said sharply. 'To have a sniff around your old place? What's all that about, then?'

Her eyes were sharp as tacks. Deeley knew, instinctively, that a lie would be spotted immediately.

'I was out of the country for a long time,' she said. 'In America. I came back and saw my sisters and I got a bit nostalgic.'

The woman snorted in derision, her eyes still boring into Deeley's. 'For this shithole?' she said, sneering. 'Pull the other one, lovey.'

'For Bill,' Deeley said simply, sticking to the truth. 'He was really nice to me. Bill was always like a dad to me.'

The woman's plucked and pencilled eyebrows rose, corrugating her forehead into a deep tracery of lines that would have had any of Deeley's old acquaintances in LA screaming in repulsion and hitting the speed-dial number for their Botox doctor.

'Right,' she commented, her voice so flat that Deeley couldn't tell what she was thinking. 'So you got no idea where he is, then, Bill? He had a soft spot for you three.'

Deeley couldn't read anything into this last statement. Was the woman making a sly comment on Bill's abuse of Maxie? Or was she ignorant of it?

Somehow it was hard to imagine this woman being ignorant of anything.

'I live just down the road,' the woman continued casually. 'Used to know Bill quite well. He really took to your mum. Met her in our local. More fool him. She was a bad lot. Very pretty, but a bad lot.'

Deeley shrugged; she couldn't argue with that.

'Dead now,' the woman said, dragging on her cigarette as if it were her main source of nutrition, never taking her eyes from Deeley's even as the thin grey coil of smoke rose between them. 'Overdosed, didn't she?'

Deeley had been too nervous of the woman to call a halt to the conversation before, but somehow the mention of her mother started to ring alarm bells inside her head. This woman knew a lot about her mother and Bill, and she had clearly not just been walking down the street when she saw Deeley standing in front of the house and stopped for a chat. She found herself glancing down at the woman's feet, and realized that what she'd taken for Uggs weren't boots at all. They were slippers. Big furry pink slippers.

The woman had seen her from inside her house, somewhere down the road. Had grabbed her packet of fags and nipped out to confront Deeley without even bothering to put some outside shoes on, though it had rained earlier and the pavement was still damp.

The alarm bells inside Deeley's skull were ringing even louder now.

'I should really be going,' she said. 'I've got a train to catch.' She would have looked at her watch, to pantomime checking the time, but it was a diamond-studded Piaget, a gift from Nicky two Christmases ago, and she sensed very strongly that the best place for it right now was tucked invisibly under the cuff of her sweater.

'We remember you girls,' the woman said conversationally, ignoring Deeley's words. 'Three of you, there were. One married some MP . . .' She spat over her shoulder, an impressive amount of phlegm spattering on the pavement. 'And the middle one's on telly. Married that rugby player, got a bit lardy. And you've done well for yourself too, eh? That isn't hard to spot. You've got a bit of a nerve coming back here all dressed up like that, Deeley McKenna.'

Deeley couldn't help it; she jumped at the mention of her name. The woman smiled slyly.

'Oh yes, not much gets past me,' she said. 'Memory like an elephant.' She tapped the side of her head with one garishly painted, long, chipped nail. 'It goes in here and it doesn't come out. Takes me a while, sometimes, but I don't forget a name or a face.'

She leaned in towards Deeley, the beer and nicotine on her breath so strong that Deeley had to try hard not to gag.

'So, Deeley McKenna, you turn around right now and go back where you came from. Somewhere a lot better than this, I'm sure. You stay away from us and we'll stay away from you. There's nothing left for you in this shithole. Is there?'

The last two words shot out like bullets from a gun; the woman's head jerking forward on her neck like a turkey's, shoving her face even closer to her target. Deeley gulped, taken completely by surprise, aware that the woman was staring up at her with absolute intent, taking in every nuance of Deeley's response and analyzing it with a precision that would have done credit to a CIA interrogator.

'No!' she answered automatically, because it was the truth. There was nothing for her here. Nothing but a crumbling pebble-dash semi with an overgrown sycamore tree in the back garden. Nothing but a few memories that she couldn't trust anyway.

The head backed away. The woman nodded, the first smile Deeley had seen on her face momentarily twisting her lips. It wasn't a nice smile at all. Deeley could happily have lived without ever seeing it.

'Good,' she said slowly, throwing the second cigarette into the street with a flick of her fingers. 'So off you go, then. First left, left again when you see Burger King, and down the parade back to the station. Back to your nice smart life with all your money and your rich men buying you things. And you tell your sisters that one visit was enough. None of us wants to see you back here, walking around all dressed up like you're better than us. If I see you round here again, I won't be so friendly. You got the fucking red carpet this time, young lady. Don't expect it again.'

She turned away, expecting no reply and getting none; her message had been delivered loud and clear. And Deeley, too, swung on her heel and walked back the way she'd come, concentrating very hard on not walking too fast, on not acting as if she were scared or intimidated.

Even though she was. That woman had scared the living daylights out of her.

Her warning had been, as far as Deeley was concerned, 100 per cent successful. She was never coming back here. The past was firmly put behind her now, and it was going to stay there forever.

Maxie

'*D*arling! You're a bloody genius!'

Olly burst into the living room, blond fringe flapping in excitement, did a comedy double take, and skidded to a halt at the sight of his adopted daughter playing on the Aubusson rug with the nanny.

'Oh,' he said, his face falling. 'She's down here, is she?'

Maxie was so used to Olly's habit of asking her questions whose answer was already blindingly obvious that it barely annoyed her any more. Most Sloane men tended to do it, she'd found; it was their tribe's passive-aggressive way of pointing out a situation they didn't like, while simultaneously indicating that it was the woman's job to resolve it for them.

'Ten minutes more,' she said, glancing at the elegant chiming clock on the mantelpiece. 'Then bath and bed.'

'She's being *such* a good girl, Daddy!' said the nanny bravely, looking up at Olly over Alice's curly head. 'She hardly ever cries, do you, sweetie?'

Alice gurgled and clutched her toy rabbit even tighter. She was indeed a very good-natured child, and as Maxie had assured Olly, very pretty, with huge, saucer-wide, liquid dark eyes and a fluted pout of a mouth.

'Probably learned it didn't do her any good at the orphanage,' Olly observed, giving both Alice and the nanny a wide berth as he walked gingerly round them to the bar on the far wall. 'Just like prep school, I imagine. More you cry, more they whack you. You learn jolly quickly not to make a whimper, I can tell you.'

The nanny, a nice Australian girl, flinched, instinctively pulling Alice into her arms for a cuddle. Alice beamed up at her; she was a quick learner and had already worked out that her nanny was the main source of love and affection in this comparatively cold country.

'No, she's working out very well,' Maxie said. She was sitting at her correspondence desk, writing emails; the desk was inlaid Georgian rosewood, had been in the Stangroom family for generations, and Maxie had coveted it as soon as she'd laid eyes on it. Though it wasn't as practical as something more modern would have been – her laptop was a little cramped, too large for the shallow surface, its rubber base catching on the inlaid surface of the desk – the desk made her feel gracious and aristocratic, like the chatelaine of a manor house, writing letters, keeping the account books, filing bills into the elaborately carved pigeonholes, making sure that every aspect of her miniature empire was perfectly organized. Like the baronet's wife she would be when Olly's father died, and they became Sir Olly and Lady Stangroom, and Maxie's mother-in-law moved into the Dower House.

Maxie simply couldn't wait.

'G & T, darling?' Olly said, reaching for the Tanqueray bottle.

'Slimline for me,' she said automatically, closing her laptop and turning to face him. 'What is it, Olly? You sound excited.'

'Promotion!' he said, beaming at her with what was probably exactly the same happy smile he'd worn when he was six and unwrapping his Christmas presents to find the Thomas the Tank Engine train set he'd wanted for months. 'It's pretty much in the bag! Junior minister! The chief whip told me today.'

'Oh, *Olly!*' Maxie's eyes glittered. 'That *is* exciting!'

'All very hush-hush, of course,' he said anxiously, glancing down at the nanny, who was blowing raspberries into the fat curvy creases on Alice's neck, making her charge chortle with glee.

'Oh, don't worry,' Maxie said, reaching out her hand for the glass tumbler of gin and tonic. 'She's signed a cast-iron confidentiality agreement.'

'You think of everything, darling,' he said fondly, bending to kiss her forehead. 'So clever. And, you know . . .' he gestured towards Alice, who was trying to purse her lips to kiss her nanny, 'that's turned out to be a great idea of yours too. He as much as said so. *Very* positive PR.' He stood back, leaning against the mantelpiece, one arm along it, the other bringing the glass of gin and tonic to his mouth: the English gentleman in his own home, master of all he surveyed.

'Bedtime for baby!' the nanny said over-gaily; she had been keeping one eye on the clock ever since Maxie's reminder ten minutes ago, ready to whisk out her charge on the dot of the appointed time. Picking up Alice and swinging her with practised ease onto one hip, the nanny came over to Olly and Maxie.

'Kiss for Mummy and Daddy?' she asked rather nervously, but Maxie smiled approvingly and tilted her head, giving Alice one smooth cheek to kiss. Olly obediently followed suit, though he was clearly awkward.

'I say, Max,' he said when the door had closed behind Alice and her only caregiver, 'it still seems bloody odd to be – y'know – her "daddy". Bloody odd. Can't really get used to it, to tell you the truth.'

'It's early days,' Maxie reassured him, stretching out her long slim legs in front of her and crossing them at the ankles; her legs were one of her best features, and she always took pleasure in looking at them. 'You'll settle in. And really, Olly, you won't be spending much time with her anyway. I'm going to organize everything just the way your mother did. She's practically given me notes.'

'Seen but not heard, eh?' Olly said more cheerfully. 'Or rather, not even seen that much? Excellent. Mummy was quite right. Small children are such ghastly bores. Have 'em down for an hour before dinner, make sure they're on their best behaviour, then pop 'em off with the nanny so the grown-ups can have their fun. Right?'

'Absolutely, darling,' Maxie confirmed. 'Your mother and I see completely eye to eye on this.'

'If it ain't broke, don't fix it!' Olly said happily in an execrable American accent.

Then he remembered something important. His mouth formed into an O of concentration, and nerves caused him to set down his glass on the marble of the mantelpiece slightly louder than he'd meant to, the rattle attracting Maxie's attention away from the happy contemplation of the neatly stockinged curve of her ankles.

'The thing is,' he started, 'and it may not really be anything at all – it's just a word Tristram had with me today . . .'

The hesitance of his tone, the slight stammer as he pronounced the dreaded name, had Maxie immediately springing to attention, her back straightening as she focussed on her husband.

'What is it?' she said sharply. 'Spit it out, Olly! What's happened?'

'Well,' Olly said, his blue eyes clouded with confusion, 'Tristram mentioned to me today that he'd like you to pop in and have a word with him in his office. At your own convenience, he said, which means—'

'Pronto,' Maxie finished, cutting in.

'Exactly.' Olly looked baffled. 'Can't think why he wants to have a talk with my wife. It's all very unprecedented. Bit of a mystery, really.'

Maxie's forehead did its best to crease, and failed. Too much Botox. Instead, little wrinkles appeared up each side of her nose; when most of your major face muscles couldn't move, the others overcompensated frantically. Sir Tristram Cavendish was the chief whip of the party, a ruthless powerbroker with a reputation for utter efficiency and terrifying intimidation skills. Effortlessly charming, cold as ice, the disapproving raise of Tristram Cavendish's left eyebrow was enough to snap wayward backbenchers into the party line once more. It was a very bad idea to defy him; Sir Tristram knew where all the bodies were buried. At this thought Maxie shivered. That expression, never a favourite of hers, had become positively taboo since Deeley had come back to London.

'I'll ring him first thing in the morning,' she said briskly, standing up; decades of practice had taught Maxie to cloak her nerves in a sheath of steely resolve. 'It's time for dinner. Roast chicken and potatoes, your mother's recipe. I taught Prabhita to make it today.'

Olly gazed at her admiringly. 'I say, Maxie, you are amazing,' he blurted out. 'I don't know what I'd do without you.'

Maxie stroked his cheek affectionately as she passed him, leading the way to the dining room.

'Not a thing, darling,' she said cheerfully. 'You wouldn't do a bloody thing.'

Maxie had been to the Houses of Parliament many times before, of course. Loyally sitting in the public gallery, watching Olly make speeches, or – more often – shout abuse at the opposition. Dressed up to the nines for the State Openings of Parliament, in a variety of elegant hats and suits. And equally smartly dressed – if rarely in a hat – for the endless round of dinners, cocktail parties and drinks on the Commons terrace, with its glorious view of the Thames below.

But she had never really been nervous visiting what MPs familiarly called 'the House' before. Her three years studying at Oxford had been such an arduous apprenticeship that everything afterwards had seemed, as Aunt Sandra used to say, as easy as winking. Maxie had officially been doing an undergraduate degree in PPE – politics, philosophy and economics – but her real subject for study was the aristocracy that she longed to join. The rich, privileged boys and girls, the ones called Olly, Alastair and Toby, or Kate, Serena and Samantha. The ones with country houses, private incomes, pink cheeks, blonde hair, butter-soft skin and the air of ineffable superiority that comes with the security of knowing that you rule the world. Some of them were quite bright, but most of them were not; and yet they were still at Oxford, the university Maxie had struggled so hard to win a place at – mostly because their families had been attending the colleges there since the dawn of time, and admissions tutors loved the old family connections.

Maxie had watched them, learned from them; she shopped where they did, talked like they did, and been clever enough not to try to mix with them socially until she had assimilated their ways. Then she had joined the Oxford Union, the famous debating society, and done well enough to be considered possible future MP material. Maxie had always been able to talk people into things. But she had preferred to capitalize on Olly Stangroom's open-mouthed admiration of her looks, brains, and naturally dominating personality, and decided to mould him, instead, into her ideal MP husband, with his mother's total approval. Lady Stangroom had been happy to overlook Maxie's common-as-dirt origins – even help her avoid social faux pas – in return for Maxie's skill in pushing, tugging and bullying Olly into becoming a suitable Member of Parliament, electable to the family seat which his father had held for thirty years.

By now, after all she had been through, all she had done to get where she was, Maxie should have felt able to deal with any situation. So she was surprised that, after her long walk down oak-panelled, oil-painting-hung corridors, as Sir Tristram Cavendish's secretary rose, smiling, to take her coat and assure her that he wouldn't keep her waiting long, her stomach was fluttering with nerves. The chief whip was one of the most powerful members of the parliamentary party, able to make and break careers, put forward his protégés for advancement, pull all kinds of invisible strings to make his puppets dance as he wanted.

Tristram Cavendish had worked his way up the ranks, one of many assistant whips, effortlessly outshining all his rivals. He'd become deputy whip very speedily, and then unseated the chief whip in a palace coup that still, years later, had people retelling the details of his utterly unscrupulous manoeuvrings in hushed, awed voices. He spoke for the prime minister, whose enforcer he was. If you voted against the party, it was Tristram you had to answer to: a terrifying prospect.

But Olly was the last MP who'd ever dream of voting against the party; he was loyal through and through, partly because of Sloane tribal dedication, partly because he was too stupid to contemplate an alternative.

That might be the problem, Maxie thought, turning over in her mind various theories as to why the chief whip wanted to talk to a prospective junior minister's wife. *Is he worried that Olly's just too thick for the job? And if so, how on earth do I reassure him?*

'Maxie! My dear! How very nice to see you!'

Lost in speculation, she hadn't even noticed the door of Tristram Cavendish's office open. Maxie was pleased with herself; she didn't jump to her feet, as one tended to on hearing his authoritative, plummy tones. Instead she stood up elegantly, smoothing down her tailored skirt, smiling at the man facing her. Tall and imposing, the chief whip had the air of a 1950s film star, an actor cast to play a politician; he radiated professional authority.

'It's a pleasure to see you too, Tristram,' Maxie said in a voice just as clipped and upper class as his.

'Daphne, I'm going to have a nice little chat with Mrs Stangroom,' Sir Tristram said, standing back and gesturing expansively at Maxie to enter his office. He glanced at the grandfather clock on the wall. 'Goodness, is that the time? Five thirty already? Just finish up for the day and run on home – don't bother to wait for me.'

'Absolutely, Sir Tristram,' the secretary said, as Tristram closed the door leading to the outer office.

'Right, let's have a drink,' he said cheerfully. 'The sun is most definitely over the yardarm! What's your tipple, my dear?'

'G & T if you have one, thanks.' Maxie settled herself in the visitor's chair behind the wide expanse of leather-topped, mahogany keyhole desk, a huge Victorian monster. The dark green leather was studded with brass, the desk boasted rows and rows of drawers with shining brass handles; its sheer scale dwarfed the modern additions of a very up-to-date computer, and Sir Tristram's mobile phone, personal organizer and various purring gadgets.

'You do yourself nicely here,' she said, her tone light, looking around at the large, beautifully proportioned room, with its vaulted stone ceilings and equally lavishly carved window embrasures. 'Even a river view. Rather beautiful.'

The last rays of the setting sun were streaking the grey waters of the Thames and turning Westminster Abbey, on the other side of the river, into a golden glowing mass. It was obligatory to act as if one were bored with the sight, so jaded one barely noticed it any more, so Maxie only let her eyes linger on it for a few brief moments before turning away to accept, with a smile, the brimming glass that Tristram Cavendish was handing her.

'Whisky for me,' he said, walking back to the bar, another huge, solid piece of elaborately carved wood, with two curving doors that opened to reveal an impressive display of bottles. It was a tribute to the sheer scale of the chief whip's office that it could accommodate furniture on an equally large scale; even the modern leather desk chair into which Tristram sank, contemplating his glass of 23-year-old Macallan with a satisfied smile of anticipation, was two feet wide, with padded arms big enough for a giant.

'Cheers!' he said, raising his tumbler to Maxie, who smiled again and raised her own in return.

But she was observing him very closely as he sipped. Tristram Cavendish was as imposing as his mahogany furniture, a big, well-built man with smooth good looks, the silver at his temples adding to his air of distinction and authority. His suit was impeccably cut; like Olly's, it smoothed over a frame that had put on some weight since his sporty university days, but he was tall enough to carry the extra pounds, and his regular tennis and squash sessions ensured that there was a solid muscle layer keeping him reasonably trim. He was, famously, something of a dandy, impeccably groomed from his sleek hair to his buffed and trimmed fingernails. His silk tie echoed the colour of his enamelled cufflinks, which were just visible under the cuffs of his jacket.

'You look most attractive, Maxie,' he said, setting down his glass on an embossed gold coaster. 'The perfect MP's wife.'

Maxie relaxed a little, enough to sip from her own glass. She glanced down at her slim-fitting navy twill suit, a silk scarf tucked in casually at the neck; a traditional outfit, but styled sleekly enough to look modern, if not cutting edge. Which was perfect. An MP, or their spouse, should definitely not look too trendy.

She smiled ironically at Sir Tristram. 'It's Armani,' she said. 'But for the photo calls and party conference, it'll be M & S. Or Bilberry, of course. We're doing a diffusion line that isn't that expensive.'

The chief whip's lightly sarcastic smile echoed her own; it was very important now, post-expenses scandals, for parliamentarians and their spouses to look as if they budgeted, had the common touch. Wearing a dress from Marks and Spencer, or supporting a British designer, was mandatory.

'Clever girl,' he said approvingly. 'A diffusion line – that's cheaper, isn't it? The populist touch. Very good.'

He drank some more Macallan.

'But you must be wondering why I asked you to pop in,' he continued, as smooth as his drink of choice.

'I was rather.'

Maxie set down her own glass, swivelled the chair a little and crossed her legs, looking as unruffled as ever, though her heart was pounding.

I so want Olly to get this promotion! Junior minister – it's the start of everything we've worked for. If bloody Deeley hasn't ruined it by blabbing to that stupid magazine . . .

'Your sister,' Sir Tristram said meditatively, swirling the whisky slowly in the heavy glass tumbler. 'Terribly pretty girl. I must say, Maxie, your family breeds pretty fillies, eh? None of you exactly hit with the ugly stick.'

Maxie smiled politely, though she couldn't help but be aware that this compliment was mainly meant for Deeley and Devon. Unless you caught both her younger sisters post-chemical peel, say, there was no way that Maxie could be considered the most attractive McKenna sister. She was good-looking, and, thanks to Botox slowing down the aging process, she didn't think she looked all of her thirty-five years. Thank God she photographed well, which helped tremendously with all the press attention for both her job and Olly's. But she could never compete with Deeley's LA glamour or Devon's sexpot appeal.

I made my peace with that a long time ago, she reflected. *I may not be as gorgeous as my sisters, but I'm a damn sight more successful.*

'But she's a bit of a loose cannon, what?' Sir Tristram was continuing, his eyebrows raised. 'I mean the American one, of course, not the luscious TV cook girl with the amazing cantilevered bosoms who always causes such a stir when she comes here for parties. Quite a bombshell. But sensible, eh? Sticks to talking about how to make cakes. That's the ticket. The other one, though, the one from the US . . .' He pulled a face. 'The trouble with Americans,' he said, 'is that they've got this rather awkward idea that no publicity is bad publicity. Which is definitely not the way we do things over here. I understand you and Olly have had a stiff word or two with her about this debacle?'

'Absolutely,' Maxie said quickly, cursing Deeley silently with every single foul swear word that she'd learned in her youth.

'Because a lot of the red tops have picked this up,' Sir Tristram sighed, using the trade expression for the tabloid newspapers, with their bright red strips across the top of the front cover. 'It's just the kind of petty salacious gossip the working classes love. Rags to riches, poor beautiful girls make good . . .' he looked contemptuous, '*not* the kind of thing we want to be associated with. Time to put a lid on your sister, Maxie. I certainly hope you didn't engineer this in the hopes of getting some publicity for your handbags, did you? I can't tell you how much the party would frown on something like that.'

'Oh God, no!' Maxie blurted out, all her carefully cultivated poise and composure deserting her at this terrifying suggestion. If she were considered a vulgar publicity seeker, it would torpedo any career chances Olly might ever have as an MP. 'I'd *never* do anything like that! Sir Tristram, you must believe me! Devon and I shot round to Deeley's as soon as that awful piece came out in the magazine, and we read her the riot act! She knows better than to do anything like that again, I do assure you.'

She bit her lip so hard it hurt as she looked anxiously across the wide expanse of desk for the chief whip's response. He had set down his glass and was steepling his fingers together, propping his chin on his manicured nails, watching her intently, his eyes cool and calculating.

If Deeley's ruined everything – everything I've planned and schemed and pushed for – Olly actually becoming a junior minister, the first step on the ladder – I swear I'll strangle her with my bare hands! Maxie thought grimly, her teeth sinking deep into the tender flesh of her lower lip.

Her ambitions for her husband were by no means unrealistic. Although Olly was hardly blessed in the brains department, he had a truly great asset for a politician: he was hugely charming. His smile could light up a room; you couldn't help smiling back at him, even though you might disagree with every word he was saying. On TV, he was very appealing; and because he was too stupid to realize when the party line he was spouting didn't make sense, his absolute conviction was very compelling.

Men just as stupid as Olly Stangroom had gone very far in politics. It was Maxie's hope that Olly would follow in their footsteps. She already had her own highly successful business; to have a husband high up in government would make them the ultimate power couple.

And the chief whip, the man whom Olly and Maxie needed to impress above all others, the one who advised the prime minister on all his most important staff decisions, nodded slowly as he took in Maxie's reaction.

'Olly told you about the promotion we've been discussing, I imagine?' Sir Tristram said, picking up his glass once again.

'Of course,' Maxie said, her entire body relaxing in a wash of relief; if the chief whip was moving on to this subject, he had accepted her assurance that not only was she innocent of scheming with Deeley to get publicity, she would make sure in future that her sister kept her pretty mouth very firmly shut about anything to do with their deprived childhood. 'He tells me everything. But,' she added pointedly, to make it clear that Olly knew how to be discreet, '*only* me.'

'Exactly right,' the chief whip said, nodding at her. 'Shows his good judgement. It's easy to see that you're the brains of the operation, Maxie, my dear.'

Maxie considered, briefly, how to respond to this. There was no point in her insisting that Olly was actually very intelligent; that wouldn't convince the chief whip, and it would make her look stupid too.

'Olly,' she eventually said, 'is terribly good at toeing the party line. He's awfully loyal. And he never says the wrong thing.'

'Very true,' Sir Tristram agreed urbanely. 'He's been absolutely gaffe-proof so far. Doesn't put his feet in his mouth. Most impressive.'

He took another drink of the Macallan.

'But, from what I understand,' he continued, 'you're very much the firm hand on the reins.'

Maxie's eyebrows raised a little. She turned her head a fraction, so she was looking him full in the face, trying to decode his words. He was staring at her very intently, she realized.

'When Olly gets out of line . . .' he continued, 'when he's a naughty boy . . .' He cleared his throat. 'Well, you know when you need to crack the whip. Don't you?'

Maxie nodded, her brain churning. She had to play this perfectly. Because if she wasn't hearing what she thought she was hearing, things would go very, very wrong indeed . . .

'Olly does need a bit of discipline from time to time,' she said carefully, pushing back her pale blonde hair from her face. 'He definitely can be a naughty boy.'

This was the crucial moment, the one where she'd know for sure what message he was sending, where she'd be able to judge the tone of the rest of this entire encounter, and whether Olly's promotion was assured or not. She picked up her glass, drained it, and set it back on the coaster. Noticing that Sir Tristram wasn't saying a word, but was waiting, utterly focussed on her.

'But,' she said crisply, 'he isn't the only one, is he?'

His eyes were bright now, his lips slightly parted, moist with whisky. Silently, he shook his head.

And there it was. The balance of power had shifted across the desk. Sir Tristram Cavendish, chief whip, who ran his party with an iron hand on the reins, had named those reins and then given them to her. He picked up his glass with a hand that trembled for the first time and downed what was left of its contents.

Maxie took a deep breath. Then she pushed back her chair and walked over to the door. There was a ridiculously old-fashioned wrought-iron lock above the handle, more suited to a Tudor mansion than an office in the House of Commons; but the key turned. She heard the wards align, the metal bolt slide into the waiting cylinder, with a clearly audible click.

And she heard, too, a sigh from Sir Tristram. A deep panting sigh of anticipation.

'Stand up!' she snapped over her shoulder.

It was very gratifying to hear how quickly he scrambled to his feet. When she swivelled back around, her posture and bearing now commanding, her back straight as a ruler, he was standing in front of his desk, staring at her eagerly, his hands still trembling.

'You pathetic little worm,' she said coldly. 'I can't even bear to look at you. Turn around and face the desk.'

He couldn't obey her fast enough. Maxie contemplated his grey-suited back for a moment, feeling calm sweep over her. This was a scene she had played many times before. Olly Stangroom had not been her first university boyfriend, and as soon as she had entered the ranks of the Sloanes at Oxford, she had been aware that many of the young men in the elite social circle were very attracted to a quality she possessed, of which she herself hadn't been fully aware.

Maxie was a natural leader. She liked to run things, to be in control. To tell people what to do. And to many posh young men, brought up by Nanny and Matron, that characteristic was very compelling. Maxie's very first Oxford boyfriend had had a marked taste for corporal punishment, brought on by years of caning at public school;

he had begged Maxie to oblige him, and Maxie, much to her surprise, had discovered that she was very good at it indeed.

It was one of the main reasons Olly had married her. Much more sensible to keep your vices in the family, rather than pay a dominatrix who might be secretly filming you to sell on to a tabloid newspaper. Clearly Sir Tristram Cavendish had much the same philosophy; only here, the family was the party to which they all belonged.

'Take off your belt,' she snapped at him, crossing the room to draw the curtains. She heard the click of the buckle, the leather sliding through the loops of his trousers, and then his hesitant voice.

'Mistress?'

She turned to see him looking at her, the belt curled into a neat coil in his outstretched hand.

'Put it on the desk!' she said angrily. 'And don't you *dare* talk to me unless I specifically order you to!'

'Sorry, Mistress,' he said humbly, ducking his head, laying the belt on the desk.

'Did I tell you to speak?' she said, snatching the belt up, seeing his eyes go wide with fear and excitement.

'No,' he said, and then clapped his hand over his mouth as he realized he had disobeyed again. A strong, elegant hand, with a gold signet ring on his left little finger, next to his wedding ring. The hand of an adult man, who at this moment was enjoying himself tremendously by behaving in a not-remotely-adult fashion.

'Naughty boy!' Maxie hissed close to his ear, watching his eyes close momentarily with ecstasy as she said the magic words. 'You need to be punished for your disobedience! Take your jacket off! And then pull your trousers down!'

The jacket flew over the back of his chair, the trousers puddled at his feet. He was wearing silk boxers in a dashing shade of emerald. *Definitely a dandy*, Maxie noticed with amusement.

It had taken her some time to learn how to use a belt properly; backhand, for maximum control and placement. By now, she was something of an expert.

'You're going to get six strokes on your bum,' she said coldly.

'After each one, you will thank me. You will not make a sound otherwise. You will stand up straight. You may not brace yourself. You may not touch yourself. And you most definitely may not come. Understood?'

He nodded frantically, shaking with anticipation by now. The first stroke made such a satisfying swish through the air, followed immediately by the lash of leather on silk, that she couldn't help smiling to herself with satisfaction. He jumped a little as it landed, babbling: 'Thank you, Mistress!' just as she'd instructed him.

She walked round to observe him; he ducked his head immediately, knowing not to look her directly in the eyes. This was by no means the first time he'd put himself in the hands of a dominatrix. His cock, which had already been hard, was now swelling impatiently against the buttoned fly of the boxers; it wasn't particularly impressive as far as size went, Maxie noticed.

'Hands by your sides,' she snapped, walking back behind him and landing the second stroke before he expected it, making him jump again, gasping with shock before the ritual thanks.

She laid the next four on hard and fast, placing each at a slightly different angle, showing off her technique, careful to avoid the base of the spine and aim for the flesh of the buttocks, a swift, expert deluge of lashes that came so swiftly he could barely thank her for one before he was flinching from the next. When the six were done, she coiled up the belt, and said softly, 'Turn around, you revolting little boy.'

Sir Tristram was unrecognizable from the smooth, groomed master of the universe who had greeted her at the doorway of his office not half an hour before. He was panting, his face suffused with blood, his lips parted, his eyes bright and moist, his whole body trembling from head to toe. His trousers round his ankles, catching on his shoes, his shirt-tails hanging loose over his boxers, his cock straining at his fly, he was utterly humiliated. And loving every second of it.

'Kiss it,' Maxie said, holding out the belt, far enough away that he had to hop and strain to reach it with his lips.

She jerked it back.

'Now kiss my shoes.'

He nearly fell, scrambling to the ground, tripping over his trousers, to kneel first and then extend his head to press a fervent kiss of worship on the tips of each of her shoes.

'Disgusting,' she said icily. 'You revolt me. You're clumsy and repellent. Stand up and turn around again. I can tell your punishment has not been severe enough.'

A lock of his hair flapped loosely over his face as he clambered to his feet again and turned to face the desk. Every part of his carefully controlled appearance was falling to pieces; she was stripping him down to the animal beneath.

'Boxers down and hold on to the desk,' she snapped. 'And pull up your shirt. You're getting six on your bare bum for being such a horribly clumsy pathetic piece of shit.'

She could see her previous work as he dragged his boxers down, hooking them over his erection. Six neatly placed stripes. She landed the first lash right over one of them, for maximum pain, and watched his knuckles, clasping the edge of the desk, go white, heard his: 'Thank you, Mistress!' moan out from between gritted teeth. He'd be sore for days. Every time he rubbed his buttocks, he'd think of her. Hopefully, he would want her to do this again, tan his bottom till it hurt. And he'd know that advancement for her husband would ensure that Maxie would return to his office, around the time his secretary was due to leave, and humiliate him thoroughly over his own desk. It was exactly what so many powerful men truly loved; a woman who would take the power away from them every so often. Under strictly controlled circumstances, of course. A window in time where they could hand the reins of power to someone else and revel, deliciously, in the suffering they spent most of their time inflicting on others.

Two. Three. Four. A fast sequence that had the chief whip shuddering, groaning, his fingers drumming on the leather of his desk, his legs trembling with the effort of keeping himself still, bent over his own desk, grabbing the sides, his hips jerking back and forth.

'Two more,' Maxie said slowly. 'Two more strokes. Beg me for them.'

'Please!' he moaned instantly. 'Please, Mistress, I beg you! Please may I have them! I've done everything you said!'

Maxie was holding the tip of the belt; she let it go, aiming for a nasty cut between the buttocks that lifted him as it landed, drawing a half-scream from him.

'I *think*,' she said, drawing it out for maximum effect, 'I *think* you might have learned your lesson by now. What do you say?'

'I have! I have!' Sir Tristram's head was turned to the side, one cheek pressed flat against the leather, his hair completely disarranged, his mouth open. Maxie held the belt to it once more and he kissed it with utter passion, his eyelashes fluttering.

'You want to come, don't you?' she said into his ear. 'Filthy, horrible little boy. You want to come now?'

'Yes! Please!'

He licked his lips, not daring to lift his head, his voice a thread of pleading.

'On the last stroke,' she said, and strode back into position.

She made him wait for it, as long as she could, until his hips were already jerking, his buttocks rising to receive the last lash. It was the hardest one yet, and for a moment she worried she'd drawn blood; but she was experienced enough by now to avoid that danger. The crack of the belt sent him stumbling against the desk, falling against it now he didn't need to hold himself up any longer, the convulsive movements of his hips, the gasping cries he was making, a clear indication of how powerful an orgasm he was having. He was spread-eagled over his own desk, his entire body throbbing with release.

Maxie dropped the belt to the carpet, a smile curving her lips. It was always hard to judge how far you could push them, how much they wanted; you had to be very alert, to read their signs, their body language, with great sensitivity.

This encounter had been an audition, she was all too aware. A payment for Olly's promotion, but an audition for his future success. And as she watched Sir Tristram Cavendish's half-naked body still spasming over his huge Victorian desk, she was pretty sure she'd passed with flying colours.

She just hoped he hadn't made a mess on the leather. That would be very hard to clean off.

'I'll be waiting outside,' she announced, retrieving her sleek Bilberry bag from beside the visitor's chair, careful not to look at him as she did so. She unlocked the office door, closed it behind her and seated herself in one of the capacious leather armchairs in the waiting area beside his secretary's desk, her heart pounding. Had she done well enough? Had it been what he wanted? With Olly, they had all sorts of scenarios worked out; she knew exactly how far to push him, which words would trigger him, how to send him over the edge and make him so grateful to her that he would do anything she wanted afterwards.

But with Sir Tristram, she had had to play it completely by ear. He had clearly sensed what she was capable of with that radar that allows people with certain, specific sexual tastes to identify each other: the misfits of society, the ones who aren't part of the happy, vanilla mainstream, have a way of signalling to each other, like calling to like in a high frequency only they can hear. He had doubtless seen the masochist in Olly just as clearly, and used code words that Maxie would recognize, while keeping Sir Tristram's secret safe in the possibility that she wasn't what he hoped she was.

Still, she'd had no time to prepare. It had all been improvised. Had it been too basic, too obvious a scenario? Had she gone too far – or not far enough?

The brass handle on his office door turned; the door swung open. It took all she had not to jump to her feet, anxiously awaiting Sir Tristram's verdict. She tilted her head and glanced up at him coolly, but one look at him had her heart singing with triumph. He had performed a small miracle, reconstructed his appearance as if nothing untoward had just happened. His suit was pristine, his hair smooth, his smile as urbane as ever. But as he walked toward her, his smile was utterly and completely satisfied.

A cat that had most definitely eaten the cream. And his voice was a positive purr of content.

'My very dear Maxie,' he said, reaching out to take both her hands, pulling her to her feet and planting a kiss on each of her hands in turn. 'What a great pleasure it is to have you visit me. We must do this again soon.'

'Oh, absolutely,' Maxie said, her voice light and friendly, perfectly pitched.

'I'll have my girl ring yours,' Sir Tristram said, just as if his 'girl' weren't a fifty-something woman in a twinset and pearls.

Maxie reached for her coat, hanging on the wrought-iron stand, but he was ahead of her, easing it off and holding it open so she could slip her arms in.

'It might be useful if you were to ring me beforehand, too,' she said very casually. 'We could discuss . . . parameters.'

What you like, she meant. *What you want. If you want me to bring anything. Paddles, whips, other things. Dress in a certain way. Say words that push your particular buttons.*

That kind of thing was always better discussed before the actual encounter, and as she settled her handbag over her shoulder and looked up at him, she could tell he knew it too.

'What a very good idea,' he said, smiling as if she were a civil servant who had come up with a plan to slash unemployment benefits without losing any political capital. 'Olly's a very lucky man. Oh,' he added, striding with a gentleman's good manners to hold the door to the outer office open for her, 'do tell him from me that you won't have to keep his promotion to yourselves much longer. The official announcement will be tomorrow afternoon.'

'That's wonderful news,' Maxie said, smiling at him. A couple of other MPs passed down the corridor, and nodded courteously at Maxie and Sir Tristram as they passed.

'Much deserved,' replied Sir Tristram, his smile in return full of meaning.

Maxie returned the MPs' nods with easy politeness. No one could possibly have told that anything remotely out of the ordinary had passed between her and the chief whip as she walked away down the corridor, her step as steady and her expression as calm as ever.

But her heart was racing like an express train. And the chief whip wasn't the only one to look like a cat that had just had an entire saucer of cream. Maxie's smile was so self-satisfied that she, rather than Sir Tristram, might have been the one who'd just reached climax in his office.

Hmm, she thought, catching sight of herself in an ornate mirror at the far end of the corridor, *that gives me an idea* . . .

She knew her way around the House of Commons by now as well as any MP. In a few minutes, she was pushing open the heavy door of the closest ladies' toilet, her heart beating, if possible, even faster than before. Maxie was very lucky in more ways than one: not only was she able to fully satisfy the whims of her husband and now the chief whip of his party, but their sexual tastes happened, very pleasurably, to coincide with her own. It had been a considerable shock to her, with that first Oxford boyfriend, to realize that with every stroke of the Mason Pearson hairbrush to his bare buttocks (he had apparently been spanked with that implement in the nursery, and never forgotten it) Maxie herself was experiencing an increase in stimulation on her own account. Afterwards, shaking with excitement, she had left him sprawled over the back of the sofa, moaning his gratitude, and retreated to the bathroom of his flat to take care of herself.

It had been the pattern ever since.

The toilet was mercifully empty: the House wasn't sitting late that day, and there were much closer lavatory facilities to most MPs' offices – or the bars, where they would usually be found at this time of the evening. The doors of the four stalls were all open. Maxie chose the last one, and made sure it was locked behind her, the metal bolt sliding across the door, secured into its slot, before, taking a deep breath, she reached down to pull up her skirt.

Maxie had always been intensely private. From childhood, she had schemed in total secrecy, never letting even her sisters into her most closely guarded plans. It was entirely typical of her that this most intensely personal act of all should be one that she only performed when alone, behind a locked door. Beating willing male victims, bringing them to orgasm while remaining in total control herself, was the perfect fit for her personality; she would rather have died than let them see how intensely aroused she became by watching their surrender to her.

No one would ever see Maxie herself let down her guard.

Her skirt was around her waist now, her fingers scrabbling at her tights and La Perla smooth microfibre knickers now, pulling them down, giving her enough room to slide her right hand between her legs as her left covered her mouth, keeping her silent. She fell back against the wall, bracing herself, wet already with excitement, her clever fingers reaching easily up inside her, coming out slick with moisture, rubbing against herself exactly where she needed it. Maxie had always been her own best lover, infinitely better than any man. No one but herself had ever brought her to orgasm, and no one would have the chance to try; Maxie wouldn't give them the opportunity. This – isolated, alone, dependent on nobody else for her own pleasure – was utterly perfect.

She was already coming, her bare bottom beating a rhythm against the cold plaster of the wall as she rode her fingers, moaning into the hand covering her mouth, her eyes closed, conjuring in the darkness the image of Sir Tristram over his own desk, begging her for more strokes of his own belt. She heard his voice in her head, his whimpers of pain and pleasure, as she reached her first orgasm, and the second followed almost immediately.

She felt completely debauched. Her tights and knickers were binding her knees close together. The hem of her skirt tickled her wrist. The smooth French twist of her hair, rubbing against the wall, was coming loose, falling down her neck, as she bit into her left hand, allowing herself, for these few minutes, to utterly let go the usual iron self-discipline she exerted over her behaviour and appearance.

Poor pathetic men, she thought happily. *Poor pathetic men who just shoot their load and come once. God, I'd hate to be a man . . .*

Because she was flicking the nails of her index and middle fingers over her swollen nub now, tickling and teasing herself, giving herself a few moments to recover, to build herself up again till she was gasping, bucking her hips, the throbbing between her legs growing more and more insistent. Until she was ready to come again, even harder this time, a deep guttural sigh of relief flooding out through the fingers over her mouth, her bottom slapping against the wall.

God, this is so good . . . so good . . .

Sir Tristram's voice was still in her head, his pleading cries. His trousers and boxers puddled around his ankles, his buttocks striped with his belt, his absolute passivity as he lay across his own desk, offering himself up to her whims. It was the biggest turn-on in the world for her, the most powerful man she had ever had under her command, and the orgasms she was giving herself now were in direct proportion to the dominance she had just exerted, the best that she had ever had. She came again and again, her eyes rolling back in her skull, her head lolling back against the wall, waves of sensation pounding through her as strongly as if she were strapped to a washing machine on spin cycle.

She had lost all control of herself. The fingers in her mouth were damp from being pressed against her tongue, the fingers between her legs were slick with her own moisture. She heard Sir Tristram calling her 'Mistress', saw him kissing her feet, felt the jerk of the leather belt in her hand as she whipped his bottom, and came again, as helpless as he had been, delighting in her ability to satisfy herself when weaker people needed to make themselves vulnerable to others to reach the same mad rush of pleasure.

How long it lasted, how many orgasms she gave herself, she didn't know. Her entire body was limp by the end, her legs barely able to support her. She slumped onto the toilet seat, wincing a little in soreness; she had ground herself down on her fingers so hard, so often, that she had bruised herself a little. She was panting, her mouth soft, her eyes glazed, as she reached out for the toilet paper and patted herself dry.

Gradually, Maxie managed to get to her feet, to pull up her

tights and knickers, wincing again as the soft fabric rubbed against the sensitive skin. She pulled down her skirt, everything happening in slow motion. It was the only time she allowed herself to relax the efficient, brisk movements with which she bustled from home to office. Almost every minute of her day was scheduled for maximum productivity; this kind of surrender to her body's urgent need for sexual release wasn't a regular occurrence.

She knew that men would often 'knock one out', as Olly put it, first thing in the morning, or maybe last thing at night, idly watching some porn on the internet, as if it were no more important to them than a bowel movement, a quick tug and then an even quicker rush of come. 'Cleaning the pipes', to use another expression of her husband's.

Maxie didn't know what it was like for other women; she had never had friends or confidantes. But she had always been a hoarder, squirrelling away her treats, saving them for the perfect time to enjoy them, and highly disinclined to share. She liked to wait until she couldn't bear it any more, until the sexual pressure was simply too great, and then to spend all her capital in a private orgy of release, like a glutton, pushing herself to come again and again until her body finally begged her to stop.

The soreness would last a couple of days, a delicious reminder of the good twenty minutes she had spent giving herself up completely to the needs of her body. *It was due some fun*, she thought, smiling as she unlocked the door of the stall and, always cautious, peered out to ensure that no one else was in the bathroom, even though she was sure she'd have heard the heavy door swing open if another woman had come in. *I starve it and make it slave away on the cross-trainer to fit into a size 8, I run round all day like a Duracell bunny, I zip and button it into tight uncomfortable clothes to look appropriate for work and the media . . . It definitely needed some fun, poor thing!*

Her hair was a mess, her make-up was smeared. But the lighting in the bathroom was good, and, being Maxie and always prepared, she had plenty of cosmetics in her handbag to repair the damage. She didn't, however, redo her foundation or layer any powder over her face, because the natural glow on her skin was the kind that you can't buy in a bottle. Heightened, radiant colour on her cheeks, a luminosity to her entire face that one usually only saw on a carefully photographed and photoshopped model in the most expensive glossy magazines.

The French twist was perfect again, her navy blue mascara equally so, as Maxie stepped out into the corridor. Her silk scarf was rearranged and tucked back into the neckline of her jacket, her skirt smooth once more. But the open stares of appreciation from everyone she passed weren't for the precision of her grooming. For the first time, MPs, researchers, secretaries, turned to look at Mrs Stangroom with a sudden realization that, as one of the deputy speakers muttered to the clerk of the House, she was a 'damn fine filly'.

And Maxie relished it. Normally, she left the sex appeal to her sisters: she prided herself on having enough intelligence and drive not to have to parade herself with her bosoms propped up on a balcony dress, like Devon, or her legs bare practically to the crotch, like Deeley. But every so often, after one of the most enjoyable sexual encounters of her life, yes, it was very nice indeed to walk through the long vaulted Commons Corridor with its soaring, white-painted walls, past the awful oil paintings of seventeenth-century political scenes – William and Mary lumpenly receiving the crown in ermine and blue velvet and horsehair wigs – and to see heads of some of the most important political players turning in her wake. To make an entrance into the Central Lobby, its ribbed and vaulted walls heavy with Venetian mosaic and endless marble statues, and call attention to herself simply by crossing the elaborately tiled floor, her heels clicking a smug rhythm, her body radiating sexual satisfaction, her skin glowing.

This is a perfect moment, she thought, smiling at everyone she passed, not slowing her step at all, wanting to be in her own little bubble of triumph, not dilute her enjoyment by pausing to talk to anyone. *Right now, this is perfect. Olly has his promotion, and more to come after that. This is the first step on a long ladder to the top. And I'm not only going to be the wife of a rising star in the party. I get to discipline the chief whip in his own office on a regular basis . . . and have my own private celebration afterwards . . .*

The mere thought of repeating this evening's activities sent an extra rush of blood to her cheeks, a delicious flush of excitement. As she tripped lightly down the flight of steps leading to St Stephen's Entrance, a peer of the realm, coming up, stumbled on a stone tread and caught himself on the stair rail, nearly taking a nasty fall, so dazzled was he by the wife of the Honorable Olly Stangroom.

Plenty of people here want a good spanking, Maxie thought, as she stepped out onto St Margaret Street and raised her hand for a passing black taxi. She knew that was what they were sensing from her aura; not just the sex, but also her capacity for dominance. As she settled into the comfortably wide leather seat of the cab, she closed her eyes, spreading her arms wide along the back of the seat, relishing, totally and utterly, the sensations still coursing through her bloodstream.

This is a perfect moment, she thought again, as the cab swung round Parliament Square, and she glanced sideways at the House of Commons, scene of her recent triumph. *Nothing can stop me now.*

I feel like the queen of the world.

Her phone was ringing. It must be Olly, wanting to know how the meeting with Sir Tristram had gone. A smile curved her lips as she reached for the phone.

'Oh, *very well, darling,*' she would say airily. '*All things considered, I think I can safely say that it went very well indeed . . .*'

Deeley

*D*eeley was in such a daze on the slow local train journey from Riseholme that she only realized they'd reached Leeds when another passenger tapped her arm and told her it was the end of the line. Her head was spinning with the aftermath of the visit she'd just made to Bill's old house, and her meeting with the unpleasant, intimidating woman in the street outside. The train to London was late, the platform cold, and when the train finally limped into the station, there were no seats to be found anywhere in second class. Deeley walked up the entire train, unable to believe that there wasn't a seat; for what she'd paid for her day return that morning at King's Cross Station, she could have flown from LA to Vegas – *And not on a crappy airline either*, she thought ironically; *on JetBlue, with leather seats and live TV.*

But no, there was not a seat to be had. It was unbelievable; this wasn't even peak time, and yet overflow passengers were sitting on their cases on the cold, juddering floor, by the doors, in front of the stinky loos, their faces grey and resigned.

You're kidding, Deeley thought in disbelief as she reached the end of the second-class section. *What's happened to the trains whilst I was in the States?*

In first class, of course, there were plenty of seats. She sank happily into a front-facing one at its own little table, the seat opposite pleasantly unoccupied, a fresh copy of *The Times* lying in front of her.

I'll just pay the upgrade, she thought, chucking her Fendi bag onto the opposite seat, stretching out her long legs in relief at being cocooned in the kind of luxury she'd grown used to in her time with Nicky. *I was so virtuous, buying a standard ticket! And look what it got me – not even a bloody seat!*

But as soon as her head rested back on the beige leather seat, her eyes shutting, her thoughts immediately returned, like a dog chasing its own tail, to the events of the day. She kept seeing Bill's face, projected on the dark screen of her closed eyelids; not a handsome face at all, battered by life, a broken nose and a cabbage ear which he'd got, she seemed to remember, from a short-lived amateur boxing career. She'd loved Bill so much, had poured all her childish, little-girl enthusiasm out to him at having finally found what seemed like a settled home with a real father figure at last. Bill truly had felt like a real father; he'd been gruff sometimes, annoyed by the shrieking and giggling and catfights of three sisters, short-tempered and grumpy when he got home, tired, from a long day's stint at the factory where he worked, hungry for his dinner.

But that was what had really made him feel like a proper dad, like the dads of friends of hers: he was normal, genuine, honestly himself. Bill never pretended to be something he wasn't – unlike their mother, whose drug and drink addiction had turned her into a liar and a fantasist, spinning wild stories, making promises she couldn't fulfil, a perpetual inhabitant of cloud cuckoo land. Deeley had been the last of the sisters to let go, with great pain and suffering, her ideal of her mother as good, caring, and loving; still grieving for the dream of a mother who actually had a maternal bone in her body, she had fixated on Bill instead as a replacement parent figure. And his lack of airs and graces, the fact that he was a straightforward man who would never promise to do something he couldn't, had been hugely reassuring to a little girl who had been lied to by her mother ever since she could remember.

But this is why I'm so fucked up! Deeley thought miserably, wrapping her arms around her waist for comfort. *I still look back and can't manage to see Bill as anything but nice and kind and caring – the dad I always dreamed of having. When I know that really he was abusing Maxie, and going to start with Devon. When I know that all the time he was being nice to me – brushing my hair in the mornings when he had time, letting me sit on his lap when we watched game shows, buying me that pink bike from Argos for Christmas, the bike I wanted for so long with the tassels on its handlebars – he was actually grooming me. That's what they'd call it now. Softening me up so he could do what he wanted later.*

She remembered the huge fight Maxie and Bill had had the night before it happened, a hissing, yelling scrap in the front room, with the TV blaring so that Devon and Deeley, even with their ears pressed to the door, couldn't hear what was going on. Maxie had finally slammed out of the room, furious, and gone straight to bed, refusing to talk to either of her sisters; but the next day, Maxie had told her and Devon they were skiving off school. They'd hidden out in the park and then sneaked back into the house when Bill had left for work, so Maxie could sit them down, tell them what had been going on with Bill, that her fight with him had been about his intention to do the same to Devon.

And she explained that the only way to keep themselves safe was to carry out the plan she'd spent last night hatching.

The trouble is, even though I went along with everything Maxie said, even though I cried and cried when she said what he'd been doing to her, I still couldn't see Bill as an abuser. I couldn't be scared of him.

No wonder I have such problems with men.

And then, of course, quite inevitably, Matt's face swam into her mind, replacing Bill's. She was still struggling with the feelings she had for Matt, the very strong and powerful attraction she had sensed from the moment he'd caught her in the lobby of Franco's, stopping her from falling; from the moment she'd looked into his eyes, and realized that she really was falling – for him.

Which was ridiculous, as she hadn't even know his name then, hadn't exchanged a word with him. Didn't have the faintest idea that he was her sister's husband.

Or maybe it wasn't ridiculous at all. Maybe it was highly significant. Maybe it indicated, more clearly than anything else could conceivably have done, that she had, in the phrase she remembered Serita, her stylist in LA, using often, a 'broken picker' when it came to men. Someone with a broken picker made really bad romantic choices. They couldn't help it. They were programmed all wrong, stuck in a bad pattern, and they were doing well if they could even acknowledge the problem at all.

'You can't change what you don't acknowledge!' Serita had often trilled, talking about friends of hers who kept dating guys she described as losers, spongers and lowlifes.

Well, OK, Deeley thought sadly. *I have a broken picker. I'm acknowledging it. But how do I change that? How do I stop fixating on Matt, who's clearly the last person in the world I should be fancying?*

Because the truth was, she couldn't stop thinking about him. She'd been at Devon's nearly a month now, and barely seen Matt at all; he had doubtless been avoiding her as much as she was steering clear of him. She had hardly gone up to the main house at all – not that Devon had invited her. Deeley had behaved as if the basement flat were an entirely separate entity, not connected with Devon's house at all; she'd never once used the back stairs to go up to the ground floor, had tried to conduct her life as discretely from her middle sister's as she could possibly manage. She'd seen Matt, of course. Through the safety bars on her basement windows, she had a good view of the street. He tended to leave for training first thing in the morning, but she'd see him coming back afterwards, in his sweats, parking his silver Jag and swinging himself out, striding up the short flight of steps to the front door with the easy, loose-knit movements of a professional athlete. Or, if he were off to a game, he'd be back later, dressed up in a nice suit for the post-game interviews. Never really late, though, never staggering home in the small hours, full of drink, having been partying at Boujis or Mahiki, surrounded by fellow players and iden-tikit blondes. Matt was a homebody, that much was obvious.

But he never once glanced down at the windows of the base-ment flat to catch a glimpse of Deeley.

She loved to watch him. She knew it was wrong, but she loved it. She'd become an aficionado of rugby, catching every game on TV in which he played, even though she didn't understand the first thing about the rules. Thank God the TV in the living room of the flat got all the sports channels. She was practically addicted to the sight of Matt, splashed in mud all over his sturdy thighs and thickly muscled calves, pounding down the field, the ball clasped firmly to his wide chest, fending off attackers with swerves of his wide, powerful shoulders. Every time he was tackled, she winced, grab-bing the arms of her chair, on tenterhooks in case he came up limping, or with blood streaming from a fresh cut or, worse, didn't come up at all. Every time he scored a try, or won Man of the Match, her heart flooded with happiness and pride in him.

Which was totally stupid, because he wasn't hers in any way, and he never would be.

Her only consolation, strange as it sounded, was that Matt was a good man. He hadn't made any effort to see her, to act on the powerful attraction that had flashed between them in Franco's. She was just down the stairs from him; it would have been the easiest thing in the world for him to drop down for a visit, making some excuse to hang out with her, try to seduce her.

Not that he'd have to try very hard, she admitted to herself honestly. *He'd just have to touch me again and I'd go up in flames. I don't think I'd have a shred of willpower where he's concerned, not if we were close to each other, in the same room, with no one else around. Especially not if he put his hands on me.*

She sighed deeply, thinking of Matt. *At least my picker can't be completely broken, not beyond repair*, she reflected. *Because I'm fixated on a nice guy, not a bastard. One who doesn't want to cheat on his wife, especially not with her sister. One who positively goes out of his way to avoid his wife's sister, in case he's tempted to do something he shouldn't.*

And then, to her absolute shock, the memory of Bill's face

returned to her once more. But it didn't obliterate Matt's. Instead, it merged with it, and for the first time, Deeley realized that there was a strong resemblance between the sort-of-stepfather she had thought so perfect when she was young, and the man to whom she was so strongly attracted in the present. Matt was much more handsome; but Bill had been a boxer in his youth, and she had thought Matt was a boxer when she'd bumped into him. Both had naturally craggy features; both had broken noses that hadn't reset completely straight; both were tall, muscular, imposing men, who carried themselves with confidence.

Oh my God, she thought, panicky. *Matt reminds me of Bill . . . how fucked up is that?*

'Tickets, please,' droned a voice beside her. 'Miss? I haven't checked your ticket yet, have I?'

Deeley started in shock, eyes flying open, jerked out of her trance. She reached across the table for her bag, fumbling inside it, producing her wallet and the return portion of her standard-class ticket.

'I'd like to upgrade this,' she said, handing it to the uniformed ticket collector.

He took it, sniffed, and started to input a series of keystrokes into the big black machine that hung around his neck. It took at least a minute; he might have been calculating the square root of an incredibly complex number, or working his way through a series of complicated algebraic equations. Eventually, without looking up at her, he announced, 'That'll be one hundred and forty-two pounds, miss.'

Deeley burst out laughing. 'God, thanks so much!' she said, when she'd stopped giggling. 'I've been having such a weird day so far – I really needed a good laugh!' She took a breath. 'How much is it really, then?'

She trailed off, because the ticket collector had raised his head from the screen of his machine and was fixing her with a very beady eye.

'It's no joke, miss,' he said coldly. 'That is the correct first-class upgrade fare for the Leeds-London leg of this train trip.'

'But that's more than my entire ticket!' she said in horror. 'Though actually . . .' she glanced at the receipt stub, 'not by much. But still! I could probably have got a cab all the way back to London for a hundred and forty-two pounds!'

Across the aisle, a businessman, ostensibly reading his paper, nodded in agreement with her.

'And there aren't any seats in the rest of the carriages,' she continued, getting cross now. 'That's why I came into first class. I mean, I bought a ticket – I should be guaranteed a seat, shouldn't I?'

'The ticket entitles you to carriage alone, miss,' said the collector wearily. 'Not to the use of a seat.'

'That's total robbery!' Deeley said, even more crossly. 'You should be ashamed of yourselves!'

'We *have* passed Doncaster,' the ticket collector said. 'It is conceivable that a seat might have opened up since you boarded the train.'

The businessman shook his head vigorously, and clearly not because of anything he was reading in the newspaper.

'Oh, come on,' Deeley said, picking up this cue. 'I saw tons of people on the platform at the last station, and they weren't just meeting friends getting off the train!'

'As I said, miss, a seat is not guaranteed with purchase of a ticket,' the ticket collector said. 'You're going to have to pay the upgrade or move.'

Sighing heavily, Deeley reached across the table for her bag. She was lifting the flap to open it when she paused. It wasn't the quality of the embossed leather that stopped her; it was the satin of the lining, the thick, heavy, utterly luxurious feel of the material beneath her thumbs, material that didn't even show for most of the time, which reminded her how much money she had spent at Fendi for this handbag. Money that she didn't have any more; money that had never really been hers.

I should sell this on eBay, she thought in a flash of realization. *Or at least, I should get all my stuff together and work out what I can sell.*

I've got tons of handbags, clothes, coats, jackets, shoes, piled up all over my bedroom in Devon's house. Most of them I've hardly even worn. It's just capital sitting there, money I could use.

Because she had no income coming in. Nothing at all. The payment from *Yes!* magazine had long since been spent. Deeley had been so excited by the approach from the journalist and the journalist had in turn been very keen; after all, Deeley was photogenic, single and a new face on the London social scene. But most importantly, she was the sister of two very well-known London celebrities. *Yes!* had hoped for a whole bounty of articles: the McKenna sisters reunited after years of separation, posing in Devon's famous kitchen in designer dresses, smiling for the cameras.

But Maxie and Devon had closed that down indefinitely. *And by the time they soften up – because they'll want the publicity too, for their TV shows and handbag lines – the magazines won't care about paying me much of anything. Because by then, I'll just be some boring ex-girlfriend. I needed to strike while the iron's hot, fresh from my 'break-up' with Nicky. In six months' time, no one will care about me. I'll be yesterday's news.*

Deeley needed a roof over her head much more than she did the payment from a few articles. She'd kept her head down, as Maxie and Devon had told her, and not taken any more calls from journalists, hoping that if she did what her sisters said, they'd forgive her. Take her fully into their lives, as she'd thought would happen when she came back to London. Let her be a part of the family again, the McKenna sisters together against the world.

But it meant that all she had financially was the lump sum that had been her pay-off from Nicky, via Carmen, sitting in her bank account, making no interest whatsoever. She needed to work out what to do with that money.

And she certainly shouldn't throw away a hundred and forty-two pounds of it on an extortionate train ticket upgrade, just so she could sit in comfort for an hour or so.

'Forget it,' she said with decision, snapping shut the clasp of her bag. 'I'm not paying your rip-off prices. I'd rather stand.'

She swung her legs out from under the seat and stood up, collecting her jacket with a dramatic flourish. The ticket collector looked her up and down, taking in the full opulence of her appearance, shocked that a woman dressed so expensively was balking at spending what would seem to be a very small sum to her. The businessman folded his paper noisily, slapping it down on the table and clearing his throat in an attempt to catch her attention. If she'd caught his eye, flashed him even the smallest smile, he'd have offered to pay the upgrade for her.

But then he'd have some rights to me, Deeley knew. *He'd talk to me, try to pick me up, buy me a drink. And that'd be fair enough – he'd have paid for it, after all.*

No. I've had enough of letting men pay for me. I lived off Nicky for five years, and I'd have gone on doing that as long as he wanted me.

Well, that's over. I'm managing on my own from now on.

Without turning her head, she stalked out of the first-class carriage, head held high. Her glow of pride in her own ability to economize didn't last long, however. She was taken aback to realize there was nowhere to sit at all, not even in the buffet car; she'd been expecting some tables there she might be able to squeeze onto. And the train, as she'd thought, was even more packed after the influx of passengers at Doncaster. One family had even commandeered a handicapped toilet, wedging open the door and camping out on the floor with their kids.

Squashed into the corridor, swaying back and forth, packed into a standing game of Sardines with her fellow travellers – all resolutely refusing to meet each other's eyes, as if that would be a step too far in acknowledging the misery of their situations – Deeley was on her feet for the rest of the fifty-minute journey into King's Cross. Her suede Isabel Marant boots weren't, thank God, stiletto-heeled, but they were high enough to be hurting significantly by the time the train finally pulled into the terminal, after waiting for an unbearable several minutes just outside, as if the driver was amusing himself by adding a final extra twist of suffering to his passengers' already horrible journey.

There was a stampede to get off as the doors opened. Deeley was carried along in the melee, stumbling over people's suitcases and prams and sobbing children, but managed to hang back on the platform until the first urgent rush of travellers escaping from their incarceration had subsided. Then, walking slowly in her now painful heels, she made her way down the platform and into the main concourse of the station. Across the crowded floor, she spotted the sign for the Tube, but after her recent journey, she couldn't face having to board two more trains to take her back to Mayfair.

And besides, I've got nothing to rush back for, she thought sadly. *Just an empty basement flat. I don't mind waiting for the bus.*

Plus, it's cheaper.

The pavement outside King's Cross Station was just as busy. It was seven by now, a pleasantly warm late spring evening, but night was beginning to fall, and it seemed to Deeley that everyone but her knew where they were going. She was buffeted back and forth as she tried to get to the traffic lights, having worked out that the bus taking her to Marble Arch would be stopping on the far side of Euston Road. Buses, lorries and taxis poured past, honking and weaving, the tails of the bendy buses whipping perilously close to the pedestrians waiting at the crossing. Deeley stepped back a little as the second half of a 73, slowing down for a stop, swung so near her she could feel the wind of its wake. Directly behind it came a double-decker number 17, looming over its predecessor, and Deeley was just glancing to see if the lights were changing when she felt a tremendous impact in her back.

Something had crashed into her, right between her shoulder blades. She went flying forward as if shot out of a cannon, throwing her arms out in an attempt to balance, whacking into the people on each side of her, but not managing to catch onto anything that would slow her down. It all happened so fast she was completely powerless to help herself: she heard herself scream in terror, mouth wide open, as the huge red front of the 17 bus bore down inexorably on her. In another split second, she would be falling in front of it, into the road, under the huge wheels of the bus. No time for it to brake, no time for the driver to even see her – she was about to die, she knew she was about to die, this was it . . .

Her left heel caught on the edge of the pavement, or maybe a loose paving stone, she couldn't tell. The impact jerked her upper body forward even more precipitately. The bus was so close she could see the dents in its metal front, the scratches on its windshield. Her hands flew up in a last-ditch, frantic attempt to protect her face. But whatever she caught her heel on saved her life. Because it slowed her down just enough for a man standing next to her to grab her round her waist and haul her backwards, a mere inch away from her seemingly inevitable impact with the number 17 bus.

It thundered past, its exhaust trailing stinking smoke, as Deeley fell against her rescuer, her scream cut off by the stranglehold of his solid arms. She struggled frantically for breath, limp against him, as he dragged her a good foot back from the edge of the pavement.

'Jesus!' he said above her head. 'You got a death wish, love?'

Deeley scrabbled her feet back under her as he loosened his grip.

'You're not going to try that again, are you?' he said, still holding onto her.

'I was pushed!' she managed to get out. 'I didn't jump – someone pushed me . . .'

'Fucking hell – you all right?' said a woman on her other side. 'You took a right old tumble there!'

'Says she was pushed,' Deeley's rescuer said.

'Oh, I believe it,' the woman said grimly. 'There's all sorts nowadays. Were they after your bag, love?'

Deeley scrabbled up her shoulder, realizing with great relief that her bag was still there.

'No, I don't think so,' she said, sighing with relief.

'Random nutter, then,' the man said, letting her go now he was reassured that she hadn't just tried to throw herself under a bus. 'Care in the community – it's a fucking joke, isn't it? I blame Margaret Thatcher. She's the one opened up the loony bins.'

'Shouldn't stand so close to the road, love,' the woman advised Deeley. 'It's asking for trouble.' She gave a valedictory nod and joined the crowd flooding across the road, dragging a tartan canvas pull-shopper behind her.

'Thanks so much,' Deeley said gratefully, turning to look up at the man who'd saved her; he was a burly construction worker, a fluorescent tabard over his work clothes.

'Glad to help,' he said, as people pushed past them, treading on their toes, complaining that their little group was blocking access to the crossing. 'You OK? 'Cos I got to rush. You all right now?'

Deeley nodded in thanks. 'I'll just take a moment to catch my breath,' she said. 'I'm fine.'

It wasn't true, but she hadn't wanted him to hang around for her. She let him shoulder his way into the crossing and waited until the bright yellow-and-orange tabard had vanished, till the next light had come and gone, until she felt recovered enough to make it to the other side of Euston Road, safely surrounded, this time, by a mass of other bodies. She had no idea who had pushed her, but she knew it had happened; a blow that stunning and powerful could only have been deliberate.

There hadn't been any point in looking back to see if there was a face in the crowd she recognized. By the time she went hurtling forward towards the bus's wheels, her attacker would have already been slipping away, back to the station and the throng of people there, completely invisible.

Someone just tried to kill me. The words rang in her head as she waited for the 390 bus to Marble Arch, as she boarded it and climbed upstairs, for the whole of the long swaying ride down Euston Road, into Gower Street, and the whole length of Oxford Street, all the endless stops and starts. *Someone just tried to kill me.*

And I have no idea who or why.

By the time Deeley stepped off the 390, she had calmed down sufficiently to convince herself that the shove in her back at King's Cross had been, as the workman who'd rescued her had theorized, a random nutter. After all, she reminded herself, both the workman and the woman next to her had taken for granted that London's streets were so dangerous that someone mentally unstable could be roaming them, shoving random targets into busy roads. They hadn't shown any surprise, any disbelief at the idea.

It wasn't personal, Deeley told herself as she turned down Park Lane.

But she was walking faster than usual, her nervousness belying her attempts to reassure herself. She could hear the quick patter of her heels on the pavement, a frightened scamper towards the security of her basement flat, with the double lock on its door and the bars on its windows. She actually darted a look back over her shoulder, like some ridiculous victim in a Victorian melodrama, being chased by Jack the Ripper.

You're being totally paranoid! she told herself firmly, clutching tightly to her bag. *Why would anyone be out to get you? You're not remotely important!*

Her footsteps were clattering along now; she swung left into Green Street, only a block away from the elegant parade of houses in which Devon and Matt lived. Two minutes away from safety.

A cab passed her, the heavy, solid ticking of its engine oddly reassuring. It pulled up just across the crossing, in front of the house, and Deeley's spirits immediately lifted. *It's Devon, coming home! I'll tell her what just happened – I mean, I know we're not getting on that well, but she's bound to be nice to me when she hears I nearly got shoved into traffic . . .*

She bit her lip. *Better not tell her it happened outside King's Cross, though. If Maxie and Devon knew where I went today, they'd kill me. I'll say it was on Oxford Street – with all the crowds, she'll believe that, no prob—*

But as she approached the cab, eager to see her sister, to throw herself into Devon's arms for a much-needed hug of reassurance, the first thing that she saw emerging beneath the door as it was thrown open was a long silver pole with a black rubber tip. It wobbled, found the pavement, and steadied itself; then a man's ankle, in a trainer as large as a small boat, edged out after it. One huge hand came out and grasped the roof of the cab. By the time

Deeley had reached it, Matt was almost out of the taxi, the crutch wedged under his right armpit now, manoeuvring carefully to keep weight off his right foot, which was wrapped in a dark blue compression bandage.

'Oh no!' Deeley exclaimed, running up to him. 'What happened?' *Idiot!* she said to herself almost instantaneously. *Isn't it totally obvious?*

'You all right there, Matt?' the cabbie called. 'Nasty one, mate!'

'Yeah, thanks,' Matt said, grimacing as he adjusted his grip on the crutch. 'Just got to rest up now.'

'Well, don't leave it too long, eh!' the cabbie said. 'The Tigers'd be a fucking shambles without you!'

Matt tried to close the cab door, but wobbled dangerously. Deeley darted forward to do it for him.

'Thanks,' he said. 'God, I'm all crocked up.'

Under his tan, Matt's face was white with strain, his lips tight with tension.

'Ripped my Achilles a few years ago,' he said, starting to hobble towards the steps of the house. 'Just messed it up again in a friendly, sod it.'

'Oh, that's terrible!' Deeley said. She hovered, feeling useless for a moment, then bravely stepped over to his good side. 'Can I help you up the stairs?'

He glanced at her, and a flicker of genuine amusement flashed in his blue eyes.

'Thanks, but if I lean on you, we'll both go down,' he said, managing a grin. 'Skinny little thing like you, I'd snap you in two if I put any weight on you. Here.' He fished slowly and awkwardly in the pocket of his tracksuit bottoms, and eventually produced a bunch of keys. 'Why don't you unlock the door? The alarm code's 2003.' He pulled a self-deprecating face. 'Year we won the World Cup.'

Deeley took the keys from him and dashed up to open the door, tapping the numbers into the alarm panel to stop the beeping. Matt was halfway up the stairs, but she went back and put a hand under the elbow of his free arm, helping him balance.

'I do a lot of Pilates,' she said, piqued by his assumption that she was weak. 'I'm a lot stronger than I look, you know.'

'Yeah? Glad to hear it,' he said between gritted teeth, his crutch stumping doggedly up one step at a time.

'There's lots of weight-bearing exercise in Pilates!' Deeley persisted, sensing that Matt needed a distraction. 'We do stuff with loaded springs, pulleys, even something called a Magic Circle . . .'

That actually got a laugh from Matt. They were entering the hall now, and he leaned against the wall as Deeley shut the front door behind them.

'Magic Circle, eh?' he said. 'I'll have to see that one of these days.'

She turned to look at him. There was a gleam of sweat on his forehead, his light brown curls a little damp with the effort he'd made to haul himself up the stairs. His lips were gripped together, his jaw tight.

'You look terrible,' she said frankly. 'Do you have any painkillers?'

'Thanks!' Matt said wryly. 'Yeah, the doc gave me some already, but I'm probably due for another dose.' He reached for his tracksuit pocket once more, but wobbled precariously, his crutch slipping fractionally on the slippery black-and-white tiles of the hall floor.

'For God's sake!' Deeley said crossly. 'What are you doing? You should be lying down! And probably elevating that foot! Come on.' She nipped to his side, taking his right arm again. 'Into the living room,' she said. 'Let's get you onto the sofa, and then I'll get you some water to take your pills.'

'Yes, miss,' Matt said meekly, hobbling along by her side, as Deeley guided him into the living room and over to the huge leather sectional sofa. He sank down onto it with a big 'ooof!' of relief as Deeley bustled around, turning on the lights and drawing the dark purple brocade curtains. The large room was scattered artfully with a mixture of tall chrome uplighters and round silver lamps on polished cherrywood tables; when Deeley had finished, a warm glow suffused the room. She bent to switch on the fire, which was an elaborate mass of fake coals around which gas flames danced, a beautiful alternative to the open-fire ban in the centre of London. The orange-and-golden flames flickered deliciously in the grate, casting glints of light against the wrought-iron frame of the fireplace.

Matt was lifting his injured leg with both hands, settling it onto the sofa, and by the time Deeley had gone to the kitchen and returned with a glass of water, he had a packet of co-codamol out of his pocket and was popping two pills out of their blisters. He swallowed them dutifully, muttering, 'Thanks,' as Deeley took the empty glass from him.

'Wasn't anyone's fault,' he said gloomily, nodding to his foot, which he'd propped up on a big suede pillow. 'It just went out from under me. I was dodging a tackle. Sprinting full out, did a bit of a twist and the next thing I knew, I was flat on my face with my ankle blown out.' He smiled wryly. 'Funniest part is, the guy coming for me was diving. I went down and he flew right over me, believe it or not. I saw it on the replays. He came back after the game to see how I was. He grazed his nose when he landed.' Matt raised a huge hand to his face, indicating the tip of his own battered nose. 'Skin's all ripped off. He looked worse than me.'

'What did the doctor say?' Deeley asked.

'Put iodine on it and told him not to whinge,' Matt said. 'He'll have a nasty scab for a while.'

'No!' Deeley actually stamped her foot. 'You, idiot! What did the doctor say about your ankle?'

Matt's mischievous grin showed her that he had deliberately misunderstood her question. But it faded fast.

'Dunno yet,' he said, sighing as he eased himself back and unzipped his fleece jacket. 'But nothing good. It was pretty much a miracle that I could play after my Achilles went. I have to rest up for a while, then they'll see.' He was avoiding her eyes, a clear sign that he wasn't comfortable with the subject under discussion. 'Look, I could do with a drink. I know I shouldn't cane it with the pills, but one won't hurt, will it? D'you mind pouring me some whisky?' He nodded over to the large antique cherrywood bar against the wall. 'And grab something for yourself. Least I can do after you've looked after me, offer you a drink.'

Deeley hovered for a moment, unsure about the situation. Devon clearly wasn't here, because the alarm had been on. And Deeley's whole policy over the last few weeks had been a complete avoidance of this very situation: finding herself in a cosy tête-à-tête with Matt Bates, sharing a drink, alone together.

But Matt's all crocked up, she told herself. *And we've been talking to each other so naturally, like we've known each other for years.*

And I could really do with a bit of company – I'm still shaken up from nearly going under a bus.

And besides, it's just one drink.

She put down her bag, shrugged off her jacket, and went over to the bar. A decorative array of bottles were ranged along the top, and when she opened the double doors, gleaming ranks of glasses swung forward, lined on built-in shelves on the inside of each door. Beyond, silver shakers, strainers, jiggers, mixing glasses and bottle openers were arranged in perfect order. Deeley pulled out two tumblers, and poured a stiff two fingers of whisky into each one. She never usually drank whisky, but she had a feeling that it might be just what she needed after the terrifying experience she'd just had.

'Cheers,' he said gratefully, taking it from her as she sat down, careful to keep a decent distance between their bodies.

She leaned over to clink glasses with him, because he was holding his glass out to her expectantly; it brought her close to him, too close. Before, helping Matt up the stairs, into the living room, gripping his elbow, her fingers only able to clasp about halfway round, she'd felt the bulk and warmth of his body, felt, also, the slight dampness of his skin post-exercise, and had done her very best not to allow it to flood her senses.

Now, leaning in, she could see his dark navy t-shirt clinging to his chest, light brown hairs curling round the V of the cotton fabric. He'd pulled off his fleece jacket, and his arms were bare now, his biceps swelling against the tight short sleeves of his t-shirt, stretching the stitching of the seams. She could see the clear, firm outline of his pectoral muscles pushing out the fabric, even the small peak of a nipple crowning one. And she could smell the soap he'd used that morning, clean and fresh, and underneath it, his own light, musky sweat.

Deeley pulled back as if he'd just held a lighter to her knuckles, doing everything she could to wipe the scent of Matt from her mind.

'Someone tried to push me under a bus at King's Cross just now,' she blurted out, too disoriented to remember that she'd told herself to lie about where the incident had happened. She swallowed a slug of whisky, which burned going down like a glorious hot fire, rich and heady.

'What?' Matt twisted at the waist to look at her, and gasped in pain as the sudden movement sent a shaft of pain down his leg. 'Ow! Shit!' he muttered. 'You're joking! You nearly went under a *bus*?'

'I was waiting at the traffic light, and someone shoved me in the back,' Deeley said, surprised at how relieved she was to say it out loud, to have someone stare at her, horrified, at hearing about her recent brush with death. 'This guy pulled me back just in time.'

'Oh my God!' Matt propped a hand on the leather of the sofa to balance himself, swivelling over his bad leg to look at Deeley. 'Are you OK?'

'It wasn't very nice,' she agreed, feeling better by the moment. Having Matt react like this allowed her to be modest, in that very British way that she'd missed living in LA; there, if you didn't make a huge fuss yourself, no one bothered to notice what was going on with you.

'Jesus!' Matt shook his head in disbelief, a few tight short brown curls bouncing on his forehead. 'There're some really bad people out there. A girl like you should be extra careful, you know? A pretty young girl in London . . . Lots of loonies out there. Probably jealous.'

Deeley couldn't help smiling at this. Matt ducked his head awkwardly, embarrassed at having let a compliment slip out, and took a deep pull at his glass of whisky, looking away from Deeley, at the flames dancing in the big fireplace.

The silence that fell was instantly dangerous. *I'll just finish this drink and go*, Deeley thought, taking another big sip of whisky, and promptly coughing as it went down the wrong way.

Matt slanted a smile sideways at her. 'Strong, eh?' he said. 'Just what you need after something like that, though. You must be all shaken up.'

'I'm OK,' Deeley muttered quickly, nervous of any more sympathy. 'So, um, when's Devon getting back?'

Matt heaved a sigh. 'Tomorrow. She's in Manchester tonight,' he said. 'She's filming that show tomorrow, the daytime one where she has to cook live. She was all wound up about it. Said she wanted to stay there the night before, be fresh for the morning.'

Deeley's eyebrows shot up. 'She's doing *1-2-3 Cook*?' she asked, trying to keep the incredulity out of her voice. Deeley had spent plenty of time in the downstairs flat watching daytime TV and *1-2-3 Cook* was one of her new favourite shows. Much as Deeley admired what Devon had achieved in her career, she had watched her sister's show as well, and it seemed pretty clear to Deeley that Devon wasn't the calibre of quick-thinking, restaurant-experienced cook who could pull off a challenge like the one she would face on live TV tomorrow.

'Yeah, that's what it's called,' Matt said. 'She'll be fine, I'm sure. She's a really good cook.'

Another silence fell. Deeley was struggling with envy for Devon, that she had Matt, who would back her up unquestioningly, assume that she could put her hand to anything she set it to.

And then the true significance of what Matt had just said hit Deeley: *He's alone in the house tonight.*

Devon isn't coming home.

No one's going to interrupt us.

She shot to her feet so fast she cannoned into the coffee table in front of her and rocked on her heels.

'I have to go!' she said loudly, bending to put her glass on the table. 'I have to, um, do things . . . ring people . . . send emails . . .'

Her voice trailed off as she glanced sideways at Matt,

overwhelmed by the sheer bulk of him, leaning against the back of his sofa, his long, wide legs stretched out along the L. His physical presence was utterly confusing. When they had been chatting just now, it had been the most natural thing in the world. She and Matt had never really talked before; they'd just exchanged a few, stumbling, uncomfortable words at that dinner at Franco's. Deeley had had no idea that they would find it this easy to talk. And it made everything infinitely more difficult.

It would have been so much better if he was just some big stupid hunk with meat for brains, she thought miserably. *Then at least I could tell myself he wasn't worth thinking about. But this guy – this guy is lovely. Self-deprecating, easy-going, really friendly. I could sit here and talk to him all night.*

Oh God. This is really dangerous now.

Her gaze slid up his body, and she realized that he was nodding slowly. More, he was looking at his glass to avoid meeting her eyes. It was hard to read his expression; the flames flickering in the grate, the soft lighting, cast shadows over his face. When he spoke, his voice was a little hoarse.

'Yeah,' he said. 'You should probably go.'

Deeley swallowed hard. 'Will you be OK?' she said, picking up her jacket from the back of the sofa. 'I mean, if Devon isn't coming back – are you going to be able to cope? With getting upstairs and everything?'

'I'll manage,' he said, setting down his glass on the coffee table. 'I've got my crutch – I've just got to get used to it.'

He reached down with his left arm to haul up the crutch, which had been lying on the floor next to the sofa. But his actions belied the casualness of his words: nerves took over, and rather than lifting the crutch, he dragged at it with much too much force, jerking one end of it up as the other side skidded across the polished floor, banging against the coffee table, the tip swinging towards Deeley. She jumped to avoid being tripped, stumbling as she tried to retrieve her balance.

'Shit, sorry!' Matt exclaimed, letting the crutch fall and shooting up his arm to catch her instead.

She grabbed onto him with both hands. It was like putting her fingers into a live electric socket. Her palms connected with his forearm, thick with muscle; she felt every vein, every slightly rough hair, with such intensity that nothing else existed for her in that moment but the sensation of Matt's warm, firm flesh beneath her hands. She clung to him as if he were a tree trunk and she were being blown away by a hurricane.

And the next second, she looked into his eyes. She was probably staring at him as wildly as a madwoman, but she was utterly unable to help herself. Deeley had never felt this lack of control over her own body; it was utterly and completely humiliating. How she would ever recover from it, manage to say goodnight and go back downstairs, she didn't know. She couldn't even let go of him – her hands were still wrapped around his arm for dear life . . .

His eyes were a brighter blue than she had realized. Brighter and more intense, as if they were burning up. Deeley couldn't look away. Her knees started to buckle under her, and he caught her with his other arm. Or maybe he reached up and pulled her down; maybe her knees didn't buckle until he did that, dragged her down onto the sofa next to him. She never knew. She just knew that one moment she was still on her feet, and the next she had landed on the sofa, her jean-clad bottom sliding across the leather right beside him.

Her hands slid up his arm; she couldn't believe how big his biceps were beneath her palms, how wide his shoulders were. Deeley was the tallest of her sisters, and despite what Matt had said earlier, not skinny. That was Maxie, who kept an eagle eye on her weight. And yet, running her hands up Matt's arms, she felt tiny, like a doll next to him. A little moan escaped her at the feel of his skin; his arms tightened around her, one huge hand round her waist, the other in her hair, cupping the back of her head, pulling her towards him, and as his head came down she tilted her own eagerly up to meet his lips, moaning again with excitement.

The little noises Deeley was making would have embarrassed her utterly if she hadn't already felt that she had lost all control over herself. She wrapped her arms around his neck, dragged his head down, tangled her fingers in his short curls, kissed him with a pent-up passion that she hadn't even known she possessed. And she realized, with a shock like a slap across the face, that she couldn't even remember the last time she had kissed a man like this. Her sexual encounters in LA had never been emotional; they had only been about scratching an itch, relieving the sexual frustration of a young, healthy woman all too aware that the boyfriend who was allegedly making love to her most nights was actually going at it on a constant basis with his gorgeous male personal trainer.

She'd hardly even kissed the guys she had casual sex with. The one thing that was absolutely banned for Deeley was for her to form any sort of romantic relationship; Carmen had made it clear that Deeley could do whatever she wanted, as long as no man could ever claim boyfriend status, because that could easily lead to precisely the kind of press story that Deeley's presence in Nicky's life was intended to avoid.

Deeley had understood completely. She'd limited herself to pool guys and tennis pros, employees who knew to keep their mouths shut. She'd even shown off about her flings to Nicky, who'd taken a lot of vicarious enjoyment from Deeley's wild stories. She'd been young, free, single, and banned from getting serious with any man; she'd done nothing wrong, had nothing to feel remorse about.

But now, kissing Matt with everything she had, wrapped in his arms, her head spinning, she did look back on those five years in LA and feel a huge wash of regret. Because, although she'd had fun, she had cheated herself of anything like this. She'd cut herself off from feeling this intense, dizzying desire. Matt's mouth, his hands on her, were hot as fire, burning her up. Her mouth opened under his and their tongues touched, the warm wet sensation making her moan yet again, her eyes closed tight so she could feel the sensations even more strongly, more deeply. A rush of heat fizzed like a Catherine wheel deep down in her, spinning, sending off sparks, driving her crazy.

His tongue drove into her mouth, and she responded by trying to pull him even closer, wrapping her arms even tighter around his neck, writhing against him. Between her legs a pulse was beating, faster and faster, driving her on, and he wanted exactly what she did, because the hand behind her back slid down, caught under her bottom and lifted her whole body, as easily as if she weighed nothing at all, snuggling her onto his lap, positioning her between his thighs, her knees pulled up to the side, so her whole upper body was pressed even closer to his.

The feel of him below her drove her wild, the sheer solid width of his thighs, the heavy muscles, strong as tensile steel. She dragged herself along them, further and closer, pushing her pelvis right into his, their mouths still locked in a frantic, deep kiss, as if they would die if they weren't kissing.

Neither of them said a word. It would break the fragile spell. Deeley knew all too well that the reason they were kissing with such desperation was that they were trying to block out everything around them. Matt was almost hurting her, his grip was so strong; his fingers dug into her bottom as she moved, as she found where she wanted to be, where she was frantic to be; and her eyelashes fluttered, her eyes were shut so tight, as she jammed herself into him, and felt his hard cock pushing up towards her through the heavy material of his tracksuit bottoms.

Oh, thank God – he's all in proportion, she thought with a flood of relief. She clung to his neck, gasping into his mouth, as she lifted herself just fractionally and then lowered herself against him, rubbing him just where she needed it so badly. A scream escaped her as she felt him slide between her legs. She felt his straining width through her jeans and knickers, through his tracksuit bottoms, and the pressure of him against the seam of her jeans sent a lightning bolt of pleasure right up her, a stab of extreme sensation that was almost an orgasm in itself.

She wasn't even straddling him. *It's like riding side-saddle*, she thought dizzily, rocking back and forth, increasing the pressure, panting hard, almost unable to breathe, because his hand clamped on the back of her head was holding her right against him, his tongue even deeper in her mouth now, echoing exactly what his cock wanted, very badly, to do to her. *I could come like this,* she realized, amazed, her hips throbbing, her entire body pounding, desperate for its release. *I could come like this, right here, right now, again and again and again . . .*

And that was what stopped her, like a bucketful of cold water thrown in her face. She froze dead where she was. If that happened, some huge Rubicon would have been crossed, and then nothing would stop them from actually doing it, from having sex right here on the sofa that Matt shared with Devon . . .

The thought of having sex with Matt was so overpowering that Deeley had to dig her nails into the palms of her hands until pain stabbed through her to distract herself from the vivid mental images that were flashing before her. Pulling away from him was the hardest physical thing she'd ever done; it was as if they were superglued together, as if she were ripping away layers of her own skin as she managed to sit back up. Every millimetre of distance she gained between their bodies was a hard-won victory.

'We can't do this,' she said in a tiny, stifled voice.

'No . . .' Matt managed to say, jerking his own torso back from her as best he could, and wincing in pain as the rapid movement sent a spasm down to his injured ankle.

She was sitting up now, catching her breath, trying to still the mad race of her heartbeats; Matt dragged his hands off her as she pulled away, dropping his hands to his sides. As she watched, he actually slid his hands under his legs, wedging them under his thighs, as if he needed to make absolutely sure that he couldn't impulsively reach out and touch her.

Deeley glanced briefly at his face, lit by the flickering firelight, and had to look away immediately. It was too painful. Swinging her feet to the floor, she scrambled off the sofa, taking a few steps away from him before she stopped and got her balance, reaching out to grab her jacket and bag. She practically ran to the living room door, each step on the polished wood floor sounding as loud as a thunderclap in the utter, funereal silence. Grabbing onto the doorjamb, she stopped for a second, feeling that she ought to say something, ought to clarify that what they had just done was terrible, horrendous, that it would never, ever happen again; but then, tears already starting, she knew that she didn't need to say a word. They were already both drowning in guilt.

Stumbling out into the hall, she ripped at the handle of the door to the back stairs. She practically fell down the steps, she was in such a hurry to get away from Matt, away from temptation; and when she tumbled through the connecting basement door, she actually turned and slid the bolt that locked it from the outside. She didn't think for a moment that Matt was going to pursue her, limp down the back stairs on his crutch to try to start things up again where they had left off. No: the lock was symbolic, a message to her. That door was totally off limits, now and forever. She was never, never going up into that house again.

Gasping for breath, she ran into the bathroom. She was so riven by different emotions that she didn't know how to cope with the physical sensations: she wanted to cry, to scream, to throw herself down on the bed and pound it with her fists like a child. And she also wanted, very badly, to go back upstairs. To fuck Matt senseless, to grind herself into him, to forget anything she'd ever learned about loyalty and honour and moral behaviour, to spend the entire night having wild sex with Matt till they both passed out, exhausted, in a tangle of arms and limbs and bed sheets . . .

No! Deeley twisted on the cold tap with quick, frenzied jerks of her wrist, then plunged both hands under it, gasping at the cold water on her pulse points. She looked at herself in the mirror, and winced. Her cheeks were flushed, her eyes bright as stars, her skin glowing golden and radiant. She looked like a woman in love, or at least the full blush of lust.

Filling her palms with cold water, she splashed great handfuls over her face. She didn't stop till she was dripping, water running down her nose and chin, splashing back into the basin. Until she had got some kind of grip on herself, taken down her temperature. Grabbing a towel, she blotted her face, not caring if her make-up was running, her hair wet. Rubbing her face as if she were trying to do an inexpert microdermabrasion, she went swiftly back into the living room and stood there for a moment, thinking fast. Almost in spite of herself, her gaze swung around the room to the locked door in the wall, the door that led up to Matt, and she felt her features soften, her body start to yearn for him.

I can't stay in this flat a moment longer. This is much too dangerous.

Throwing the towel on the floor, she strode into the bedroom, pulled out a big soft leather Anya Hindmarch overnight bag, and started throwing clothes into it. Jeans, t-shirts, sweaters. Nothing smart. A handful of her favourite lace Leigh Bantivoglio French knickers, a couple of bras, some sports clothes, an Etro swimsuit, silk La Perla pyjamas, socks, her cashmere slub-knit Signoria throw in pale heather, big as a blanket but fine enough to pull through a slender bracelet, her ultimate comfort wrap.

Comfort clothes, in fact. Not only nothing smart, definitely nothing sexy. Picking up the bag once it was nearly full, she ran into the bathroom and scooped everything into a big Clinique toiletry bag. Dumping that on top, she closed and zipped the overnight bag and slung it over her shoulder. *Pale yellow leather,* she thought with a flicker of humour, looking down at it. *Get me, what a rich bitch! What the hell was I thinking, spending all that money on a bag that's bound to get dirty as soon as I actually travel with it!*

Oh, that's right. It wasn't my own money. She pulled a face. *Well, enjoy this bag while you can, Deeley. And keep it clean. Because you're going to be selling it on eBay soon enough, just to get a roof over your head.*

All her vital documents were in the Fendi handbag. She added that to the weight on her shoulder, and made sure everything was turned off before she locked up. Deeley didn't know where she was going, but one thing was sure: when she came back to Green Street, it would be just to clear out the rest of her stuff from the basement flat. No way could she spend one more night under her sister's roof, accepting her sister's hospitality, when she had nearly just had sex with her sister's husband.

The memory of what she had just done was a smack across the face. Flinching, she dashed up the outside steps and practically sprinted along the street to where it debouched into Park Lane; she was bound to find a cab there. Her hand was flung up as soon as she reached it, and almost instantly a black taxi squealed to a halt.

'Where to, love?' the cabbie said, swivelling to look at her, as she tumbled in, setting the bag on the seat beside her.

'Heathrow,' Deeley said. 'No . . .' She had a feeling that Heathrow was more for big international flights; wasn't Gatwick the airport that served closer locations, did more charter flights? She'd have a better choice of last-minute destinations with Gatwick, surely?

'Gatwick,' she said, sinking back into the seat, closing her eyes, grateful that it was dark outside, that he wouldn't be able to see her expression. 'Take me to Gatwick, as fast as you can.'

Tears started to flood out, dampening her eyelashes, pouring down her cheeks. Finally, she could give way to some sort of physical release, and the relief was tremendous.

Deeley cried all the way to the airport.

Devon

Sod them all, Devon thought defiantly, staring at herself in the dressing room mirror. *I'm going to be amazing.*

She looked wonderful, which was the main source of her confidence. In the two-and-a-half weeks since her blowout at the meeting with the BBC, Devon had embarked on a crash diet, and it had definitely stripped away some of her excess weight. She'd spent hours on the internet, working out which regime would best suit her; she'd immediately ruled out anything that involved fasting (she knew she couldn't manage that) or juicing (she needed to chew on food to feel satisfied). The meals that you could have delivered to your home on a daily basis all seemed to require you to put in extra vegetables, and for the amount they charged, that seemed a con.

Of course, she could have gone really upmarket, had a personal chef cook tiny diet meals for her every day, but how would it look if that leaked out to the papers? *FAT PIG DEVON CAN'T COOK SLIMMING FOOD*. She shivered at the mere idea.

No, she had to be discreet about this. And what she'd finally settled on had a simplicity that she liked a lot: plus, she could eat as much as she wanted. Which, for someone as naturally greedy as Devon, was perfect. It was an egg-only diet, which meant exactly what its name indicated. You hardboiled vast amounts of eggs, and you ate as many of them as you fancied. Nothing to dress them, no oil or, God forbid, mayonnaise. You could put spices on them. Devon had gone a bit mad with salt and sweet paprika, just to give them some interest.

There was only one downside to the egg-only diet. It played havoc with your digestion. In other words, it blocked you up and made you very farty indeed. Devon had started to add in cherry tomatoes, too, on the principle that they were pretty much calorie-free and would give her some fibre; they'd helped with the first issue, but not the second. For the last fortnight, she'd been sleeping in the guest bedroom; Matt had been noble and uncomplaining about the situation, but she got sick of apologizing.

And, to be honest, she hadn't minded having an excuse not to share a room with Matt. The state of her marriage was not a subject she wanted to examine too closely at the moment. She was beginning to wonder whether her reluctance to have sex with her husband was really all down to her dislike of her own body, or a more fundamental sign that her marriage was in deep trouble . . .

'Devon?' A runner for *1-2-3 Cook* poked his head into the dressing room. 'We're almost ready. Can I take you to the green room?'

He jerked his head back just as abruptly, having sensed a certain odour in the air.

'Um, I'll wait in the corridor,' he said quickly. 'Till you're ready.'

Damn, Devon thought, standing up. *Is it that bad?* She'd lit a Space NK candle as soon as she got in here, Blue Hyacinth; she'd thought the sweet, heady scent would have covered any smells she had been making. *Well, apparently not. Oops.*

She shrugged as she surveyed her body in the mirror. *I may be a bit gassy, but I've lost nearly half a stone already. So sod it – I'm thinner! That's all I care about!*

Devon had literally spent days picking out the clothes she would wear on live TV. A black crêpe Ghost blouse, fitted close to her now slimmer body, with a pretty Victorian round collar and black mesh yoke, slightly transparent. It was unbuttoned just to the start of her famous cleavage, giving a hint of bosom without showing so much that it would be unsuitable for daytime. Her denim Karen Millen pencil skirt smoothed down her bottom, and black patent knee-high boots drew attention to her newly slim legs. Underneath, of course, she wore a skin-tight slimming slip whose heavily-Lycraed material sucked her in as much as humanly possible. Its constriction meant she couldn't make any sudden movements, but you didn't want to do that on TV anyway. And it reminded her to keep pulling in her tummy, which was definitely a good thing.

Her hair and make-up were perfect. She'd brought Gary up from London with her for the purpose. Gary knew exactly what daytime TV required: he had blended on even more foundation than normal so her skin looked preternaturally perfect, while dialling down the eye make-up and lipstick. The women who watched afternoon TV would be alienated from a Devon who was made-up as if she were on the red carpet; what Gary had done so superbly was to make her look like a heightened, naturalistic version of herself. Only flawless.

'All right, love?' he said now, popping back into the dressing room, giving her a quick once-over, and rummaging through his silver train case for some lip stain, which he reapplied to her mouth. 'I just saw Elton John in the corridor – oh dear, all that money, and he's still got jowls hanging under his chin! I wanted to say, "Oi, bulldog-clip it, dear!"' He giggled. 'Now some more lip gloss,' he continued, dabbing it expertly onto Devon's reddened lips. 'Ugh, it pongs in here! That candle really hasn't worked, has it? You'll have to hold them in while you're filming, love. You don't want to be farting all over the food.'

Devon couldn't help giggling back. 'Shut up, Gary,' she said, slapping him. 'I've lost seven pounds on this diet.'

'Oooh, I know! Good for you,' he said. 'Close your eyes.' He gave her hair – pulled off her face and tonged into artless-seeming ringlets which hung down her back – a last misting of Elnette. 'Right, off you go.'

Devon turned to him for a moment, the colour draining from

her face; not that anyone could have noticed, as her skin was so thoroughly plastered with foundation and gel blusher.

'Gary . . .' she started nervously. 'I'm – I'm going to be OK, aren't I?'

'Of course you are!' Gary said instantly. 'You started on live TV, didn't you? Just do what you always do, silly girl. Wiggle your tits around and have a good old flirt with the cameraman. Works every time.'

Devon giggled again; she didn't just keep Gary around for his excellent make-up skills. He could always cheer her up. His brand of tart-tongued honesty was as good as a tonic. She walked out of the dressing-room – or, rather, wiggled, as Gary put it, because her slimming slip was so tight she could only take small steps – and followed the runner along the corridor to the set. Gary was hard on her heels, carrying a small bag of make-up for emergency touch-ups: powder, lip stain, lip gloss. If Devon had glanced back at him, her confidence boost might have faded fast; because as soon as she'd turned her back, his bright, encouraging smile had disappeared, replaced by a grimace of concern.

The runner led Devon into the backstage area of the TV studio, which was like every other one in the world: black floors, black flats, heavily scuffed white tape marking out seemingly random sections of the floor, thick cables running across them, full of bustling, over-weight tech guys in baggy black clothes.

'Watch your step,' the runner muttered automatically, as he guided her across the floor to where Barry, the presenter of *1-2-3 Cook*, was standing by a monitor, talking to the director and the producer.

'Devon! You look fantastic, darling! Ready to rumble?' said Barry, spotting Devon and coming towards her with a big welcoming smile. 'We're all so excited to have you on the show! You know Stan, of course?'

He indicated the chef with whom Devon would be competing, a veteran of this kind of programme. Stan had his own restaurant, his own pasta sauces and his own cookbooks, but, unlike Devon, he didn't have his own series. Tall, thin, white as a peeled onion, Stan wasn't prepossessing enough to be considered prime-time TV material, and he resented it; he'd made various snarky comments about Devon's cooking abilities over the years, all of which Devon's publicist had firmly told her to ignore.

'Hi, Devon,' Stan said, stepping over a coil of trailing electrical wires to shake her hand with extreme formality. His palm was sweaty, his bald head already a little shiny. 'May the best man – or woman . . .' he added, rolling his eyes sarcastically, 'win!'

'Oh, I'm not really seeing this as a competition,' Devon said quickly, withdrawing her hand. 'I mean, we're just here to have fun and be entertaining, right?'

Stan smirked down his long pointed nose at her and did not deign to reply.

'Absolutely!' Barry said, jumping into the awkward silence, beaming at Devon. 'Your job is to have fun out there! Now, we've just got a couple of minutes – let's get you miked up and intro-duced to your teammates, shall we?'

As a tech fixed Devon's microphone pack in place and handed her the little mike to clip invisibly onto her bra, the runner reap-peared, chivvying two people in front of him. It was immediately apparent, from the hesitance with which they gingerly picked their way over the trailing cables and the comparative lack of make-up on their faces, that they were the members of the audience who had been chosen to participate in the cook-off.

'Here we go,' the runner mumbled. 'We've got, uh, Jim and Shirley. OK?' Without waiting for an answer, he dashed off again, consulting his clipboard.

'Fantastic!' Barry said with unabated cheerfulness. 'Do we know who you're with, Jim and Shirley?' He looked over at the producer. 'Thoughts?'

Swiftly, Devon assessed the two contestants. Jim was thirty-something, slight and unprepossessing, but with an alert glint in his eyes that indicated intelligence; he was staring at her apprecia-tively, too. Shirley was in her sixties, with an old-fashioned perm, a novelty sweater with a duck knitted into it, and an apprehensive expression.

Please let me get Jim! Devon thought, crossing her fingers. *I can do my flirting thing with him – it worked really well on* Wake up UK. *Plus, he looks like he's got some brains . . .*

'Oh, Shirley's with Devon, and Jim's with Stan,' the producer said brightly. 'Girls against boys! It'll be a good laugh!'

Oh shit. Shirley turned to look at Devon, taking her in from head to toe: the patent-leather boots, the snug skirt, the partly-transparent yoke of her blouse, the red lip-stain, the richly-coiffed hair. Shirley's lips tightened into a thin, judgemental line, and she shook her head fractionally from side to side.

Slut, her expression now said, as clearly as if she'd spoken the word out loud. *No better than she should be. Dressed up like a dog's dinner.*

'Hi, Shirley,' Devon said, smiling at her, doing her best to turn on her legendary charm.

'Can't I be with Stan?' Shirley asked, in a tone that, if she had been a teenager, would most definitely have been described as petulant. 'I see him on the show all the time. I was hoping I'd get Stan.'

'Whoops, no, sorry!' the producer said, looking not at all apologetic; in fact, she was practically rubbing her hands together in glee at this reaction. Conflict always made better television. 'You'll have a lovely time with Devon, I'm sure! Now, everyone, we're on in just a couple of minutes. You all know how this works. Barry welcomes Stan and Devon, then we bring on you two . . .' she smiled patronizingly at Jim and Shirley in lieu of remembering their names, 'we get the two mystery ingredients you have to use in your dish, and we start the clock. OK? Brilliant!'

She nodded at Barry, which was his cue to chivvy Devon and Stan onto the set. The warm-up man had done a great job: the studio audience broke into riotous applause at the sight of Barry and the celebrity chefs. Barry had been beaming and jovial backstage; now, under the bright TV lights, feeding on the roar of the crowd, he seemed to swell up like a puffing toad, his smile almost as big as his face, his teeth gleaming white.

'Hellooooo Manchester!' he yelled, throwing his arms wide. 'Glad you could make it! Are you having fun yet?'

The whoops and cheers that answered him went on for almost a minute; Barry stood there, arms still open, lapping up the appreciation. Then, just as it was ebbing, he jerked his arms down, giving the impression that the applause might have gone on forever if he hadn't brought it to an end.

'We're live in ten,' the floor manager said.

'You heard that, Manchester!' Barry said. 'Get ready to make some noise!'

Devon was suddenly unable to breathe. She stared out at the blinding bright lights, at the faces beyond, twenty rows of them in tiered seating; she could hardly see any details, just a mass of people, all watching her. Looking right at her. The camera nearest to her swung round, ready for a close-up on her. *Flirt with the cameraman*, Gary had reminded her, and Devon automatically tilted her head to him and winked. Cameras she was used to, lived with for large parts of her life; cameras she could manage. And live TV she could manage, too; she'd done this before.

It was the live studio audience that was terrifying her. Their reactions, their approval or disapproval. *They're totally Barry's*, she realized. *They'll do anything Barry tells them to: laugh, clap, anything. They're like a mob that he controls.*

Her hands clenched on the bright red countertop in front of her. The set was done up in primary colours: daffodil-yellow walls, a shiny white central podium, where Barry stood, and then a red kitchen and a blue one, each with its own sink, oven and hobs. They'd been shown round the set before, to make sure they knew where all their ingredients and pots and pans were; Devon had done her best to remember everything, while Stan had made a point of chatting to the floor manager the entire time, to indicate that he already knew the TV kitchen as well as his own.

Stan was standing in the centre of the blue kitchen, parallel with her; as she glanced over at him, he stared back at her, blank-faced, for a moment, before his mouth twisted into a derisive smile. Lifting his hand, he raised it to hip level, where only she could see it; the work counter in front of them was at waist height. He stuck out his thumb and turned it downwards like a Roman emperor pronouncing judgement on a defeated gladiator, his smile positively malicious now.

Devon stared at his thumbs-down, feeling nausea rise in her throat. *I'm totally out of my depth here. And Stan's clearly going to do everything he can to make me look like an idiot.*

Oh God, what have I done?

The red light above the studio doors flashed on, and stayed on. They were live. There was no going back now.

'Welcome to *1-2-3 Cook!*' Barry bellowed over the renewed applause. 'Settle down, you lot! We've only just begun!' He flapped his hands at the audience, pretending that he was annoyed by the noise they were making. 'Blimey, you're loud, aren't you? Well, we've got a real treat for you today! Not only do we have the dashing and handsome Stan The Man in the house today . . .' he gestured to Stan, who flourished a long and elaborate bow, instantly becoming a showman as the camera panned to him, 'but we have a really special guest! Back on live TV for the first time in donkey's years . . .'

Which makes me sound as old as the hills! Devon thought crossly.

'The lovely Devon McKenna! You've bought her books, you've watched her shows – well, now you can watch her cook!'

And that makes it sound as if I haven't cooked before, Devon realized. Her head jerked back in shock. *Am I being set up?*

Three cameras were on her. Adrenaline shot through her, powerful as a taser to her chest. She put back her shoulders, tilted her head to the side, and flashed her best smile. As many whoops of appreciation came from the crowd as cheers, for which she was very grateful. But her heart was drumming so hard against her ribcage that it hurt.

'Right, let's bring in our dauntless contestants!' Barry continued, turning to face the left side of the set. 'Battling it out for the chance to win their own incredible *1-2-3 Cook* apron . . .' he turned to wink at the crowd, who, obligingly, laughed, '*and* five hundred pounds for the charity of their choice!'

Jim and Shirley were herded onto the set, blinking slightly as the sheer wattage of the lights hit them in the face. They were now dressed in the show's aprons – Jim in blue, Shirley in red – and carrying an extra one each. Barry walked over to meet them, putting his arms around their shoulders, and guided them over to the central podium.

'Jim and Shirley, two brave souls who are going to cook with us today! So, Jim, you're with Stan!' he announced. 'Hand him his apron, will you?'

Stan took the blue apron from Jim and donned it as Barry asked, 'How do you feel about being with Stan, Jim?'

'Well, I'd rather be with Devon!' Jim said, which drew loud appreciative laughter from Barry and the crowd. Stan pulled a comical face, which made people laugh even harder.

'I think we'd all rather be with Devon, Jim,' Barry said, milking it happily. 'But hey, Shirley's the lucky one today. Eh, Shirley? Will you give Devon her apron, please?'

Resentfully, Shirley walked over to Devon and gave her the apron.

'Now, Shirley, I've been told you're a regular watcher of our show – is that right?' Barry said, grinning at her.

'Yes,' Shirley said over-loudly. 'I watch it every afternoon. And I like *him*.' She pointed at Stan. 'He's a good cook, he is. Not some jumped-up dolly bird in a tight skirt.'

A brief, awkward silence hung in the air for a moment. Devon, easing the red apron over her head, froze with it halfway on.

Barry clearly made a lightning-fast calculation, decided to leave this well alone, smiled so widely that the audience could practically see his molars, and said, 'Right! Let's get on with the meal! Who wants to know what the mystery ingredients are?'

Devon finished pulling on the apron. Automatically, she reached behind her and tied it round her waist, moving as if she were in a trance.

It's only a half-hour show, she told herself. *Just half an hour. I'll bosh something out, get through this and then I'll never have to see any of these people again.*

'Eggs!' Barry boomed, as a screen behind the set flashed a huge image of eggs in a basket. 'And . . . aubergine!'

Ah, dammit! Devon thought. *I hate aubergine.*

'Red team, blue team, you have a minute to confer and plan your dish, starting . . . now!' Barry said.

Devon stared rather hopelessly at Shirley. 'Um, do you have a favourite dish featuring aubergine?' she said as cheerfully as she could.

'Never eaten it in my life,' Shirley said, folding her arms in satisfaction, her eyes beady with dislike.

'Right! Well, we'll do, um, a brunch dish! Because of the eggs!' Devon's voice was going higher and higher. 'Something Mexican!' They'd already been shown the store cupboard and fridge, which gave the contestants plenty of basics for their recipes. 'Why don't I get you to cube up the aubergine, and we'll flash fry it?'

'And . . . time to start cooking, everyone!' Barry swivelled to Devon and Shirley. 'So, red team, what are you two cooking up for us today?'

'Mexican brunch eggs!' Devon announced, smiling at him.

'Ooh!' he said, the audience chorusing an echo of 'Ooohs!' behind him. 'Sounds great! And blue team, what about you?'

'We're going to be making Imam Bayildi, Barry,' Stan drawled, giving Devon a challenging look over Barry's shoulder. 'That's a fantastic Turkish dish which means "The Imam Fainted". We're roasting the aubergines and making nests to bake the eggs inside. Very ambitious, but we're up to the task!'

'Wow! Can't wait to try that!' Barry said, as Devon scrabbled for a knife and chopping board for Shirley, who seemed to have embarked on a tactic of passive resistance.

'Can you chop it into small cubes, Shirley?' she asked nervously. 'The tinier the better. It's going to be sort of aubergine caviar. They do that a lot in the Middle East.'

'I thought you said we were doing Mexican,' Shirley said loudly. 'Changed your mind, have you? Copying him now?'

She jerked her head towards Stan and Jim's side of the kitchen. Devon stared at her, horrified.

'No!' she said quickly, though that wasn't exactly the truth: as soon as she had heard Stan's words, she'd realized that actually, aubergine was much more Middle Eastern than Mexican. It was just so hard to make up stuff on live TV, with no time to correct yourself. Devon had a sudden rush of sympathy for the contestants on game shows who blanked on completely obvious answers.

Stan was much better at this than she was; he'd given a really good answer to Barry, whereas Devon had just blurted out the first thing that came into her head. And he and Jim were already chopping and slicing away, while she and Shirley just stood there, facing off.

'Right, Shirley! Off you go!' Devon said, grabbing the aubergines and slapping them down in front of Shirley. 'I'm just going to sauté some onion . . .'

She had got the onion sliced and into a pan by the time Barry strolled over, two cameras tracking him, to see what they were doing.

'I'm just browning some onion,' she announced, 'while Shirley chops the aubergine . . .'

'And how's it going, Shirley?' Barry said, his face now pantomiming seriousness.

Shirley sniffed. 'It's Mexican one moment, Middle Eastern the next – I don't know *what* we're doing!' she said snappishly. 'Madam can't make her mind up!'

'Oh dear! Having some issues?' Barry said delightedly, turning to Devon, who had dashed across the red kitchen and was rummaging in the spice rack for anything that remotely resembled a Mexican spice.

'No!' she corrected him, her voice rising to a squeak. 'We're fine! How's that aubergine coming, Shirley!' Grabbing some chilli powder and cumin, Devon nipped back to the hobs, only to see in horror that her onions had burned round the edges. She whipped the pan off and dumped a tin of tomatoes into it to stop the onions burning any further, and then realized that she'd meant to fry the spices up with the onions . . . and aubergine.

'Right, I need another pan . . .' she muttered, grabbing one at random from under the counter. 'And some more oil . . .'

'Weren't you going to put these in with the onions?' Shirley asked, hefting the board of chopped aubergine aloft. 'Did you forget?'

'No! No, I meant to do that!' Devon said, much too quickly, realizing that she still needed to cook down the tomato sauce. She dragged the pan back onto the heat again. 'Shirley, why don't you stir that while I do the aubergine?'

'Looks burned to me,' Shirley said, picking up a wooden spoon.

I'm going to kill her, Devon thought, trickling cumin and chilli into the second pan and setting it onto the hob next to the one Shirley was using. She smiled brilliantly at Shirley, tossing back her hair.

'Careful that doesn't get in the food,' Shirley said dourly, drawing a laugh from the audience.

I'm going to pick up this pan and smash it across her face, Devon fantasized.

'God, she's a right old bag, isn't she?' Gary, watching, muttered to the runner standing next to him. 'Where did they dig her up from?'

'Oh, mate . . .' The runner, who was making a roll-up on the top of a speaker, paused for a second as he tipped out the Golden Virginia into the Rizla paper. 'She's a fucking nightmare is what she is. Every time she comes she volunteers to be on. She's never been let do it before, because she's a grumpy old cow.'

Gary stared at him in horror. 'You're kidding,' he breathed. 'So why'd she make it on today?'

The runner shrugged. 'Barry thought it'd be a laugh to put her with Devon,' he said. 'Good TV, you know?'

'Fuck. Dev's totally buggered,' Gary mumbled. 'I can't watch this.'

'Car-crash telly,' the runner said. 'Got to love it.'

By now, petrified of what Shirley would say next, equally terrified of the dog's dinner she was cooking up, Devon was in such a state she could barely focus on the pan in front of her. The aubergine seemed to be scorching without cooking through; she lifted the spoon and tasted a bit. It was absolutely foul.

'Mmm!' she exclaimed, smiling at the closest camera. 'Delicious!'

'Five minutes left!' Barry announced. 'Time to finish your dishes, teams!'

'Shirley, dump your sauce in here,' Devon said swiftly, practically grabbing the pan of tomato sauce from her reluctant teammate. 'I'll cook it all down. And why don't you fry up a couple of eggs? You can fry eggs, can't you?'

'Of course I can fry eggs!' Shirley said, offended. 'What do I look like?'

Devon bit her lip, hard, to avoid telling Shirley exactly what she did look like, as Shirley, humphing loudly, pulled out a frying pan and poured some oil into it.

The tomato sauce, mixed in with the aubergine, looked awful; the watery tomatoes – Shirley had barely cooked them down – were studded with tiny greyish dots of aubergine, which floated in the sauce, blackened and charred. Devon stirred it frantically, hoping that the more it cooked, the tastier, at least, the tomatoes would get. Beside her, Shirley was dourly frying a couple of eggs in oil that was smoking so hard now that Devon started to cough; Shirley seemed utterly immune to it.

'Two minutes!' Barry positively yodelled, his voice brimming with glee. 'Red team, how's it coming? I've gotta tell you, the blue team are cooking up a storm over there!'

He took in the grim little scene at the hobs: Devon and Shirley working away, not exchanging a word. Across in the blue kitchen, Devon could hear Stan and Jim chatting and laughing together as they cooked in unison.

'We're doing great, Barry!' Devon said, beaming at him. 'Delicious brunch eggs coming right up!'

'Shirley?' Barry asked, swivelling to Devon's teammate. 'Having fun?'

'Not really,' Shirley said. 'I might as well be working in a caff.' She sniffed again. 'Frying eggs! It's not exactly gourmet cooking, is it?'

Devon ladled the sauce out onto a waiting plate and nipped over to the fridge, where she'd seen a bunch of parsley. Pulling it out, picking off some leaves, she arranged them on the side of the plate; that was one skill Devon did possess, making a plate look pretty. She'd done it so often for her own shows that she was fully confident; her heart racing, she grabbed a small red chilli from the fridge too and set it among the parsley, shaping them to look as if the chilli were a flower and the parsley its leaves. The audience, who could see everything she was doing on a huge monitor, oohed and aahed its appreciation.

I might be in with a chance! Devon thought, adrenaline spiking through her. *At least it'll look good – and that's almost all that counts on TV . . .*

And then she saw Shirley's eggs.

Shirley was sliding a spatula under them, holding it out towards Devon. The eggs were a crucial ingredient, one of the two that had to be used; no matter how awful they looked, Devon couldn't avoid them. Miserably, wanting desperately to cry, Devon picked up her pretty plate and carried it over so that Shirley could dump the eggs on top. They had been fried to within an inch of their lives, their edges frilled, brown and curling; the whites hard and rubbery. Delicate, lattice-like fried eggs, their yolks golden, their whites soft, might just have worked, sitting elegantly on the sauce, and concealing most of it; but Shirley's eggs were exactly like the ones you would get in the caff she'd just mentioned disparagingly. All they needed was a red rubber tomato, filled with ketchup, sitting next to them.

Devon managed to arrange them so they didn't block the view of her chilli flower, but that was all she could do to redeem the situation. She stared at the plate in horror as a buzzer beeped loudly and repeatedly, and Barry sang out, 'Cooks . . . put your spoons down, *now*!'

It was a catchphrase and the audience chorused along with him. Devon stepped back from the counter, wiping her hands on her apron, plastering a happy smile to her face. Then she glanced over at the blue team's counter and her smile froze.

Because Stan and Jim's creation looked absolutely amazing. How they'd done it in the time, she didn't know; somehow, they'd cooked and stuffed an aubergine, a poached egg resting invitingly in each hollow. The dark purple skin of the aubergine glistened deliciously, a rich sauce puddling at the base; a golden cheese gratin on top, beneath the eggs, was the perfect finishing touch. It looked totally professional.

While mine looks like something two drunken students made at four in the morning, then chucked in the bin because they thought they'd puke if they had to force it down. Devon averted her eyes from her own plate, unable to look at it any more.

Over in the blue kitchen, Barry was talking to Stan and Jim about their Imam Bayildi, mmm-ing and ooh-ing as he tasted it: 'Pan-roasted . . . flash-grilled . . . reduction of aubergine and onion in a creamy sauce . . . pecorino and feta gratin to reflect the Middle Eastern theme . . .' Stan was chanting happily over the top.

'Deee-licious!' Barry said happily. 'Tastes as good as it looks! And now, let's see what the red team have cooked up . . .'

The next minute went by in a blur. Devon just kept smiling. It was all she had left, and if she stopped, she knew she'd burst into tears instead.

She smiled as Barry looked at the plate, and commented that at least the flower looked pretty. She smiled as Shirley said that no, she didn't want to try the food they'd just made, because it looked like a mess and she didn't fancy it. She smiled as Barry gamely cut into the egg, splattering sauce over the plate and her chilli flower, and made a big production of chewing through it, raising his eyebrows as he did so to indicate how tough it was. She smiled as Barry coughed, mentioned that maybe the chilli powder hadn't been cooked enough, and that the aubergine tasted raw. She smiled as Barry thanked her and Shirley, went back to his podium, and asked the audience to hold up red or blue cards to vote on who had won today's cook-off. She even managed to keep smiling when a wall of blue promptly rose in front of their eyes, and Barry exclaimed that it was the first time ever – 'a *1-2-3 Cook* record!' – that not a single person had voted for one of the teams.

Devon smiled as she hugged Shirley as the credits rolled, as she shook Stan and Jim's hands, as she stood behind the red counter waving goodbye to the viewers. And then she walked off the set like a zombie.

Gary, bless him, was waiting for her, his train case and overnight bag already stacked next to the suitcase she'd brought up from London the night before.

'Here's your coat and bag,' he said, his face grim. 'I've got them to book us a cab – it's outside, waiting. Let's get you out of here. We'll get to the station and hop on the first train for London, OK? I've got an emergency hip flask in my case – you can have a nice old nip of voddy on the train.' He hesitated for a moment. 'And then you should probably hole up for a few days. Or take a little break somewhere. Get away from it all.'

Go somewhere they don't have the internet. Or TV. Or newspapers, he added to himself silently, as he shepherded the dazed and broken Devon out of the studio, everyone falling aside to let them go. Nobody could meet their eyes.

'Wow,' the runner mumbled, nipping out the back to smoke his roll-up. 'That's a first. I've never seen someone totally fuck over their career on live TV before.'

1993

*B*ill's corpse hit the ground with a thump. His head thudded down last, drawing a whimper from Deeley.

'Ssh!' Maxie hissed furiously.

But the whimper had been as instinctive as an animal's whine of distress: Deeley couldn't control it. Maxie glanced at her. Even in the faint moonlight, she could see how upset her little sister was. It was a reasonably warm late spring night, but Deeley was shaking as if it were twenty degrees below freezing.

Carrying Bill's body outside had been awful for all of them. Maxie and Devon had taken one of his ankles each, and started to pull him across the floor of the lounge, but the way his head bumped across the carpet tiles, lolling at a dreadful angle because of his broken neck, had been too much for Deeley, who had started crying. Maxie had curtly instructed Deeley to go outside and wait for them, but she couldn't blame Deeley for her distress. The only way she could get through this was by telling herself this was the worst thing she'd ever have to do in her entire life, and that wasn't helping much. She'd had to pinch Devon hard to stop her bursting into tears too, and now Devon was as white as a sheet and clamping her lips together in an effort not to break down.

By the time Devon had helped drag Bill through the lounge, into the kitchen, and out the back door into the garden, she was in pieces. Even *if she looked only at what was directly in front of her – Bill's ankles, in the socks and John Lewis slippers they'd bought him for Christmas – she could still hear the back of his skull knocking against the lino of the kitchen floor, whacking into the wooden riser on the threshold of the open back door, thudding down onto the stone patio outside, a relentless punctuation.*

Maybe his head wouldn't have hit so loudly if they'd been stronger, if they'd been able to pull Bill more smoothly along the floor. But they weren't very strong and Bill was a solid, heavy man. So they had hauled him along in a series of jerks, a big heave, a stop to catch their breath, another heave. And every time they stopped, that sound came. Bill's skull, banging to a stop.

Right on the bald patch at the back of his head, Devon thought, choking back her tears. He hated that bald patch, he was so careful to brush his hair around it to cover it over as much as possible. And now they were wearing it away even more . . .

Devon glanced over at Deeley, whose face was so wet with tears by now that the moonlight made it gleam like glass. She rubbed her eyes roughly with the arm of her school sweater.

'Right,' Maxie whispered, darting a look back at the houses on either side of them; no lights were on, no one seemed to be awake. They'd waited till three in the morning, and the entire street was dark. Just a few sputtering streetlights on the road, very faint in the distance. If there hadn't been a reasonably full moon, the girls wouldn't have been able to do what Maxie had so carefully planned.

'In there,' Maxie said, nodding towards the big hole by the crumbling garden wall.

There were sycamore trees all along the gardens behind Thompson Road. Bill had hated them because they sent out so many seeds every year, which did their best to pollinate on his lawn; he spent hours during the spring and summer months picking out the little seeds, each with twin wings of green leaves that enabled them to glide on the wind. He'd taught the girls to look for them and how to pinch them out of the ground where they were trying to take root. And he'd chased the council, wanting them to uproot the sycamore in the back garden of his house, because it was gradually beginning to tear up the low stone wall that ran along the boundary of the garden.

They hadn't answered his letters. Eventually, Bill had given it up as a lost cause. But Maxie had taken notice of everything: the tree roots, digging a hole at the base of the wall; the stone, beginning to crumble away, exposing the foundations of the wall. Leaving a space big enough to hide the body of a man.

'We need to roll him in there,' Maxie said grimly, nodding towards the tree. She knelt down on the grass and slid her hands under Bill's torso, getting ready to heave.

But Deeley and Devon were still standing there; they hadn't moved.

'Come on!' Maxie hissed angrily. 'It's too late to stop now! We can't leave him out here in the open!'

Devon obediently dropped to her knees beside Maxie. So did Deeley; but when she reached out to touch Bill, she started crying all over again.

'Deeley, go and sit on the step if you're not going to help,' Maxie said impatiently, still under her breath.

Crying silently, tears flooding down her face once more, Deeley obeyed, as Maxie and Devon heaved Bill's body up and over, onto his face, towards the hole. They shuffled forward on their knees, slid their hands under him again and heaved once more, Bill turning on his back again, beginning to slide down into the hole.

'You take his feet,' Maxie whispered, knowing that Devon wouldn't be able to handle moving Bill's head, lolling grotesquely on its broken neck. Maxie shuffled round to his shoulders, clambering over the loose stones, getting herself at an angle where she could haul and drag his upper body deeply into the hole under the wall. She could smell his hair, the Head and Shoulders shampoo he used, and faint traces of the Mitchum deodorant he'd put on that morning.

She'd have to get rid of all his personal stuff, she realized. His deodorant, his shampoo, his toothbrush, his passport; stuff he'd have taken with him if he'd left. And she'd have to do that herself. Neither Devon or Deeley would be up to the task of going through Bill's things.

Maxie suddenly felt so weary that she could have lain down on the grass and gone to sleep right then and there.

But she couldn't. There was so much more to do tonight before she could finally crawl into bed.

She looked over to see what Devon had managed with the other end of the body, and was relieved at how well Devon had done: she'd pulled and hauled one leg after the other, stacking them on top of each other to squash Bill underneath the wall as much as possible. Maxie wriggled round to join Devon, braced herself, and, both hands firmly against Bill's torso, gave him a last, massive shove that sent him right into the hole, as deep as possible, landing on the soil below with a heavy thud.

It was a very final sound. From the kitchen step, Deeley gave a tiny, choking gasp, which Maxie ignored. Instead, she picked up a clod of earth, and Devon followed suit. They piled up the earth till it looked exactly as Maxie had planned, as if the wall had crumbled outwards, hiding the sycamore roots, loose stones dotted over the top. It took another half an hour, but by the time they'd finished, Bill was thoroughly buried. Even looking at it in the dark, Maxie knew that her plan had been successful. No one would ever suspect that a body was lodged in there, under the wall, wedged between the roots.

The sycamore would grow and spread out, covering Bill's body more and more. The wall would crumble further, onto the corpse, driving it deeper into the soil below. The only way he would ever be found was if the council tore up the entire garden, ripped out the wall, uprooted a huge tree, and found the bones lying underneath.

Maxie stood up, rubbing her hands together to wipe as much dirt off them as she could. Even by the faint moonlight, she could see how filthy her nails were, and she couldn't help wincing; she tried so hard to keep her hands clean at all times, nicely painted. To show that though her mum was a drug addict, and currently banged up, she, Maxie, was better than that, was going to make something of herself.

'Come on,' she said softly, holding out her hand to Devon, who took it and clung on so hard Maxie winced. They walked over to Deeley, who was curled up in a ball on the step, rocking back and forth. She looked up at her sisters with a tear-wet face, her eyes huge and dark.

'It's all over, Deels,' Maxie said. 'He's gone now. We'll never see him again.'

'What if they come round? The council?' Deeley whispered, so quietly they had to bend down to hear her. 'Like Bill wanted? What if they come round to dig up the tree?'

'They never even got back to Bill, not once,' Maxie said reassuringly. 'They've got tons of other stuff that's much more important than some old tree in some crappy back garden, believe me. No one'll ever dig that up. We're completely safe.'

'I hope so,' Devon mumbled, her fingers digging even deeper into Maxie's hand.

'And even if they did – which they won't,' Maxie added quickly, feeling Devon stiffen beside her, 'they'd never suspect us. Not in a million years. Three nice sisters like us. We're never in trouble, we do well at school, we're nice to our teachers. Look.'

She pulled Deeley up with her free hand and guided them all back into the house, through the kitchen, into the living room; to the mirror on the far wall, over the sofa. They stared at their images in the mirror. Seventeen-year-old Maxie in the centre, the tallest, the most dominant, her jaw set with resolve. Thirteen-year-old Devon, softly beautiful, even despite the terrible events that they had just gone through. And Deeley, the smallest and most vulnerable at just nine, her plaits coming loose, her round childish features smudged and damp with tears, her eyes swollen from crying. All of them still in their school uniform sweaters, Maxie and Devon with their sleeves pushed up to their elbows, to avoid getting them dirty, because they only had one each.

'Look at us,' Maxie said, her voice full of reassurance. 'We're good girls. Good sisters. No one's ever going to think we'd do something like . . .' She hesitated, choosing her words. 'No one's ever going to think we'd do anything wrong. We just need to stick to our story, and we'll be fine. We're going to say that Bill went away on a trip and didn't come back, and after a week or so, we're going to go and live with Aunt Sandra. Because we can't stay on here with Bill missing. OK? People will think something weird happened to Bill, but they won't ever imagine that we might have had something to do with it.'

She reached her arms round her sisters, drawing them even closer.

'We're good sisters,' she repeated to their faces in the mirror. 'We just need to stick together, and we'll be fine. OK?'

'Yes, Maxie,' Devon and Deeley chorused, hugging Maxie tightly. Maxie nodded.

'We look after each other,' she said, her voice utterly serious. 'We're good sisters.'

Part Three

Part Three

Deeley

*P*anic flooded through Deeley as she opened her eyes. Everything was in the wrong place. The door wasn't to the left of the bed; there were curtains in front of her that seemed, as though by some sort of optical illusion, to be running all round the room; and the bed itself was huge, so wide that she couldn't feel the edges of the mattress. For a moment she thought she was still dreaming, some *Alice-in-Wonderland* illusion of a bed as big as a field, white and snowy and crisp, that she could crawl over for days and still never escape; then the last remnants of her confused and complicated dreams mercifully faded away. She'd dreamed of Matt and Bill, somehow blended into one person, her sisters in school uniform, tangles of memory twisted round one another, woven into weird, frightening designs. She sat bolt upright, wiping the sleep from her eyes, blinking hard, determined to wake up fully.

She was in a hotel room. A beautiful sprawling hotel room, with sage green walls and dark chocolate curtains. Her head was heavy; she had no idea how long she'd slept, and only a hazy sense of where she was. Slipping out of the ridiculously comfortable bed, she padded across the room, her feet sinking into the deep, rich pile of the carpet, and flung open the curtains.

Her jaw dropped as she took in the view: she was looking out onto a stunning expanse of steel-blue sea. A wide esplanade ran along the seafront on which the hotel stood; waves lapped at the breakfront, leaving white flecks of foam as they ran up the sandy beach below and pulled away again in endless rhythm. But further out, like a magical, extraordinary mirage, was a grey stone castle, which seemed to be floating on the water.

Deeley knew she wasn't dreaming now. It was a cloudy, overcast day, but the sun behind the cloud cover was still bright enough, after the padded, luxurious darkness of the bedroom, to make her eyes water a little as they readjusted to the light. She squeezed them shut and opened them again: yes, the castle was still there, a little out to sea. Now that she looked more closely, she realized it was actually a little island, with a castle at its peak, heavily fortified, its stone walls sheer, ready to defend it against intruders. Seagulls wheeled around it, diving and twisting in the winds, their caws clearly audible, like a wild chant. It was melancholy, isolated, and utterly beautiful.

I'm in exactly the right place, Deeley thought, wrapping her arms around herself, hugging herself through her silk pyjamas. *This is perfect.*

She'd walked into Gatwick, her bags slung over her shoulder, and stood in front of the Departures board, staring up at it hopelessly, jostled by an endless stream of travellers, watching the display update as it changed, as flights took off, as new ones came up on the board, as the people around her headed off and new ones arrived. She had no idea how long she'd stood there, staring blankly at one destination after another.

Finally, after a particularly hard bump on her ankles from a trolley, she turned away, walking at random, thinking that she might find an airline office and book a flight to somewhere. And then she saw the sign to the tourist information office. Deeley had never in her life asked for tourist information and she had been amazed at how helpful the woman behind the desk was, especially since all Deeley could manage to say was that she wanted to get away, somewhere quiet and peaceful, money no object. Ten minutes later, she had a flight booked and a hotel reservation made.

'People don't really think about going to Jersey, the first time,' the woman had said, smiling at Deeley. 'But once they do, they keep going back.'

Deeley hadn't even known where Jersey was – one of the Channel Islands, apparently. Nearer to France than to Britain, though the plane took off and landed almost immediately. From her window seat, dazed with everything she had been through that day, Deeley could see the little island floating into view, bright orange lights blazing through the velvet dark. A small, pretty airport, everyone friendly, everything clean: she was in a cab in just a few minutes, and at the Grand Jersey Hotel in a bare fifteen more. It had all happened so fast she was still in shock as she entered the lobby; it was as if she had been whisked away on a cloud.

She hadn't even heard the sea last night. She couldn't believe it. She remembered the lobby, like a jewel box, all red and black and fuschia, with its rich polished wood staircase; she remembered checking in, being shown to her suite, stripping off her clothes, climbing into the big bed, and falling fast asleep, so exhausted by her long, eventful day that she passed out immediately.

But how could she not have realized that the hotel was on the seafront?

She was starving. Tearing her eyes reluctantly away from the sea view, she looked around her, found the room phone, and ordered breakfast. Eggs Benedict, toast, juice, cappuccino, croissants, everything she could think of, diet forgotten. Twenty minutes later she was showered, scented with a whole range of the ESPA toiletries ranged in the bathroom, and devouring a huge breakfast in the living room of the suite, still looking out at the sea through the long windows that ran over the mirrored Art Deco cabinet along the wall. The suite was a lush, cosy haven, utterly peaceful, with velvety sofas on which Deeley could have curled up all day in complete comfort and solitude.

But comfort wasn't available to Deeley, not after what had

happened yesterday. *After what I did yesterday*, she corrected herself firmly; she couldn't hide behind the passive tense, pretend that kissing her sister's husband had just happened like a natural disaster, a tsunami or an earthquake for which no one was really responsible.

I did it. I did the worst thing one sister can do to another. Devon gave me somewhere to stay, and in return, I kissed her husband as soon as she went away for the night. And yes, he kissed me back, but that doesn't mean I'm any less to blame.

Deeley shivered from head to toe with guilt and remorse. She couldn't stay in the room any longer; she was already beginning to pace back and forth, memories of everything that she and Matt had done last night flooding back in, torturing her with their vividness. She pulled on trainers and a jacket and practically ran out of the suite, down the main staircase, through the lush, red-carpeted lobby to the revolving doors. The doorman told Deeley that the tide was going out, and when it did, Deeley would be able to walk to the castle, across the sands.

He apologized for the weather, saying it was usually much sunnier than this in mid-May; but it was perfect for Deeley's mood. There was a beautiful melancholy about the bare, deserted sands, the distant castle, the cawing seagulls, that echoed exactly how she was feeling. Hands shoved in her pockets, hair already blowing in the sea breeze, she dodged across the road that separated the Grand Jersey from the esplanade and almost ran down the stone steps that led to the beach.

The scent of the sea, the ozone in the air, was fresh and clean, just the thing for a guilty conscience. Salt and seaweed, sand damp beneath her feet, her trainers sinking in so deep it was hard to walk, and that was good too: instinctively, Deeley knew she needed to exhaust herself, tire herself out as utterly and completely as she could manage. It was as if she were punishing herself with each heavy step, trying to make her body feel as bad as her brain.

First I betrayed Devon – and Maxie – with that stupid magazine interview. I wasn't thinking, but that's no excuse. I just chattered away without watching what I was saying, and it could have been really dangerous for all of us. And then, even worse, I kissed Devon's husband . . .

Not just kissed, she corrected herself, wanting to be brutally honest, not to minimize her appalling behaviour. *Much more than kissed*. She remembered Matt's hands on her, hers on him, and found herself walking even faster, as if she could physically outrun what she had done, leave it behind her, have it washed away as the sea, coming back in, would eventually wash away her footprints.

But I can't outrun it. I have to live with what I've done. For the rest of my life. That's my punishment. I'm the worst sister in the world. Of all the men in London to choose from, how on earth could I do that with my own sister's husband?

Deliberately torturing herself with her thoughts, Deeley tramped along the seafront as the tide ebbed away from the castle. Far across the wet sands, she watched a bright blue vehicle drive out from the castle. At first she thought it was a boat then, as it cleared the surface of the water, she realized it was a big van, cantilevered four feet off the ground on thick stubby wheels, bumping slowly along a winding track that led back to the mainland, spray flying up and spattering the windows as it went, carrying tourists back and forth to the castle at high tide.

She must have walked for hours. Eventually, once the tide was low, she picked her way over to the castle track, and followed it out along the sands, climbing up the shale and shingle to Elizabeth Castle. There was a guide in an old-fashioned army uniform, red coat, white trousers, and tricorne hat trimmed with gold braid, jovially telling visitors all about the castle, and Deeley avoided him like the plague; she wanted to be completely alone. There were endless stairs to climb, towers to scale, and a huge concrete pillbox on the top, a Second World War relic, on which Deeley sat and stared out to sea.

She wasn't even close to processing what had happened with Matt yet. She was still in the middle of it, unable to step back and get any kind of perspective, trembling with shock as she remembered every single moment of what had taken place last night. His hands on her, hers on him. His mouth, his kisses, the scent of his skin. His muscles, the sheer strength of him. Even her overpowering guilt faded temporarily as she let the memories come back; she felt completely obsessed, as if she were on drugs, in the grip of an addiction so powerful that she could think of nothing else. She couldn't even close her eyes, because when she did, she saw Matt's face immediately, felt his mouth on hers, the feel of his skin under her hands, the tight curls of his hair twined through her fingers.

It was too much: she couldn't bear it. She had never felt anything like this before. She hadn't even known that it was possible to feel so strongly attracted to someone.

It was terrifying. Deeley would have been frightened by the strength of her emotions even if Matt hadn't been her sister's husband. Instinctively, she felt that this was the kind of passion that people wrote books and plays and ballads and operas about: stories that always had unhappy endings, that were meant to make you cry. Stories about passion that was a curse, sent by the gods to torment mortals, that dashed you on the rocks like the ones below her, sharp jagged teeth that would smash your skull open if you were unlucky enough to tumble onto them.

And that just went to show how crazy last night had been, how insane she was to be thinking like this: because all those images were of star-crossed lovers. High up on the castle fortification, the brisk sea air blowing round her head, whipping strands of hair around her face, Deeley was managing to keep clear-headed enough to acknowledge that she and Matt did not fit into that category. They barely knew each other. The fact that she had instantly felt comfortable with him last night, laughing and joking, making conversation as easily as if they'd known each other for years – the instant, violently powerful attraction they had felt from the moment they had met – neither of those signified anything close to being in love.

I shouldn't be using that word. I shouldn't even be letting it cross my mind for a moment. It's probably just because he's the one man I can't have, ever. Forbidden attraction, all that stuff that seems so romantic in books, or films, but is sheer torture in real life.

Thank God at least I got away from London.

Deeley knew that she couldn't stay any longer in the house that Devon and Matt shared as husband and wife. Even in the flat below, separate as it was, she couldn't sleep there one night longer. It wouldn't be right to accept her sister's hospitality after what she had done.

Shame welled up in her again at the thought, her face hot with embarrassment and self-disgust even though the breeze should have cooled her down. She needed to find somewhere else to live, straight away. She had her BlackBerry with her; she'd go online and spend some time looking for a place to rent, line up appointments with estate agents, book herself into some sort of B & B where she could live temporarily until she signed a lease on a flat.

Just a small studio, nothing too expensive. She crossed her fingers that she could afford something reasonably central. *And then I need to work on getting an agent. I'll ring that woman who did the article in Yes! – she offered to help with an agent, someone who specializes in celebrity clients.*

Deeley pulled a wry face. She was self-aware enough to know that in no universe, apart from the bubble of glossy magazines, could she ever be described as a celebrity. She hadn't achieved anything in her life but looking pretty and dressing up in the latest fashions. Her ex-boyfriend was a talented actor, her middle sister was a famous TV cook, her older sister a successful businesswoman. Compared to all of them, Deeley was just a silly fluffball.

I need to start earning my own money. Taking care of myself. Not living rent-free in my sister's basement – and, my God, making out with her husband as soon as she goes away for the night!

The sheer guilt of that thought drove Deeley to her feet. She jumped up and bounded down the stairs from the tower, dashing back through the wide courtyards of the castle, between its houses and archways, down the ramp back onto the sand, sliding over marker stones dotted with dark slimy kelp, pounding the walkway back to the hotel. She was panting by the time she reached it, her legs heavy and tired from hours of walking, her trainers so thickly clotted with wet sand that she took them off on the hotel steps, and under the amused gaze of the doorman, beat them against the wall to get most of the sand off them.

'Is there a spa here?' she asked him, holding her trainers by their backs. 'Maybe even a pool?'

The doorman looked genuinely shocked at her ignorance. 'We have a five-star spa here, miss,' he said. 'It's famous – it cost over a million pounds to build. Pool, gym, saunas, everything! It's won awards every single year.'

The spa was just as luxurious as this description, and the smiling girls on the front desk offered her a whole range of treatments, but Deeley turned them all down; panic rose in her at the thought of having anyone's hands on her. She was terrified it would bring back memories of Matt; it was all she could do to strip down to the swimsuit that, mercifully, she had thrown into her bag the night before, wrap herself in a big robe, and find her way to the pool. It was softly lit, with glowing candles in niches, so relaxing that Deeley felt stress slipping away from her shoulders as soon as she stepped inside. She managed twenty lengths of the pool before she climbed into the exquisite mosaic Jacuzzi.

Oh no, she realized immediately. *This is a mistake.* It was too warm, too soothing; she stretched her arms along the tiled walls of the Jacuzzi, leaned her head back, closed her eyes and immediately found herself thinking of Matt.

It's like he's haunting me. Her body instantly responded, pulling up images of Matt from the night before. Sitting in his lap. Pressing herself against him, winding her arms around his neck; feeling him hard underneath her bottom . . .

No – no, no, no, no . . .

She was out of the seductively warm water in two seconds, and looking for a shower to cool herself down; she was overheated, burning up from head to toe. And, tucked away behind the pool, she found a huge, circular shower – it was like walking inside the spiral of a snail's shell – with a panel of buttons on the far wall. She stabbed at one of them at random, marked *Atlantic Ocean*, then gasped as orange and blue LED lights started to play round the inside curve of the shower, while water shot out of jets at waist height around her; another flow of water poured down on her head, softly scented with a fresh, ozone perfume. Jets came and went, the infusion of scent surrounded her; by the end of the programmed sequence, Deeley was laughing with enjoyment and surprise. She hit another button, *Caribbean Rain* and tangerine lights accompanied a tropical downpour on her scalp, like a rainstorm of droplets, the scent of passion fruit warm and stimulating.

She tried the *Cold Mist* button, bracing herself, and even though she'd guessed what was coming, she squeaked at the bright blue lights and the cool water, fragranced with mint, that made her teeth chatter and her scalp tingle; it was so stimulating that she kept running the same sequence, three times, till she was shivering from head to toe and giggling as the jets caught her in the small of the back every time, no matter how she turned to avoid them.

'Sounded like you were having a great time in there!' said a man's voice as she finally, reluctantly, exited the shower.

Deeley jumped.

'Sorry,' he said, reaching up politely to get her robe from the peg where she'd hung it. 'I didn't mean to startle you.'

'No, I'm sorry,' Deeley said, completely embarrassed, taking the robe from him and pulling it on. Not only had she hogged the shower, she'd been in there for ages making silly squeaking noises. 'Did I make you wait for hours?'

He grinned, long and slow. Deeley's eyes, which had been dazzled by the LED light display in the shower, were accustoming themselves by now to the muted illumination outside, but she blinked as she took in the sight of him. He was tall and his skin, the colour of the rich polished dark wood of the Grand Jersey's imposing central staircase, was dewed with fresh beads of sweat which glinted against his smooth shaved head, his bare imposing chest, like tiny crystals. The short white towel wrapped around his waist set off his dark skin, and called attention to the flatness of his stomach and the narrowness of his waist.

'Yeah, well, I could hear the noises you were making,' he said, his teeth flashing as white as the towel. 'You were having such a good time, I didn't want to interrupt you . . .'

'Oh God!' Deeley covered her face with her hands in embarrassment. 'I'm so sorry! And you've just been in the sauna – you were waiting to cool off, and I kept you out here . . .'

'No, don't apologize,' he assured her as she took her hands away; he was grinning even wider now. 'I was having a lot of fun listening to you. I had a little bet with myself, actually. Want to know what it was?'

Deeley shook her head, pink in the face by now.

He winked at her. 'I bet myself that you were pretty,' he said, untwisting the towel from his waist; he was wearing a pair of short red trunks that left very little to the imagination. 'Just the way you were yelping – I thought, that girl's bound to be pretty. Don't ask me why.'

As he turned to hang up the towel, Deeley couldn't help checking out his bottom, tight, high and impossibly round, two firm handfuls moving temptingly under the snug red Lycra.

'But I was wrong,' he added over his shoulder. 'You're not pretty. You're totally gorgeous.' His grin widened. 'Look, I'm staying here. Maybe I'll see you in the bar later. What do you say? If you're still feeling guilty, you can always buy me a big fruity cocktail to make up for it . . .'

And then he disappeared round the corner of the shower. Deeley was unable to help watching his lean dark shape until he had gone round the curve; a moment later, the shower went on, orange lights glowing off the brown mosaic walls.

Belting her robe, she looked around for her hotel flip-flops, smiling. He was cheeky and funny; *Maybe that's exactly what I need. Some cheeky guy to have a flirt with.* She went upstairs slowly, smiling to herself all the way.

Because in the shower, and talking to the mystery man outside, she hadn't thought about Matt Bates once. And in her current state of mind, anything that distracted from her sister's husband, even for twenty minutes, was an absolute godsend.

Devon

*D*evon had always loved being recognized before. Who wouldn't? That was part of the deal when you were famous; people whispering about you, knowing who you were, knowing your name before you told them, coming up to you to tell you how much they liked your show, to ask for your autograph, or to pose with you in a picture on their camera phone.

You could call Devon a lot of things, but she was no hypocrite. She had always wanted to be a celebrity, had worked hard to get there, and now that she was one, she had never complained about the fact that it inevitably meant that you lost a considerable amount of privacy. She didn't have much respect for the famous people who did complain – they ought to know what they'd signed up for, in her opinion. And if they really didn't like it, they were more than welcome to stop appearing on TV, or pretending to write books, and let someone else, who really wanted their fame and fortune, fill that slot instead.

Even now, getting off a flight at Florence Airport in sunglasses and a silk headscarf tied over her very recognizable glossy mane of hair, she didn't regret the fact that everyone who'd checked her passport and boarding card at Gatwick had given her knowing glances, more than aware that Devon McKenna was escaping the

UK the day after her humiliating appearance on *1-2-3 Cook*. The press had relished describing in the most embarrassing detail how many mistakes she'd made; videos of her on the show were already all over YouTube, with links posted on broadsheets, tabloids and gossip sites.

Although every article did express sympathy for Devon at getting stuck with Shirley for a partner – *The Times*, which had always been nice to Devon, had a columnist suggesting she'd been set up – the trouble was that this disaster came directly on the heels of the failure of *Devon's Little Bit Extra*. *1-2-SHE CAN'T COOK!* had been the *Sun*'s headline. Gary had told her not to Google herself, but she hadn't been able to help it; this morning had been like crawling over broken glass. Every time she hit a computer key, it was like the Little Mermaid taking another step on her new feet; sheer agony. But she hadn't been able to stop.

Matt had begged her to stay off the laptop, but she hadn't listened. And because he was laid up with his ankle injury, he wasn't mobile enough to follow her around the house, snatching the MacBook away. He'd yelled a lot, listening to her sobbing, telling her to stop reading; eventually, she'd run upstairs, right to the top of the house, knowing that he wouldn't be able to reach her up there on his crutch, and had an orgy of self-pity, tormenting herself with every nasty thing she could find about herself on the internet. It was as if she had to go right down to the depths, as far as possible, know exactly how bad it was in one fell swoop. Because after that, the only way would be up.

But it doesn't feel like up, she thought gloomily as she queued up for passport control. *It just feels like running away.*

It had been Rory's idea. Devon had been amazed that he would come to her rescue after that appalling meeting at the BBC a couple of weeks ago, but then she'd realized that what he was actually doing was getting her out of the country and off the media radar, while he had time to strategize frantically and try to work out how – if it was remotely possible – to salvage the disaster that was *Devon's Little Bit Extra*. The BBC still had six episodes to air, and

British TV, unlike American television, didn't pull failing shows. So they were stuck with a prime-time slot – 9 p.m. on Tuesday nights – filled with a series that was tanking in the ratings.

At least Rory could ship its troubled star off to Tuscany to lie low for the rest of the run. That was the deal: six weeks in Chianti, holing up in Rory's villa. Staying away from the UK, in total retreat from the media. No interviews, no phone calls or emails to anyone who might pass information on to the eager, waiting press. Rory had already spoken to Devon's manager, editor and publicist, and they were all in agreement; Devon had chosen to go against their advice and appear on *1-2-3 Cook* – and look how that had turned out. Now it was time to do things their way.

She could have taken Matt, of course. Ironically, Matt's ankle injury was perfectly timed for travelling with his wife to Italy and holing up in a luxurious villa, nothing to do but eat, drink, and work on his tan in the late spring sun. But Devon didn't want Matt with her; she didn't want anyone with her. Not her husband, not even Gary, who would have happily come along. Matt had been in pieces when he'd heard how long she was planning to be in Tuscany, all alone.

'I've got nothing to do here, Dev!' he'd pleaded. 'I can't train, I can't do anything but stay off my ankle. I'm just on the sofa, watching rubbish TV, hoping the lads'll come round and cheer me up a bit.'

Devon looked at her big, handsome husband, sprawled on the sofa, ankle elevated, the expression on his face agonized in a way she had never seen before. She knew it wasn't due to physical pain; Matt had been crocked up many times during their relationship, and he'd been nothing but good-tempered when injured. Besides, he had plenty of painkillers if his ankle was that bad.

Her guess was that Matt was going through a really bad time at the prospect of his rugby career being over. From what she'd understood, this ankle blowout might well mean that he couldn't play again professionally; no team could risk one of their stars suddenly taking a header because his ankle went out from under him. She felt for Matt, she really did. It was one thing to know, as a sports-man heading into his thirties, that his body was gradually declining from its physical peak, and that his days on the rugby field were numbered. It was quite another to be tearing down the field one moment, about to score a try, a British rugby hero, and the next to find yourself washed up on your living-room sofa like an enormous beached whale, your occupation effectively gone.

She'd knelt down beside him, taking a deep breath. 'I need to be by myself,' she'd said hopelessly. 'It's not about you. It really isn't. It's all about me.'

'Dev – when *isn't* it about you?' Matt had said, rearing up against the back of the sofa. 'I've been telling you for months that we're in trouble! We haven't had sex in so long I can't remember when – now, with this diet, you're sleeping in the spare room, so we don't even get to cuddle! I'm lonely, and I need to be with my wife! For better, for worse, remember?'

Devon buried her head against the leather sofa. 'I'm just so miserable,' she said against its side. 'I've totally fucked up. I hate myself at the moment, I really do.'

'But that's what I'm for!' Matt leaned over to stroke the top of her head, clumsily, because it was hard for him to move with his ankle propped up on two pillows. 'I'm your husband – you're supposed to lean on me when you need me.' He cleared his throat. 'And Dev, I need you now, really badly.' His voice was hoarse. 'Things have been . . . I've been in a really weird state . . .' He took a deep breath. 'I need my wife,' he continued in heartfelt tones. 'I really do. Let's go away together. We don't need to go to Italy – we can go anywhere we want. What about the Maldives? We've always wanted to go there!'

'Do you know how much that'd cost, the Maldives for six weeks?' Devon had said, raising her head and looking at her husband. 'My series is a total failure, my book's not selling – God knows when you'll be able to play again – this is *definitely* not the time for us to go spending huge amounts of money . . .'

'*Dev*! It's our *marriage* I'm talking about!' Matt had lunged for her hand, and managed to get hold of it, clinging onto her so tightly he ground the small bones in her palm against one another. 'How can you put a price on that? Dev, if you can't turn to me when you're in trouble – and you won't comfort me when I'm all messed up – what kind of marriage *is* this?'

He looked haunted. And big, handsome, rugged Matt was the last man in the world who was suited to that expression; it would have been much better on a gaunt, high-cheekboned French actor, with three days' stubble, pulling on a Gauloises and staring off into the distance, remembering the last woman who had broken his heart. Matt's craggy features, his clear blue eyes, were made to be happy, carefree; seeing him so miserable, so broken-down, drove home to Devon very powerfully how badly she was behaving. How much she had messed things up.

But all she did was pull her hand away from him and stand up. 'I just don't like myself,' she said in a small, pathetic voice. 'I *despise* myself. And I don't . . .' She swallowed. It was really hard to get the words out, especially because they sounded so pathetic. 'I don't want to be around someone who'd want to be with me.'

'But Dev – where the hell does that leave us?' Matt sounded ready to explode with frustration. 'What the hell am I supposed to do when my wife says something like that to me?'

'I don't know!' Devon jumped up, barely able to meet her husband's eyes. She was already in her coat; she pulled it around her, realizing with a degree of relief that since the egg-only crash diet, she was just about able to fasten the buttons.

'Also, you're leaving me stuck here!' Matt added, grabbing his crutch. 'I can barely get up the bloody stairs to get to bed, or make myself something to eat – what kind of wife leaves her husband by himself in this state?'

He was frowning now, his forehead deeply lined, grimacing as he managed to get the crutch wedged under his armpit enough to swing first one leg, then the other, off the sofa. Devon didn't know whether he was intending to try to come with her; she practically bolted for the door.

'A really bad one!' she yelled over her shoulder, tears starting to form in her eyes as she hauled the suitcases she had stacked in the hall to the front door. 'A really bad wife! I know I'm a terrible wife! I know I shouldn't be leaving you like this! I feel like shit, OK?'

'It's all about you, Devon,' Matt said sadly, managing to hobble across the living room in time to see her bumping one of the suitcases down the front steps to the waiting cab. 'You don't say "us" – you say "I". All the time.'

He was absolutely right. And Devon couldn't deny it. Pulling up the handle of her carry-on case as the cabbie stacked the rest of the suitcases into the ticking vehicle, she paused on the steps for a moment, looking back at her husband, who was leaning half on his crutch, half against the living-room doorjamb. It was as if she were staring at him from a very long distance away, not just the width of their hallway.

Matt's such a good husband. But maybe a good husband's the last thing I need.

'Look,' she suggested, at least trying to deal with the fact that she was abandoning him when he was injured. 'Deeley's downstairs – she's living here rent-free, and as far as I know all she's doing is taking Pilates classes and going shopping. Why don't you ask her up here to help you out, give you a hand with stuff? She could have the spare room.'

'*Jesus*, Dev!' Matt exploded, the strong cords of his neck popping out in frustration, his forehead creasing into a mass of lines. He banged his crutch on the floor for emphasis. 'What the hell is *wrong* with you? You don't give a shit about me, do you? You haven't bothered to take a moment to *see* what's going on with me – what I'm trying to tell you!'

'I'm sorry,' Devon said feebly. 'I'm really sorry, Matt.'

He heaved the longest, deepest sigh she had ever heard. It was only when he eventually spoke again that Devon realized he'd been waiting for something. For her to say or do something that seemed incredibly obvious to him, but simply hadn't occurred to her.

'Just go, Dev,' he said very sadly. 'You're already out the door. Just go and do whatever you're going to do.'

And she had.

Devon had reached the top of the Italian passport control queue. Pushing her sunglasses up onto the crown of her head, so her face was visible, she stepped forward and handed her passport to the smartly uniformed man behind the Perspex screen. Taking her in, he flashed a huge, appreciative smile as he looked down to her photograph and up again to its original.

'*Benvenuta in Italia, signora,*' he said, sliding the passport back to her. '*Veramente, molto benvenuta.*'

Devon's Italian was extremely basic, mostly limited to restaurant vocabulary, but she knew that he was saying 'Welcome to Italy', and she smiled back at him charmingly enough that he swivelled to watch her walk round his booth to the luggage belts before, reluctantly, returning his attention to summon forward the next person in the queue.

It was the same with the customs officials, lounging against the wall, looking as bored as the German shepherd dog lying at their feet; on catching sight of Devon, doing her best to manoeuvre a trolley piled high with matching suitcases past them, they brightened visibly, standing up, their hands automatically rising to straighten their caps, staring at her blatantly while muttering comments on her figure, walk and – being Italian – her clothes to each other as she went by.

In England, this would have been highly annoying. In Italy, for some reason, it wasn't. Devon had been to Italy several times, but always with Matt; this was the first time she had travelled here alone, so she had never experienced before the full surge of attention that its heterosexual men directed to unaccompanied women they considered worthy of attention. To her surprise, Devon realized that she definitely liked it. Maybe it was because she didn't feel treated like an object. They weren't just staring at her boobs or her bum; they took in the whole of her, from head to toe, and a definite part of their assessment, she could tell, was how she was dressed, how she presented herself.

Which is actually really nice, she thought, wrestling the trolley towards the automatic doors at the end of the customs corridor; it kept trying to veer left, rather than straight ahead. *I mean, if you make an effort, they notice. It's every woman's dream.*

Rory had said that she would be met at the airport by Gianni, the husband who, with his wife Laura, ran Villa Clara for him; they lived in a cottage down the drive, and managed the grounds and the house. Rory left a car in Italy which Gianni would drive to the airport to collect him; Devon could use it when she was there to get around. She paused a little way through the doors, looking around her. There were no barriers, just a motley crowd of people staring expectantly past her, waiting eagerly for their loved one to come through the doors. A few men in shirtsleeves were holding up signs with names written on them in black pen, but even allowing for misspelling, there was no way that she could make 'Devon McKenna' out of any of the names on offer.

Devon's heart sank. Gianni hadn't turned up after all. She'd jumped on a flight at the last minute, paid an extortionate price to Meridiana, the only airline that flew to Florence, which was closer to Villa Clara than Pisa; maybe, despite Rory's assurances, Gianni simply hadn't had enough notice. She was fumbling in her bag for her mobile phone, aware that she was blocking the way out but not sure where she should be heading, when a man's hand landed next to hers on the bar of the trolley, pushed it down, and started to move her firmly through the crowd towards the exit doors ahead.

'*Madonna*,' he said cheerfully, 'this is a communist *carrello*, eh? He only wants to go left.'

Devon jerked back, grabbing her phone tightly in case he were an unusually well-spoken mugger.

'Who are you?' she said suspiciously, glancing at him. First she saw the light blue shirtsleeve, rolled up to mid-forearm. There was a dull gold bracelet on his wrist, its heavy links snagging a little in the dark curly hairs. Rearing back, she saw a head of curly hair, thick wild ringlets, almost like an Afro. He wasn't much taller than her, but he walked so confidently the crowd cleared for them and the trolley as if by magic.

'You are Mees Devon, *non é vero?*' he said, his entire attention focussed on piloting the trolley. 'I am here to take you to Villa Clara.'

Devon started to say something, but he was still talking, his light tenor voice rising and falling in cadences, almost as if he were singing.

'And Mees Devon . . .' they exited the flight terminal, and Devon blinked in the sunlight before sliding her sunglasses back onto her nose, 'you are welcome to Italy.'

He turned to smile at her, and Devon got her first glance of his face. But his features weren't the first thing she noticed.

Wow, Gianni is so hairy! she thought, almost giggling to herself. His narrow dark eyes were framed by long, curly eyelashes; his chin was stubbled as heavily as if he hadn't shaved in days; and the cloud of curly ringlets that floated around his head was like something out of a Renaissance painting. It almost, but not completely, distracted from his nose, which dominated his face: aquiline, with a magnificent hook, the famous Roman profile which featured on so many historic statues of generals or emperors.

He does carry it well, she had to admit. *And, to be fair, the hair does balance the nose . . . Still, if he has a sister with a nose like that – well, I bet she had it fixed a long time ago.*

'The car is over there,' he said airily, waving his hand ahead of them, as he bumped the trolley into the road and started pushing it along the centre line, oblivious to a taxi behind him honking crossly.

'Um, I think you're supposed to walk on the pavement,' Devon said, hesitating for a moment, then stepping down to follow her suitcases.

Gianni waved his hand again, dismissively this time. 'In Italy,' he said, drawing the 'I' of Italy out so long the word sounded like 'Eeeetaly', 'we design the roads very well and the pavements very badly.'

Devon waited, but that seemed to be all he was going to say on the subject. The taxi honked again; Gianni, without slowing his pace, waved his hand again behind him, this time with an unmistakable gesture.

'Won't he get cross?' she asked nervously, glancing behind her at the taxi, whose bumper was barely two feet away from them. The driver scowled at her.

'Of course! It means nothing,' Gianni said cheerfully.

He bumped the trolley across another road, over a concrete walkway, and down the other side, to the short-stay parking lot; after a brief but vigorous argument with the official at the ticket kiosk, he returned with a validated ticket, frowning deeply.

'*Ma vaff*',' he muttered. '*Che ladri!*' He glanced at Devon as he pushed the trolley towards a battered old Golf. 'Thieves,' he said darkly. 'All thieves, all corrupt. Italy is a very sad place.'

'You don't look sad,' Devon ventured, which made him burst out laughing. He looked, she noticed, just like a little boy when he laughed. A very hairy little boy with a very big nose.

'No!' he said, his eyes slanting and bright. 'No, you are quite right, Mees Devon! I am not sad! In fact, I am very happy!' He pronounced his 'h's with great care, as if it were a very difficult task. 'It is a sunny day, I am with a beautiful woman – how can I not be happy!'

He beeped open the Golf and started throwing Devon's expensive suitcases into the boot with a brio that made her wince.

'And now,' he said, opening the passenger door and bowing to her, 'I drive you to Chianti!'

The seat of the Golf was saggy, the plastic dashboard chipped. A Magic Tree in the shape of a pineapple hung from the rear-view mirror, looking as old and battered as the car. Gianni fired up the engine, hit the button to turn on the CD player and shot out of the parking space in what felt like one continuous movement. Devon squealed, reaching frantically for her seatbelt.

'*Ah si, bene,*' Gianni said, glancing over at her. 'Is the law now, the belt. I forget always.'

He fastened his own seatbelt, rolled down his window, extracted a packet of Marlboro Red from the breast pocket of his shirt, and held it out courteously to her, all the time firing the car around a roundabout, through an amber light and into a stream of traffic.

'No, no, thank you,' Devon said faintly, cringing back in her seat. Some sort of Italian rock music was playing, a man with a very loud, hoarse voice yelling about something that sounded very important over the thump of drums and guitars.

Gianni tipped a cigarette into his mouth, clicked down the car lighter and settled his left arm comfortably onto the open window embrasure, squinting happily into the sun.

'This is Vasco Rossi,' he said, gesturing at the CD. 'A very famous Italian singer. You know him?'

Devon shook her head, which made Gianni turn enquiringly to her, not having heard a response.

'No!' she practically screamed. 'No, I don't know him! *Please* keep your eyes on the road!'

Gianni laughed in the most amiable way possible and leaned further towards her.

'He is the most famous Italian singer,' he informed her. 'This song, it is about a man alone with a woman. She is crying, and he tells her to stop.'

The cigarette was hanging precariously out of the corner of his mouth; Devon squirmed back in her seat to avoid having any ash spilled on her.

'*Please!*' she said, in total panic now. 'The road!' She flailed her arms towards it, indicating where he should be looking.

'Oh, I drive these roads since I am a little boy,' Gianni said breezily, still barely glancing towards the road ahead. 'I can drive them *con la benda*. How do you say that?'

He took both hands off the wheel and put them over his eyes to pantomime what he meant. Devon screamed, which didn't faze him in the slightest.

'It's a blindfold!' she shrieked. 'That's how you say it!'

'*Grazie*,' he said airily, replacing one hand on the wheel and spinning it to send them towards one of the motorway tollbooths.

He squealed to a halt in front of the barrier, pulled out a ticket, muttered curses under his breath at how long the bar was taking to lift, and shot away again when it was only halfway up, barely avoiding smashing into it with the roof of the car.

'Look,' Devon said, furious now. 'Rory pays you, right? He's your employer, and I'm his guest, so you have to do what I say, and I'm telling you to slow down! OK?'

Gianni shot up the entry ramp to the motorway, nipped across two lanes, straight across the path of two huge lorries, and settled into the fast lane.

'*Certo, signora,*' he said affably. '*Ecco!*'

He took his foot momentarily off the accelerator, bringing the speed down from 140 to 130 kilometres per hour. Behind them, a BMW flashed its lights and honked impatiently, yelling, '*Ma va a cacare!*' Gianni twisted the wheel, shot in front of a lorry in the middle lane, and gave the BMW the finger out of the window as it whipped past, doing at least 180.

'What's the speed limit here?' Devon asked in a tiny voice.

'*Cosa?*' Gianni asked blankly. 'I don't understand.'

'Never mind,' Devon muttered.

Too frightened to look at the road any more, she pulled down the plastic visor and slid open the mirror cover; the mirror was scratched and bent, but she could see herself well enough as she untied her headscarf, shook out her hair, and speared her fingers through her curls to rearrange them. Then she picked up her big silver Hayden-Harnett bag and rummaged through it to pull out her transparent Clinique cosmetics case. Reapplying make-up always calmed her down, but that was impossible in a car with a bad suspension bumping at high speed along a motorway. Instead, she extracted a purse vial of Marc Jacobs' Lola, popped off the top, and sprayed herself liberally with the rich perfume: the scent of rose, fuschia, peony and geranium filled the car. Normally she would have thought it very rude to spray herself with such a strong perfume in a comparatively enclosed space, but Gianni hadn't asked her permission before he lit up his stinky cigarette, had he?

He sniffed the air appreciatively. 'Mmm!' he said. '*Molto buono! Molto feminile*,' he added approvingly. 'Very feminine. That's the right word, yes?'

'Yes!' Devon said quickly, before he turned to look at her again.

'A woman should be feminine,' Gianni said, whipping the Golf sharply left, across another lane, to take the motorway exit. 'A man should be a man and a woman should be a woman. You, Mees Devon,' he added, looking at her as he fired the car at one of the exit tollbooths and squealed to a halt mere inches from the barrier, 'are very feminine. This is a very good thing.'

Devon was about to tell him off for making personal comments when she realized that he wasn't even listening to her; he was chatting with the man at the tollbooth, a big guy with a shaved head who was giggling at something Gianni had just said.

'This is Aladino,' Gianni said to Devon, gesturing at the man. 'He lives in our village, Greve. He is very funny at parties.'

'*Ciao!*' Aladino said, bending to get a good look at Devon. 'Ooh! *Bellissima!*'

Gianni said something which made Aladdino laugh even harder; he handed Gianni his change and called to Devon, '*Ciao, bella! A presto!*'

'He says see you soon,' Gianni informed her as he gunned the Golf again. 'Greve is a very friendly place.'

Oh great, Devon thought. *What, I'm supposed to hang out with tollbooth attendants and caretakers while I'm here?* She knew this was snobbish of her, and she was ashamed of it. But she had grown up in such poverty, such reduced circumstances, had struggled so hard to better herself and put those days behind her that she felt as if it would be a huge step backwards to find herself making friends with guys who collected motorway tolls, or picked other people's guests up from the airport for a living.

'Are you hungry?' Gianni asked, as he wove the Golf at high speed down a series of back roads. 'We can stop for a little *aperitivo*, if you would like.'

Devon did want a drink and a snack, but she had no intention of spending a moment longer with Rory's annoying caretaker than she had to.

'No, thank you,' she said stiffly, as the car whipped round a curve at terrifying speed and then shot over a pretty little stone bridge.

'You are tired from your flight,' Gianni said, unabashed. 'Laura has put food and wine for you in the house. And tomorrow she will come to ask you if you want to go with her to the village, to see the shops.'

'I look forward to meeting her,' Devon said pointedly, to indicate that Gianni was flirting with her in an inappropriate manner, considering that he had a wife at home.

The car jerked and then corrected itself; Devon grabbed the bottom of the seat in panic. The singer called Vasco Rossi was howling now. Gianni tapped another cigarette out of the packet and lit it up.

'You will like Laura very much,' he said cheerfully. 'She, like you, is very beautiful.'

'Oh good,' Devon said sourly, rolling down her own window to ventilate the car. She had to admit that the view was exquisite; she had been to Tuscany before, but only on a whistle-stop tour of Florence and Siena. She had never been into the countryside before.

'This is not the pretty part,' Gianni, who seemed to have a disconcerting ability to read her thoughts without even looking at her, informed her. 'This is the industrial road, down in the valley. Here we make *cotto* – terracotta – and press the oil. That is very smelly. It is nice to do it not so close to where most people live. Up in the hills,' he took both hands off the wheel to gesture expansively, 'it is very pretty. Much more than this.' He smiled at her. 'I think you want to arrive at the villa quickly, so I take the fast road. It is very straight.'

Devon, who was almost getting whiplash from Gianni's driving, could only be grateful that he had taken what he considered the less curvy road. They passed through a charming-looking village, low white-painted buildings with red-tiled roofs, bustling squares and several bars and restaurants: one bar, called Va! Va!, had little wrought-iron tables on the pavement, by the roadside, with people sitting at them, chatting and smoking. Gianni braked to a screaming halt, leaned across Devon to wave at everyone, yelled something at a table occupied by a dark-skinned man with a thick head of hair and a skinny girl in tight trousers, high heels and an entire eye pencil's-worth of black liner round her eyes, yelled abuse at the drivers behind him who were honking because he was blocking the road, and sped away again, throwing his cigarette out of the window as he went.

'It is a very nice bar,' he said to Devon. 'That is the owner, Remsi. He is Turkish. Very nice. Also they have *calcetto* – football on the table. Do you play?'

'No,' Devon said coldly, as the car zipped out the other side of the village.

'I will teach you,' he offered.

'Lovely,' Devon said even more coldly. 'We can all go to the bar with your wife.'

The Golf bumped over a bridge, jerked hard left and up a dirt road so steep that Devon gasped in shock.

'*Perfetto!*' Gianni said, laughter in his voice. 'You, me and my wife – we will all go to play *calcetto!* Very nice. Oh, *guarda* – look! A *fagiano!*'

A cock pheasant rose, whirring, from the side of the road. Devon could barely look, though; on the far side of the car, the hill dropped away so sharply she was terrified. The wheels were bouncing over huge potholes, she was being tossed from side to side like a boat in choppy water; silver-grey olive trees and twisted vines thick with bright green leaves fell away on each side of the narrow dirt road. They tilted up a wide avenue lined with thick oaks and pines, and at the top more vine groves drew a gasp of appreciation from her, because each was planted with a rose bush at the end, which were blooming richly in the warm weather.

'The roses are lovely,' she exclaimed, unguarded for a moment.

'They warn us if the mildew is coming to the grapes,' Franco said, bouncing the Golf between the groves, past a field of walnut trees, the green grass thick with bright red poppies. 'Also, they are beautiful. You like roses?'

'Who doesn't?' Devon said frigidly again, back to warning him off flirting with her.

The car turned between two big stone pillars, up a winding gravel drive, and her heart lifted. It positively soared as she took in Villa Clara, a large, elegant house painted pale cream, sitting in a nest of stacked green ornamental gardens, a small fountain playing in the centre of the little lawn in front of the villa.

'*Eccoci!*' Gianni said, spraying gravel everywhere as he pulled the Golf to a halt next to the arched wooden front door below a wrought-iron balcony. 'Welcome!'

He lugged her bags out of the boot and carried them into the house; for a lean, wiry man, he was unexpectedly strong.

Well, he does work in the fields all day, I suppose, Devon reflected, following him up the stone staircase, very much amused by the fact that his shirt was tucked neatly into his jeans. *Very Italian – no English man would dress like that. He does have a nice bum. But I expect that's all the manual labour.*

'Rory, he stays in there,' Gianni said, gesturing to a high door as they emerged into a stunning anteroom with pale salmon walls and an elaborately tiled floor. 'But you do not sleep with Rory, no?'

'No!' Devon said furiously. 'I'm a married woman!'

Oh God, Matt – what am I going to do? she thought with a deep pang of guilt.

'And your husband? He comes with you?' Gianni said, lugging the bags into a huge, white-painted room, its large bed made up, neat piles of stacked towels resting on a wooden antique trunk at its foot. 'It is a big bed! Room for a husband!'

He grinned at her as he dropped her bags on the stone floor.

'He has to stay in London,' Devon snapped, fishing in her handbag. Gianni might be unspeakably annoying, but she still had to tip him. 'Here.' She handed him a ten-euro note.

Gianni's thick eyebrows shot up till they disappeared behind the mass of curly hair over his forehead. He shoved the note in his jeans pocket: then he took her still-outstretched hand, bent over it, and planted a warm kiss in the palm.

'*Molte, molte grazie, signora,*' he said softly, looking up at her, still holding her hand, his thumb lightly stroking her palm. '*Ci vedremo presto, lo prometto.*'

Devon was riveted to the spot. Her jaw dropped. She stood there, amazed, as Gianni dropped her hand, stepped round her carry-on case and strode out of the room. She listened to his footsteps crossing the tiled antechamber and running lightly down the stairs, the front door slamming behind him; then she ran over to the window and peered out to see him walking across the drive, presumably back to the cottage she could see across the lawns, the cottage he shared with his wife. His curly hair bounced in the breeze, his slim figure moved easily as he tapped another cigarette from the packet. He was whistling; she could hear it clearly.

Oh my God – I'm watching the caretaker walk away. I'm watching the caretaker's bum walk away. I can't take my eyes off it.

Gianni didn't even turn round to see if she was looking at him. He had to be the most confident, annoying, self-centred man she had ever met in her life. The first man ever to pay her compliments while simultaneously absolutely ignoring her requests. He'd disregarded half the things she said, she realized. He'd ridden roughshod over her. And then he'd kissed her hand – not even her mouth! Her hand! – and held it for a moment, and that had been the single sexiest thing that had ever happened to her in her life.

She hadn't even realized she was attracted to him until that moment. And now she couldn't think about anything else but him – Rory's caretaker. His married caretaker. Who chain-smoked, drove like a maniac, had a beautiful wife, and who had looked up at her with his slanted dark eyes, for that long moment holding her hand, as if he was longing to do a series of unbelievably filthy things to her. All of which, God help her, she would let him do without breathing a word of protest. Things she had never done with anyone.

Devon sank down onto the wide, soft mattress, staring straight ahead of her, but unseeingly, the elegant framed watercolours of fruit and vegetables hung on the white walls completely invisible.

My God. If I feel like this just because he kissed my hand, I'll go to pieces if he kisses me anywhere else!

What the hell am I going to do?

Deeley

*I*t was grey outside again the next morning and raining, but Deeley didn't care. In fact, she preferred it. The low dark clouds made her feel cut off from the rest of the world, reminding her that she was on a small island off the coast of France, and that nobody knew where she was. It was strangely comforting being marooned in five-star luxury, in a suite as plush as the inside of an expensive jewellery box; thick carpets, heavy curtains, velvet armchairs, silk cushions, all in rich tones of chocolate and chartreuse and plum. She had come back to it yesterday afternoon after her spa visit, put on her silk pyjamas, and curled up on the big sofa, watching TV and dining on room service in solitary splendour. This morning, she'd swapped the dinner tray for the breakfast one; she was eating more than she ever had, steak and fries, eggs Florentine, toasted muffins, food she had barely touched in her years of living in LA.

It was lovely. She'd forgotten how delicious potatoes were. She'd had a big glass of claret too last night. Her head was a little heavy, but who cared; she could crawl back to bed for as long as she needed to.

Or she could go for a long walk on the beach in the rain.

She stood up, pushing back the breakfast tray, and walked over to the long wraparound window of the sitting room of her suite, staring out at the view. Bare wet sands and grey sea still surrounded

Elizabeth Castle, whipped by the wind, white horses riding the waves; it was perfect. Superimposed on the wild view was her own face, her unbrushed hair falling around it, her eyes huge and dark. It looked like something out of a film, a melancholy European film with subtitles, where the heroine did nothing but walk on the beach and think about the man she couldn't have, the man she absolutely, positively had to stay away from for the rest of her life.

Deeley heaved a deep sigh. That made her situation sound romantic, when actually she had enough good sense to know that it wasn't. Fancying the pants off your sister's husband was not some version of tragic, forbidden love; it was actually more like a sort of horrible curse.

Especially when he fancied you back.

You can't think about this, she told herself firmly. *You just can't. Beep! Banned! Banned subject!* Turning away from the window, she stripped off, pulled on her walking clothes and dashed out of the room, grabbing her iPod as she went. *No gloomy music. Nothing romantic. Nothing sexy. Shit, what does that leave me?* She ended up tramping across the sand to Paramore, four albums' worth, right from one side of the curving bay to the other and back again along the esplanade, blown back and forth by the strong sea breeze. By the time she reached the Grand Jersey once again it was hours later, and her legs were as tired as if she'd done a Pilates class with nothing but jumpboard exercises.

But Deeley still wasn't done. *I need to be so tired I can't think about anything*, she knew instinctively. *So tired that all I can do is sleep.* She went back to the suite, changed into workout clothes, and hit the gym in the spa; having walked for hours, she concentrated on upper body exercises, shoulder presses, tricep dips, press-ups and plank holds until her arms and shoulders were aching as much as her legs. Then, grimly, she knocked out two hundred crunch sit-ups. Thank God for lifts: without one, she couldn't have made it back up to her room afterwards. She showered, fell into bed and slept for hours, utterly exhausted.

By the time she woke again, it was dark outside, the view even more beautiful by night. Lights glittered down the esplanade, illu-minated the façade of the castle in the sea, wrapped around the seafront houses that rose above the bay; it was enchanting. And the lights called to Deeley. She sat up, rubbing her eyes, the room dark, staring out into the evening; light wisps of cloud scudded across the night sky, stars bright in the velvety black, a small curve of moon just visible in the distance.

I can't stay shut up here moping forever, she thought suddenly, jumping out of bed. *And I really doubt that the person who tried to push me in front of the bus has followed me to Jersey to have a go at poisoning my cocktail in the hotel bar . . .*

By now, Deeley had made her mind up that the shove at King's Cross Station must, as her rescuer and the woman next to her had assumed, have been some random maniac. It did happen; in her short time back in London, she'd read about a couple of released mental patients stabbing people in shopping centres, or on train platforms.

And my idea of dressing down isn't exactly London style. I know I look rich-bitch and glitzy compared with most people here. Someone probably took against me, someone who thought I needed teaching a lesson . . .

It can't have been personal. I barely know anyone in London, not enough for someone to want to hurt me that badly.

Apart from Devon, of course, Deeley reflected grimly. Devon would have a very good reason to want to injure, maim or kill her younger sister, if she knew what had gone on between her husband and Deeley just forty-eight hours ago. But the push into traffic had happened before Matt and Deeley had had that terrible, wonderful make-out session on the sofa, and as far as Deeley was aware, Devon had never had psychic precognitive skills.

Besides, she was in Manchester, getting ready for her show. No, it couldn't possibly have been Devon.

Logic dictated that that push into traffic must have been some sort of freak incident, never to be repeated. And logic also told Deeley that she couldn't hide out indefinitely in a hotel suite, even if it was one of the loveliest she had ever been in. Defiantly forcing herself off the bed, she went over to the big walk-in cupboard and pulled out the simple little black DKNY dress she had brought with her.

Let's see what kind of cocktails the hotel bar on this little island can drum up . . .

But as soon as she stepped into the champagne lounge, her jaw dropped. She hadn't made much effort with her appearance, just pulled on her LBD and a pair of heels, brushed her hair and added simple make-up. And yet again, she'd got it completely wrong. It was Saturday night and the bar was hopping with young, sexy partygoers dressed to the nines. Deeley was elegantly understated, by minimalist LA standards, but Jersey, clearly, did not do minimalism at all. Whoever had decorated the champagne lounge had been much more influenced by baroque and rococo; if Deeley's suite were like a jewellery box for an aristocrat, rich, discreet and opulent, then the champagne lounge was a jewellery box made for Drag Queen Barbie.

It was pink, silver and black: suede, velvet and glass. The bar was a curve of Italian silvered mosaic tiles; behind it, a huge cut-glass mirror frame wrapped around a gigantic TV screen showing *Casablanca*, bottles of bright liquor glittering in front of Ingrid Bergman's iconic face. Black glass chandeliers hung from the high ceiling, their pendants glittering dully in the soft, enticing lighting; suede fuschia sofas curved around circular silver tables with ice buckets in the centre, filled with champagne bottles. And the clientele seemed to consist entirely of very curvaceous, very blonde young women in dresses as short and tight as their heels were high, and their smart, aftershaved, very appreciative male escorts.

I'm definitely underdressed, Deeley thought with amusement, surveying the scene before her. *I should have worn one of my Hervé Léger bandage frocks.* Deeley wasn't intimidated. She had attended the Emmys and the Golden Globes, and the MTV awards in LA; she'd been photographed on countless red carpets and hobnobbed with TV and movie stars. It had all been totally superficial, naturally; she'd been too sensible to think for a moment that the actresses whose mansions she went to for charity brunches, who posed cheek to cheek with her, smiling widely, were her friends in any way, or even remembered her name for more than a minute (if they'd known it in the first place).

Still, having spent five years battling for attention with some of the most competitive, cut-throat women in the world, it was child's play for Deeley to enter a bar on her own. She picked her way through the lively mass of beautiful people, enjoying the experience of having no one waiting for her; and she was quite happy, too, to wait in the crowd at the bar until she could make her way to the front and be served. Men glanced at her, but beautiful though Deeley was, by Jersey standards she was almost dowdy; clearly, they preferred a girl who was showier, flashier, sparkling from head to toe, throwing her head back and laughing to show every single whitened tooth in her brightly lipsticked mouth.

So when someone tapped her on the shoulder, she was genuinely surprised. She swivelled, as much as she could in the press of bodies, to see the man from the spa, dressed in a very smart pale grey suit and bright blue shirt, smiling at her with great enthusiasm.

'Hey! I looked for you last night,' he said. 'What happened to you?'

'I crashed,' she said simply.

'What?' He cupped his hand to his ear, leaning towards her and Deeley couldn't help smiling. She knew this ploy of old; it was a man's way of getting closer to a woman in a noisy bar, brushing up against you under the pretence of wanting to hear what you had to say, when actually, listening to you was the last thing he was really interested in doing . . .

'I crashed!' she said more loudly, still smiling. 'I was really tired!'

He wasn't pushy. She'd already realized that in the spa; he'd been very cool. He didn't try to touch her any further, put his hand on her to draw her closer to him; instead, he tilted his head away and said, 'I have a table over there by the window – would you like to join me? We might actually be able to hear each other.'

'OK,' she said, as he effortlessly caught the eye of a passing waitress, said something to her, and guided Deeley through the melee to the high windows on the far side of the bar, to a table with a small curved love seat in front of it, facing the windows. The suede was soft beneath her bare thighs, and the view out of the window hypnotic: clouds in the dark sky, the sea at high tide lapping up to the breakwater, lights glimmering around the bay. She couldn't help glancing out, rude though it was not to look at her host, who had sat down next to her, hitching up the knees of his well-cut trousers.

'Stunning, isn't it?' he said, quite unoffended. 'That's why I come here so much. I just can't get enough of this place.'

She looked back at him, taking in once again how handsome he was.

'I'm Jeff,' he said, reaching his hand out to shake hers; it was so sweetly formal that she giggled as she took it.

'Deeley,' she said.

His hand was warm and dry, his handshake light; he didn't try to hold on to it too long. And he hadn't tried to put his hand on the small of her back as they walked across the room, that awful, possessive gesture men used on women they wanted to have sex with. He'd barely touched her, in fact. Already he was way ahead of almost all the men who had tried to pick up Deeley in bars . . .

'Deeley?' Jeff looked at her closely. 'I know this sounds really cheesy, but you look familiar, and that name rings a bell. I'm pretty sure I'd remember meeting you, though. In fact,' he flashed his cheeky grin, 'I'm *completely* sure I'd remember meeting you! Are you a model or something? I'm in image consultancy – I spend much too much time looking at ads . . .'

Deeley shook her head, but he interrupted before she could speak.

'Oh God, that sounded like the worst chat-up line in the world!' he exclaimed, pulling a comical face. 'I'm sorry! Ignore it, OK? That was really naff.'

'No!' Jeff was very easy to talk to and Deeley found herself leaning towards him, patting his knee briefly in reassurance. 'It wasn't naff! You probably saw me in magazines – not the ads, though. I used to date Nicky Shore – he's on *Cooking up Murder*,' she added, in case Nicky's name didn't ring any bells with him. 'We were in all the gossip mags. And then we broke up and now I'm back in London. I did a shoot for *Yes!* a few weeks ago . . .'

She wasn't going to mention her famous sisters; neither of them seemed to want any connection made between Deeley and them at the moment, and besides, the last thing Deeley wanted, for pride's sake, was to be seen as the least well-known of the McKenna siblings.

'Phew!' Jeff said. 'That makes sense. I read a lot of those magazines – well, skim them. I'm in something called trend-mining, believe it or not. We're always looking for the latest hot fashion.' He pulled a self-deprecating face. 'Seeing what celebrities are up to is a big part of that.'

'Oh, I'm not a celebrity!' Deeley said quickly, not wanting him to think she was boasting. 'I just dated one for a while.'

'Two Grand Jerseys!' the waitress said, rounding the edge of the love seat and sliding a tray onto the table; it held two cocktails, an enticing shade of pinky orange, and various little silver bowls of bar snacks. 'And I brought you some nibbles as well, Mr Jackson.'

'I took the liberty of ordering you my favourite cocktail,' Jeff said, picking up one of the champagne flutes and handing it to Deeley. 'It's champagne, limoncello and passion fruit – oh, and Chambord..'

'Ooh, that sounds lovely!' Deeley said eagerly. 'Champagne cocktails are my favourite thing!' She flashed him a gorgeous, flirty smile. 'But didn't you say that I should buy you a drink, for making you wait for the shower? Shouldn't I be paying for this?'

Jeff, who had taken his own glass and was raising it to clink with hers, looked horrified.

'Oh my God, no!' he exclaimed, spilling some of his cocktail. 'I invited you to sit at my table – this is absolutely on my tab. Please!' He realized that Deeley was giggling naughtily. 'You're having me on,' he accused her, his eyes sparkling with amusement. 'You evil woman. You're totally having me on.'

Deeley winked at him and sipped her Grand Jersey.

'Mmn, delicious,' she said appreciatively. 'You have very good taste.'

'I do,' Jeff said, raising his to toast her. 'Very good taste in evil women.'

They sat back, looking at each other as they drank their cocktails, smiling at each other over the top of their champagne flutes. After years in LA, Deeley was very used to meeting someone for the first time in a swimsuit, nearly naked, and then encountering them later, fully dressed, but it was always enjoyable – as long as they had a good body, of course. She was remembering what Jeff had looked like yesterday in his tight red trunks, his smooth dark skin glistening, damp from the sauna. It was a very pleasant image. The day before, he had looked like a sportsman; today he was every inch the creative professional in his impeccably tailored suit.

'So, Deeley,' he said. 'This is a bit of a personal question, but you mentioned that you just broke up with your boyfriend – Nicky, right?'

Deeley nodded, still smiling, still sipping her drink. She was very much enjoying his gradual approach. As far as she was concerned, he was doing everything right. Deeley hadn't thought about Jeff since their meeting in the spa; her mind had been full of what had happened with Matt, and her near fatal collision with a bus at King's Cross. She wasn't arrogant, but she was used to men chatting her up, and she'd taken Jeff's flirtation the day before for a light-hearted moment of fun; it hadn't occurred to her to come down to the bar last night, looking for him.

And this was still light-hearted fun, a stranger in a bar, buying her a cocktail, coming onto her in the nicest way possible. *Much better than sitting in my suite, staring out of the window, trying not to think about Matt . . .*

'I'm single too,' he said easily. 'I have this incredibly pressured job, you know? Endless meetings, lots of travel, always having to spot the next big thing before someone else does.' He flashed her a big smile. 'No complaints – I love my job. But years ago we came here for a seminar, and I fell in love with this whole place. The island, the hotel. It's like being cocooned, you know?'

'That's exactly how I feel,' Deeley agreed, surprised; it was as if he had read her mind.

'You know the spa's completely underground?' he asked, summoning the waitress with a deft wave of his hand, indicating that they needed two more cocktails. 'That's why it feels so . . . sheltered, you know? It's a complete refuge. I mean, the view's fantastic, but I go in there, work out, get a massage, a facial, soak in the Jacuzzi . . .' He grinned at her.

'I know *exactly* what you're going to say,' Deeley said with dignity, 'so you don't need to bother—'

'Have a nice shower with essential oils, as long as some random girl isn't hogging it, of course—'

'I *said* you didn't need to bother!'

'Every few months, I just need to recharge my batteries,' he was saying, laughing now. 'So I get away from it all here. Fantastic food, great cocktails, walks on the beach—'

'Picking up girls in the spa . . .' Deeley added, setting down her empty flute.

Deeley was definitely flirting back now; she uncrossed her legs and slowly recrossed them the other way, knowing that Jeff would be unable not to look at them. Her long, golden, toned legs were one of her major assets, and the pretty little black kitten-heel sandals, tied at the ankle with fine suede strips, showed them off to perfection.

'I don't actually expect you to believe this,' Jeff said, earning major points by not staring at her legs with his tongue hanging out, but returning his gaze to her face, 'but I don't come here to pick up girls. No offence to the local lovelies.' He glanced over at the big table in front of the mosaic bar, which was brimming with platinum blondes. 'They're very pretty girls, and dressed to kill, but my tastes are less footballers' wives, and more – well, more *Vogue* model.'

The waitress arrived with their new round of drinks, and Jeff raised his glass to Deeley again. She clinked with him.

'I'm flattered,' she said demurely.

'That was the idea,' Jeff said, waggling his eyebrows at her comically. 'So, Deeley, what's a *Vogue* model lookalike doing by herself in Jersey? Getting away from it all too? And why here?' He looked a little embarrassed. 'I must admit, I asked the front desk about you. They were pretty discreet, but I'm a regular, and they did tell me you were here on your own.'

Deeley nodded, giving him more points for admitting he'd been interested enough to ask after her.

'*Definitely* getting away from it all,' she said in heartfelt tones, drinking half of her second cocktail in one go and coughing a little on the bubbles.

'Oh, hey,' Jeff leaned forward, his knee touching hers. 'Something happen? You don't sound good.'

And then almost all of it came spilling out: Deeley left out anything to do with Matt, of course; she didn't mention Bill, or even the backstory to her arrangement with Nicky . . . But there was enough, she realized with considerable surprise, more than enough to be upsetting, even leaving out the worst parts. Her 'break-up', and being ousted unexpectedly from her lovely life in LA. Her return to London, and the discovery that she wasn't exactly welcomed back with open arms by her sisters. Her trip to see her childhood home – well, one of them – the weird feelings it had induced; the push in front of the bus at King's Cross, and then her dash to the airport, which she made sound as if it had happened directly afterwards.

'Jesus!' Jeff, who had been listening very sympathetically, exclaimed at this. 'You must have been really shaken up!'

Deeley nodded so fervently she nearly spilled what was left of her drink; Jeff took it and put it on the table. Then, somehow, he was holding her hand, and she was holding his right back, more grateful than she could say for the reassurance of human contact.

'Hey,' Jeff said gently, leaning towards her a little.

Light gleamed on his smooth scalp, glossy red-brown, like a sculpture carved from cherrywood. Deeley found herself reaching her free hand up to touch it; his skin was incredibly soft, like oiled suede. Jeff closed his eyes as she stroked his head, her fingers reaching round his head, cupping it; he butted his scalp against her palm like a cat being caressed. She'd never been with a man with a shaved head before, and the sensation was new and delightful.

Her hand slid down to his neck as Jeff's fingers closed tighter around hers, pulling her a little closer to him so that as his head lifted, he was near enough to her that his lips found hers. His mouth was wide and soft, like a ripe plum, and he kissed her as lightly as a man can kiss a woman; she felt his warm breath on her lips, the tip of his tongue, so lightly that it made her want more. Made her want him. She drew him fractionally towards her, her mouth opening under his, her eyes fluttering closed, relishing the physical sensations that were flooding through her as smoothly and easily as sliding into the warm bubbling water of the Jacuzzi in the hotel spa. Jeff's hand was on her shoulder, stroking her skin, his fingers running up and down her neck, and she murmured her appreciation of what he was doing, how lovely it felt.

Kissing, Deeley thought dreamily, *is one of my favourite things in the world. I could do this all night long* . . .

Jeff's lips, his tongue, tasted as sweet as the cocktail, of passion fruit and the raspberry Chambord. Deeley wasn't used to drinking that much; LA was not a big drinking town. People there drove themselves to bars and clubs, and unless you were a drug-addled starlet, you didn't want a DUI. Besides, everyone had early morning starts; 6 a.m. workout sessions were the norm. Nicky and Sean, who were very into clean-living, often trained even earlier.

One and a half glasses of champagne, laced heavily with liqueur, was making Deeley's head swim deliciously. She licked the champagne traces off Jeff's full lips with the tip of her tongue, as delicately as the cat she'd compared Jeff to, making him grip her more tightly as he kissed her harder, his arms wrapping around her, pulling her along the suede love seat, her bare thigh, below the hem of her dress, rubbing against the fabric of his trousers.

'Jesus!' he said against her mouth, taking a deep breath, raising a hand and stroking her hair back from her face. 'What are you doing to me?'

Deeley could feel him smiling; he planted a kiss on her lips and pulled back a little, taking an even deeper breath, running both hands over his scalp. She opened her eyes and saw him shifting to sit with his legs slightly parted, adjusting his trousers; he caught her glance and raised his eyebrows at her, throwing his hands wide, flashing her a self-deprecating smile.

'Just needed to – um, take a moment,' he said, reaching for his drink and finishing it in one long swallow. 'Wow.' He shook his head in disbelief. 'That was . . .' He shook his head again. 'Making out like teenagers in a bar on a Saturday night. Believe me, I haven't done that in a *long* time.'

Deeley did believe him; he looked genuinely taken aback. *But I have*, she thought, embarrassed. *I had quite a few times making out with near strangers in LA; sometimes going home with them, too.* She couldn't feel too guilty; she'd been in her early twenties, and banned, by her situation, from having anything resembling a real boyfriend. *I was young, free and single; I had my fun; They were industry parties so no one would gossip; I wasn't cheating on anyone or doing anything I shouldn't.*

But now it felt different. She glanced sideways at Jeff. He was a really nice guy. Sweet, handsome, and a great kisser. Definitely possible boyfriend material.

And as soon as he stopped kissing me, I started thinking about Matt again.

Oh God, I'm such a mess.

Jeff had got himself calmed down enough to look at Deeley again. To the long list of his assets, she could add an extra one: he wasn't a fool. He could tell immediately that something was on her mind. He grimaced.

'Look, feeling up a woman I've just met in a bar isn't exactly how I like to think of myself behaving,' he said. 'So I was going to suggest that maybe we take a walk along the esplanade, under the stars. It's stopped raining . . .' He gestured out of the window. 'But I can tell from your expression that maybe you're not OK being alone with me.'

'It's not you,' Deeley said immediately. Now she definitely felt guilty.

'Really?' Jeff pulled a face; his features were very mobile, Deeley thought. You'd never get bored watching him. 'Because that's how it's feeling. I came on much too hot and heavy.' He looked earnest. 'You're just so gorgeous. I don't mean that to sound like I'm blaming you—'

'Oh no, it was me, really! I touched you first!' Deeley said, wriggling in embarrassment. 'I mean, I stroked your head . . .'

'Oh yeah, so you did.' Jeff grinned at her, his teeth very white and even. 'It *is* a very nice head, isn't it?' He stroked it complacently for comic effect, making her laugh. 'I'm not surprised you couldn't keep your hands off it.'

He had a really nice way of using humour to deflate a moment of tension. Deeley felt herself relaxing.

'It's the ex-boyfriend, isn't it?' Jeff said. 'The one in LA you just broke up with.'

Deeley nodded. It was a lie, but in a way it was the truth; she was confused over a man, messed-up enough not to be able to let herself go with Jeff, see where the evening led them. Just because it wasn't Nicky in LA, but Matt in London, the core was the same. There was another man in the picture. And Jeff was too nice for her to use him like a Band-Aid to plaster over the wound that her stupid behaviour with Matt had made.

She opened her mouth to try to explain this to him, or as much as she could, but he was ahead of her.

'I get it,' he said gently. 'You came away to get over someone, and it's way too early for you to think about someone else. Even if it's just making out with some near stranger in a bar. Look.' He raised a hand to summon the waitress. 'I'm going to sign the bill and go for that walk myself – I need some cold air.' He grinned. 'You're more than welcome to come with me if you feel the same. And all I'll do is let you hold onto my arm, OK? I won't touch you at all. Not even if you beg me. Not even if you stroke my head the whole time.' The waitress arrived, and he signalled to her that he wanted the bill. 'So.' He looked back at Deeley. 'Feel like joining me for a totally chaste, utterly kiss-free night-time stroll?'

Deeley was smiling now. Jeff was too funny; she couldn't help it. 'I'd love to,' she said.

Devon

*D*evon met Gianni's beautiful wife Laura the very next morning.

Devon had gone to bed early, after foraging in the enormous kitchen for a very basic dinner. The last thing she wanted to do was cook; frankly, she couldn't imagine ever wanting to cook again. But Laura had left the huge fridge stocked with cheeses, salamis and prosciutto; there was a large bowl of ripe red tomatoes on the kitchen table, and a fresh loaf on the olive-wood breadboard. Devon had assembled a delicious sandwich, sunk most of a bottle of local red wine, and crashed. It was a tribute to the lack of additives in the wine that this morning she had woken at nine with a clear head.

Wrapping herself in a dressing gown, she had padded downstairs, made herself a big pot of espresso on the stove-top Bialetti, toasted some bread to eat with the chestnut honey she'd found in a cupboard, and wandered outside to have breakfast on the terrace. The kitchen's big double French doors gave onto a sheltered stone patio, an outdoor staircase behind it thickly clustered with pots of herbs and trailing geraniums; Rory had placed a wrought-iron table there, so that he and his guests could eat outside even in the heat of the day.

Devon sipped her coffee and stared out across the valley in

front of her. The lawn glimmered with dew, the fountain in its centre playing lightly; a decorative stone wall hemmed the lawn, and below it the ground dropped away to a vineyard ten feet below, where she could just about see a squarish man in a battered old hat spraying something on the vines. In late spring, the foliage was at its most lush, the grass still green, the oaks and silver birches thick with leaves, the olive trees feathery and full, looking from a distance like pale green-grey puffballs. The last faint wisps of cloud were burning off in the haze of morning sun. It was going to be a warm day.

'*Signora? Buongiorno! Signora?*'

Devon turned, startled, to the kitchen doors, hearing a woman's voice call, and footsteps bustling across the terracotta floors. '*Cotto*,' Devon remembered Gianni calling that tile yesterday. She thought she remembered every single word he had said to her. God, what a mess! And this was bound to be—

'*Sono Laura*,' the woman said, appearing on the terrace with a beaming smile. 'I am Laura. Good morning! You sleep well, yes? Everything is good?'

Devon's jaw dropped. She stared at Laura with what in England would have been utter and total rudeness. Because Gianni's wife was not at all what she would have expected.

After Gianni's comments to her yesterday about women looking like women, she'd assumed that his wife would be voluptuous, with cascading dark hair and heaving bosoms. Instead, Laura was more Jamie Lee Curtis than Sophia Loren. Skinny, wearing a tight white stretch shirt tucked into equally snug jeans, her cropped hair was dyed a frightening shade of orange streaked with blonde, and big gold hoop earrings dangled almost to her bony shoulders. She wore absolutely no make-up at all, and could not have been a day under fifty.

'*Benvenuta, signora!*' she said happily, rushing forward to kiss Devon on either cheek, smelling strongly of perfume. 'Welcome to Chianti! We take good care of you here, I promise.'

'You're Laura?' Devon could only say, still utterly taken aback by the sight of Gianni's wife.

'*Ma si, certamente*! I am Laura! I look after you. I cook, clean, what you need I do. So!' Laura clapped her hands, smiling. 'I go to Greve now, to shop. Do you want to come? I show you our town.'

'Oh, no, no thanks,' Devon said distractedly; she was by no means ready to face the outside world, let alone a bustling, gossipy Italian village in the company of a woman with the energy of someone who had just sunk three Red Bulls back to back. 'Um, I met your husband yesterday. He seemed very nice.'

She felt the colour rising to her cheeks, and she hadn't even said Gianni's name. *This is awful*, she thought grimly. *I have the worst schoolgirl crush on him.*

'*Si?*' It was Laura's turn to look surprised now. 'You meet Gianni?'

'Yes,' Devon frowned. 'He picked me up from the airport. In Rory's car.'

'Oh!' Laura simultaneously clapped her hands and cackled with laughter; it was quite a trick. '*Ma senti che buffo!* You think 'e is Gianni?' She cackled again. '*Ma quello e veramente divertente*!'

'I don't speak Italian,' Devon said through gritted teeth, sitting up on the edge of her chair. 'What are you saying?'

Laura didn't seem to mind her rudeness at all: still laughing, she pointed into the field below the lawn.

'*Quello e Gianni*!' she said happily, indicating the stout man in the ancient hat. 'That is my 'usband! Yesterday, you meet Cesare. *Il nostro principe.* He says *Signor* Rory has telephoned to him, to say that you come to visit, and he takes the car to meet you. 'E is a friend of *Signor* Rory. *Molto simpatico.*'

Devon's heart almost exploded from her chest with relief. It was like a blow in the ribs, but from inside, a physical sensation so strong it paralyzed her for a moment. Laura was still cackling away, however, and didn't seem to notice that Devon had collapsed back into her chair, reaching for her coffee cup.

''E is very funny, Cesare. *Molto buffo*,' Laura was saying cheerfully.

Devon didn't drink the coffee; she just needed something to do with her hands. Cradling the cup, she said as casually as she could manage, 'Oh! Does he, um, live near here?'

Laura's plucked eyebrows shot up and she stared in amazement at Devon.

'*Ma si!*' She pointed across the valley, beyond the stand of oak trees at the bottom of the vineyard, to a pale pink villa on the hill beyond, surrounded by cypresses. '*Di la*! Vignamurlo – the villa, is very famous, many tourists go to see it. 'E is *principe*. Prince. Very old Tuscan family. *Come i Gucciardini-Strozzi*,' Laura added incomprehensibly. 'Well, OK! I go to Greve now. I buy you milk, eggs, bread. You want other things?'

'Um, maybe some fruit?' Devon said, on autopilot now.

'*Benissimo*!' Laura said, bustling away. '*A presto*!' She shot a quick look at Devon, remembered the latter's lack of Italian, and added kindly, 'See you soon!'

Devon sat there, unable to move, listening to Laura's car start up, somewhere beyond the house; a minute later she saw a flash of white winding its way down the drive, half-hidden by the cypresses that lined it.

On the plus side, he isn't Rory's caretaker, she thought. *And he isn't married – well, not to Laura, anyway. And on the negative, I tipped him ten euros. And he took it! Oh God, how embarrassing!*

She took a deep sip of coffee, the bitter strong liquid coursing through her. Not that she needed it to wake her up; every nerve ending in her body was pinging with sensation.

He said 'presto' *to me before he went. Which means 'soon'. 'See you soon'. So he must be planning to come back and see me, mustn't he?*

Soon?

She wasn't going to ring Cesare. Wouldn't, couldn't, wasn't going to. Devon had avoided Laura on her return from Greve, because she knew all too well that she would be unable to resist pumping the housekeeper for information about Cesare; did he live here full time? Did he have a girlfriend? Was he married? *He probably has both,* she thought gloomily. *A wife and a girlfriend. He's so bloody flirty, he probably has a string of women all over Tuscany.*

Devon's own husband was like a thorn in her side to her;

whenever she thought about Matt, she flinched. She knew perfectly well that she had treated him appallingly, that he had been nothing but wonderful to her. She didn't deserve Matt, and she knew it. She was hiding out here in Chianti, putting off the awful moment when she would have to be honest about the state of her marriage. The last thing she had expected was to be this attracted to another man. *And*, she realized with dawning surprise, *I don't think about being fat at all when I'm with Cesare. At least, I didn't yesterday. How weird. With Matt – with anyone else – it's all I'm aware of . . .*

Devon was determined to eat healthily here. No pasta, no cake, no fatty foods. She made a salad for lunch from artichokes and sundried tomatoes, rocket and mozzarella, and then, bravely, went upstairs to put on her swimsuit. She couldn't sunbathe – as the palest of the McKenna girls, her skin couldn't take the sun – but she loved to swim, and she knew Rory had a pool. Snagging a couple of thrillers from the shelf in her room, she took a beach towel from the pile in the laundry room – Laura's sheet- and towel-folding was a work of art – and, in a cover-up and flip-flops, headed out to find the pool.

Villa Clara was built against the side of a hill, for shelter in the winter and for protection from the sun in the summer. A series of ornamental gardens were cut like terraces into the soft slope of the hill, each one a few steps up from the next, and the pool was above them all, perfectly placed for the best views of the gardens and the villa, its stone border surrounded by loungers with parasols. Devon found the striped padded cushions for one of the loungers, adjusted the sunshade, and curled up there, distracting herself from thoughts of Cesare by immersing herself in a Lee Child. After an hour or so, feeling restless, she stepped into the still cool water of the swimming pool and ploughed up and down its length in a steady breaststroke.

She had lost count of how many lengths she'd done, her arms pulling at the water, her legs scissoring together, her inner thigh muscles working harder than they had for years; the exercise took her over. She didn't hear the swing of the little iron gate that led up to the pool, the footsteps on the stone. She didn't even notice his leather-shod feet standing on the edge of the pool surround. He had to squat down and wave his hand in front of her face as she swam up to the shallow end to get her attention.

Thank God it's the shallow end, Devon thought fervently, coughing up the water she had swallowed in shock. She got her feet under her and stood up, slicking back her hair with both hands. Cesare's eyes immediately dropped, appreciatively, to her breasts, which were raised and amplified by the gesture.

'Do you always swim in sunglasses?' he inquired.

'I don't like getting water in my eyes,' Devon said, more grateful than she could say that she was wearing them; it gave her some protection, some defence against him. Stopped him reading, instantly, how happy she was to see him.

'I came to see if you were having a nice time,' he said, strolling over to a lounger and sitting on its edge. 'You are a guest in Chianti. We want our guests to have a nice time.'

'I am, thank you,' she said, walking over to the edge of the pool and resting her arms on it, propping her head on them; she was incredibly self-conscious, suddenly, about the fact that she was almost naked, whereas Cesare, in white jeans and a denim shirt, was fully clothed. Some lucky star had warned her to wear her Miracle Medium-Control swimsuit, with its ruching that sucked in her stomach and love handles, its concealed bra that flattered her breasts, its aubergine colour that set off her white skin and dark hair so well; but no matter how miracle a swimsuit was, it couldn't hide your cellulite.

I should have worn a wetsuit, she thought with a flash of amusement. *That would have done it*. The idea made her smile, and the smile, parting her naturally red lips, made her look so beautiful that Cesare, stared at her in open admiration.

'The first time I see you,' he said, 'you have all your clothes on. The second time, you wear only a swimming suit. Maybe the third time . . .'

'You're outrageous!' Devon said crossly.

He smirked. 'In Italy,' he informed her, 'we say what we think. In England, perhaps you do not. *Moh.*' He shrugged, raising his palms to near shoulder height, clearly indicating which way he thought was preferable.

Gasping at his arrogance, Devon jumped back and splashed him with water; her aim was good, and his white jeans were promptly splattered.

'*Capisco,*' he said airily, standing up and starting to undo his belt. 'You get my clothes wet because you want to see me *nudo.*'

'No!' Devon screamed, giggling, covering her eyes with her hands. 'No! I didn't mean that!'

'*Aspetta un' attimo,*' he said, walking around the pool and disappearing into the green-painted pool house.

As soon as he had gone, Devon leaped out of the pool and dashed to retrieve her towel, desperate to cover her bottom and upper thighs. She wound it round her as tightly as possible, so she didn't look too bulky, and wrapped it in the most Grecian-like way she could manage.

What just happened? she thought frantically. Cesare was extraordinary: somehow he had managed to escalate the situation in the space of barely a minute to the point where he had vanished, possibly to take his clothes off. Thinking about him all yesterday evening and today, she had built him up in her mind, picturing him as irresistibly handsome, and the revelation, seeing him again, was twofold.

Firstly, no, he wasn't handsome. His nose was too big for that, his hair too wild, his mouth too wide. And secondly, he was even sexier than she'd remembered. He looked at her as if he were picturing her naked, and it made her weak to her core.

He's not really going to come out of there nude, is he? she wondered helplessly, torn between excitement and nervous anticipation. *I'll definitely run away if he does. He can't chase me if he's naked.*

My God, this is totally insane!

And then, as Cesare emerged from the pool house, a complacent smile on his face, she burst into complete hysterics.

'It is not mine,' he said, looking down at the bright blue Speedo he was wearing. 'But it fits, yes?'

He was definitely hairy, Devon saw between the fingers she had clapped over her eyes. But, thank goodness, in the right places. After Matt, Cesare looked very slim, lean and muscled, the dark curly hairs on his chest failing to conceal his pectorals and the absolute flatness of his stomach – *it's almost concave*, she realized, sitting up to suck in her own. There was a definite line of dark hair down to the waistband of his Speedos, which actually sat on his hipbones, perilously low; she blushed, even behind her hands, as she checked out the Speedos' contents.

Not huge, she thought, rather disappointed. *But maybe he's a grower, not a shower . . .*

'It fits?' Cesare repeated, doing a slow pirouette so she could see the back.

Oh thank goodness, not a hairy back! She almost sagged in relief. *And his bum – oh, wow . . .*

It was just as tight and firm as she had imagined, watching it yesterday as he climbed the stairs in front of her. Devon was sure her face was as red as a turkey-comb by now.

'But you have got out!' he said, hands on hips, staring at her with an outraged expression. 'This is not fair! I put on my swimming suit, and you get out of the pool!'

His hair stuck out in all directions; his nose, for some reason, looked even larger when he was almost naked. The muscles in his forearms flexed. He looked more confident in those ridiculous shiny blue Speedos than any of the men Devon had dated did fully clothed. He wasn't Devon's type at all; too slight, too lean. She liked them big, handsome, chunky with muscle. Action heroes.

And she was melting, totally melting, for this arrogant, almost-skinny, curly-haired idiot. She felt as if she were drunk, as if her entire body were filled with bubbles, airy and weightless.

Cesare was walking across the grass now, to the twin flights of stone steps that led down into the pool. Gingerly, he put his toes into the water, and jumped back, an appalled expression on his face.

'*Ma e gelida, l'acqua!*' he said, looking outraged. 'Is freezing! How do you swim in that?' He shook his head sadly. 'English people are cold,' he said. 'Cold like the fish. Cold hearts, too.'

Devon wasn't going to fall for that obvious trap. And she didn't want him to see her in a swimsuit; she hugged her towel around her and said firmly, 'That's why I got out. It's too cold. You should get dressed,' she added hopefully.

Because if he does, I can too. I really don't want him to see my cellulite.

An expression of extreme calculation narrowed Cesare's dark eyes. He looked at her as if he were working out a complicated equation.

'So if it is warm, you get in?' he demanded.

'Yes, of course!' Devon said, feeling that this was a safe answer: what could he do, suggest they take a hot bath together? 'I love being in the water.'

'*Perfetto!*' He raced over to her, grabbed her hand, and pulled her to her feet, dragging her back to the little gate. He was so close to her, and so nearly naked, that it made her even dizzier; she could smell his scent, feel his bare, hairy arm against her smooth one, rasping and so masculine that she had to bite her lip, hard, to stop herself rubbing against him. She snatched at her towel, which was coming loose, but to her disappointment Cesare didn't even notice that it was falling off her.

'*Bene!*' he said. 'You go to the villa, you put clothes on – simple clothes, some jeans, a *pull* – and you bring your swimming suit, and I take you where the water is very warm.'

'I don't—'

'*Zitta! Vai!*' He smacked her towel-covered bottom. 'Hurry! Then you meet me in the *parcheggio*. The parking lot.'

'How dare you—'

'Go!' Cesare crossed his arms over his chest and frowned intimidatingly at her, his thick brows coming together over his nose. The Speedos hanging off his hipbones rather undercut this attempt at authority. Devon giggled all the way back to the house.

* * *

It turned out that Cesare owned a bright yellow Lamborghini, which had been undergoing some sort of complicated electrical checks the day before, and hadn't been available for his errand collecting Devon from the airport. It made short work of the switchback of sharp curves that hugged Chianti's steep hills on the left side and dropped away on the right to breathtaking views. It was like driving through a series of postcard photographs; the stone house on the hill, a cypress-lined drive arrowing up to it, surrounded by terraced olive groves and vineyards, their lines of green-leaved vines marching in perfect symmetry. It was a sea of lush green, with the odd bright flash of stronger colour: blue glints of swimming pools that echoed the blue skies above; bright red poppies and roses; yellow-petalled early sunflowers. Mercifully, at the wheel of his own car, Cesare was fully occupied with the serious business of whipping it around each corner as fast and efficiently as possible. Chain-smoking happily, humming along to the CD, which seemed to be the same hoarse-voiced male singer as the day before; he ignored Devon almost completely, limiting himself to the occasional informative comment.

'Now we go round Siena. It is very small and the people are not very interesting – they talk only about their horse race, the *Palio*. Moh. *Chi se ne frega?* Always the same. The horses run round the square. Sometimes the horses fall down. Moh.'

And, ten minutes later: 'Here we are in the *Creti Senesi*. Siena white hills. It is the only interesting thing about Siena.'

'They look like the white cliffs of Dover,' Devon said.

'*Che cosa?*' Cesare, visibly uninterested, overtook a white Panda so fast that its outline almost blurred as he sped past. '*Panda di merda,*' he muttered. 'Panda shit. I hate the Pandas.'

They were driving along a ridge now, the road falling away to each side, and Devon gasped at the views; the landscape here starker than Chianti, which was very heavily forested. Beyond Siena, the chalky cliffs shone a lunar white; the houses were much fewer, scattered over peaks of hills.

'Imagine in the *Medioevo*,' Cesare said cheerfully. 'Up this hill with no one but your family and some animals, all winter long. Maybe a priest, if you are unlucky. Nothing to do if you are a young man but fuck the sheep. *Ah si,*' he said, turning his head for the first time to look at Devon, who had snorted in shock. 'Sienese men, they like to make love with the sheep,' he added very seriously. 'It is well known.'

'What about Florentine men?' Devon asked, not wanting to seem like Cesare had it all his own way; if he could tease her, she could tease him. 'What animals do you like to make love with?'

It was Cesare's turn to snort. 'We do not make love with the animals,' he said with great hauteur. 'But in the old days, we make love with the back of the woman. The *culo,*' he clarified. 'That way, she is still *vergine* for the husband, but she has still fun with a lover. It is very common. My uncle, he made love that way with half the women in Greve.'

Devon rolled her eyes. 'More fun for him than them,' she muttered.

'It is obvious,' Cesare said austerely, lighting another cigarette with his right hand while the Lamborghini shot through a village at sixty kilometres an hour, its inhabitants turning to stare enviously at the yellow sports car, 'that you have not made love with a man of the Montigiani family. *Ecco!*' He gestured with his cigarette to a sign they were passing at speed, which read: *RAPOLANO TERME, SAN GIOVANNI. SPENGERE SIGARETTE, FONTE TERMALI.* '*Siamo arrivati.* The sign, it says no smoking, because there is hot gas from the earth here. It makes the water hot.'

'Shouldn't you put that out then?' Devon said, looking at his Marlboro.

'It is not *pericoloso,*' Cesare said casually, throwing the lit cigarette out of the window into the ditch. 'See? That sign, it is for tourists.'

He drove past a No Entry sign, past a hotel and round its side to a parking lot, where he pulled up the Lamborghini in a No Parking zone and jumped out lightly. The hotel doorman stared over at the car, and Devon longed for him to make Cesare move, but he just called something appreciative to Cesare, who raised a hand to him in response.

'OK, as the Americans say!' Cesare announced, leading Devon up a flight of stairs to a long low elegant white building. 'You like hot water, I bring you to hot water!'

Inside it looked like a cross between a spa and a Swiss health club; stripped down simple wooden walls, pale green and white fittings, a reception desk staffed by elegant women in black uniforms. Cesare chatted away to them, handed over some money, hired himself and Devon a dressing gown, towel and flip-flops each, and bustled her along into the women's changing rooms.

There was nothing for it, she was going to have to strip to her swimsuit again. Bundling herself into her robe, Devon emerged to find Cesare lounging like a Roman emperor against the wall. He had the very annoying air of being the master of all he surveyed. Leading her upstairs, through a bar and restaurant, out onto a terrace, they passed groups of people in dressing gowns and towels, or just wandering in their swimsuits, their faces pink and relaxed. They exited onto a wide terrace, and Devon gasped at the sight below.

It was a huge blue swimming pool, surrounded by loungers. Water poured down into it from a series of much smaller pools, terraced down the side of the hill, cascades of lightly steaming hot water. A higher narrow pool led into a wooden dome, Swedish-style, whose glass windows were translucent with steam. Everything was as simple and elegant in style as the reception had been, the cushions in shades of white and grey, the parasols aqua blue, the bodies of the clientele tanned and shiny.

'We have many hot springs in Tuscany,' Cesare said, bounding down the flight of stairs that led to the pool. '*Terme.* Is very good for the skin, and the circulation. *Vieni!*'

Devon followed him, and in an effort to put her cellulite on display as little as possible, she chucked her towel on one of the loungers, kicked off her flip-flops, pulled off her robe and dived inexpertly into what she assumed would be like a warm bath. She came up screaming in shock, wiping the hair off her face, to see Cesare standing on the side, laughing his head off at her surprise.

'This is the coldest part,' he informed her, stripping off his own robe and diving in as easily as a merman. 'Aah!' He emerged, shaking his head so vigorously that water sprayed off his wild mop of hair in all directions; it was like being next to a sheepdog shaking itself. 'Up there,' he added, 'it is more hot. Here! *Vieni!*'

He swam the length of the pool to the first waterfall, white chalky water pouring down into the blue-tiled depths of the pool. Cesare stood underneath it, gesturing for Devon to join him. She squealed as the water pounded down on her head, heavier than the most powerful shower, dazing her with its force.By the time they climbed up and into the next, smaller pool, to stand under that cascade, she was already so relaxed she could barely speak. The pools grew hotter, the water on her head warmer. By the time they reached the last one, resting their arms on the marble side to look down over the landscape, the series of waterfalls below them, the tanned bodies on the loungers, the swimmers in the big pool, Devon had forgotten all about her cellulite, her love handles, the extra little squeezes of flesh just next to her armpits, pushed sideways by the boning of her swimsuit. Her hair was plastered to her skull, her skin already feeling softer after immersion in the opaque white water. Everyone seemed to be floating, disappearing at the waist, or sinking down till just their faces were floating like happy masks in a bath of milk-pale water. There were old and young, beautiful and ugly, all Italians, bronzed already by the Mediterranean sun; many had curly hair and big noses, but no one's hair was as wild, no one's nose as large as Cesare's.

'*Ti piace?*' he asked, turning to look at her. His face was very close. She could smell the cigarettes on his breath, something that would have repelled her before, but now, because it was Cesare, she found herself leaning towards him. Longing to taste the tobacco on his mouth.

Oh God, I really have it bad, she thought despairingly.

'It is very beautiful,' he said softly. His eyes gleamed, so dark she couldn't distinguish the pupil from the iris. His arms, propped next to her on the marble surround of the pool, were lean and muscled, distractingly patterned with moles; she longed to take a pen and connect up the dots, make painstaking drawings on them. It was a ridiculous thought, but everything about this situation was ridiculous; she had known him for less than twenty-four hours, and she was obsessed by him to the point that she could quite imagine herself buying cigarettes and burning them slowly to invoke a scent that reminded her powerfully of him. She was Alice down the rabbit hole, tumbling into a world where all the rules were reversed, and her perfect, handsome, considerate husband was ignored for a scrawny Italian who rode roughshod over her.

It was almost funny. Devon couldn't help smiling.

'You look just like your photographs,' Cesare said, still very softly. 'On Rory's books in his kitchen. I see you on the cover and I ask, who is that, this very beautiful woman? And Rory says you are a famous cook in England. And I remember. So when he rings me, listen, Cesare, my friend the cook comes to Italy, she has some problem and needs to escape to stay at my house, maybe you have a drink with her, I think, no, *ancora meglio*, I will go to the airport like an Italian gentleman and drive her to Villa Clara. And that will make her happy, and maybe she will kiss me to say thank you.'

He raised his hand and pointed to his face. '*Due baci*. Two kisses on the cheeks, as we do here to say hello and goodbye. And that will make me happy. But instead . . .'

The talk of kissing had made Devon feel that her lower body was melting away into the warm water. Heat flooded between her legs, made her torso liquid. She couldn't speak. She stared at him, hypnotized, her eyes very wide, her red lips parted, as he continued.

'Instead, she gives me ten euros. It is a very sad story.'

He had slid closer to her, his body turning to face her. He was so good at this, he must have done it hundreds of times before, thousands maybe; taken out foreign women visiting Italy, driven them very fast in his car, brought them here, and talked nonsense to them until they literally couldn't think straight. The thought of being just another in a long line of women seduced by Cesare woke her up from her trance enough for her to protest.

'I was expecting Gianni. And you were driving that old Golf! How was I to know who you were?'

Of course, he ignored her objection, focussing instead on his own goal.

'But now you know,' he said. 'I am a friend of Rory. So I am your friend too. And friends kiss each other here in Italy. *Così.*' He raised his hand to his face again. Looking at the light sprinkling of dark hairs on the back, she pictured that hand on parts of her body, so vividly she was again struck dumb.

Leaning forward in the heavy white water, she kissed him on each cheek. It was like taking a shot of tequila; sensation raced through her as fast as alcohol down her throat. Her breasts brushed against his chest; her lips touched his stubble, one hand braced herself on his shoulder for balance, so that she didn't fall into him. It was exquisite torture, trying not to give in completely, to cling onto him as she wanted to, to kiss his mouth, to taste that tobacco on his lips.

And Cesare didn't touch her at all. He let her kiss him, and when she pulled back, her heart racing, pounding as if she had just sprinted desperately to catch the last train of the night, he smiled at her, his dark eyes slanting, full of enjoyment.

'So now,' Devon said, piqued beyond endurance at his self-control, 'you owe me my ten euros back.'

He threw back his head and laughed so loudly that the other people in the pool turned to look at him curiously; even by Italian standards, it was a very noisy laugh. He had to wipe tears out of his eyes with the back of his hand; he looked at her again, and clapped, one, two, three times.

'*Signora* Devon,' he said, every line on his face creased with amusement, '*sei meravigliosa*. You are marvellous. Come. We go to boil ourselves like *aragoste*. Lobsters,' he translated after a moment's thought.

He still didn't touch her, though she was longing for it, for him to take her hand and pull her through the water, maybe to put one hand on her back and guide her. But no, he just indicated the entrance to the big wooden dome she had seen before, a passage-way covered with big plastic strips she had to push aside and walk through blind. Inside the dome it was instantly ten degrees hotter still, an open steam room, with a waist-high bath of water at its centre; she stepped down into it and gasped at the heat enveloping her like an embrace.

'This is the *percorso*,' Cesare said just behind her, no more than a centimetre away from her back. She could feel his hair tickling the tip of her ear, and it took all the willpower she had not to lean back against him, feel his entire body pressing against her. 'The journey we take from the cold to the hot. You finish in the hot, and then you jump into the cold again, and then it all begins once more, the journey . . . Ah, *bene! Vieni!*'

He gestured over her shoulder to two fountains of water at the far side of the pool, set into a marble slab; the water pouring out was steaming hot, clearly directly from the natural thermal springs which fed this resort. People were standing under both fountains, letting the water pour on their backs, but a group was leaving one. Cutting deftly ahead of another hopeful, Cesare strode across, setting his back against the marble slab, indicating that Devon follow him.

The other fountain was occupied by a couple, young and totally absorbed with each other; the boy was standing where Cesare was, the girl facing him, embracing him, her head on his shoulder, his arms around her slim, tanned waist. God knew what they were doing, half-hidden from the rest of the world by the constant silver stream of thermal water, by the hot steam rising around them. It was a deeply erotic sight, and Devon longed to be in Cesare's arms, just like that, wound tightly against him. As she watched, the boy's hand slid slowly down the girl's body, to the base of her spine, then under the white water, opaque as pearly stained glass. The girl gasped and wrapped herself even closer to her lover.

'Devon! *Vieni qua!*' Cesare was calling, rather crossly now. She could hardly see him through the flow of water in front of him and desperately, not wanting to seem like she was begging for a kiss, she turned around and backed into the fountain instead, the water hitting her shoulders with an impact that almost winded her.

Cesare's arms came round her waist, pulling her against him, arranging her so that the water streamed down her back.

'*Perfetto*,' he said, his mouth against her ear. 'The hot water is for here . . .' One hand came away from her waist and traced a line over both shoulders. '*Le spalle*. And for the *scapole* . . .' His finger ran across her shoulder blades. 'And the *spina dorsale* . . . to make better any stress . . .'

His hand slid down once more to her waist, pulling her between his legs, wrapping around her.

'You have stress now, Devon?' he whispered into her ear.

Everywhere was hot and wet; the touch of his lips on her skin was one more sensation streaming down her like the torrent of water. His mouth closed on her ear, his teeth a light pressure that made her moan softly and arch against him, her bottom moving against something hard between his legs, something which made it very clear that Cesare was, indeed, a grower. Her eyes closed in utter pleasure. She was leaning against Cesare, Cesare against the wall, the marble that was no harder than him. If he'd wanted to, he could have had sex with her then and there, slipped his fingers under her swimsuit, pulled it to one side, slid himself up and into her, and all she would have done was brace her legs and try not to scream with ecstasy.

His hands were in her hair now, stroking her scalp, massaging it, the tips of his fingers cleverly finding all the points on her skull that craved to be touched. It was the most sensual experience, a scalp massage. And a scalp massage under hot thermal springs, in the arms of a man you were attracted to as you had never been attracted to a man in your life . . . it was transcendent. Everything seemed to fall away. The disaster she'd made for herself in England, her career, her weight, her marriage, poured off her like the steaming cascade of opalescent white water.

Her worries about Deeley, whether she would be OK, what her younger sister could say about her childhood, about Bill, streamed away too; who cared what had happened all those years ago? Nobody. If they did find Bill, the McKenna sisters would tell their story, tell the truth, and everyone would understand. Maxie worried too much. Maxie worried for all of them, and Devon had not only let her, she'd allowed Maxie's worries to dominate her life. Well, no more. No more worrying. Deeley would find her way through life, would find a nice guy, and hopefully some sort of job that made her happy. Everything would work itself out, if she'd only let things pour over her like pounding cascades of hot water.

Devon had been so ambitious all these years, worried about the future, driven to succeed, to make her glittering career; television, books, spin-off merchandise, she'd achieved everything on which she'd set her sights. The perfect husband, the wonderful house. And now, at this moment, none of that seemed to matter at all. Devon relinquished her iron grip on ambition without even a sigh of regret.

Cesare's strong hands in her hair, massaging her temples, then working out the tension in her neck as her head sank forward, were the only thing she could focus upon, the only thing that mattered. She could leave everything in England behind without looking back, become Cesare's mistress as long as it lasted, say goodbye to everything she'd once thought was important.

Her forehead smoothed out, her face became utterly serene. It felt as if there weren't a knot left in her shoulders; Cesare was gripping them now, shaking her very gently, easing out any last wisps of stress that might remain, any regrets, any glances back at past mistakes. By the time he said that they were done, that other people were waiting to take their place under the fountains, she was a husk of herself, her eyes dreamy, her lips curved in a smile of utter relaxation. They ran back down to the big pool and jumped in, screaming, to cool themselves back down.

Devon had entirely forgotten any consciousness about her body flaws and now all she could do was smile. She smiled as they wrapped themselves once more in their robes and walked up the flight of steps to the bar, where Cesare bought them each a glass of *spumante*, dry sparkling wine. They stood out on the balcony, sipping it in contented silence, watching the sun set behind the far hills in streaks of Campari red and blood orange. She smiled as she pulled on her clothes in the changing room, ran a brush through her hair and pinned it back, as she outlined her eyes briefly with a dark pencil, brushed some mascara onto her lashes and some gloss onto her lips, and was done in five minutes, too relaxed to battle the other women there for mirrors and hairdryers. She even smiled as Cesare sent the Lamborghini flying down the Siena road on the way back, the speedometer easily reaching 150 kilometres per hour, other cars whipping out of the fast lane at his approach, headlights flashing impatiently. And she smiled when he thrust the car into a probably illegal parking space in front of a police station in a little village called Castellina-in-Chianti, jumped out, and came round to the passenger door to hand her out, saying cheerfully, 'Now, we eat the best pizza in Chianti!'

'Pizza!' Devon said happily. 'I'm starving. How did you know?'

He shrugged, taking her arm and wrapping it through his as they walked up a little cobbled street and into a pretty little square. It was dark now, and soft lights glimmered in shop windows, high-lighting antique sideboards and modern steel Alessi gadgets.

'*I* am starving,' he said. 'So it is time to eat.'

The pizzeria was set in a high stone arch, a deep pizza oven built into one corner; it was warmly lit, decorated with wine bottles from floor to ceiling, and had a huge buffet table in the centre piled with plates of different antipasti. Devon drank red wine and nibbled on sundried tomatoes and slices of ham until their pizzas arrived. Cesare had ordered for them: Devon's was simply fresh mozzarella and freshly made tomato sauce, sprinkled with basil leaves, the golden oil of the mozzarella staining the crispy edges of the pizza. It was as wide as a wheel and as thin as a sheet of paper. She moaned repeatedly in pleasure as she ate it, which brought an extremely smug expression to Cesare's face.

'I tell you it is the best pizza in Chianti,' he said complacently, tucking into his own. 'But maybe it is the best in all Toscana. *Il Fondaccio*, this place is called. *Veramente delizioso, non é vero?*'

Devon nodded, her mouth full. *I must learn Italian*, she thought. *Rory has some books and CDs at the villa. I'll start tomorrow. Tomorrow* . . . Her eyelids fluttered as she imagined the night that would pass before the sun came up the next morning. She had thought of nothing else since Cesare drew her under the fountain in the hot pool. Of what they would do together, all night, alone in Villa Clara. The anticipation was exquisite. She drank more red wine, and for dessert spooned up a lemon sorbet served in half a lemon, sliced lengthways and hollowed out; with it they served her a *limoncello*, lemon liqueur, bright yellow from infused lemon rind, sweet and tangy like the sorbet. She was floating as Cesare settled the bill and took her back to the car.

He drove a little slower now, down the long switchback of curving road to the river at the bottom of the hill that was the border between the provinces of Siena and Florence; he steered the car with perfect efficiency, a couple of fingers on the wheel, a flick of the other hand on the gearstick, up the equally steep hill on the other side of the bridge, to Greve-in-Chianti and the cypress-lined drive of Villa Clara.

He helped her out of the car and walked her, arm in arm, to the big wooden door of the villa, and waited while she fumbled in her bag for the door key and put it in the lock. As the door swung open, he turned her towards him, hands on her shoulders, and pressed her against the stone doorjamb. She looked up at him in the moonlight, still floating on the red wine and the liqueur as if she were drifting on the hot waters of Rapolano Terme, and saw his head come down to hers, the wild tangle of his curls silhouetted against the night sky. Her head tipped back, her lips parted; she was ready for his kiss, had been ready for hours, welcomed his mouth on hers, his tongue sliding confidently, possessively between her lips, as if they had kissed many times before. Cesare had no hesitation about anything, it was clear. He kissed her without a single moment of question, of waiting for consent. He kissed her like a conqueror taking possession of territory which has already surrendered to him.

And Devon kissed him back with all the passion that had built up in her over the last months, maybe even years, of denying herself and denying Matt. She felt completely released, completely free. No self-consciousness, no withholding; she pressed her body against him without worrying for a second that he might think her breasts were too big, or feel the paunch of her stomach. She wrapped her arms around his neck, felt his hairs crispy beneath her fingers. His stubble rasped at her soft skin, but she didn't care; she wanted the sensation, craved it, dragged him even closer to her, cried aloud with pleasure as he kissed down her jawline and buried his head in her neck, his lips hot as fire as they bit and teased her skin, his stubble scraping like sandpaper, the stone blocks of wall behind her digging into her, holding her up.

'*Madonna,*' Cesare gasped into her neck. '*Madonna santa . . .*'

His hands were in her hair, gripping, twisting, reminding her so powerfully of the scalp massage he had given her earlier that she was almost fainting with the remembered sensation. Their rasping, panting breath was the only sound in the whole night around them. They were utterly alone. Devon wanted to fuck right there, pull down her jeans, have Cesare drive into her against the stone pillar . . . *No, I weigh too much, he couldn't pick me up, I could sit on the wall, we could fuck like that, out here in the moonlight, I could wrap my legs around him* . . . She writhed against him at the thought, picturing the two of them having sex so vividly that she felt Cesare's rigid cock throb against her through his jeans, working itself between her legs, which parted immediately for him; he pushed her even closer to the wall, slamming her into it, his hands twined in hers now, kissing her mouth so hard they were bruising each other, the backs of her hands against the stone, above her head, Cesare's fingers wrapped so tightly through hers it felt as if something were about to break . . .

'*Oh Dio, Madonna mia . . .*' he said against her mouth, like a desperate prayer, and dragged his head back enough to gasp in some breath, put a little distance between them. He lowered his hands, bringing hers down too, and turned them, kissing each of her fingers in turn before releasing them, stepping back.

'*Vai dentro,* Devon,' he said, clearing his throat. 'Go inside, OK?'

Devon stared up at him, utterly confused and frustrated, her entire body throbbing for release.

'But . . .' she started, not knowing what to say, but most definitely wanting to register a protest.

'I see you tomorrow,' he said, taking a long, deep breath. 'We go to dinner. Like civilized people, not peasants who fuck against a house, OK?'

He looked down at her for a long moment, drawing his thumb slowly across her lips. Devon bit at it crossly, and Cesare winced in pleasure.

'*Cattiva*,' he muttered. 'Bad girl.'

Devon licked the tip of his thumb, and groaning now, Cesare reluctantly withdrew it from her mouth.

'We are not peasants,' he repeated, as if trying to convince himself. '*Cazzo di Jesu.*'

'I am,' Devon muttered. 'I am a peasant.'

But Cesare was already turning her, pushing her inside the villa, sending her on her way with a firm slap to her bottom.

'*A domani, bella,*' he called. 'I see you tomorrow. Dress smart – I take you somewhere nice, not a pizzeria.'

Typical of him, Devon thought sourly as he shut the big wooden door behind her with a definite slam. *He can't even say goodbye without telling me what to wear next time he sees me.*

She was burning up with sexual frustration, unable to believe that Cesare had gone so far, turned her on so much and then abandoned her like this, on fire. She ran up the stairs, threw herself on her bed and pulled her jeans and knickers down to her knees; she was wet for him, dripping wet, and as soon as her fingers slid between her legs she started to cry out with her first orgasm. She came and came, lying on the big white bed, moonlight drifting through the windows, outlining the shadows of the silver birches beyond the lawn outside. She pictured herself and Cesare fucking under the hot springs, against the wall outside, on the staircase, her gripping onto the iron rail as he drove into her; on this bed, her straddling him, holding down his hands as he had just done with hers. She cried out again and again, like an incantation, imagining the sound of her orgasms echoing across the valley to his house, driving him as crazy as he was driving her. On the inside of her closed lids she saw him with his hand wrapped around his cock, imagining it was her palm rising and falling, making him gasp as he came, wishing he were deep inside her, her mouth, her pussy.

She only stopped when she was beginning to hurt herself, when she had come so many times that she was almost bruised from the endless friction. *He can't do that*, she thought triumphantly, collapsing back onto the white linen of the pillows, utterly exhausted. *He can't have so many orgasms that he couldn't even count them up if he tried*. It felt like a victory over him that she relished; he might have decided that they weren't going to have sex tonight, but she had taken a kind of revenge by glutting herself with pleasure.

And tomorrow, she told herself, making a resolution as she fell asleep, *I'll make him wait for it like he's making me wait now. I'll make him beg and plead and crawl to me. Today he took me by surprise; tomorrow I'll be in charge. I'll turn the tables on him.*

The only problem was that she genuinely thought she might go mad waiting for him.

Deeley

As soon as the plane had taken off, circling over Jersey before heading back over the Channel, Deeley's stay there had seemed like a dream, which faded with disappointing speed as soon as the dreamer awoke. To her surprise, after a few days being cocooned in the luxury of the Grand, with nothing to do but eat, sleep, walk on the beach, and take long scented showers in the spa, she had found herself getting restless. Real life was waiting for her back in London, with all its stresses and messy complications; she would have to face it sooner or later. And she couldn't live like a princess forever, spending money as if it were water without ever checking the state of her bank account.

Jeff had left the day before, off to Cologne, Dusseldorf and Berlin on a business trip. He had been a wonderful companion, and they had dined together every evening, but, apart from a few brief kisses, nothing more had happened. Jeff had taken her number and pressed all of his contact details upon her; he'd ring, he said, as soon as he got back to London.

Deeley hoped he would. But right now, poor Jeff had been relegated to a distant cubbyhole at the back of her mind. *Somewhere to live*, she thought firmly. *And a job. I have to get settled, start earning some money, stand on my own two feet.*

And get out of Devon and Matt's basement.

The thought of Matt was like a raw wound; maybe it would start to heal if she could manage not to touch it. But she knew that was impossible. He was married to her sister. Her entire worldly possessions were in his house. She was going to be scrambling around rental agencies today in a panic, just to avoid him. How could she not think of him? How could she not worry about him, with an injury that looked as if it had messed up his chances of ever playing rugby again?

He belongs to another woman, she told herself severely, as she jumped off the bus carrying her from Victoria, halfway up Park Lane. Deeley had taken the Gatwick Express back to London; no more taxis for her. After the extravagance of Jersey, she was on a new push for economy. She went quickly down the stairs that led to the underpass. *Matt's not yours to worry about. All you can do is leave him the hell alone.*

She emerged full of good resolutions on the other side of Park Lane, next to the car showroom. Green Street was just a few turnings up on the right, and after all her walks on the beach in Jersey, her feet sinking deep in the wet sand, she was practically flying along the pavement, even with her heavy overnight bag slung over her shoulder. *In and out, as quick as possible. Grab a change of clothes, some clean underwear, do the rounds of rental agents . . .* She'd made a list in Jersey, had the printout ready in her pocket. *Hopefully I'll find something I can afford today, move right in . . .*

She tumbled down the iron stairs to the basement flat without even looking up at the windows of the main house, her key in her hand.

And then she stopped as if she had run into a wall.

Because, sprayed on the front door, were the words: *KEEP YOR FUCKING MOUTH SHUT.*

Deeley stared at the graffiti in utter shock. It hadn't been here when she left for Jersey. Even in her rush, she couldn't have failed to notice these bright red letters splayed across the door. So it had been done while she was away.

Instantly, her thoughts flashed to the shove in front of the bus at King's Cross, reconstructing the timeline. She'd come back to London, been attacked, fled Green Street for Jersey as if the hounds of hell were after her, and been away for four days. During which, perhaps, someone had come round to try to finish what they'd started at King's Cross. And, failing to find her, they'd sprayed a crude but effective warning to her instead.

A warning that only she would see. The door had originally been the tradesman's entrance; it was set back into the stone stairs that led up to the front door of the house. The below-ground area was fenced off from the street by black-painted iron railings; someone would have to lean over them and twist their body back on itself to squint down and see the door below, hidden by the overhang of the stairs. Whoever had done this had known that they wouldn't be observed, and that only the inhabitant of the flat would see what they were writing.

It's that woman, Deeley thought immediately. *That scary woman from back home. She told me to stay away. She didn't actually say to keep my mouth shut, not that I remember. But it has to be her.*

Deeley pushed at the front door; it didn't yield, which hopefully meant that no one had broken in. Past experience from her youth made her examine the lock for splintering, or footmarks where someone had tried to kick the door in, but it looked as pristine as before. She thumbed 999 on her phone and kept her thumb on the green phone button that would place the call, before she inserted the key into the door. Nerves racing, on the balls of her feet in case she needed to turn and sprint away, she pushed the door open.

She knew instantly that she was safe, that the flat was empty, though she couldn't have said how. There was an absence to the atmosphere that was immediately reassuring, and a second later, she realized why: the woman from Riseholme had stunk of cigarettes. Cigarettes and cheap perfume, the rip-off stuff you got from pound shops or market stalls. Vividly, Deeley remembered Devon being mad about her fake Calvin Klein Eternity, which smelled like the real thing when you sprayed it on but turned to what Maxie had cruelly compared to cat's pee after ten minutes or so.

If that woman had been in here, the flat would smell of her. No question. But all that hung on the air was the faint, sweet aftermath of the candle Deeley had burned the night before she left, Votivo Redcurrant.

She needed to move quickly, though. Dumping handfuls of dirty laundry onto the tiled floor of the kitchen, next to the washing machine, she dashed into the bedroom to grab more t-shirts, jeans, sweaters, underwear and socks. In the bathroom, she emptied the contents of the shelves into her matching gold quilted Elizabeth Arden toiletry bags; on her way out, she snatched a pair of boots and two pairs of ballerina flats.

Time's up, Deeley. Get out of here now. She was no stranger to sudden moves – a dash-and-grab of her possessions before the bailiffs evicted them, or the people they were staying with couldn't bear their mother's drinking and drugging any more, or their mother had to up sticks before someone to whom she owed money tracked her down. Taking off at a moment's notice had characterized much of her childhood. And at least now she didn't have the torture of being terrified she would leave Brown Bear, her precious stuffed toy, behind; she remembered the scenes, the tears and hysteria, when she was told by their mother they were packing up again, had only ten minutes to collect her things, and Brown Bear was temporarily missing.

She'd always found him in the end, with the help of her sisters. And it was the memory of Maxie locating him down the back of the sofa, or in a tangle of cheap duvet, and shoving him at a sobbing Deeley, that gave her the impetus, as she ran out of the flat, locking the door behind her and dashing up the area steps to the comparative safety of the street, to cancel the 999 she'd tapped into her phone and ring her oldest sister instead.

Maxie

*I*t was two in the afternoon, and Maxie should have been at work. To be precise, she should have been ensconced at her glass desk in her beautiful office, designs spread across it for the latest range of Bilberry wallets, key fobs and luggage tags, scribbling comments across each drawing, editing the spring/summer line of accessories till each one was a coveted collectable. It was the part of her job she loved the most: honing, pruning, pushing her designers to polish the Bilberry range till it shone.

So it was not only quite unprecedented, but contrary to her entire perfectly run life, that when her mobile rang she was actually in her living room, holding a sobbing child and dabbing inexpertly at its face to try to dry the tears. That was the least of the leakage problems the child was having, if the smell rising from its lower regions was anything to go by. Maxie had put calls into every agency she and her PA had been able to contact and now, hearing the trill of her mobile, she grabbed for it, hoping that it was the good news she'd been waiting for. That a substitute nanny had been found for her adoptive daughter.

Instead, it was her younger sister. Maxie's heart sank. It was never good news to hear from Deeley. *She's barely more use than Alice*, Maxie thought savagely, looking down briefly at the tear-splotched face of the child in her arms. *Less, actually. At least Alice is excellent for PR.*

'Maxie! Oh, thank goodness you're there!' Deeley sobbed down the phone.

'*Not* a good time,' Maxie snapped between clenched teeth. 'I'm in the middle of an emergency.'

She refused to say 'childcare emergency'; she'd scorned so many women in business over the years for using that very phrase. And now here she was, bang in the middle of one, dammit. Why on earth had she thought it was a good idea to buy a baby?

'Oh no! Is everything all right?' Deeley said. 'I am too, sort of – well, definitely—'

No, no, no, Deeley. I've looked after you enough. I absolutely do not have time for your emergency as well as my own.

'Really can't talk, Deeley,' Maxie said sharply. 'I'm not even in the office. I've had to come home. The nanny's walked out.'

'Oh no! That nice Australian you mentioned? I thought she was working out really well!' Deeley said.

She was, Maxie reflected, *until she decided to launch into a speech over breakfast about how little Alice was having difficulty bonding with her new mummy and daddy because she barely saw them*. Olly had laughed, finishing up his kipper, and said that was precisely the point of having a nanny and it hadn't done him any harm. Maxie, seeing the nanny's eyes well up, had said swiftly that Mummy and Daddy were awfully busy with work at the moment, but that they'd have a nice holiday all together in Cornwall that summer. (It looked better for the voters if MPs holidayed in the UK.) The nanny had asked if Mummy and Daddy could try to get home before little Alice's bedtime, and Olly, pushing back his chair and throwing his napkin on the table, had stood up, saying impatiently that they'd spent a fortune bringing the child over from Africa in the first place and that Whatsherface was very well paid to take care of her, so what the hell was all the fuss about? If this kind of thing kept up, he'd ban the child from coming in at breakfast time as well.

The nanny, deeply offended, had whisked Alice out of the dining room. Maxie, whose car was waiting outside, had called up to her to say that they'd have a chat that evening; but a few hours later, the sobbing Australian had rung Maxie's mobile to say that her conscience wouldn't allow her to bring up a child that never even saw the people who were supposed to be its parents, and that Maxie needed to be at home in the next half hour, as her bags were packed and she was standing by the door. Maxie had rushed home, reminded the ex-nanny tersely that she had signed a cast-iron confidentiality agreement and that Maxie would not only sue her for everything she had but would make sure her work visa was revoked if she breathed a word about the Stangrooms' domestic arrangements, and, very reluctantly, had taken her sobbing child from the girl's arms.

'Yes, well – things didn't quite go as smoothly as I'd hoped,' Maxie informed her sister. Politicians and their spouses quickly became very skilled in the art of understatement. 'I have to go, Deeley. We've got calls in to every agency in town – I need someone to take this child off my hands, pronto . . .'

Lucia, their very competent Romanian cleaner/housekeeper/ cook, was out that afternoon doing errands, and though, technically, Maxie could have summoned her back and left Alice with her, it would only have been a very temporary solution. Lucia had a full-time job of her own, and Maxie had no desire to see Lucia cosily playing with Alice instead of carrying out the ironing and flower-arranging that was on her schedule for today.

'I'll come over!' Deeley said, jumping at the idea. 'I'll come over right now and look after her! If I jump in a cab, I can be there in fifteen minutes. Tell you what, I'll bring an overnight bag and camp out in the nanny's room. I can stay for a few nights – that'll give you time to interview a replacement and make sure you have the right one. Otherwise,' she continued, 'you'll just take on the first one who shows up and maybe have this problem all over again. If I look after Alice till you find someone you really like—'

Maxie had never wasted time in her life.

'Enough!' she said, holding up one hand, making Alice scream even louder and cling to her, afraid of falling. 'Oh, for God's sake,' Maxie muttered, putting the child down on the carpet. 'Deeley, fine. Great. Come over here right away.'

She disliked being indebted to her sister, but what could she do? It was an emergency, and Deeley was quite right; this would solve the problem. Besides, Deeley did owe her for persuading Devon to take her in . . .

'Oh, not at all!' Deeley sang out, sounding surprisingly ecstatic for someone who had just committed herself to days of changing nappies and calming down a screaming child. 'I mean, we help each other out, don't we? That's what sisters are for!'

Oh, fabulous, Maxie thought caustically. *I knew there must be something.*

But when Deeley arrived, Maxie experienced a sensation so new to her that it took her some time to identify it. *Gratitude*, she realized finally, with considerable surprise. *It's gratitude.*

Deeley had chucked her overnight bag in the hall and gone immediately into the living room, where Alice was lying on the carpet, sobbing at a volume that, if it went any higher, only bats and dogs would hear. She had been trying to teach herself to stand by hauling on the legs of every single precious antique side table one by one, making the carefully arranged objects on their surfaces wobble dangerously. Maxie, who had been on her phone with her PA, had limited her childcare to barking a series of ever louder 'No's at Alice, which the latter had ignored completely; eventually, Maxie had used the tone of voice in which her mother-in-law ticked off naughty dogs, a steel lance of reproach which had made Alice collapse to the floor in hysterics, grabbing at a sofa tassel which promptly came off in her chubby little hand.

It had all been utterly horrendous. Maxie would have carried Alice back up to the nursery, which was completely free of Sheraton occasional tables bearing cut-glass vases, but she simply couldn't bear to pick the child up any more. She was really beginning to smell now.

'Oh, poor baby! Look at you!' Deeley said, running over to her sobbing niece. 'Poor little mite!' She picked Alice up and the baby immediately stopped crying, looking up at her aunt with huge dark wondering eyes. 'She probably needs a change, doesn't she, Maxie? Why don't you tell me where the nursery is, and I'll take her up there and you can get back to work? Eew!' She planted a smacking kiss on Alice's forehead, making her niece giggle with pleasure. 'Aren't you the pongy one? Never mind, darling, we'll get you all cleaned up in two secs.'

Maxie looked at her sister with something resembling awe.

'I never thought I'd say this, Deeley,' she said, 'but you're a lifesaver.'

'Just show me where Alice's stuff is and then leave it all to me,' Deeley said cheerfully, settling Alice on her hip as her niece pulled inquisitively at her aunt's hair. 'Maybe we'll go out for a walk later. It's a lovely day.'

'Thank you, Deels,' Maxie said with complete sincerity; it was the first time she'd ever really been grateful to her younger sister. 'If you're sure you'll be all right . . .'

But she was already dropping her phone and keys in her bag and looking round for her coat. The sooner she could put this horrendous, never-to-be-repeated experience behind her, the better.

Devon

You could spend a really long time getting ready for what promised to be the best date of your life, if you had absolutely nothing else to do. And Devon's calendar that day was completely empty. She had sat down in front of her laptop a couple of times and tried to compose an email to Matt, but she was no writer; her books had been constructed by the expedient of having a writer follow her around, listening to her enough so that she could capture her voice on paper. Devon had had very little to do with them, really.

And if she couldn't manage a cookbook, something as hard as an email to your husband telling him that you probably, on balance, thought you wanted a divorce, because you just didn't think it could work out between the two of you, was completely out of her range. She got as far as 'Dear Matt. I have something to say which I don't think will be a massive surprise to you,' which was the best opening she had managed to come up with; but following those words seemed impossible.

Particularly because Matt seemed to her a thousand miles away, a tiny speck on a very distant horizon, not even visible with the naked eye. When had she fallen out of love with him? When had she begun to realize that, lovely though he was, he simply wasn't right for her – nor she for him? *Probably longer than I know*, she thought guiltily. *I suppose I was as much in love with the idea of us as a perfect media couple as I was with Matt himself. Me and him in magazines, looking gorgeous, in our lovely house.*

She hadn't been a total hypocrite: she'd married Matt because she thought she loved him, and she'd definitely fancied him madly. But she knew, in this brutally truthful spate of self-analysis, that he had never really satisfied her emotionally, never made her feel as easy and relaxed to her core as Cesare had managed in a mere twenty-four hours, without even trying. Matt was always worrying about her, wanting her to be happy. Sensing, probably because he was an intelligent, sensitive man, that she wasn't as fully happy as she could be.

While Cesare was the opposite of her husband. All too clearly, Cesare just assumed that being with him, doing what he decided, would make Devon happy. *And if it doesn't*, Devon thought acutely, *he'll assume that we'll have a blazing row and I'll shout at him a lot, and he'll shout back, and we'll wave our hands around madly while we yell insults. Which he'll enjoy tremendously.*

And, she had to add in the interests of honesty, *so will I*. Devon had always hated that Matt didn't want to argue with her; he got really upset instead, which completely ruined any attempt to shout insults and wave one's hands around. *With Cesare*, she realized, *I feel that I can be myself. And with Matt, I was always pretending. Trying to be the person he wanted me to be. Maybe the person I wanted myself to be.*

Well, it's time to face up to who I really am. I'm a bit of a cow. I'm selfish and self-obsessed and vain and if you put me with a nice man, I'll ride roughshod over him and make our lives a misery. Matt will be much better off without me. He needs a nice sweet girl who wants to have babies straight away, someone he can lavish care and attention on. While I need a man who isn't half as nice as Matt, so I don't have to pretend to be sweet when really I'm a bit of a bitch. I need someone as selfish and self-obsessed and vain as I am.

Which, of course, brought her straight back to Cesare. His hands, his mouth, his body against her. His nose. His hair. Her face creased into a stupid grin whenever she thought about him, and since she thought about him almost all day, she walked around grinning like a mad clown.

She had barely eaten; she had no appetite at all. Her clothes seemed looser. She had the feeling that the adrenalin surging through her was burning off some pounds; all she could manage to get down were a few small balls of mozzarella, light and melting on the tongue, floating in milky water that reminded her of the thermal springs yesterday. She had gone for a walk that morning, careful of the sun on her pale skin, and then for a swim in the pool; she needed to keep moving, because if her body wasn't occupied it started craving Cesare so badly that she became frighteningly restless. She'd tried a glass of red wine at lunchtime to calm her down, but it tasted like acid and after that first sip, she'd thrown the rest of it down the sink.

She found herself going up and down the stone stairs of the villa, rambling from room to room, exploring the whole beautiful house; the little terrace overlooking the formal gardens, the various sitting and dining rooms, sinking into a chair for a little while, then standing up again to wander further, picking up objects and putting them down, unable to settle to anything. Rory had the usual bookshelves of crime novels discarded by previous tenants and guests, and she tried a Swedish detective story but couldn't get past the weird surnames and all-pervading gloom. When you were in a seventeenth-century Italian villa in early June, the warm early summer sun streaming in through the windows, casting rhomboids of warmth on the cool stone; when each window yielded a view breathtaking enough to make an entire collection of postcards; when you were waiting for your Italian lover to come by in his Lamborghini, take you to dinner and then, hopefully, ravish you till dawn – well, it was impossible to focus for more than a few seconds on whether a group of depressed alcoholic detectives called things like Smorgasbord and Fjordsdottir had found a body at the bottom of a frozen lake.

At least Devon could spend hours on her appearance. Painting her nails, letting the various coats dry, took plenty of time; she chose a deep rose, as anything darker would look Gothic against her white skin, and Cesare might tease her about being a vampire. Then she took a shower, loofahing herself within an inch of her life, and a long soak in a hot bath with essential oils, her hair coated in conditioner. By the time she was clean and dry she was already gleaming like a pearl. She moisturized with Ralph Lauren Glamorous lotion, which had a faint gold gleam that made her sheen opalescent.

Devon felt as if she were in a film; it was perfect and it was unreal. Villa Clara was like a film set, or maybe a backdrop for a play. Her bathroom and bedroom were decorated simply, in utterly neutral shades, stone floors, white walls, huge white bed, an equally huge white porcelain bath, marble sinks. She herself, wrapped in a huge white towel, was the only colour; she floated back and forth between the rooms, spraying on Glamorous perfume, finger-curling her heavy dark hair into loose ringlets, checking her appearance in silver-backed mirrors as she gradually made herself more beautiful than she had ever looked in her life. She spent ages on her make-up, blending in foundation, dotting a rosy glow onto her cheeks, dusting shades of purple and gold onto her eyelids, outlining her eyes with dark pencil, painting onto her lips a deep rose lip stain that exactly matched her nails. She was her own canvas.

Thank God I packed everything I could think of! Devon was vain enough to have brought clothes that showed her in her best light, and she had very luckily packed sheer black thigh-high stockings, lace underwear, high heels. She posed in them in front of the mirror, imagining Cesare's face when he saw her in them; and then she had to throw herself onto the bed, literally so weak at the thought that her legs wouldn't hold her up.

I wish I could wear Spanx, she thought wistfully; for a moment she contemplated pulling them on over her lace French knickers, taking them off in the toilet of the restaurant, so that she'd fit perfectly into her dress at the early stages of the evening; by the later part alcohol would smooth over the lumps and bumps, much like the Spanx themselves. *But what if Cesare puts his hand round my waist and feels them – you can tell when someone's wearing slimming pants – and what if I forget to take them off – Oh God, he'd laugh like a drain, he'd tease and tease me, I'd be totally embarrassed . . .*

No, the Spanx were out. But when she pulled on her dress, a black cap-sleeved lace Nougat dress that was one of her favourites, she was hugely excited to find that it slid down smoothly, without getting caught on any rolls of fat along the way. She had definitely lost some weight. Devon would never be slim enough to wear the kind of bright, fashionable, body-hugging clothes than Deeley could pull off, let alone Maxie's fitted suits; Devon had literally never been able to tuck a blouse into a waistband in her life, because it made her look like the Michelin Man. The best she could hope for was to be able to wear a size 12 dress. And here it was. Her bosom spilled up at the neckline, cut straight across, which always flattered a woman who was well-endowed; two perfect white swells, like the cover of a romance novel set in the 1700s. White skin, black dress with a wide white grosgrain ribbon threaded through lace eyelets at its empire-line bodice, black hair; the only colour was Devon's dark rose mouth and her painted nails. She was hugely complacent as she went down to the formal sitting room on the first floor and arranged herself on one of the sofas as alluringly as possible.

An hour later, her nerves were completely shot. She had been ready by seven, not knowing when to expect Cesare; by eight, she was pacing back and forth, having gone down to the kitchen and poured herself a glass of Prosecco to help with the nerves. She thought she might be sick at any moment. What if he hadn't really meant it? From her single days, she remembered the men who had said they'd ring you, or see you tomorrow, and then had never turned up. What if he had meant it, but changed his mind? Decided to take another woman out instead? He must have a whole string of possibilities. What if he'd thought, in retrospect, that she was much too easy? An Italian woman would surely not have kissed him like that, made it so obvious that she'd let him do whatever he wanted. Especially not the aristocratic Italian women with whom a prince would usually spend his time.

I may be all dressed up, with an acquired posh accent, but really I'm just a working-class girl from a small Northern town, Devon thought, pouring more Prosecco into her glass, her heart hammering against her ribs. *All dressed up and nowhere to go. I'm a peasant, basically. I even told him I was one, last night. And he must have decided that he doesn't fancy a peasant after all . . .*

By the time she heard car wheels clattering up the gravel of the drive, all the calm she had achieved when looking at herself in her bathroom mirror was lost; she was an utter bundle of nerves. Shoving the glass back on the kitchen counter, she dashed upstairs again to the living room, determined to let herself be found as she had planned, lounging elegantly on the formal sofa. She grabbed the Swedish crime novel as she went, thinking it would look better if she were absorbed in a book, not just sitting there counting the minutes till his arrival. She was barely back on the sofa, face flushed, trying to smooth down her hair, relief flooding through her like a tidal wave, when she heard the front door swing open.

'*Ciao, bella! Dove sei?*'

The sound of his voice sent a spike up through her; she twisted on it, momentarily unable to speak. She wanted to punish him for being so late – she looked at the clock on the mantelpiece. It was almost eight thirty. How dare he keep her waiting so long?

Cesare was coming up the stairs now; she heard the leather soles of his shoes on the stone treads. '*Sei qui?* Are you here?'

He entered the living room and stopped dead at the sight of Devon on the sofa, the book in her hands; with horror, she realized that it was upside down, and quickly she put it down on the coffee table.

'Goodness,' she said coldly, 'what time is it? I wasn't expecting you for hours!'

She looked at him, and her breath caught in her throat at the expression on his face. He was staring at her as if he wanted to eat her up, his eyes glinting almost savagely.

'*Sei bellissima*,' he said quietly, looking her up and down, from the toes of her black suede Kandees stilettos to the crown of her head. '*Bellissima*. You are the most beautiful woman I have ever seen in my life.'

Devon gripped onto the arm of the sofa for support; even sitting down, when Cesare stared at her like that she felt weak. Especially because he just kept staring, and she knew that he was taking in every detail of her appearance, the silver necklace glinting at her throat, the diamonds in her ears, the pretty painted fingernails. The silence grew, like a cloud, a bubble enclosing both of them, from which his intensity was sucking out all the air; she could barely breathe. She stared at him just as greedily, looking him up and down; dark blue silk shirt tucked into slim black trousers, showing off his narrow, lean frame. Smart: he had dressed up for her too. And it even looked as if he had shaved before coming out. His jaw was remarkably free of stubble. She wondered if he had put on aftershave, and if so, what it smelled like, and the idea of being close enough to smell him made her shiver.

'Shouldn't we go?' she said eventually in a tiny voice, staring back at him. Still holding the arm of the sofa, she stood up, adjusting her dress, tugging down the hem to hit just below her knees. It was hard to move, though. She was actually frightened to approach him, to walk towards the door; the idea of them going downstairs, of her collecting her wrap and her bag from where she had placed them in the front hall, seemed unimaginable.

'*Si*,' Cesare said, as if he had been hypnotized and was responding automatically. 'We have a reservation for nine o'clock.'

'Is it far?'

Why am I asking? Devon thought hopelessly. *I don't give a damn how far away the restaurant is . . .*

'*Un po' di strada*,' he answered, still staring at her.

And then she knew why she'd kept asking questions. Because when she stopped talking, when she simply stood there, looking back at him, the silence was overwhelming. The bubble pressed in around them, tighter and tighter, enclosing them in a space that wasn't about speech at all, but something much more basic. Neither of them dared to move. It was, Devon realized, the calm before the storm. And she did, for one long, breathless, endless-seeming moment, feel strangely calm.

If Cesare had turned away, broken the spell for a little while, headed out of the living room and down the stairs, gesturing for her to follow him, they might have managed to maintain the civilities of proper behaviour for a little while longer. Might even have reached the restaurant. And as soon as Devon realized that, she couldn't bear it, couldn't wait a moment longer. *I've been waiting since last night for this. No, since he kissed my hand in my bedroom and I fell hopelessly in lust with him.*

No. I've been waiting my whole life for this.

She took a step towards him. He stared at her wildly, almost like a nervous horse, eyes rolling. She took another step; she was very close to him now. And she could smell his aftershave; he hadn't stinted on it. Dry and citrussy, like crushed lime leaves, with a tang of something stronger behind them; bay rum.

'I thought,' she said, still in a tiny voice, because it was all she could manage, 'I thought in Italy you kissed people on the cheek to say hello and goodbye? I don't want to be rude and have you shout at me again.'

And, propping one hand on his shoulder, she leaned in and kissed his right cheek. His body was as tense as a wire; his shoulder muscles felt like steel under her palm, but he didn't react in any way. Disappointed, persevering, she turned to his left side, deliberately brushing her breasts against his chest, kissing his other cheek now. And when he still didn't, as she had hoped, crack and kiss her, she summoned up her courage, and trailed her lips along his cheek, slowly till she reached his mouth. She planted a single light kiss on it, feeling how taut he was; his lips were actually clamped together, wouldn't respond to hers at all.

Pulling back, taking her hand away, she looked at him; as she was wearing heels, he was probably no taller than her, if you didn't take the shock of his hair into account.

'Well then,' she said, smiling at him as enchantingly, as seductively as she could manage. 'Have we said hello properly now?'

Cesare's lips unclamped. He muttered something Devon couldn't hear, but which, from its tone, she assumed was a string of curses. And then he reached out for her, clamping her against him. She practically threw herself into his arms as their mouths met, gasped with happiness as he kissed her and she kissed him back. It was all she could do not to burst into tears with sheer relief. The kiss was just as powerful as she remembered from last night. It hadn't been the drink, the hot springs, the intoxication of an Italian early summer evening with a half moon in the velvet night sky; it had been all Cesare, the chemistry between him and her, which was now eating them both up like flames licking over their bodies.

And, as if they had really been on fire, frantic to strip burning clothes off before the flames ate into their flesh, they grabbed at each other, tearing impatiently at buttons and zips, grabbing and pulling to reach bare skin. Cesare reached down and with one pull tugged the hem of Devon's dress from where she had demurely smoothed it below her knees. He lifted it right up to her waist, making her gasp at the shock of the cooler air on her skin, and then, a split second later, at the heat of his hands on her lace-covered bottom, fingers sinking in, pulling her even closer to him. He gasped too, his hands roaming up and down, finding the tops of her stockings, exploring the bare skin between them and the edge of her French knickers.

'*Madonna mia,*' he groaned against her mouth. '*Che cosa mi fai . . . sto impazzendo per te . . .*'

'Oh God, yes,' Devon begged, ripping at his shirt, running her hands over his chest, sinking her fingers into the curly hairs, trying to pull the shirt off his shoulders as best she could. 'Keep talking Italian, Cesare, please . . .'

'*Ti piace?*' he asked, sinking his tongue into her mouth, his fingers into the round curves of her bottom, kneading the soft skin. '*Ti piace, signora?*'

She thought that meant 'Do you like it?' and, as soon as she could speak again, as soon as her mouth was free, because he was kissing her neck, down to her breasts, pulling her dress off her shoulders so he could bare her lacy bra, she managed to moan out a 'Yes, yes!' that was all the answer he needed.

'*Allora, parlero Italiano per te, bella mia,*' he said, his hands behind her back, undoing her bra as she ran her own over his small, firm buttocks, cupping them as he had cupped hers. '*Ti parlo Italiano quanto vuoi, basta che continui a toccarmi cosi . . .*'

He dragged her bra up, baring her breasts, groaning in pleasure as he saw them for the first time, his hands closing round them, lifting them so he could kiss and lick one taut nipple and then the other. Devon's legs gave way under her in slow motion at the sensation; there was absolutely no way she could keep standing up while Cesare was doing this to her. She grabbed at the coffee table on the way down, Cesare collapsing with her, bracing their fall; they landed on the carpet in a tangle of limbs, Cesare's mouth still, miraculously, kissing and nipping at her breasts.

And suddenly, Devon realized something. They were in a villa, empty apart from them, in the middle of the countryside. However much noise she made, no one would hear. She could do what she'd always dreamed of doing during sex, what Cesare was making her want to do more than ever before; she could scream as loudly as she wanted. In a complete rapture of abandonment, she opened her mouth and shrieked in ecstasy and appreciation of what Cesare was doing.

He loved it, as she had assumed she would. He redoubled his efforts, which sent her into an even higher pitch.

'*Si, bella,*' he groaned into her breasts, '*si, grida per me – dimmi che ti piaccio, grida per me . . .*'

His hands were on her thighs now, pulling down her knickers. Devon raised her hips to help him, and, not to be outdone, managed to get her hands up to his waist, half-sitting up, kissing him madly as she undid his belt, and, with huge relief, felt not only the size and girth of his cock as she unzipped his trousers, but the unmistakeable outline of a condom wrapper in his pocket.

'Oh, thank God,' she muttered, pulling out the latter and biting it to tear it open frantically, in a desperate hurry to have Cesare inside her. Then she screamed again as her wish was immediately granted, his fingers deftly parting her and sliding into her, finding her wet and more than ready for him.

'*Jesu santo, sei cosi bagnata,*' he groaned, as she clung to his shoulders, momentarily paralyzed by the sensations rushing through her. Then she started to move, to ride his fingers, her face buried in his hair, her eyes closed, concentrating utterly selfishly on what she wanted, working herself against him and his clever fingers till in a moment she came in a spasm so intense it was like a stab up through her, leaving her collapsed and panting with relief against his body. Only dimly did she register him snatching the unwrapped condom from her limp fingers, rolling it on and pressing her down onto the carpet, positioning his cock with his hand and then driving it into her with one long motion.

If Devon had screamed before, it had been nothing compared to the volume that she achieved now. With every thrust Cesare made inside her, she shrieked in ecstasy, her hands wrapped around his forearms, which were braced on either side of her. She dug her fingers in, feeling the hairs on his arms, the muscle, the throbbing veins, managing to keep her eyes open to watch his face above her, contorted now in his efforts not to come immediately, but to draw this out as much as he could; she delighted in every tortured line of his face, his eyes drawn into dark slits of concentration.

And then she realized why she was screaming so very loudly. Cesare's cock had a curve to it; she had felt it just now, running her hands over him. And that bend in his cock was hitting what must be her G spot, or at least a particular place inside her that felt better than anything had ever felt before. It was as if he were a sex toy made specifically to fit her, ramming and ramming against that sensitive nub of flesh till she felt herself letting go utterly, her fingers slipping from his arms as her hips bucked against him in spasms of orgasm, her head beating against the carpet.

With a yell of '*Ti vengo – cazzo, ti vengo!*' Cesare plunged into her in a last few pounding strokes, even more strong and overwhelming than before, sending Devon completely over the edge. She'd wanted to feel him coming inside her, but was so lost in her own orgasms that she missed it. He collapsed on top of her, their bodies still jerking and throbbing against each other's, reluctant to finish. Devon came again in a final little extra of release that drew a squeak of surprise and pleasure from her and made Cesare grunt as his still-hard cock felt her briefly spasm around him again.

'*Mio Dio*,' he muttered into her breasts. '*Mai sentito qualcosa cosi.*'

'What?' she said, her eyes closed, reaching up to stroke his hair.

He planted a kiss on each breast and rolled off her; she whimpered, feeling his weight withdrawn. Carefully, he pulled off the condom.

'*Ma, guardo quanto*,' he observed smugly, looking at it before he discarded it on the stone floor. 'I make a lot of *sperma*,' he said, lying back down next to her on the carpet and pulling her into his arms. 'I am very manly with you. I come a lot.'

Devon started to giggle. 'Only you,' she said, 'would boast about how much you'd come.'

'It is a compliment to you,' Cesare said, kissing her hair. 'With you, a man makes a lot of *sperma*. You are very much a woman.'

'Thank you,' she said, still giggling. 'That's really beautiful.'

'*Ero cosi eccitato, sono ancora duro*,' Cesare added. 'I am still *duro*.' He took her hand and reached it down, between his legs; it was true, his cock was still hard. 'I am very excited for you,' he said matter-of-factly.

Devon's dress was entirely bunched around her waist, her bra hanging off one arm; Cesare's trousers and silk boxer shorts were round his knees. They were both still wearing their shoes; they must have looked completely ridiculous. But all Devon could think about was Cesare's cock in her hand, hot and slippery, and still, amazingly, as hard as if it had a bone inside it. She couldn't stop herself. She ran her hand up and down it, slowly, twisting and stroking, drawing a series of groans and picturesque Italian swear words from him. Eventually, he reached over and slid a couple of fingers between her legs, finding her equally slippery nub and bringing her to orgasm as slowly as he could, again and again, a series of heady, gradual climaxes that built on each other, one not quite finished before the next began. She never let go of his cock; she was proud of that.

'*Ti trombo di nuovo,*' he said, finally coaxing her to her knees. 'I fuck you again now.'

'Oh, yes please,' Devon said with great enthusiasm; but then she froze as she felt his now dripping fingers leaving her pussy and running between her buttocks instead, parting them gently, one finger sliding in, and then two before she even realized what he was going to do. It felt wonderful, but she couldn't help stiffening; this was something that men she'd been with before had begged to do, and considered a huge favour on her part if she had agreed. And she'd seen it as a favour, too; she had definitely always seen it as something she should be asked for, something that she enjoyed much less than them, and should be cajoled, flattered, persuaded into bestowing on rare occasions.

And now Cesare was acting as if he could just do it without even asking her permission! She was outraged. Even more so when she heard him unwrap another condom.

'Wait a minute,' she started to say, but then he bent over her, his mouth closing round her ear, breathing hot against it, licking and biting her lobe, the hand not at her rear wrapping round her, descending between her legs, sliding into her again, making her stop talking and moan and rear against him instead, her hands reaching out to hold onto the back of the sofa.

'*Eccola,*' he said softly against her ear. '*Eccoti. Ora mi prendi.*'

Somehow, his fingers had come out of her bottom, and his cock was easing into it, very slowly, letting her tighten in resistance, waiting cunningly until his fingers, making her come slowly, tricked her body into relaxing; and then he pushed in further, in stages, each orgasm making her looser, more helpless, till she realized that she was pushing back against him, wanting him further inside her, taking him in.

'*Brava,*' he said complacently. '*Bravissima.*'

'You *bastard,*' she said, deeply annoyed at how effortlessly he had achieved his goal, but unable to resist pushing back against him harder now, the sensations flooding through her utterly, overwhelmingly positive. 'You absolute, twisted, fucking *bastard.*'

But those were the last coherent words she managed to utter. After that she started to scream. She held onto the back of the sofa for dear life, screaming what was almost an aria of release as Cesare began to move faster now, sliding in and out, never stopping the work of his fingers between her legs, making sure that she was entirely under his spell. By the time he was ready to come, she was limp and utterly satisfied, feeling him plunging inside her, his hands rising to close over hers on the sofa, gripping and twining through her fingers, his entire torso pressed tightly into her back, his mouth on her neck, as he yelled his climax into her sweat-drenched skin, jerking up again and again as he came.

I will never be happier than this, Devon knew, as his curly head collapsed onto her shoulder, as they slid, once more, entwined, back to the carpet in utter exhaustion, their bodies throbbing with overloaded sensation and damp with sweat, lying side by side, Cesare still inside her. *It would be impossible. I will never, ever, be happier than this.*

Deeley

*I*t had been three days now, and Deeley was still too terrified to go back to the flat in Green Street by herself. She felt horribly alone. If she'd had a friend she could trust to come with her, even just to stand guard on the street, ready to let her know if someone was following Deeley down the steps to the flat's front door, it would have been a different story. She could at least have cleared the flat of her things, moved them into Maxie's nanny flat upstairs; she was dying to get the rest of her clothes.

No, that was a silly overstatement. She wasn't dying. But she was scared that she might be, if she made another mistake. Deeley was absolutely sure that going up to Riseholme had set this whole train of events in motion; the push into traffic at King's Cross, the warning on the door of her flat. She had been followed the whole way back to London. And who would do that but the terrifying woman she'd met in Thompson Road? She'd told Deeley to back off, and then made sure of it by setting someone else to trail Deeley to her home. *No way could that woman have followed me herself*, Deeley knew. *I walked up and down the Leeds to London train, looking for a seat; I'd have seen her, I'm sure.*

Which meant that the woman was as powerful as she had intimated to Deeley. She had people she could summon up in an instant, from the moment Deeley turned to head back to Riseholme Station. And not only to follow Deeley, but to menace her by shoving her in front of a bus.

She thinks I know something. Deeley had worked out that much. *But what is it?*

What could I possibly know that could make me dangerous to her? The entire situation was loaded with irony; surely the boot was on the other foot. It was Maxie, Devon and Deeley who shared a terrible, guilty secret. If anyone should be threatening people, it was the three McKenna sisters. And yet there was no mistaking that woman's message. Stay away from Riseholme. Keep your mouth shut.

It's not just me, that's the real worry, Deeley knew, blaming herself utterly for this whole mess. *I've brought them to Devon's. They know the house now, where Devon and Matt live. And maybe someone even followed me here . . .*

She drew a deep breath, telling herself that now she'd gone too far. Devon and Maxie were public figures; it wouldn't be hard to find out where they lived. That woman in Thompson Road had known about them, said they'd done well for themselves.

Besides, Devon's still off in Italy. Safely away from this whole nightmare. Deeley, like everyone else in the country, had watched Devon on *1-2-3 Cook*, and cringed at the sight. When Devon had texted her and Maxie, saying that she was off to hide out in Italy, Deeley had thought it was the best thing that could happen.

But then the press had been shocking over the next couple of days, tearing poor Devon apart. They had gone so far, in fact, that Deeley had thought Devon might be able to turn the situation to her advantage. Deeley had seen this before in LA, when actor friends or acquaintances of Nicky's had been hyped in a new series that had proceeded to tank in the ratings, and been pulled by the network after only a couple of episodes. It could be a career killer, but it could also be a stepping stone, because the sheer amount of publicity that had been poured into those actors had to go somewhere. Their faces had been all over billboards, buses, TV promos.

People knew who they were, recognized them, would feel a friendly familiarity if they saw them again.

And there was already a backlash building against *1-2-3 Cook*, which a clever publicist working for Devon could use and spin to help restore Devon's reputation. With plenty of time on her hands, Deeley spent a good deal of it on the net, and she'd come across several comment pieces suggesting that Devon had been set up. The contestant she'd been paired with had, apparently, been a known grump, who'd kept auditioning for the show but had only been selected when Devon, a novice to the format, had been on. Devon wasn't known for her live cooking skills, it was plucky that she'd tried at all, another article had said, and she should be commended for it. Catch Nigella or Nigel on one of those daytime shows!

Deeley had emailed Devon, expressing her sympathy, and telling her, too, that she didn't think Devon's career was by any means in tatters. Telling Devon she should think about coming back to London and planning a triumphant comeback. It was all true: Deeley had meant every word. But it was also to expiate her own guilt at having nearly had sex with Devon's husband.

Deeley closed her eyes for a split second; it was hard not to when she thought, even briefly, about Matt. It would have been so simple for her to make an excuse to see him – tell him about the graffiti on the flat door, ask him to stand guard as she packed up her things. But she was nobly refusing to do it, though it was an awful, sinful temptation that nagged at her every waking minute. Matt had no idea where she was, and he couldn't get in touch with her, even if he'd wanted to. As long as she stayed away, she was safe. They were safe.

It was incredibly depressing how lonely it was sometimes to do the right thing.

Jeff had been ringing her; he was in Strasbourg, travelling for work, but due back in London in a couple of days. They were going out to dinner at the weekend. *Thank God*, Deeley thought. *I've got a date lined up with a nice guy – even better, one who knows that I'm*

*on the rebound, and won't expect more from me than I can manage. I
need all the distraction from Matt I can get . . .*

Deeley's hands, pushing Alice in the baby swing, had slackened
as she remembered Matt: Alice, sensing a lack of attention, yelled
impatiently, a 'Wah!' that Deeley knew meant 'Go faster!' She
redoubled her efforts, looking down at the tight head of dark curls
below her, rocking back and forth, small chubby hands doing their
best to hold onto the bars of the swing.

At least it isn't all bad, she told herself, as she had done ever since
she came to Maxie and Olly's. *At least I have Alice to hang out with*.

She lifted her niece out of the swing and took her over to the
baby slide, setting her on the top, holding her as she slid down to
the bottom, screaming her approval and a clear desire to do it again.
Deeley had a strong feeling that Alice's first word might well be
'again', or as close to it as she could manage. She was a very happy
child, which was a miracle when you considered that she'd been
given up by a family that couldn't afford to feed her, and housed in
a so-called orphanage for months before being selected from a
picture by Maxie and flown to London by two government officials.
What on earth her life would be like with Maxie and Olly, Deeley
couldn't imagine.

'Don't worry, Alice in Wonderland,' she said now, hoisting her
niece into the air and back onto the top of the slide again. 'Auntie
Deeley will always be around. You can come and stay with me any
time.'

She pulled a face. 'Actually, you may not need to run far,' she
added, as Alice swooped down the slide again. 'Auntie Deeley may
be living upstairs at Mummy and Daddy's for the next twenty
years, the way her life's going.'

Since Deeley's instant bond with Alice, Maxie had definitely
slackened off her emergency efforts to find a nanny; she was going
through a protracted interview process, as far as Deeley could see,
but seemed perfectly content to have her younger sister looking
after her daughter for as long as it suited everyone. And being with
Alice was utterly absorbing for Deeley. She'd always wanted

children, but had never really spent time with one; the few kids of friends or work colleagues of Nicky's in LA had been surrounded by nannies and housekeepers, kept well away from any kind of social life. Deeley knew how the game was played: you had a baby, sold the newborn pictures for charity (which meant great publicity for you) and then arranged for the paparazzi to photograph you out buying pumpkins with the kids at Hallowe'en, or taking them to the beach, so you could demonstrate how in shape you were for having just given birth. The trick was, of course, that in return for the tip-off, the paparazzi made sure to keep the hovering nannies out of shot, to make it look as if you were taking care of your child all by yourself. Which never happened: it was quite common for movie stars to have two nannies per child. Just in case.

So this was the first time Deeley had spent with a child. And she loved it. Not the nappy-changing and occasional tantrums, of course: she wasn't a saint. But at twenty months, little Alice was so engaging, so lively and interested in the world around her that Deeley adored her already. Alice's noisy but non-verbal company gave Deeley all the time she needed to get herself together. Reflect on the total mess that, so far, she'd made of her life. And start to think about what she could do to turn it all around.

Alice was beginning to get wilful, her cries more plaintive; signs that she was tiring out. Deeley looked at her watch. Definitely nap time. She loaded the protesting child into her stroller, waving good-bye to the other nannies in the little park. They'd already made acquaintances, the Filipinas and Jamaicans and Eastern Europeans finding it utterly hilarious that Deeley was the only white nanny looking after a black baby in SW1; it was a complete anomaly. 'Always the other way around,' Rosa from Trinidad had said the first day, giggling her head off. 'Always black nanny and white baby here.'

'I'm unemployable,' Deeley had said, making them all laugh harder, but, she'd known ruefully, it wasn't far from the truth. She was seriously thinking of asking Maxie to give her the job of being Alice's nanny. Deeley loved it, found it hugely satisfying – *and honestly, what else could I do? This or waitressing!*

Alice was asleep in five minutes, conked out after a hard morning's play in the park. Reaching Maxie and Olly's house, Deeley went up the steps to unlock the door, then descended them again, bending down to pick up the stroller and carry it up into the house; she might even let Alice nap in it, if she really seemed fast asleep. Deeley had changed Alice's nappy in the park toilets so she should be fine to sleep for an hour or so without being woken up by a cold wet bottom . . .

Absorbed with the usual calculations of looking after a small child, Deeley was too busy settling the stroller in the living room, undoing Alice's jacket so she wouldn't be too hot, and pulling off her own, to realize that Lucia, the housekeeper, was hovering in the hallway with a worried expression on her usually calm face.

'OK if I leave Alice here, Lucia?' Deeley asked, drawing the living room door to, leaving it cracked enough so she could easily hear Alice when she woke up. 'She's conked out, and it seems a pity to wake her up just to carry her up to bed . . .'

Her voice trailed off as she took in Lucia's look of concern.

'What's wrong?' she asked quickly. 'Are Maxie and Olly all right?'

Lucia was actually wringing her hands, Deeley saw; it must be very bad.

'It's the police!' she exclaimed, her wide forehead corrugated. 'They came twenty minutes ago, to see you and Mrs Stangroom!'

Grabbing Deeley's sleeve and dragging her into the office, where two men, one in uniform, one in plain clothes, were sitting in front of the large keyhole desk, Lucia announced: 'Miss Deeley – Mrs Stangroom's sister,' and dashed out of the room again, closing the door behind her.

'My God, what is it?' Deeley stood there, looking frantically from one to the other.

Both men had automatically got to their feet on seeing her. The uniformed one just stared, momentarily dumbstruck at the long jean-clad legs, the cascading caramel hair, the extremely pretty face; the older one, collecting his wits much sooner, said, 'Miss McKenna? Don't worry, miss. None of your family are hurt. It's not that.'

He had read Deeley's thoughts perfectly. She sagged against the door with relief, drawing in a deep breath.

'God, I was so worried!' she said.

'Or rather . . .' He indicated the chair behind the desk. 'Maybe you'd better sit down, miss. I'm Detective Inspector Wenn, and this is DC Davis.'

Deeley walked around the desk, sitting in Olly's huge leather swivel chair, which was big enough for two of her.

'Well, it's not exactly family,' he continued, and as Deeley recognized the familiar accent of her childhood, an awful suspicion began to grow in her. She stared at him wide-eyed, praying she was wrong, as he continued. 'Do you remember a friend of your mother's you lived with for six months or so in 1993? You'd have been a kid then . . .'

He glanced sideways at DC Davis, who was already flicking through a notepad on his lap.

'Nine years old, I make it, sir,' he said promptly.

'Nine, or thereabouts,' DI Wenn said. 'With both of your sisters. I'm referring to a gentleman called Bill Duncan. He lived at 42 Thompson Road, in Riseholme. Any memories of him at all?'

There was no point denying that she remembered Bill. Her mouth dry, Deeley nodded, unable to take her eyes of Wenn's stolid face.

'Well, the thing is, we've just found his body,' DI Wenn said, watching her very carefully as he delivered this news. 'Buried in the back garden, of all things. Is this a surprise to you, Miss McKenna?'

Deeley fumbled desperately for the right words. She was nowhere near finding them when the office door burst open, and Maxie appeared, looking like the wrath of God in human form. Wearing a pale stone belted raincoat, her blonde hair pulled back off her face, her make-up perfect, she projected such an imperious air of command that both policemen jumped to their feet at her appearance.

'What on *earth* is going on?' she demanded. 'Deeley, what have you *done*? Honestly, I leave you with Alice for a couple of days – I thought at least you could manage to look after a baby without too much trouble—'

'Mrs Stangroom,' DI Wenn interjected, 'this isn't about your baby, or Miss McKenna's care of her. I'm Detective Inspector Wenn, of the Greater Leeds police force, and this is Detective Constable Davis. Would you mind taking a seat so we can discuss why we're here?'

Maxie didn't take off her raincoat; she didn't even unbutton it, clearly indicating that she did not intend to be detained for long. She stalked across the office. Deeley jumped up from the desk chair, looking around her for another; not finding one, she stood awkwardly as Maxie sank into the leather chair, swivelled it to face the policemen, and snapped, 'Well, what is it? I haven't got all day, you know!'

'It's about a body, Mrs Stangroom,' DI Wenn said, and Deeley saw he was watching Maxie closely, trying to read her reaction. 'The body of a gentleman called Bill Duncan, with whom you and your sisters lived for a while when you were younger. It's just been found in the back garden of the house in which you lived with Mr Duncan.'

Maxie's eyebrows shot up, but otherwise she betrayed nothing. Deeley, watching Maxie anxiously, was hugely relieved by her sister's poise.

Thank God Maxie's here, she thought devoutly. *Maxie will know what to say. She'll make everything all right*.

'I don't understand,' Maxie said after a moment. 'That was so long ago. I was, what, seventeen or so when we moved out of there? Deeley, you must have been . . .'

'Nine,' Deeley chimed in, feeling she should say something.

'Exactly!' Maxie looked back at DI Wenn. 'Almost twenty years ago!'

'Not quite,' the DC mumbled, but Maxie ignored him.

'How many people must have lived in that house since then?' she demanded. 'Are you interviewing all of them? What a colossal waste of time!'

'Oh, we can narrow it down reasonably accurately,' DI Wenn said, making Deeley's heart sink as fast as it had risen at her sister's defiant words. 'Mr Duncan's disappearance was recorded at the time. His brother reported it to the police. Mr Duncan was an upstanding citizen, Mrs Stangroom, very respectable – bills paid on time, steady job, good pension plan, all the bells and whistles. Not the sort of bloke to go disappearing from one day to the next. You must have felt that too, you and your sisters. Must have been quite a shock to you all.'

He looked from Maxie to Deeley, his expression inquiring. Deeley started to say something, then bit her tongue as Maxie leaned forward.

'DI – Wenn, is it?' she said coldly. 'It's no secret that my sisters and I had a troubled childhood. We have never tried to conceal it. But that doesn't mean that I will stand by and see our humble origins dragged through the dirt for the benefit of the tabloid newspapers. My husband is the junior minister for the Department of External Affairs. It would look very bad to the party if they felt this were simply an attempt to smear him by the opposition.'

DI Wenn's eyes flickered; Deeley could see that Maxie's words had hit home.

'Mrs Stangroom, please,' he said, shifting in his chair. 'I'm only doing my job. You and your two sisters were living with Mr Duncan at the date he was reported missing. Now his body's turned up and our forensic guys say that they think he went into the ground more or less at the time he disappeared. Which puts the three of you on the spot, as it were. I'd be neglecting my duty if I didn't ask you these questions.'

'If *anything* leaks to the press, my husband will have you sacked,' Maxie said levelly. 'Do we understand each other?' She glanced at DC Davis, who looked petrified. 'And that includes you,' she added nastily.

'Mrs Stangroom!' DI Wenn raised both his hands in the universal gesture with which a man tries to calm down an angry woman. 'Please, let's not get ahead of ourselves! Can I just ask you some questions about you and your sisters' knowledge of the timeline around Mr Tennyson's disappearance?'

Maxie stared at him narrowly. 'Under what circumstances was his body discovered?' she asked. 'It seems very odd that it should just have been – what? – in that back garden, for all this time? Wouldn't people have seen a grave, or something?'

Oh, very good, Maxie! Deeley thought approvingly. She was resting her hands on the desk for support, her palms beginning to dampen the wood; but that was OK. Anyone would be nervous under these circumstances. *And Maxie's such a good liar. She'll get us all out of this.*

Rattled now, DI Wenn made the mistake of answering.

'It was buried under an old wall, Mrs Stangroom. Sort of in the roots of a tree. Very well concealed.'

Maxie pounced on this immediately. 'So how was it found?' she demanded.

'Mrs Stangroom, I'm not at liberty to—'

'*Please,*' Maxie said with such acid in her voice that even Deeley flinched; DC Davis actually flattened himself against the back of his chair, looking terrified. 'My husband is *just* promoted to junior minister . . .'

God, Deeley couldn't help noticing, *Maxie loves saying those words!*

'. . . and bang on cue, some body's unearthed in a house my sisters and I used to live in? The timing is very suspicious, Detective Inspector! I want to know how this body was found! Otherwise I, my husband and the party will *assume* that this is some kind of opposition conspiracy to start a scandal!'

She had DI Wenn on the run now; he couldn't meet her eyes. Instead, he glanced nervously at his sidekick, who was no help at all, before eventually stammering, 'Look, Mrs Stangroom, I really can't—'

'It will look *much* better if I hear it from you,' Maxie said crisply, 'than if my husband has to demand answers from your chief constable.'

DI Wenn sagged visibly. He sighed, long and hard.

Poor man, Deeley thought, almost sympathetically. *He should have known better than to say no to Maxie.*

'We apprehended several individuals in the process of digging up Mr Duncan's body last night,' Wenn said reluctantly. 'They were under the command, as it were, of Linda O'Keeffe, who is well known to all of us in the local police force.'

Maxie didn't react to the mention of the name, but Deeley held onto the desk hard to stop trembling. That was the name of the woman she'd met outside Bill's house: Linda O'Keeffe. She'd seen her before, when she was little; she had vague memories of her mother in the pub with her, heard her name mentioned as someone you never crossed if you knew what was good for you.

Oh God, if Maxie finds out I went back to Riseholme and bumped into Linda O'Keeffe, she'll kill me! Deeley thought frantically. *Because I have the awful feeling that's what started all of this . . .*

'When arrested, Mrs O'Keeffe denied that she had anything to do with the death of Mr Duncan,' DI Wenn was continuing. 'She told us that she was looking for something that she believed Mr Duncan to have in his possession when he disappeared in 1993.' He stared hard at both Maxie and Deeley in turn. 'Something that he was actually keeping for your mother, who was in prison at the time.'

'What?' Deeley couldn't help blurting out, her eyes wide. 'Bill was keeping something for Mum? He never said anything about that!'

Maxie shrugged her shoulders dismissively. 'Why should he say anything to us?' she said. 'I never wanted to know what our mother was up to,' she added, directing this at the policemen across the desk. 'It was never good. Believe me, we all got away from her messes as soon as we could and never looked back.'

'I do understand that, Mrs Stangroom,' DI Wenn said swiftly. 'And we're very sympathetic to your position. But these are questions I have to ask. Mrs O'Keeffe has told us that your mother had an old canvas bag containing about thirty grand in cash which she gave to Mr Duncan to keep for her. Mrs O'Keeffe's story is that this was, in fact, her money – Mrs O'Keeffe's – given to your mother by her to store with Mr Duncan, who was considered trustworthy. Mr Duncan was keeping the money for your mother and Mrs O'Keeffe as they were both going to prison, having been convicted of receiving stolen goods in the same court case.'

He looked down briefly at his notes.

'When Mrs O'Keeffe came out of prison, according to her, she immediately contacted Mr Duncan, or tried to. On finding out that he was missing, she assumed that he had run away with the money, and did her best to track him down, to no avail.'

He looked from one to the other of the sisters, gauging their reaction.

'Description of the bag, Davis?' he said to the constable.

'Green fabric, white plastic handles, white straps running around the sides, in poor condition,' DC Davis read from his notes.

'Ring any bells, ladies?' DI Wenn asked. 'See any bag like that in Mr Duncan's house?'

Deeley was gaping, completely taken aback. Thirty grand! She'd had no awareness of any of this. She looked at Maxie, whose eyebrows had risen, but whose smooth, Botoxed face was relatively unaffected.

'No, Bill never said a word about that to us,' Maxie said, shaking her head. 'But hold on . . .' Her eyes narrowed. 'This money – even if it existed, it was obviously obtained illegally. How do you know she's telling the truth – about the money, about everything? How do you know that she didn't kill him herself? She might have been digging up the body to move it, because she thought someone suspected it was there, and just concocted this whole story when you caught her at it.'

Brilliant, Maxie! Deeley thought, shooting a swift glance of congratulation at her sister for her quick wits. But her surge of confidence was short-lived.

'Because Mrs O'Keeffe was a guest of Her Majesty at the time Mr Duncan disappeared,' DI Wenn said dryly. 'Together with several of her known associates. Of whom, naturally, your mother was one. Neither she – nor your mother – could have been involved in killing Mr Duncan or concealing his body.'

Maxie's face was expressionless as she processed this information.

'She thinks you and your sisters had something to do with this,' DI Wenn continued. 'She informed us that she met Miss McKenna in Thompson Road a few weeks ago, standing outside number 42.'

Deeley's breath caught in her throat: the look Maxie shot her was terrifying. And now everyone was staring at her, waiting for an explanation.

'I've been away from the country for years,' Deeley managed. 'Living in LA. I got nostalgic when I came back here, that's all – seeing my sisters again, remembering old times. I had the impulse to go up to Riseholme and see it again.'

She swayed a little.

'Can I sit down?' she asked, and DC Davis instantly got up to offer her his chair, moving it round the desk so she could sit next to Maxie.

'Thank you,' she said, collapsing into it. 'This has been an awful shock.'

'It's perfectly normal for my sister to go back and revisit somewhere that was a childhood home,' Maxie said, reaching over to pat Deeley's hand in a show of sympathy that was all for the police's benefit. 'Nothing odd in that at all.'

'Mrs O'Keeffe told us that Miss McKenna was staring fixedly at the tree and the crumbling wall in the garden for some minutes,' DI Wenn said, leaning forward and staring hard at both sisters. 'Enough to make her extremely suspicious. According to her, that was what gave Mrs O'Keeffe the idea to wait till the occupants of number 42 were away for the weekend, and enter the back garden to dig up the wall.'

'Oh, *please*,' Maxie said again; she sounded casual, dismissive, but her nails were digging into Deeley's hand now. 'My sister *stared at a wall?* That's what you're accusing her of? While someone who's been in prison is caught digging up a body – which might, for all you know, have died of natural causes! I don't know why you even bothered us with this!'

'There was a dent in the skull,' DC Davis, now standing behind his superior, piped up. 'The victim's neck was broken. He didn't die of natural causes.'

Maxie's nails were leaving deep, painful dents in Deeley's palm now. Memories of that awful night came flooding back: Devon wielding the vase, smashing Bill over the head; Devon and Maxie dragging his body out into the garden. Tears welled up in Deeley's eyes. The next thing she knew, she was sobbing, great gusty sobs of fear and panic.

'Look at what you've done!' Maxie snapped immediately, taking full advantage of the situation, scooting over to wrap her arm round Deeley's shoulders. 'Can you not understand how upsetting this is for us? We're not *like* those people! We made something of our lives! We got away from all that!'

DI Wenn tried to say something, but Maxie was in full flood.

'My poor sister!' she stormed. 'She was just a baby at the time! I remember Linda O'Keeffe – she was a drug dealer, the scum of the earth. And a madam too, I wouldn't be surprised. The way she looked at me and my sisters was downright nasty.'

Both DC Davis and DI Wenn flinched at this; Maxie had obviously hit the nail on the head with her speculations about Linda O'Keeffe.

'Some convicted criminal's caught red-handed digging up a body,' Maxie went on furiously, 'and points the finger at me and my sisters, because she's jealous of us! And you fell for that? It's so obvious! She's seen me and Devon on the television, and she's jumped at the chance to try to drag us down! And all the evidence she has is some allegedly missing money that no one can even prove existed, and the fact that my sister went back to visit a home that had some childhood memories for her. This is ludicrous!'

Deeley's sobs were abating as she heard Maxie make mincemeat of the police; Maxie was fighting the McKenna sisters' battles, as always. It was the most reassuring thing in the world. She took the tissue Maxie was handing her and wiped her eyes, sitting back in the chair, drawing deep breaths.

'We will need to take statements from all of you,' DI Wenn finally said in a smaller voice. 'You were living in the house at the time Mr Duncan disappeared. I'm afraid that's unavoidable.'

'We thought he'd abandoned us,' Maxie said, as if rehearsing the statement she would give. 'It was very frightening for all of us. And this news, after all these years, has been a total shock. You'll have to give us some time. Our sister Devon is in Italy at the moment, and will have to make her arrangements to return to London. And of course,' she levelled an icy dark gaze at DI Wenn, 'we will be accompanied by our solicitor.'

'That's not necessary . . .' DI Wenn began, but trailed off immediately as Maxie stood up.

'*I* will be the judge of what's *necessary*,' she said in biting tones, 'since you insist on dragging my sisters and myself into a matter that has nothing to do with us. If you leave me your contact details, I will have my solicitor contact you in due course.'

DI Wenn reached humbly for a card as Maxie said, tightening the belt of her raincoat, 'And now I will have to ask you to leave. I've wasted much too much time on this. I had an appointment to see Sir Tristram Cavendish, the chief whip of the party, for which I am now very late. I don't imagine he'll be best pleased when I explain the reason for my delay.'

Wenn and Davis couldn't leave fast enough; they practically tripped over their own feet getting out of the study. Maxie stood like a statue behind the desk until she heard the front door close, and saw them getting into their waiting car down the street. Then she rounded on Deeley like all three of the furies in one.

'You little idiot!' she yelled. 'You went *back to Riseholme!* You stupid little idiot! Did you say *anything* to that bitch Linda O'Keeffe about Bill? Anything at all?'

'No! I promise, Maxie! I didn't!'

Deeley felt nine years old all over again, looking up at her sister, whose cheeks were bright with livid spots of fury.

'I can't believe you did that!' Maxie fumed, striding up and down the office on her high red patent leather heels. 'Ugh! Well, one thing at a time. I'll deal with you later. Right now, you ring Dev and tell her she needs to get back here immediately and not to speak a word to *anyone* until she sees me, understood? *Anyone*. I'll ring the solicitor myself and explain the situation – by which I mean, give them the official story. After my appointment.' She looked at her watch. 'My God, I have to run!'

She swivelled to point a menacing finger at Deeley.

'You, keep your mouth shut, OK? And don't leave the house. You can take Alice into the garden, but that's it. Don't answer the door – journalists might get hold of the story and come round for a quote. Get Lucia to answer it and tell them no one's home. If you need anything, Lucia goes out to get it. You *do not leave this house for any reason at all.*'

Deeley nodded obediently as her sister dragged her phone out of her bag and tapped in some numbers.

'Hopefully Sir Tristram will understand,' she muttered as she dialled, walking towards the office door. Over her shoulder at Deeley, she snapped, 'Do everything I said and not a *thing* more!' as she whisked out of the room.

Alice, woken up by her adoptive mother's yelling, started to whimper in her stroller. Deeley was almost relieved; having Alice to look after, to comfort and play with, would distract her from her own guilt and fear at what she'd brought down on her sisters' heads. Maxie had slammed the front door and was running down the steps and Deeley watched her through the office window. A gust of wind caught Maxie's raincoat and blew it open. For a dizzying moment, Deeley actually thought that, underneath it, Maxie was wearing some sort of PVC miniskirt: white, with a red trim. *Almost like a nurse's outfit. A naughty nurse. As if she were going to a costume party, not an appointment with the chief whip.*

Deeley blinked, unable to believe her eyes, and when she looked again, her sister was as elegant and ladylike as ever, her raincoat demurely closed, raising her hand to stop a passing taxi.

My God, I'm so messed up by all of this I'm seeing things! Shaking her head, Deeley went into the front hall, bending down to unfasten her crying niece from the stroller. *I'll change her first*, she thought, reaching down to feel Alice's nappy: yes, it was damp. *And then I'll ring Devon, to tell her she needs to come back to London – not just for this awful situation with the police finding Bill, but for her husband too.*

She'll be glad to come back to Matt, I'm sure. She must be missing him so much.

Deeley took a deep breath, and picked up a sobbing Alice, trying very hard not to burst into tears herself.

Devon

*D*evon wasn't really in Italy. She wasn't in Tuscany, she wasn't in Villa Clara, she was barely on earth; she was on Cloud Nine, floating in a golden bubble of utter and total infatuation, her feet barely touching the ground, her eyes glowing like stars. She had never looked so beautiful in her life, and she hadn't worn make-up for three days; she felt light as a feather, and was sure she must be losing pounds, even though she was eating three times a day, proper meals, for the first time she could remember.

Because although she and Cesare had not left the house and grounds of Villa Clara since he came round that evening to take her out to dinner, and although they had spent what felt like pretty much every waking moment having sex wherever the mood took them (the marble shower had been fantastic, but they both had bruises from the stone staircase), Cesare had been insistent on not letting standards slip. They were going to eat properly in the intervals between sex sessions, and he was taking charge in the kitchen. The morning after his arrival, he had rung Laura, told her not to set foot in the villa, but to go shopping and to leave the bags outside the door: he had dictated a list of provisions to her, and told her to expect another list the next morning. Then he had hung up, because Devon was doing something to him that demanded his full attention, and also because he was making the kind of noises that would not be appropriate on a phone call to Rory's housekeeper.

After that, however, he had waited impatiently for Laura's arrival, and the ring on the doorbell that signalled the delivery of his order, then he had tripped happily downstairs, calling to Devon that breakfast was here. Cesare liked a sweet pastry in the morning, preferably a *torta di riso*, a little custard tart with a filling of cooked rice, which sounded bizarre, but was delicious, served with a cappuccino which he whipped up by beating air into heated milk until it foamed as richly as any Gaggia machine could manage. Lunch was light, but they still sat down to it; a salad, a pasta, a plate of *bresaola*, air-cured beef, rolled around soft white creamy cheese and served on a bed of rocket. Dinner was two courses, always, an antipasto or a pasta course, followed by meat or fish, and then, sometimes, a sorbet.

Devon ate everything he served. She had tried to protest about quantities, about her weight, about trying to avoid pasta and bread, but Cesare had just laughed at her, and she had caved in. *After all*, she'd thought, *I'm fucking five times a day, that has to be burning loads of calories.* And she'd forked up every exquisite meal Cesare had made. It had only dawned on her gradually that this food was actually not fattening; the little *torta di riso* in the morning was tiny, and that was all she had till a light lunch. Pasta servings were small, and the occasional piece of bread, laced with green extra-virgin oil, was a treat, rather than an entire basket-full. She was drinking much less than she usually did; they had a glass or two of wine with lunch, and the same with dinner. Maybe a Prosecco before dinner, and a Muscat afterwards, but the latter was served in a tiny dessert-wine glass, just a taste. Cesare did not approve of being drunk, or of drinking without food being served; when the food was finished, the wine was too.

Devon had originally been horrified by this: now she took it for granted. As she sat on the stool at the kitchen counter, watching Cesare make their lunch, she didn't say a word about the fact that he was proposing to serve toasted breadcrumbs over pasta in what sounded like a carbohydrate frenzy.

'This is a peasant dish,' he said, shaking the cast-iron pan in which the breadcrumbs were turning golden over a low heat, ensuring they toasted evenly.

'I thought we weren't peasants,' Devon said pertly. She was acutely aware that part of her charm for Cesare was the way she teased him, picked him up on things he said, refused to take him seriously; she sensed that this was something he wasn't used to with Italian women. He complained bitterly about her English sense of humour, but clearly loved it.

Now his eyes gleamed as he said over his shoulder, 'I was wrong, *cara mia*. You are English, so you are a peasant. You eat like a peasant. You think it is all right to use Martini for cooking if we have no white wine!' He shuddered theatrically, turning off the heat under the breadcrumbs. '*Che schifo!* Disgusting!' He grabbed a breadboard and a head of garlic, splitting off several cloves with his thumb.

'I just said it's a good backup,' Devon said rather sullenly. Cesare had taken to reading her cookbooks and quoting aloud extracts he found particularly amusing. 'You should try it sometime.'

'*Mai*,' he said firmly. Devon was rapidly learning Italian, and this, meaning 'never', was a word Cesare used very often indeed. '*Mai, mai e poi mai*,' he added, as if she needed extra clarification, while he deftly flattened the cloves with a wide-bladed knife, slid them out of their skins, and dropped them into another pan in which olive oil was heating.

'Also, you say to cook with extra-virgin olive oil!' he said, hooting with laughter, reaching for a jar of spaghetti, measuring the amount he wanted in the loop of his thumb and index finger, and then dropping it into a pan of boiling, salted water. 'All the taste of extra-virgin, it is lost when you make it hot! You are *pazza!*'

'What's *pazza?*' Devon asked crossly.

Cesare tapped the side of his head. '*Lunatica*,' he said cheerfully, stirring the spaghetti to separate the strands.

You couldn't give in to Cesare – not outside the bedroom, anyway. He'd run roughshod over you. Devon had worked that out very early on.

'*You're* mad,' she said firmly. 'How can you possibly call something "extra-virgin"? It doesn't make sense!'

Cesare giggled as he crumbled a few whole dried red chilli peppers into the oil, which was beginning to smell deliciously of garlic.

'*Certamente,*' he said, 'there are no extra virgins in Italy. Even the nuns, they make lots of fun with each other. But there are English virgins, maybe?' He leered at her. 'I tell you when we go to the *terme*, it is obvious you have not made love with a man of the Montigiani family. Now you are not a Montigiani virgin any longer.' He smirked. 'It is much better, no?'

'Absolutely not,' Devon retorted. 'You're terrible in bed. I'm only being polite when I say I like it.'

'*Bugiarda,*' Cesare said complacently, draining the pasta, dropping it into a large white ceramic bowl, and dressing it with the oil. 'You are a liar, Miss English.'

He sprinkled the breadcrumbs over the pasta, added some chopped parsley, and tossed it expertly with a pair of forks, disdaining Rory's designer utensils. 'Now we eat. I hope you are angry.'

Devon slid off the stool and followed him to the table.

'Angry,' she said, making a furious, frowning face. 'Hungry.' She rubbed her stomach. 'Try it again.'

'Aah!' Cesare slapped down the pasta bowl on the table. 'Always I say it wrong! *Haaangry!*'

'Huuungry.'

'Huangry.'

'Better,' Devon said. 'But still not perfect.'

Cesare scowled theatrically. 'You,' he said, 'make me aaangry.' He looked at her crossly. '*Donne,*' he said. 'Women. All they do is make a man angry.'

'Oh dear,' Devon said sadly. 'You should probably go, then.' She lifted her hand and flicked her fingers at him. 'Bye-bye. Thanks for lunch.'

'*Mi fai incazzare da morire,*' Cesare said, grabbing her shoulders and kissing her so hard her teeth rattled. By the time he had finished, she was weak at the knees; she had to grab onto the back of the chair for support. '*Ecco*,' he said, looking satisfied as he pulled up his own chair and sat down at the kitchen table. 'Now eat your *pasta-sciutta*. It is simple but very nice. And afterwards, we make love. When,' he added, twisting up a forkful of spaghetti, 'we have digested properly, of course.'

Devon sank into the chair, a flush of happiness pink in her cheeks. Every time Cesare referred to 'making love', her heart sang. It was ridiculous, of course, and she knew it. She was married; she still hadn't been able to get any further with that email to poor Matt; for all she knew, Cesare was married too, with children and a string of other mistresses, just amusing himself for a few days with some visiting Englishwoman before he resumed his normal life.

On every level, it was much too early to even think of the word 'love'. What they had might be just sex, which would burn itself out as quickly as it had caught fire.

And yet, whenever Cesare said '*fare l'amore*', or 'make love', Devon melted with sentiment. She wasn't brave enough, or Italian enough, to use those words herself; she'd whispered them to herself, tested them out, but she was much too English to say 'make love' as casually as she would say 'have sex'.

She took a bite of spaghetti, and moaned, taken aback at how good it was. Cesare looked at her smugly across the table.

'It is what we eat when we are young,' he said. 'When you have been out dancing with your friends, and you come home at *alba* . . .' He clicked his fingers to help him remember the English word. 'Dawn,' he said triumphantly. 'You come home at dawn, and you are angry – *huuungry* – so you make something to eat that will be good for you. It is restorative. Garlic, chilli, some parsley. *Molto buono.*' He gestured with his fork. 'We have not been dancing, but we need to eat restorative food, I think.'

Devon was smiling at how serious Cesare's expression always was when he talked about food – much more serious than when he talked about making love – when her phone rang. It had rung a few times over the last few days, and she had ignored it every single time: but this was different. It simply kept ringing. Whoever was calling didn't let the phone go to voicemail; they cut off as soon as they heard the message, and rang back. Three times, four times, five times: by the fifth, Cesare said firmly. 'Devon, *cara*, it is important. You must answer your phone. *Almeno*,' he added, 'to make it stop. It is annoying me.'

Devon sighed, pushed back her chair, and stood up, feeling as reluctant as a sulky child. She went into the hallway, where her bag was lying, with her phone inside; she was actually surprised that the phone still had any charge, as she hadn't plugged it in since she'd arrived in Italy. There was a list of missed calls, but the most recent were from Deeley, which was something of a relief. *At least it's not Matt*, she thought, her stomach sinking at the mere thought of talking to the husband she had so comprehensively betrayed.

The phone jumped in her hand as it started to ring again. Devon clicked on the button and said. 'Hi Deels,' as her sister's voice babbled over her.

'Dev! You're there! Oh my God, I was beginning to think you'd never answer! Devon, it's really serious. You have to come back to London, right away. Dev, the police have been to see us. They've found Bill's body! They want us all to make statements about what we know about him disappearing!'

Devon could barely take it in. From her paradise in Tuscany, stone floor warm under her bare feet, sunlight flooding in through the open door, her lover pouring them each a glass of red wine, it was almost impossible to picture the scene back in comparatively cold England. Crime-scene tape round the garden of 42 Thompson Road; Bill's corpse being carried out on a stretcher; Deeley and Maxie having to deal with the police.

'You're joking,' she said, knowing how stupid the words were even as she uttered them.

'No! Dev, you have to come back, now! We have to work out what we're all going to say – Alice, I'm coming . . . oh, you want Dolly? Hold on, I'll get her for you . . .'

Devon shook her head sharply, trying to get her brain into focus.

'Dev, are you there?' Deeley was back, as urgent as ever. 'Can you get back here right away? I mean, you're not doing anything there, are you?'

Devon looked at Cesare, who had inserted his large nose into the wine glass and was taking a long sniff of it. He looked absurd, like a caricature of a shock-headed Italian. Scrawny, by comparison with her big, muscular husband. Not half as handsome or as photogenic.

And yet the idea of leaving him was like tearing a vital organ out of her chest.

'Dev! Are you *listening*? You *have* to come back!' Deeley was squeaking at her. 'Alice, please, don't cry, sweetie! Auntie Deeley doesn't mean to shout!'

Devon had no choice. 'OK,' she said slowly. 'I'll try to get on a plane tomorrow.'

'No! Today! As soon as possible! Maxie's talking to a solicitor right now – Dev, just go to the airport and get on a plane, *please*!'

'All right.' Devon yielded, feeling the fight drain out of her. Miserably, she said, 'OK, OK. I'll come back.'

'Text me when you know what plane you're on,' Deeley said with huge relief. 'Oh, I'll be so happy to see you, Dev!'

I wish I could say the same, Devon thought sadly, walking back into the kitchen as if she were going to the gallows, feet dragging, head low. Cesare jumped up.

'*Madonna*, what is it? *Cara*, you have had bad news?'

'Sort of. Yes.' Devon reached for the glass of wine and took a long gulp. 'I need to get on the next plane to London. It's sort of a family emergency.'

The word 'family' worked on an Italian as powerfully as 'beer' did to a German. Cesare swung immediately into action. He instructed her to sit down and finish her pasta, saying that no one should travel or hear bad news on an empty stomach, while he launched into a series of rattlingly fast-paced phone calls. By the time Devon had finished her lunch and thrown her clothes into her suitcases, he had a flight booked for her and the Lamborghini was ready to take her to the airport.

'*E Pisa, non Firenze,*' he announced, as he loaded her cases into the car. 'But don't worry, I get you there very fast. I book you a business-class seat, and if we are there in an hour we are sure they put you on the flight.'

'An hour?' Devon said. 'I thought Rory said we were an hour and a half from Pisa—'

'Ssh,' Cesare said, ushering her into the passenger seat. 'I drive, you don't worry, *va bene?*'

Cesare was determined that she not miss her flight: the Lamborghini took off, accelerating so fast that Devon's back shot into the leather seat. Apart from the brief occasions when he slowed down to avoid getting photographed by a speed camera, his foot was permanently down, and he didn't say a word to her. He didn't even play a CD by Vasco Rossi. He screeched to a halt in the middle of the No Parking zone at Pisa Airport barely an hour after they'd left Villa Clara; Devon would have been a nervous wreck at the speed at which he'd driven if she hadn't been swamped in misery at the fact that, not only was she was leaving him, he seemed to have accepted it with such ease.

'*Eccoci!*' he said, dragging her bags out of the car and striding off towards the Departures entrance doors, Devon following reluctantly. It felt almost as if he were packing her off, which was absurd, of course; he was being fantastic, helping her to get back to her family emergency as swiftly and efficiently as possible.

What did you want him to do – beg you to stay? she thought, trailing behind him miserably. *How could he do that, when your family needs you at home? He's doing exactly the right thing!*

Except . . . except he hasn't asked me how long I'll be away. Or if I'm coming back.

Or even said he wants me to.

Cesare was already at the British Airways check-in desk, speaking in rapid-fire Italian to the woman behind it. He took Devon's passport from her, handed it over, and in a minute had loaded her bags onto the belt and was giving her back her passport and boarding card.

'*Presto, presto,*' he said, taking her hand and dragging her through the airport towards Security, which was just around the corner. She didn't have time to say a word before he stopped, looked at her, put one hand on each cheek and kissed her deeply on the mouth.

'Come back soon, *bella*,' he said. 'Italy will be sad without you.'

Devon couldn't say a word. She stared at him, her eyes almost on a level with his, hating to leave him so much that she was terrified to speak, in case she blurted out something much too revealing. Cesare looked as cheerful as ever.

'You must hurry,' he said. 'Or you will miss your flight.'

'I owe you for the ticket!' Devon said, finding her voice. 'I need to pay you back—'

'Pffft,' Cesare said, frowning theatrically. '*Zitta.*'

He'd used this word enough for Devon to know what it meant: be quiet.

'OK,' she said quickly. 'Then I owe you ten euros for carrying my suitcases.'

Cesare put back his head and laughed so loudly that people turned to look.

'*Va bene!*' he said happily. 'You give me ten euros when you come back, OK? And who knows, maybe I carry your suitcases again! I make twenty euros!' He pulled her towards him and kissed her forehead. 'Now,' he said, spinning her around and pushing her towards the official who was ready to check her boarding card, 'you must hurry. Go safe!'

Devon was determined not to look back as she walked towards the security gate; but as she was loading her handbag onto the belt, she couldn't resist. She scoured the area for Cesare's unruly dark curls, but couldn't see them anywhere. He was long gone. Already ringing the next woman on his list, probably. Tears formed in her eyes as she walked through the arch and collected her bag on the other side, her passport and boarding card still clutched tightly in her hand. It was only when she reached the departure gate, and the British Airways official waiting to bustle her onboard practically snatched the documents from her, that she realized there was something else there too.

A card. It fell from inside her passport as the woman opened it to check Devon's photograph. Devon caught it as it tumbled to the counter, snatching it up as eagerly as if it were a love letter.

CESARE MONTIGIANI, it read in small, elegant lettering. And underneath, an Italian phone number. No address, no email. No personal note.

But still, it was a way to contact him. Cesare hadn't asked for her contact details, her email, nothing. *But he gave me his card and he said Italy would be sad without me . . . Still, that might be just a nice way of saying goodbye. He's probably really grateful it ended like this, so neatly . . .*

Despite the gravity of the crisis that was summoning her back so urgently to London, Devon could barely focus on it. She sank into the business-class seat, fastened the seatbelt, and rapidly tapped out a text to Deeley, telling her what flight she was on, as the steward shut and locked the plane door. He nodded at her mobile, but she was already turning it off and slipping it back into her bag. She closed her eyes. Suddenly she realized she was exhausted; it wasn't as if she and Cesare had been doing much sleeping over the last few days. Devon knew she should be thinking about the nightmare situation that was calling her back to London, or worrying about the mess she'd made of her marriage. But all she could do was close her eyes, fall asleep and dream about her Italian lover.

'Dev!' called an instantly familiar voice as Devon pushed her trolley out of the last-ditch duty-free shop just after Customs. Devon looked over to see Deeley standing there and she blinked as she realized that her sister had a small child propped on her hip. She was so disoriented that it took her a few more moments to realize that this must be Maxie and Olly's adopted little girl, who she hadn't actually met yet.

She pushed the trolley towards her sister, who, as usual, looked as if she had walked straight out of the pages of *Grazia*, in a trendy, long, belted grey sweater over slim faded jeans tucked loosely into studded ankle boots. Long, cascading caramel-streaked hair, pulled back with a wide suede band, framed Deeley's face perfectly; she and Maxie's little girl made an arresting picture, one so dark and the other so fair, both of them so pretty in their very different styles.

'You look like Angelina Jolie at a photo shoot, Deels,' Devon said with irony.

'And you look wonderful,' Deeley said, staring at her sister. 'Italy really agrees with you, Dev. You look absolutely amazing. You've lost weight, haven't you!'

'Yes! Um, thanks!' Devon said, blushing, and hoping that Deeley wouldn't guess exactly what Devon had been doing to give herself this post-coital glow of satisfaction.

'This is Alice,' Deeley said, hefting her charge a little higher on her hip. 'Say hi to Auntie Devon, Alice.'

Alice stared at Devon with wide, dark, heavily lashed eyes; she was definitely a little beauty.

'Trust Maxie to pick a pretty one,' Devon said cynically. 'What did she do, get her out of a catalogue?'

'Dev!' Deeley said, shocked.

'Oh, come on, Deels. Maxie didn't even go to Rwanda herself, did she? She got her brought over by people from the government. You can't tell me this is anything but a PR thing,' Devon said, rolling her eyes. 'Poor little mite,' she added, looking at Alice's serious face. 'Maxie isn't exactly cut out to be a mother.'

Deeley couldn't deny a word of this, much as it was clear she wanted to.

'Well, Alice has me now,' she said firmly, dropping a kiss on her niece's curly head. 'And I'm taking very good care of her. Dev, we should go. Maxie's really worried about journalists. She sent me to meet you and make sure you didn't get waylaid. I don't see anyone, but you never know, I suppose . . .'

'I'll just grab a coffee,' Devon said quickly; with everything waiting for her, she needed a pint of Caffè Nero's finest to keep her alert.

'Ooh, get one for me too!' Deeley said, sitting Alice down on top of Devon's suitcases as their owner dashed off. 'Look how tall you are now, baby Alice,' she crooned cheerfully. 'You're as tall as me!'

God, Deeley was born to be a mum, Devon thought as she returned with the two largest cappuccinos-with-extra-shots that Caffè Nero's barista had to offer. Deeley was singing to Alice, who was giggling, delighted, back at her.

They found a black cab and settled in, Alice on Deeley's lap, staring out of the window or playing with her aunt's long hair as the cab took off for central London.

'I've had to stop wearing earrings,' Deeley said fondly, bouncing her niece. 'Little madam here pulls them all out and then tries to eat them.'

'Ouch,' Devon said, putting her hands up to her ears to check she wasn't wearing anything dangly. No, just her diamond studs. She remembered Cesare running his tongue round one, biting her lobe, and shuddered with a rush of sensual memory so strong she could feel it from her fingers to her toes.

Stop it! she told herself, raising her coffee cup and drinking deeply, the rich brew jerking her back into harsh reality.

'Tell me what's been going on, Deels,' she said, looking at her sister over Alice's head. 'And don't leave anything out, OK?'

Deeley took a deep breath, looked as if she were about to cry, leaned forward to check that the partition between them and the cab driver was firmly shut, and then spilled it all. It took most of the drive back from the airport, and Devon listened in silence, reaching out to wind her fingers through Alice's from time to time to distract her niece from pulling at the neck of Deeley's jumper. She winced on hearing about Deeley's visit back to Riseholme, but didn't say a word of reproach, for which Deeley was clearly grateful.

When Deeley had finally ground to a halt, as the cab was coming off the flyover, Devon said slowly, 'I remember Linda O'Keeffe. I couldn't have told you her name, but I remember her. She was a really nasty piece of work. Stank of smoke. And looked at all of us like we were pieces of meat.'

'That's right,' Deeley said. 'She scared me.' She looked as if she were about to say something else, then bit her lip.

'So what are we going to do, Deels?' Devon asked.

The two sisters looked at each other with identical big, dark McKenna eyes.

'Maxie's talking to her solicitor now,' Deeley said. 'Giving her the official line – pretty much what she told the police. But she's being very careful. She's going to tell us exactly what to say in our statements. And the solicitor will be with us to make sure we don't make any mistakes.'

'Won't that look a bit suspicious?' Devon said, concerned.

'No, because Maxie was really clever and made it sound as if she thought this was all a set-up to make the government look bad,' Deeley reassured her. 'So the police think we have the solicitor because of Olly being a minister and not wanting any scandal.'

Devon guffawed. 'I can't *believe* Olly's a minister!' she said. 'It just goes to show anyone can get into power as long as they went to the right school and have enough money.'

'Junior minister,' Deeley corrected, unable not to smile at Devon's tart words.

'He won't be that for long,' Devon said. 'Maxie'll push him up the greasy pole faster than you can say prime minister. With her hand up his bum like a puppet, making him talk.'

'Dev!' Deeley covered Alice's ears with her hands. 'Don't listen, Alice,' she said, giggling. 'Auntie Devon's being naughty about your mummy and daddy.'

'Where are we going?' Devon asked suddenly, as the cab followed a swaying line of buses around the Shepherd's Bush roundabout.

'Back to Maxie's,' Deeley said. 'She'll come back when she's finished with the solicitor. She said to all meet there.'

'No, wait . . .' Devon leaned forward and slid the Plexiglass open, giving her address to the cab driver. 'I want to go home first. Drop off my stuff.'

'Maxie said—' Deeley started, shifting uncomfortably.

'Maxie isn't God, Deeley,' Devon snapped crossly. 'I'm going home first, OK? It won't take long.'

I'm being a coward, Devon thought. *I want Deeley and Alice there when I see Matt again, if he's home. I can't face him on my own, not after Italy. I'll grab enough stuff for a few days and go to a hotel, or sleep at Maxie's. I can't stay in the house with Matt. It wouldn't be fair.*

Not when I'm going to tell him I want a divorce.

Deeley was looking very unhappy. Devon knew her too well for Deeley to be able to hide her feelings.

'What's up?' she said, staring narrowly at her younger sister.

Deeley went red, and then white. Finally she blurted out a story about the front door of the basement flat having been vandalized, and her conviction that it was Linda O'Keeffe, or someone working for her, who had done it; she tagged on some crazy story about having been pushed under a bus at King's Cross. It sounded much too lurid to be at all likely. *Probably just fell over on her high heels*, Devon thought meanly.

'So you haven't been back there since?' Devon asked.

'No – I went to Jersey, and then to Maxie's – I've been looking after Alice since the nanny left . . .' Deeley was hanging her head, unable to meet Devon's eye.

Poor thing, she's embarrassed at having to be her sister's nanny, Devon thought. *I bet Maxie's treating her like a member of staff.*

'But what about Matt?' Devon asked. 'I sort of thought he'd have you around to help him a bit . . .' She was embarrassed, in turn, at having left her husband crocked up, with no one in the house but the daily cleaning lady. Especially since she had run off to Italy and promptly started a torrid affair. Colour rose in her cheeks; she was too busy thinking of Cesare now to realize that her sister had turned bright red again at the question, burying her face in her niece's hair to avoid answering.

The cab pulled up outside the Green Street house. Deeley hung back as Devon set her jaw, marched up the steps and unlocked her front door, calling, 'Matt? Matt, it's me . . .'

The cabbie carried her cases into the house; by the time she'd tipped him and sent him on his way, Alice was trying to crawl up the stairs, and Matt's crutch was tapping its way out of the kitchen to meet his wife. He stared, confused, at the scene in front of him, his eyes going from Devon to Deeley to Alice, trying to work out what was going on. His foot was still in its wrap bandage, grubby round the edges now, and he was in pyjama bottoms and a t-shirt, his hair messy, his chin unshaven, looking exactly like a man who had been left to fend for himself by his wife, and who had gone slightly feral as a result.

'I didn't even know you were coming back!' he said to Devon. 'What's going on?'

'Family crisis,' she said briefly.

'That makes sense.' Matt's expression was unreadable. 'Somehow, I didn't think you'd come back to see how I was getting on.'

'We should get going,' Deeley said quickly, shifting from one foot to the other. 'Maxie'll be wondering where we are.'

Matt looked over at Deeley, and then glanced away swiftly, *as if he were angry with her*, Devon observed. Maybe Deeley and Matt had had a fight while she was away, and that was why Deeley hadn't wanted to come back to Green Street; why she was desperate to get away as fast as possible.

Well, I can't worry about that now. There are much more important things at stake.

Devon drew a deep breath.

'Not yet,' she said slowly. 'Matt deserves to know what's happening. He's my husband. He's a part of this whether he likes it or not.' She finished the last dregs of her takeaway cappuccino and realized that she still needed more caffeine to help her cope with all this drama. 'Come on,' she said. 'We'll go into the kitchen, I'll make a big pot of coffee, and we'll tell Matt everything. All about our sordid childhood. We can trust him.' She gave her husband a long, clear look. 'I'm really sorry about this, Matt. You're going to get dragged into a lot of stuff that's nothing to do with you, and it isn't fair. Especially when you and I are in such a mess at the moment. But the least I can do is tell you the whole truth.'

It was the most honest, direct thing she'd said to Matt in a long time, and she could see him taking it in, appreciating it.

'Thanks, Dev,' he said, nodding at her, his blue eyes clear. Something passed between them, something like a goodbye with no hard feelings. *Or maybe I'm just imagining that. Hoping for it,* Devon thought, as she walked into the kitchen. *But right now, it feels as if Matt's decided he doesn't want to be married to me any more either.*

'Who's this lovely little thing?' she heard Matt asking Deeley, as she filled the kettle.

'This is Alice,' Deeley said, a note of pride in her voice. 'Isn't she gorgeous? She's Maxie and Olly's new daughter. Come on, Alice – we're going into the kitchen, sweetie. I've got some toys for you in my bag . . .'

'Looks like she'll be walking soon, eh?' Matt said. 'Oi! Get off my crutch!'

'Alice! Naughty girl!' Deeley chimed in.

Deeley and Matt were both laughing as they came into the kitchen. *Wow, they get on really well,* Devon noticed, as she scooped coffee into the cafetiere. Deeley was hefting Alice, who was leaning over to grab at Matt's crutch, which seemed to fascinate her. Deeley put her down on the kitchen rug, and Matt, heaving himself onto a stool, handed Deeley his crutch so Alice could crawl over it happily. He propped his foot awkwardly up on the foot-bar of the adjoining stool, swivelling to face his wife.

'Right then,' he said simply. 'Spit it out.'

Deeley

Sitting on Devon's big cranberry velvet sofa, making sure Alice didn't fall on the crutch and cut her head open, Deeley was more grateful than she could say for the distraction of needing to constantly supervise her niece; it gave her something to do with her hands, somewhere to direct her attention. That way, she could avoid looking too obviously at her sister and her sister's husband, desperately trying to read their interaction. *You and I are in such a mess at the moment*, Devon had said to Matt, and he'd tacitly agreed with it.

What does that mean? Deeley speculated frantically. *How much does it mean? Is Devon going off to Italy, not caring that Matt was injured, just a blip? Or something more serious?*

Deeley had been so good, so careful to avoid Matt ever since that evening. It wasn't she who had suggested coming back here, to the house that he shared with her sister; that had been Devon's idea. And now she had to be just as cautious. She couldn't stare at Matt, shouldn't even talk to him.

But now, so close to her sister's husband, Deeley knew that her flirting with Jeff, her date to meet him at the weekend, were just an attempt to put a tiny Band-Aid on a gaping wound. Deeley wanted Matt as badly as ever, and she didn't dare to look at him, in case

Devon saw the longing in her eyes. He was so big, so lovely, so sweet; she wanted to wrap her arms around him, hug him, look after him – *And yes, to finish what we started in the living room*, she admitted to herself, knowing that her cheeks were going red as she tried not to think about it. He'd smiled so adorably at Alice, dimples forming in his cheeks, that Alice had gurgled and immediately reached out for him, her chubby hand connecting with the top of his crutch; Deeley and Matt's eyes had met over her head, and the connection had been instant, a jolt of happiness and recognition.

Like a husband and wife who've been apart for a while, and are really happy to be back together, Deeley thought with great wistfulness. Out of the corner of her eye she could see Matt's long, wide thigh, propped at an angle on the bar stool to rest his hurt ankle. She realized that she was staring openly at the swell of his quadriceps muscle through the thin cotton of his pyjama bottoms, and dropped her gaze; but then she saw the white piping on the cuffed hem of the pyjamas, which for some reason filled her with immense tenderness. They were like pyjamas a granddad would wear, probably bought from Marks and Spencer. The thought of Matt going to M & S, picking up a pair of navy blue pyjamas with white piping, made her heart melt.

I want to be buying his granddad pyjamas, Deeley thought with a rush of wistfulness. *And his socks. And his boxers.*

Oh God. This isn't just lust, she realized, wanting to cry. *I'm in love with him.*

She hadn't heard a word that Devon had been saying to Matt. She'd only vaguely registered the fact that Matt had been making sounds of upset and sympathy and concern as Devon told him about Bill abusing Maxie, sounds which had muted into utter silence as Devon wrapped her hands around her cup of coffee, gathered her strength, and gradually, haltingly, told him about that night in 1993 when she, Maxie and Deeley had killed their stepfather to keep themselves safe.

'Jesus God,' Matt said slowly, when Devon had finished. 'I can hardly believe it.'

He turned awkwardly on his stool, looking from Devon to Deeley. 'I wish I'd been there,' he said softly. 'I'd've sorted that bugger out for you. Makes me ashamed to be a man when I hear stories like this.' He reached out and squeezed his wife's hand. 'You did the right thing, love. Men like that never change. He'd've gone after you and Deeley, or found some other girls to mess with instead. You kept a lot of people safe.' He drew in a breath through clenched teeth. 'God, when I think about it, my head wants to explode. I've never warmed to Maxie, you know that. But when I think about what she went through – poor cow. No wonder she's a bit cold.'

'The thing is,' Deeley said slowly, 'I don't think she actually did go through it.'

She must have been mulling this over subconsciously, ever since she had been back to Riseholme; or maybe even before. Because why had she been to Riseholme in the first place? Why had she brought back all those memories of the worst moment of her entire life? She wasn't a masochist. She had come back to the UK after years away, and she had started to think, once again, about those events when she was nine years old. She had remembered Bill, and her memories of him hadn't been anything but kind and good and loving.

And she had realized that she simply didn't believe that Bill had abused Maxie.

'What do you mean, Deels?' Devon stared at her over the counter, completely taken aback.

'I was thinking about Bill,' Deeley said. 'Remembering what it was like to live in his house.'

Both Matt and Devon were staring at her now, and it was as if she were being taken over by a force stronger than her, that was speaking through her. *No,* she realized. *This is me. This is the grown-up Deeley, the person who wants to tell the truth. To trust her own instincts, instead of being told what to think and say by her eldest sister.*

'We had all sorts of weird "uncles" who came and went with Mum,' she said directly to Devon. 'Didn't we? We knew which ones were dodgy. We were careful to keep out of their way, not to be alone with them. But Bill? We never thought that, you and me. You know we didn't. We were absolutely amazed when Maxie told us what he'd been up to.' She swallowed. 'I felt I had to believe Maxie. She'd always looked after us, kept us safe. I couldn't admit that I didn't believe her. Because without Maxie, we wouldn't have anyone. But I never did believe her. I never did.'

She stared back at Devon, willing her to admit the truth.

'And Dev, I don't think you did either,' she said quietly.

There was a long pause.

'No,' Devon said finally, in a tiny voice. 'No, I suppose I didn't.'

'But I don't understand!' Matt shifted on the bar stool. 'Why would she make up something that horrible? It doesn't make sense!'

His handsome face was contorted with confusion. *Matt's so sweet*, Deeley thought. *He can't understand why anyone would lie, or make up an awful story about someone.*

Matt's awkward movement had knocked his crutch, lying on the floor. Alice had crawled to the rubber end and started to chew on it; distracted, Deeley hadn't seen what her niece was up to. Alice, bumped by the crutch, started to wail, and Deeley picked her up, rocking her.

'I think she's tired,' she said. 'She hardly had a nap today.'

'Deels, tell me everything that happened with the police this morning,' Devon said, leaning intently towards her sister.

Dark had fallen, but no one had drawn the heavy curtains yet. Beyond Devon, Deeley could see the shadows of the trees in Devon and Matt's garden, tall and strangely menacing against the deep violet pink of the London night sky. *Trees. Oak, ash . . . sycamore.* She saw again the sycamore in the back garden of the Thompson Road semi; she remembered the sight of Bill, lying on the carpet. Of Devon, bringing down the vase over his head. Deeley closed her eyes for a moment, hoping to make the awful memories fade.

It didn't work. She opened them, looking at her sister, and recited everything the police had said to her and Maxie that morning in a dull monotone. A horrible suspicion was running through her, sweeping over her. It was the idea that the worst thing she had ever done was based on a lie she had been told – a lie that she hadn't even really believed. Deeley could see, from Devon's frozen expression, that the exact same emotion was sweeping through her. She was almost at the end of her narrative when Devon interrupted her.

'The bag the money was in,' she said, almost in a whisper. 'They said it was green?'

'With white handles. And a white stripe, I think,' Deeley agreed.

'I saw a bag like that at Thompson Road,' Devon said.

She was naturally pale – all the McKennas were, with their white Irish skin. But there was a difference between having a pale colouring, and being as white as a sheet. All the blood seemed to have drained from Devon's face. She had come back from Italy that afternoon glowing, so beautiful and full of life that Deeley had caught her breath to see her sister looking so stunning, only a short time after that debacle on live TV. Tuscany, it seemed, had been better than a rest cure, lighting Devon up like a firework. Heads had turned in the airport, not to gawk at Devon McKenna, who'd made an idiot of herself on a cooking show, but in dumbstruck appreciation of her beauty.

She'd been radiant. And now, just a few hours later, all that luminosity had drained from Devon; her face was like a greyish mask, her eyes two dark holes punched through it.

'In Bill's room?' Deeley asked in a tiny voice. She already knew the answer.

'No,' Devon said. It seemed as if she could barely move her lips, as if her body was resisting her getting the next two words out. 'In Maxie's.'

Devon

*I*t was deathly quiet in Maxie's living room. You could almost
have heard a pin drop, though its sound would probably have
been muffled by the denseness of the draperies. There were two
sets of curtains, heavy taffeta ones looped back with big draping
tassels, and lighter silk ones, now drawn across the floor-to-ceiling
windows that faced onto the back garden. A thick wool carpet,
scattered with Persian rugs inherited from Olly's family, covered
the floor, and in the centre two long sofas, upholstered in slub silk,
faced each other elegantly, a glass coffee table between them, on
which Devon's soft suede bag lay, next to a couple of untouched
glasses of water. Everywhere you turned, there were straight-back
chairs, placed next to occasional tables holding ornamental vases
filled with fresh flowers. It was done in perfect taste, in shades of
pale yellow, pale green and cream that complemented the polished
wood tables, ready for a photographer from *The World of Interiors*
to appear at any moment and start snapping away.

The only discordant notes were Deeley and Devon, in their jeans
and dark tops, looking much too casual for the smart, cocktail-party
decor. Deeley had kicked off her flats and curled up in the corner of
one of the sofas, trying to get comfortable, but the hard sofa, its
fabric caught at regular intervals with a series of small, silk-covered

buttons, defeated her. It wasn't a sofa to curl up on; it was for sitting up straight, knees together, a cup of tea or martini in hand, as you made polite conversation with an MP or an influential party donor.

Alice, exhausted from a long day, had been fed and put to bed some time ago, and had fallen asleep with barely a whimper of protest. Olly was in the House, which was sitting late, and Maxie was still in a meeting with her solicitor. Devon and Deeley couldn't even look at each other; they felt like conspirators, utterly disloyal, turning on their leader. To disbelieve Maxie, to challenge her, was like *lèse-majesté*, the crime of disrespecting a reigning monarch. They both felt shocked at their daring and when Maxie's key finally sounded in the front door, they jumped like naughty schoolgirls caught in their older sister's room, trying on her clothes and make-up.

It's ridiculous, Devon thought dryly, bracing herself for battle. *Maxie still has us feeling as if we're barely teenagers.*

She shot a glance at Deeley, encouraging her to keep their resolve. Deeley's eyes were as big as saucers: she looked like a terrified puppy. *Come on, Deels, it's time to grow up. Be a big girl.*

'Great, you're both here!' Maxie called from the hallway, glancing into the living room, unbelting her raincoat and hanging it in the cupboard. Maxie had always been meticulous about her possessions. She kicked off her heels and walked into the living room to join her sisters, crossing to the built-in bar at the far end of the room, which was set into a recess where a bookcase had once been. 'God, I'm dying for a drink! You two have one already?' She didn't wait for an answer, just poured herself a very stiff vodka and slimline tonic, gulping half of it down in one practised swallow.

'Well!' she continued, turning to face her sisters, propping her skinny bottom against the wooden edge of the bar, swirling her drink as she looked from Devon to Deeley. In a slim navy coat-dress, cinched at the waist with a shiny leather Bilberry belt, her hair as smooth and groomed as ever despite the drama of the day, Maxie was definitely intimidating. Devon felt as if she were an erring student in a posh girls' school, summoned to see the headmistress.

'You changed your outfit,' Deeley said, quite unexpectedly.

Maxie's body jerked back against the bar; if she hadn't drunk so much of her V & T, it would have slopped out onto the carpet.

'What?' she said, her plucked eyebrows shooting up.

'I saw what you were wearing earlier,' Deeley said bravely. 'It looked like a white shiny skirt. White and red. Like a nurse's outfit.'

Maxie opened her mouth, gaped at her youngest sister like a fish, and finally said, 'Nonsense! You've had a very hard day. We all have. You were seeing things.'

She swivelled to top up her drink with more vodka, her narrow shoulder blades poking through the navy fabric. Devon looked at Deeley, who shook her head firmly and swung her legs down, sitting up straight, her jaw set resolutely.

'Maxie,' Devon said, clearing her throat. She settled her suede bag on the arm of the sofa. 'We need to talk to you.'

'Of course we need to talk!' Maxie turned back, pulling a face. 'We need to have a bloody summit meeting! I've got all the gen from the solicitor. She's coming round here tomorrow and we'll go over everything with her before we give our statements. She's arranging for the police to come here at one – that should give us plenty of time.'

'I thought we had to go to the police station,' Deeley said.

'Oh God no!' Maxie laughed. 'That's for the riff-raff, darling. We're People Who Matter. We make them come to us.'

When did she turn into this person? Devon wondered, staring at her older sister. *This awful, entitled, braying Sloane? I know we all really tried to lose our accents, but Maxie's gone much further than us – she sounds like she was born and bred in the Home Counties with a silver spoon in her mouth. And she thinks like them too – Olly and all his friends. It's as if she's completely forgotten where she comes from.*

'*We're* riff-raff, Maxie,' Devon said. She was dying for a drink, but she wouldn't have one; she needed to be utterly clear-headed for this.

'Yes,' Deeley chimed in unexpectedly. 'We are.'

'Not any more!' Maxie snapped, her dark eyes flashing. 'Not any more! I made bloody sure of that, didn't I? I pulled us up out of there with my bare hands! Look at all of this!'

She gestured around her with the cut-glass tumbler, a sweeping motion that encompassed not only the living room, with its swags of pale golden brocade curtains and its family antiques, but her entire house, her entire existence, her brilliant career, and her husband, junior minister and baronet's son.

'That's what we have to talk about, Maxie,' Devon said, fixing her sister with a stare. It was even harder than she had thought to stand up to Maxie; it went against the ingrained habit of her whole life. *Maxie knows best. Mum's a train wreck, but Maxie will look after us.*

Do what Maxie says, and we'll be safe.

'What do you mean?' Maxie said impatiently. 'We don't have anything to talk about! I'll tell you what we're going to say to the police tomorrow, we'll rehearse it tonight and go over it again tomorrow morning, and then this whole bloody mess will be over! There's nothing to discuss!'

'Yes, there is,' Devon said bravely, her heart pounding. 'We have to talk about the money. The thirty grand that was in the canvas bag.'

An absolute silence fell after those words. Standing by the bar, Maxie froze as if they were playing a game of Musical Statues. Devon held her breath; she shot an agonized look at Deeley, and saw that she was doing the same. It was terrifying to finally confront the person who had always been your authority figure. *I've never done this before,* Devon realized. *Never stood up to Maxie, never disagreed with her, not once.*

It wouldn't have been safe.

Even now, I don't feel safe. Thank God Deeley's here as well.

'What are you talking about?' Maxie eventually said, pinning Devon with a hard glare. 'I have no idea what you mean.'

'The money, Maxie,' Deeley piped up. 'The police told us about it this morning. They said Bill was holding it for Linda and Mum while they were in the nick – in prison,' she corrected herself swiftly. 'But then it would still have been in the house when we left. And no one ever found it.'

'Someone else must have taken it,' Maxie said, shrugging. 'When we moved out to Aunt Sandra's, and the house was empty. One of Linda's lot. They weren't all in prison, were they?'

'But they could have taken it any time,' Devon said quietly. 'When we were out at school and Bill was at work. Any weekday. They wouldn't have waited till Bill went missing and we were gone, would they?'

There was a pause. Then Maxie said curtly, 'I really don't know. What difference does it make? Bill's dead, and we have to make sure that no one suspects we had anything to do with it. The solicitor said—'

'Maxie, that's not good enough,' Devon said as steadily as she could manage. 'We need to know what really happened. I saw that bag in your room, after Bill . . .went missing. Under your bed. We were getting our stuff together to pack, and I thought you'd borrowed my trainers. I was looking for them. I remember the bag. I hadn't seen it before.' She grimaced. 'And we didn't have much, you know? You couldn't help noticing anything new.'

'Oh, for God's sake,' Maxie said dismissively, finishing her vodka and tonic and setting the glass down on the bar with a smack. 'That was over eighteen years ago! How can you possibly remember something like that?'

'Well, I do,' Devon said simply. 'And I don't want to.'

Those words hit home. Maxie walked over to the mantelpiece and looked into the Venetian glass mirror, making a show of smoothing down her hair, avoiding her sisters' eyes.

'And then I remembered, when you went off to Oxford,' Devon continued, 'you came back with all these new clothes. Your hair was done, your nails, everything.'

'You looked really rich,' Deeley added.

'You said it was your boyfriend, that he was buying all this stuff for you,' Devon said. 'But you didn't meet Olly for ages after that. And you had those clothes almost from the beginning.'

'I worked,' Maxie said, still to the mirror. 'I got a job straight away.'

'Oh, come on, Maxie!' Devon burst out, beginning to lose her self-control. 'That's bollocks! You couldn't have afforded all those things working in a tea room!'

'You had jewellery too,' Deeley said. 'That pearl necklace and the earrings. Just like all those posh girls on TV.'

'And dyeing your hair blonde,' Devon said, fingering her own dark locks. 'It looked really natural. That costs a fortune. I never even saw any roots.'

'What *is* this?' Maxie clearly decided that attack was the best form of defence. She swung round furiously, propping her elbows behind her on the mantelpiece, looking down on her two younger sisters, as she had always done. It was the old-fashioned man's position, the power pose: in front of the fire, dominating the room.

'Are you two picking this moment to gang up on me?' she demanded, looking from one to the other of her sisters. 'You must be insane! Don't you realize we need to stand together – like we've always done? It was always us against the world, wasn't it? We have to keep going, don't you realize that? We have to be strong – the McKenna sisters against the world! We can't let them drag us down!'

It was a passionate, fervent plea. Maxie's eyes were sparkling; she leaned forward, her demeanour utterly convincing, totally authoritative, even in her stockinged feet. Devon and Deeley looked up at her, and then at each other; Deeley's pretty, Bambi-face was a picture of confusion.

'Oh no,' Deeley moaned, bringing her hands up to her face. 'I'm so messed up – I don't know what to think . . .'

'You *do*, Deels!' Devon said urgently. 'It was you who started it when you said you didn't believe what Maxie said Bill did to her—'

'*What?*' Maxie rounded on Deeley, coming off the mantelpiece in a lunge towards her youngest sister, striding towards the sofa. 'You said *what?*'

Deeley's hands were still over her face. Devon willed her to stay honest, to push for the truth. Finally, Deeley said in a tiny voice, 'But I *don't*, Maxie.'

Her hands came down. Maxie was standing next to the arm of

the sofa, arms folded, glaring intimidatingly. Deeley turned to look at her, swallowing hard.

'I don't,' she repeated. 'I've been thinking and thinking, ever since I got back to London. I've been asking myself why I feel so weird – confused, really. That's why I went back to Riseholme. I didn't realize it at the time, but that's why.' Her big dark eyes were huge and haunted. 'I feel like I'm torn between you and Bill. I look back, and I just don't remember him the way you said he was. Grooming us, being nice to us to get what he wanted, when he was secretly really creepy – he wasn't *like* that. He was like a *dad*. He ticked us off and worried about us and got cross when we didn't do our homework.' She drew a long, juddering breath. 'I felt safe in his house,' she finished simply.

'I did too,' Devon said, equally simply.

'So what are you saying?' Maxie glared from Devon to Deeley. 'What are you saying? That I made it all up? Why would I *do* that?'

Deeley stammered; she'd just shot her bolt, and had no courage left.

I'll have to say it. Devon gathered up her resolve, bit her lip, and said, 'To keep the money, Max. That's what we think. You wanted to keep that thirty grand, so you could go to university and make a big splash, buy your way into the posh people's parties. And Bill didn't agree with you. He was going to give it back when Mum and Linda got out. We think that's what you and Bill were arguing about, the night before you got us to kill him.'

Devon's voice cracked on the last words. *I was doing so well!* she thought, furious with herself, as the tears began to form. *I really was!* But all the memories came flooding back now, overwhelming her. She remembered grabbing the vase, as Maxie had told her to. Bringing it down on Bill's head. Hearing the impact, his neck snapping under the blow.

It was too much. She started to cry. Maxie saw weakness, and pounced on it immediately.

'*You* killed him!' she said cruelly, pointing at Devon. '*You* broke his neck! That's what did it! How dare you go throwing accusations at me!'

'You told her to!' Deeley actually jumped to her feet, her hands on her hips, confronting Maxie, impatiently tossing back the hair that had fallen over her face. 'How dare *you* talk to her like that – tell her she killed him – when you were the one that planned it all! I bet you meant all along to get Dev to hit him, so you could blame it on her too!'

Maxie gasped in shock. 'I can't believe you're turning on me like this!' she said furiously. 'After everything I've done for you! I made sure you two were OK, always! When Mum was fucking up, it was me you came crying to, both of you! It was me who planned ahead and found us safe places to go and shoved chair backs under door handles so none of Mum's creepy boyfriends could get into our room!' She was panting now, her hair beginning to come loose from its immaculate French twist. '*I* looked after you! *I* did everything for you two ungrateful bitches! I made sure we stayed at the same school, and did our exams, and had clean clothes to wear, and weren't split up and taken into care! I *deserved* that money!'

Maxie pounded on her chest with a fist.

'Yes, OK, I took it!' she screamed. 'All right? Satisfied now? I *deserved* it, after everything I did for you! Mum owed it to me – I did her job for her, bringing you two up. I earned it! I took that money and I spent it on stuff to help me fit in at Oxford! I needed to look right – like I was one of them. And I got a good boyfriend, and the right kind of job—'

'And Bill wouldn't have let you spend it on that,' Devon prompted, wiping away her tears.

'No! No, he bloody wouldn't!' Maxie yelled. 'He wasn't going to let me touch it – he said Linda would tear us into pieces if we spent it! He never wanted it in the house in the first place, he was so bloody honest – but Mum said she'd tell the social services he was fiddling with us if he didn't keep it for her. That was what gave me the idea.' She was gasping in her efforts to spill out the words, determined now that her sisters should hear everything, every last sordid truth. 'So yes, you're right about that too. OK? Happy now? Bill and I had a big fight, he said I couldn't take a penny from that thirty grand to buy stuff for university, and I *had* to. You remember how poor we were! Or do you? Do you even remember?'

She threw her arms wide, gesticulating at the luxury of her house.

'This dress is Jil Sander,' Maxie said. 'My hair is done by Nicky Clarke, every three weeks. My shoes, Bilberry. Which would cost an absolute fucking fortune if I had to pay for them. My nails . . .'

She flapped her hands furiously at her sisters. Deeley, with her stunning head of artfully streaked hair, her trendy cobweb-knot Nougat sweater, her Seven for All Mankind jeans, her Louboutin boots. And Devon, her pretty diamond studs sparkling, her skin perfect from Dermalogica facials, her lips red with her favourite Fresh lipstick.

'Get it? And look at the two of you! *Look* at yourselves! You're sitting on top of the world now! Think about how far you've come! If it hadn't been for me, you'd have been taken into care – we'd have been split up, abused, all sorts! You know what goes on! Deeley,' she rounded on her younger sister, who flinched, 'you'd have been easy meat for anyone! You could never take care of yourself. Without me, you'd be on the streets now, or dead!'

Deeley bit her lip, knowing this was true, her face a picture of unhappiness. Her shoulders slumped. It was Devon who got to her feet to answer this, pulling down her striped silk sweater to cover the bulge of flesh at the top of her jeans.

I feel twice the size of Maxie, she thought miserably. *There's no way you can stand facing your size 6 sister if you're just about fitting into a size 12 and not feel huge by comparison.*

Maxie got thinner, and I got fatter, she realized with a flash of understanding. *It's like I was tied to her in some way. As if we needed to balance each other out.*

Well, not any more. If I can stand up to Maxie and say the truth, then I can be free of all of this, finally. Whatever the consequences.

'You made me kill someone,' she said, confronting her sister directly. 'You made me and Deeley help you kill Bill and hide the body. We've had to live with that our whole lives, keep it a secret.

Sometimes I was bursting to confide, to talk about it – weren't you, Deeley?'

Deeley nodded miserably.

'But we couldn't,' Devon said quietly. 'We had to live with it, and not say a word, pretend that nothing had happened. And we did, Maxie, because we thought we'd done it to keep you safe. It was worth it for that.'

'More like to keep yourselves safe,' Maxie interjected sarcastically. 'I told you that Bill was coming after you next. That's why you helped me kill him, why you went along with it when I told you what we had to do – you were saving your own skins.'

'God, you're *horrible,*' Devon said furiously. 'Bill never laid a finger on you, did he? He never touched you like that, and he was never going to touch us either. He was a good man, and you killed him so you could have thirty thousand pounds to spend on turning yourself into a Sloane.'

'He *was* a good man,' Deeley said, echoing Devon. 'He really was.'

'Right! Fine!' Maxie's stockinged feet rasped on the carpet as she turned round and stamped back to the bar, tipping more vodka into her glass. 'Here you go!' She lifted her glass to her sisters, her eyes black now with anger. 'This is what you want, is it? Bill never fucking abused me, OK? He never did! He was a do-gooder! He'd never have done anything like that! You two were bloody idiots to think for a moment that he would!'

She toasted them, holding up her glass, before drinking what was now neat vodka.

'It was his own fault,' she said, coughing a little as the strong spirit went down. 'He should never have stood in my way. What business was it of his? How dare he stop me trying to make something of myself!'

'You *had* to kill him,' Deeley said slowly. 'Because he was a scapegoat. Linda had to believe that Bill had gone off with the money. Otherwise, she'd have come straight after us.'

'Oh my God,' Devon said, realizing the truth of this. 'It

wasn't even about you having a fight with Bill. You'd always have had to kill him to keep that money. You probably planned it like that all along.'

She looked at Deeley, their expressions equally horrified. Deeley was pale as bone. Devon found herself walking towards her younger sister, and Deeley came to meet her. They fell into a hug, their heads together, their arms wrapping around each other. Deeley was choking back tears; Devon raised her hand and stroked her sister's hair as Deeley's head rested on her shoulder.

Over Deeley's head, Devon looked at Maxie. She thought of the clichéd expression, 'seeing someone for the first time', and rejected it. Devon had always, truly, known who her sister was: she'd seen her ruthlessness, her ambition, her willingness to step on anyone who got in her way. Devon was ambitious, too, always had been. She couldn't judge Maxie for that. But the rest of it – the lies, the way Maxie had twisted their childhood, killed the only adult who'd ever tried to be decent to them, involved them in it and made them feel as guilty as her – that was unforgiveable.

Deeley was crying now. But she raised her head from Devon's shoulder, and turned to look once again at Maxie.

'Who pushed me under the bus?' she asked, her voice choked with tears. 'Who sprayed that warning on my front door? Because I've been thinking about it, and I don't see how it could have been Linda. She'd already warned me off. I don't see why she'd get some-one to follow me down to London, or even how she'd have someone who could do it that quickly. She knew she'd scared me enough. She didn't need to go to all that extra trouble.'

Devon stared at Deeley, taken aback. 'I don't get this,' she started, confused. 'What are you . . .'

'I think it was her,' Deeley said, pointing accusingly at Maxie. 'I think *she* did it. Maxie was the one who wanted to scare me off, much more than Linda. Maxie was the one who had everything to lose by me being stupid and poking around at Riseholme.'

'But how would she have known you'd gone to Riseholme in the first place?' Devon said.

This is a turnaround, Devon realized. *Deeley's the one who's willing to believe worse of Maxie than I am. Little Deeley, who couldn't say boo to a goose when she was small – who certainly couldn't say boo to Maxie.*

And here she is, managing to stand up to Maxie. She's being braver than I am.

Despite the horror of the situation, Devon realized that she was deeply proud of her younger sister.

'Fine,' Maxie said coldly. 'Let's get it all out, shall we? Devon, to answer your question, I had someone following Deeley. After that mess with the magazine article, I didn't trust her. Not in the least. I wanted to make sure that she didn't do something else equally stupid and irresponsible.' She glared at Deeley. 'And guess what? She managed to do something even more stupid! She went up to Riseholme, gawked at Bill's old house until she attracted the attention of Linda O'Keeffe – *Linda*, of all people! – and stirred up this whole bloody shitheap! How bloody idiotic was *that*! I told the detective agency I wanted reports whenever Deeley did anything that was out of the ordinary, and the guy they had following Deeley rang me from the train back. He thought it was definitely out of the ordinary for her to travel all the way up there, turn around after half an hour and come all the way back. And the way he described the woman you'd talked to, I could tell it was Linda. I was so angry with you I could barely *breathe*.'

'You had someone *following* me?' Deeley said, eyes widening.

Maxie shrugged. 'I run a very successful company,' she said. 'And my husband's an MP. Sometimes one needs information that one can't get from normal sources. It's fairly standard to have a detective agency on call.'

Devon shook her head in frank disbelief. 'I honestly don't know what to say, Maxie,' she murmured, as her older sister finished off her drink and continued, gesturing with the glass.

'*So*, what did I do?' Her jaw set. 'I asked him what time the train got into London and went to meet it. And I told him he was off the job the moment the train pulled into King's Cross. I waited by the barriers and saw you come through,' she glared at Deeley again, 'and I followed you out of the station, and I gave you a bloody good shove when you were waiting at the lights. I didn't mean to kill you, just to give you a scare. Make you sorry you'd ever gone up to Riseholme.'

'I could have been killed,' Deeley said, her voice rising in anger. 'Or really badly hurt.' She gulped. 'And you painted those words on the front door as well, didn't you? While I was away in Jersey?'

Maxie nodded. 'You needed a good fright,' she said callously. 'And you deserved even worse. If you hadn't gone up to Riseholme, none of this would have happened, you stupid little bitch!'

'Hey!' Devon said, just as angry as Deeley by now. 'Don't you talk to her like that! How dare you call her names!' She stared Maxie straight in the eye. 'I always thought you were looking after us, Maxie. But I was wrong. You were the worst thing that ever happened to us. Worse than Mum, worse than any of her boyfriends. Because we trusted you, and you lied to us and betrayed us. You made murderers out of your little sisters.'

She turned away, pulling Deeley with her. 'We're going now. There's nothing more to say.'

Deeley nodded. Devon was right. There was no point continuing this. But suddenly a crucial thought occurred to her, and she exclaimed, 'Oh God, wait . . .' Deeley dashed out of the room. 'I have to get Alice!' she called over her shoulder. 'I can't leave her here, without anyone who cares about her! I have to take her with me!'

Devon picked up her bag as Deeley ran upstairs. Her head was heavy, her legs felt as if she were dragging lead weights behind her as she walked into the hall. Maxie's silence was all she needed to hear, confirmation that Devon was right; there really was nothing more to say.

Deeley came down the stairs as fast as she could with a sleeping child in her arms, Alice's nappy bag slung over her shoulder. She grabbed the stroller as Devon opened the front door for them.

And then Maxie exploded into the hall.

'How *dare* you say I'm worse than Mum!' she yelled, her face blotched with red spots of anger. 'How *dare* you! That's the *worst thing*, the *worst thing* you could say to me – you bloody *cow*—'

Maxie's arm was crooked back behind her head, the heavy cut-glass tumbler in her hand. Devon had a split second to react as she realized what was happening: she shoved Deeley out of the door and slammed it behind her, hoping to hell that her sister wouldn't lose her footing on the steps and hurt herself and the baby. There was no time for Devon to save herself; she ducked down instead, her hands covering her head, her face, as the glass crashed against the door and onto Devon.

'Get out!' Maxie was screaming. 'Get out of my house, you bitch! Get out and never come back!'

Scrabbling for her bag, her left hand screaming in pain where the glass had hit it, Devon grabbed for the door handle, twisting it, frantic to get out before Maxie attacked her again. She fell out into the London night, panting in relief at the sight of Deeley on the pavement, holding Alice, safe and sound.

'Are you all right?' Deeley said, her voice so high and scared that its pitch made Alice wake up and wail a protest on realizing that she wasn't in her nice warm bed.

'Just about . . .' Devon tumbled down the stairs to her side.

'And you got your bag? Tell me you got your bag!'

Devon held it up. Inside was the digital recorder which her assistant used to tape all her interviews; it lived in Devon's home office, and it had been easy enough for her to bring it in her handbag, switching it on when she placed it on the arm of the sofa.

'It's all on tape,' she said. 'Everything we said.' She set her jaw. 'And we're taking it to the police station, first thing in the morning.'

Epilogue
Two weeks later

Deeley

*I*t was a beautiful English early summer day: a few white cotton wool clouds scudding lightly across the clear, Wedgwood blue sky, the sun sparking glints of gold off the green blades of grass and the small stained-glass windows of St Bartolph's parish church. The press photographers and the TV crews, their vans laden with satellite dishes and antennae, were clustered at the end of the old cracked stone path that led through the churchyard, its verges planted prettily with lavender and roses. Bordered by a low stone wall, secured by a creaky old iron gate, the boundary was patrolled by two policemen, who were also there to keep out local inhabitants who might never have been to church in their lives, but couldn't resist the opportunity to snatch a view of the biggest celebrities who had ever come to Riseholme: a TV star, a rugby player who'd been capped for England, an It girl from the glossies.

The police had also had to clear the graveyard of all the disaffected teenagers who usually substituted school attendance for slumping on the tombs, smoking joints, drinking cheap booze and shouting abuse at each other; none of them had gone too far, though. They were sitting further down the wall, distant enough for the police not to bother them, still pulling openly on their roll-ups.

That was Riseholme for you in a nutshell; the police were too worn down to even bother with kids smoking spliffs in public.

But the teens, like the press, were mostly obscured by the ancient oaks whose heavy foliage pressed its branches almost to the grass below. It was the first time Deeley had ever been into the church-yard; she'd always been too nervous of the wild kids who hung out there. Now, as they walked out after the ceremony, she was dazzled by how pretty it was, like a tiny green oasis in the centre of ugly, built-up Riseholme. Sunlight dappled shadows across the grass and the grey stone of the gravestones; some late bluebells still clustered in the shadow of the oaks. It was the perfect spot.

She glanced over at Devon, who must have had the same thought, because their small smiles mirrored each other's. The pall-bearers were leading the procession, six men who had been hired by the funeral director, all in cheap dark suits, badly cut and too shiny in the bright sunlight, pulling across their shoulders. But the coffin itself had been the most expensive in the local funeral parlour's range, a deep, polished walnut wood with burnished brass handles, solid and substantial without being showy.

Just what Bill would have wanted, Deeley thought approvingly.

On top of it was a big white wreath, roses and lilies on a bed of deep green foliage: simple and beautiful. They'd only managed to find a few relatives of Bill's to attend the funeral, and they hadn't sent flowers; Deeley and Devon's wreath was all there was.

Maybe we should have made it a bit bigger, Deeley fretted. But Bill had hated ostentation, lavish displays of money. *He'd have had a heart attack if he'd known what that wreath cost, let alone the coffin.* Devon had paid for it all, of course, but Deeley had made the arrangements. Devon had enough on her hands, what with leaving her husband, moving out of their house, and shacking up at the Dorchester with her new Italian lover. *Who's apparently a prince*, Deeley thought with great amusement. *Trust Dev to go on holiday and promptly snag an Italian aristocrat.*

The cortege had reached the graveyard now, the freshly dug plot gaping open like a wound in the lush green grass, ready for the coffin. Deeley stepped to one side of the grave, the vicar passing them to stand at the head, by the newly cut stone. The pall-bearers lowered the coffin carefully onto trestles, and stood respectfully to one side while the last of the service was read. As the few mourners took their places, Deeley found herself facing Devon and Cesare across Bill's grave.

What would Bill have made of Cesare? Deeley couldn't help wondering, looking at Cesare, with his mad mop of curly hair, his big nose, the stubble already beginning to show on his chin, and his Italian suit, which would certainly have been cut much too tightly for Bill's taste. Still, she had the feeling that Bill would have liked Devon's new boyfriend. Cesare was most definitely a man's man. Deeley had already heard him talk to Devon in a way that Deeley would never have thought that anyone could get away with; Devon had always had to be the boss, and now here she was, letting herself be ordered around by an Italian man half the size of her husband, and giggling happily as he did it.

Mind you, she gives as good as she gets, Deeley reflected. *I've seen Devon slice Cesare into pieces with her sarcasm, and he giggles too. They're a perfect couple.*

She looked at her sister. It was an ironic thing to think at a funeral, but Devon truly had never looked so beautiful. Black suited her like no other shade; her pale skin was luminous against the shoulder-skimming neckline of the simple dress, her glossy hair a cascade of dark curls framing her beautiful heart-shaped face, her heavily lashed dark eyes and red lips.

And she seems so confident, Deeley realized. *I know Devon's always been worried about her weight, but ever since she came back from Italy, she doesn't seem to care about it any more. Mind you, she's drinking less, and I'm sure that helps . . .*

Cesare's arm slipped round Devon's waist, pulling her against him. He whispered something in her ear that made her turn her head towards him, smiling gratefully; he dropped a quick kiss on her lips.

The evening after their terrible confrontation with Maxie,

Devon, Deeley and Alice had taken refuge back in Devon's basement flat, settling Alice to sleep in Deeley's bed, propped up with pillows, while Deeley and Devon curled up on the living-room sofa, talking all night. Crying, hugging, drinking endless cups of tea, telling each other everything that had happened in their lives, ever since Devon's TV career had taken off, since Deeley had gone to LA.

And before then, too. Confronting Maxie with her crime, her betrayal of their trust in her, had opened floodgates that Devon and Deeley hadn't even realized existed. Their murder of Bill, the awful secret Maxie had forced upon them, had estranged the sisters from each other ever since. Devon had theorized that they'd been frightened to be as close as before, because if they were, they would start talking about that awful night, and if they did, they might never stop . . .

And Maxie kept telling us never to say a word. Never to say a word to anyone. Or we'd all go to prison for the rest of our lives.

So Devon and I stopped talking to each other. Confiding in each other. Maxie didn't just kill Bill, she killed my relationship with my middle sister for eighteen years.

Devon had spilled out everything. How messed up her marriage to Matt was, how, even before she'd fled to Italy, she'd been sure that there was no chance they could reconcile.

'Matt's so lovely,' she had said earnestly. 'He didn't do a thing wrong. Maybe he was too nice, but that's not exactly his fault, is it? It's *my* fault for being a cow, and not appreciating a really nice guy!'

She'd twisted her hands in her lap.

'And then I met Cesare . . .' she confessed. 'I don't know how he feels about me, or if he wants to see me again – but I can't stop thinking about him. And I can't be married to one man and be thinking like this about another.'

Deeley had held her breath, waiting for her sister's conclusion. To her amazement, Devon had stood up, taken a deep breath, and marched up the internal staircase to the main house. Deeley'd looked at her watch: a quarter to ten. She'd waited, her heart pounding, pacing up and down between the kitchen area and the living room, unable to sit still, dreading the sight of Devon bouncing happily back downstairs, hand in hand with Matt, announcing that they'd miraculously reconciled, and were going to start trying for a baby straight away.

Or, even worse, not coming downstairs at all, because they were too busy making up by having wild sex all over the house . . .

Deeley had been trying so hard not to picture Devon and Matt in each other's arms that she didn't even hear the upstairs door open, or her sister's footsteps on the treads of the stairs. She turned in her pacing to see Devon standing there, in the doorway, looking very subdued.

'I did it,' she whispered. 'I went up and told Matt that I want a divorce.'

'What happened?' Deeley's heart was pounding nearly out of her chest. Had Matt tried to talk Devon out of it? Had he pleaded, begged her not to go, told her he couldn't live without her?

Devon heaved a weak little laugh.

'He said he'd been meaning to ask me the same thing!' she said, flopping into the armchair. 'He said he'd known for ages things weren't right. He said the more time he'd had to think about it, the more he could see that we just weren't compatible. We want really different things. And, to be honest, we get on each other's nerves.' She looked up at Deeley with wide, shocked eyes. 'So it's official. I'm getting a divorce. What a day, Deels,' she said slowly. 'What a day it's been.'

And then Devon had broken into tears, and Deeley had run over to sit on the arm of her sister's chair, hugging her and telling her that everything would be all right.

At least I wasn't lying when I said it would all come out right, Deeley thought now, looking at Devon, who, even at the funeral of their sort-of-stepfather, couldn't stop glowing. The vicar had finished reading the eulogy, but Deeley was ashamed to admit that she'd barely heard a word. Her head was full of thoughts and speculations. She had caught the words 'In the midst of life, we are in death', or something like that. *For me, it's the opposite*, she had to admit. *Here I am at a funeral. I should be taking the time to think about Bill, to tell him how sorry I am about how he died. How grateful I am for everything he did for us.*

But it's really hard to focus on Bill, when I know Matt's just come up the path behind me.

Devon had told her that Matt would be coming: he'd said he wanted to attend the funeral out of respect for what she and Deeley had gone through. 'He's *such* a nice guy,' Devon had said on the phone that morning. 'He insisted. I said I'd be driving up with Cesare, and he was totally OK with it. Said there were no hard feelings.'

Deeley had come with Devon and Cesare, who had shot over to London in his Lamborghini, making the drive in a mere sixteen hours, as soon as Devon had rung him to say she was getting a divorce. Devon had told Deeley, beaming from ear to ear, that Cesare hadn't pursued Devon to London out of respect for her married status; he'd hoped that she would come back to Italy after her emergency was resolved, but had left the ball firmly in Devon's court. However, once given the green light, he had jumped into his extremely fast car and driven straight to London; he was planning to take Devon back to Italy as soon as possible. The food in London, he announced, was getting better, but it was still scarcely on a par with Italy.

Deeley had assumed that all she would be able to think about on the drive was that she would imminently be seeing Matt again, as a free man, but Devon and Cesare's constant bickering had been so distracting that it had fully occupied Deeley. Although the dialogue had mostly consisted of them hurling insults and telling each other to shut up, interspersed with Devon screaming at Cesare to slow down because of speed cameras, it was clear that they were an extremely happy couple; Deeley had never seen her sister so glowing, so full of laughter. *And so obviously having vast amounts of very good sex*, she thought wryly.

Matt must have noticed that, too, she thought, finally turning to look at him. She had barely glanced in his direction in the church, but now that she wasn't sitting next to her sister, she felt more free to look at him. He was still using his crutch, she'd noticed that before, and winced for him, because it must mean that his ankle injury was pretty serious. She could hear it tapping up the path, Matt walking carefully on the uneven stones. As he reached the foot of the grave there was a moment when he paused, looking at the mourners, and then chose, quite deliberately, to limp his way over to Deeley's side.

He was wearing a black suit, not quite as well cut as Cesare's, but you couldn't compete with a slim Italian man when it came to clothes; Matt had to have his suits specially made to wrap around his bulky muscles. He dwarfed even the pall-bearers as he passed them. Deeley noticed that none of them could resist darting glances at him, thrilled to be so close to an England international. It was extraordinary, the effect he had on her; with every step closer, Deeley's heart beat faster, her legs felt weaker. By the time he reached her, she was concentrating so hard on looking normal that she felt paralyzed. In a bare minute, she had lost any sense of what a sister-in-law would normally look like when greeting a soon-to-be-ex-brother-in-law at the funeral of her sort-of-stepfather – in whose death she had been very much involved . . .

Did you just hear yourself? she couldn't help thinking. *And that's not even including the fact that you're madly in lust with him, at the very least! There is no normal in this situation!*

'Hello Deeley,' Matt said quietly, as the pall-bearers took up the straps lying on the trestles beneath the coffin.

It was such a solemn occasion, Deeley should have felt horribly guilty at the rush of excitement that fizzed through her on hearing Matt say her name. It was schoolgirl-ish, silly and stupid, to feel such exhilaration at such a simple thing. Especially at Bill's funeral.

Of course Matt's going to say hello! she told herself firmly. *What else would he say? And of course he's standing next to you – he's not going to join his wife and her new boyfriend, is he? Don't let this give you any ideas!*

'How've you been?' Matt asked.

'I don't know, really,' Deeley said simply, looking up at him. The sight of his handsome, craggy face was like a blow. All she wanted to do was reach up and kiss him, and that was completely out of the question. His clear blue eyes were questioning, concerned, completely focussed on her; no one else existed in that moment.

'It's all been such a mess,' she continued. 'God, that's such a huge understatement.'

'I can imagine.' Matt grimaced in sympathy.

'But at least we *know*,' Deeley said in a heartfelt tone. 'At least we know everything now. We can bury Bill properly. Tell him how sorry we are.'

Deeley choked a little on those last words; the realization of what she and Devon had been tricked into doing by Maxie was still very hard to deal with. Matt shifted his weight, wedged his crutch into the grass, and reached out his hand to her for comfort. It was so big her own disappeared into its warm grasp; tears pricked at her eyes, and she blinked them away.

'He knows you're sorry,' Matt said quietly, as the pall-bearers lowered the coffin into the waiting grave in front of them. At its head, the simple stone was engraved with Bill's full name, the dates of his birth and death, and then the words: BELOVED STEPFATHER. 'Believe me, he does.'

Deeley's fingers gripped his convulsively.

'Deep breaths,' he said gently. 'Take deep breaths.'

It was as if Matt's hand was the only thing holding her up, giving her strength. As the coffin disappeared into the ground, as the pall-bearers pulled out their straps and discreetly backed away, Deeley met Devon's eyes across the open grave. Devon was clinging to Cesare now, both his arms around her; he was smoothing down her hair, whispering in her ear. Devon wiped tears from her eyes and managed a smile for Deeley. Devon took in her husband, standing next to Deeley, holding Deeley's hand; she looked from one to the other, processing the sight with a tiny nod.

Matt didn't let go of Deeley's hand, even with Devon looking at them. She hardly dared imagine what that might mean. Her heart was pounding; there was an odd, metallic taste at the back of her throat, a haze of nerves enfolding her. The vicar was saying something; now she'd closed her Bible and was walking back, passing them, touching Deeley lightly on the shoulder in sympathy. Devon, half-leaning on Cesare, was already following the vicar back to the church.

Matt looked at Deeley. 'Can I give you a lift?' he mumbled. 'I'm going back to London . . .'

'Yes!' Deeley almost squealed, then caught herself in horror at the sound she had just made. 'Um, yes, thanks,' she said in an artificially formal voice. 'That would be very nice.'

He grinned, his hand leaving hers, as they started to walk back down the church path, the paparazzi cameras snapping away.

'I saw a very flash yellow car parked up there, next to the hearse,' he said, a glimmer of amusement in his voice. 'Thought you might have had a bit of a Mario Andretti time coming up here.'

'Just a bit,' Deeley said, smiling. 'And there's not much room in the back.'

'He seems like a nice bloke,' Matt said, his tone deliberately casual.

'Yes, he does,' Deeley agreed. She was watching her step; she didn't want to trip on the loose stones in her kitten heels. But she was watching what she said about Devon and Cesare just as carefully – and even more so, what Matt said about them.

'That's what she needs,' Matt went on, looking straight ahead. 'Some Italian guy in a Lamborghini. Lots of drama, lots of waving hands around and yelling. Like in the films.'

Deeley glanced up ahead, at Devon still leaning on Cesare, dabbing at her eyes now with a tissue. Matt was quite right: Cesare was the perfect fit for her sister.

'I was always too boring for Devon,' Matt continued.

'Oh, I'm sure that's not—'

'No, really!' Matt shot her a sideways glance that was brimming with humour. 'No need to deny it. We were never the best match. An Italian prince and the jet-set life, that's more her speed. I never even wanted to live in London – that was all Dev. I'd've been in the countryside. Wiltshire was my pick. Or the Cotswolds.'

'Oh, lovely,' Deeley said unguardedly.

'Yeah.' He wasn't looking at her now, but Deeley had the sense that he was choosing his words very carefully. 'I'm all crocked up now, you know. I've played my last game. Saw the doctor and the coach yesterday. I'm officially retired.'

'Oh, Matt, I'm sorry.'

And why can't I start a sentence without saying 'Oh'? she thought, furious with herself. *I sound ridiculous!*

He held up the hand not grasping the crutch. 'No worries. Honestly. I've had my time, done everything on the field I wanted to do. Some blokes might go into coaching, but I've thought it over and that's not me. I fancy a fresh start. Buy a farm in the country. Pigs, cows, sheep, the works. Orchards.' He grinned. 'I fancy making my own cider, believe it or not.'

'It sounds wonderful,' Deeley said, trying as hard as she could not to gush, and worrying that she'd failed.

'Really?' He glanced at her again. 'I wouldn't have thought you'd've fancied that kind of set-up. You know, farms are mucky places. A glamour puss like you . . .' His swift look took in her black Issa jersey dress, her suede kitten heels, her hair twisted up into an elegant chignon. 'I mean, you're a party girl, aren't you?' he said. 'Devon used to point you out on telly, at all those awards ceremonies in LA, dressed up to the nines. Country life might not exactly be up your street.'

'Oh, it *is*,' Deeley said, realizing that she'd done it again, started a sentence with an 'oh', she could have kicked herself. 'The happiest I've been in London is going to Green Park.'

And as she said it, she realized, with great relief, how true it was: *I mustn't make things up just to please Matt, or say what I think he wants to hear*, she told herself firmly. *He's had enough of lies, and so have I. We have to be honest with each other from the beginning.*

'You know,' she admitted, in the interests of full disclosure, 'that wasn't really my boyfriend in LA. It was all fake. He didn't want to come out – he thought it would hurt his career. So he asked me to pretend to be his girlfriend.'

'Poor sod,' Matt said compassionately. 'Can't blame him, can you? I mean, it's getting better, but there're still a lot of crappy people out there.'

'And I was pretty wild then,' Deeley continued bravely, very glad that Matt had been so nice about Nicky and her LA set-up. 'I *was* a party girl. Like you thought I was.'

'Well, fair enough,' Matt said. They had slowed down, were walking as slowly as they could, but they were almost at the church now. 'I mean, you were single, weren't you? You've got a right to have your fun.'

'And I thought I'd do that when I got back to London as well,' Deeley said quickly, determined to get this all in before they reached the others. 'Be a party girl. But then I realized that I didn't really want to. I didn't know *what* I wanted to do. But just dressing up and going to parties – I'd done all that solidly for five years, you know? I didn't need to throw myself back into it. The best time I've had in London has actually been looking after Alice – you know, Maxie and Olly's daughter. Taking her to the park, playing with her. It's been really lovely.'

Matt looked at her, his expression unreadable.

'I haven't seen much of her, but she seems like a nice little girl,' he said. 'Poor mite, what's going to happen to her now?'

Deeley took a deep breath. 'I want to adopt her,' she said simply. She'd been thinking about this ever since Maxie's arrest. 'I don't think Maxie gives a shit about her, and I know Olly doesn't. I can't imagine they'll make a fuss if I take her on.'

They had come to a halt now by Matt's car, and were staring at each other so intensely that everything else faded away in a haze. The vicar, talking to Devon, Cesare and the funeral director; bird-song from the wood pigeons and starlings nesting in the church gables; cars starting up as the pall-bearers drove away – all the sounds around them melted into nothing. All they could see were each other's faces, all they could hear were each other's words.

And, of course, the words that they weren't saying.

'That's great,' Matt said with complete sincerity. 'That's really great. That little girl'll be so much better off with you.'

He had the nicest face she'd ever seen, Deeley thought, looking up at him. Not the handsomest; she'd met the handsomest men in the world in Los Angeles. But the nicest. She would never get tired of looking at Matt, at his slightly smashed-in nose, his craggy cheekbones, his square, solid jaw, his blue eyes . . .

'Deeley! Matt! We're heading off now,' Devon called from the passenger door of the car. 'Matt, you're giving Deels a lift?'

'Yes,' he answered, without even looking over at Devon. 'I am.'

'Great!' Devon beamed happily. 'Ooh, and Deels, I forgot to tell you – Rory says they've greenlighted that series idea! Isn't it exciting? We'll start filming in Italy next month!'

Impulsively, she ran over and threw herself at her sister, kissing her.

'I'm so happy,' she said into Deeley's ear. 'I'm *so* happy, Deels, and I want you to be just as happy as I am!'

She squeezed Deeley's arms, hugging her tight. 'Be happy, Deels,' she whispered, glancing sideways at Matt. 'I'm not completely blind, you know. I can see how the two of you are together. You're much better for him than I ever was. Go for it. Be happy.'

And, with a swirl of black jersey skirt, leaving a cloud of expensive perfume behind her, Devon turned and ran from Matt and her old life to Cesare and her new one, jumping eagerly into the passenger seat of the Lamborghini.

'We do *not* start to make the film next month,' Cesare said as he closed her door and walked round to the driver's side. 'You are not ready. You are not ready till you learn not to overcook the pasta.'

'I do *not* overcook pasta!' Devon said crossly as he got in and wound down the window, lighting a cigarette. 'You're such a liar!'

'*Stai zitta, perche é meglio,*' he said, slamming the door and sending the car flying out of the parking lot; even Matt turned his head to watch the Lamborghini in motion.

'What's that all about?' Matt asked Deeley, as the Lamborghini zipped past the gateposts in a streak of bright yellow; oohs and aahs could be heard from the kids on the churchyard wall as it passed them.

'Oh!' She couldn't help smiling. 'Rory – you know, the producer who makes Devon's shows – he saw Dev and Cesare together and thinks they're hilarious. He pitched a series where Cesare teaches Devon Italian cooking. They're basically going to bicker all the time and throw things at each other. The BBC loves the idea. I think Cesare'll be chain-smoking, too. He says he looks forward to showing the British people how you really cook Italian food.' She giggled. 'Franco's passed muster, but it's run by Italians, which makes a difference. Cesare's really taken against Jamie Oliver. They went to his Italian restaurant last night and Cesare made a big scene about meatballs in the carbonara, apparently.'

'Sounds a blast,' Matt said, raising his brows. 'I won't be watching, I shouldn't think. Might be a step too far, watching my ex-wife cook spaghetti with her new man. But I wish them all the luck in the world.'

'You *do*?' Deeley breathed. She was absolutely unable to prevent herself from sounding like some girlish idiot; if anyone played back this conversation to her, she knew, she'd be cringing in total embarrassment. *But it's working, isn't it?* she told herself, crossing her fingers tightly in the draped folds of her skirt. *This is going better than I ever dreamed it could* . . .

Matt nodded soberly.

'Yeah,' he said, 'I do.' His jaw tightened. 'It was over for much longer than I let myself admit,' he said sadly. 'I've been flogging a dead horse for a long time now. Too proud to see it, you know? And I didn't want a divorce. No one in my family's ever been divorced, and I didn't want to be the first. But you've got to face up to things sooner or later.'

He looked over to where the Lamborghini had been.

'We always wanted different things, me and Dev. I couldn't make her happy, no matter how much I tried.' He smiled crookedly. 'I'm a simple man, Deeley. I just want to be married, settle down. Make my wife happy.'

Deeley couldn't say a word. She couldn't breathe. She just stood there, staring at him, her lips slightly parted. *I don't just sound like an idiot*, she thought. *Now I look like one too.*

'Miss McKenna?' The vicar bustled over to Deeley's side, startling her out of her trance. 'I'm so sorry for your loss.'

'Thank you,' Deeley said, turning to her; the vicar took Deeley's hands and pressed them firmly.

'Very sad,' she said, shaking her head sympathetically. 'Very sad circumstances. I'm sorry that we couldn't see your eldest sister here as well.'

'She's, um, awaiting sentencing,' Deeley said, her eyes widening in surprise that the vicar had mentioned the disgraced Maxie.

The vicar nodded, her expression kindly.

'It's still a shame that she couldn't be here,' she said. 'We do see criminals at funeral services sometimes, with a police guard if that's considered necessary. And I must say, I take it as a blessing if they attend. For true repentance, one needs to make amends as much as possible. I would have liked to see your sister at this poor man's funeral. Hopefully she will come and visit his grave, when she can.'

Deeley nodded; she didn't know what to say.

'She confessed, I understand,' the vicar said, giving a last press to Deeley's hands and then releasing them. 'That's a very good sign, isn't it? A trial would have been very distressing for her family. And of course, it indicates an acknowledgement of her crime. I hope you will be visiting her in prison.'

Still unable to speak, Deeley made an ambiguous motion with her head; Matt put his arm around her, moving her back, away from the vicar.

'They're still very upset by all of this,' he said, gesturing that Deeley should get into the car. 'But the family does appreciate all your help, Vicar. It was a very nice service. Very moving.'

Shepherded firmly by Matt, Deeley gratefully got into the car. Matt limped as briskly as he could round to the driver's side and got in too.

'I didn't know you had a convertible,' she said, fastening her seatbelt, taking in for the first time the dark green BMW 3-series with its beige leather interior.

'I don't.' Matt swung himself in and slung the crutch into the back seat, closing the door. 'This is an automatic – I borrowed it from the garage for a month or two. Can't drive a manual with my foot messed up like this.' He grinned. 'I might keep it, though. Nice, isn't it?' He started it up. 'Never had a convertible before, but I really like it.'

He shot her a glance of concern. 'You all right with the top down? Put on your coat, it'll get cold,' he said, nodding to the black fake fur jacket she was carrying over her arm. 'Will the wind mess up your hair?'

He's so sweet! Deeley thought with a rush of pleasure.

'I couldn't give a shit if my hair gets messed up,' she said happily. 'But,' she realized that they were going to drive past all the photographers and news crews, 'with the top down, they'll get tons of shots of the two of us.' She nodded towards the church-yard wall.

'I couldn't give a shit if they take photos of us,' Matt echoed easily, raising a hand to the vicar as he drove away, rounding the gateposts considerably slower than Cesare had done.

Deeley settled back in her leather seat, still almost unable to believe that she was driving away with Matt. Sitting next to him as the paparazzi called their names, trying to get them to turn and look at the cameras. *He must know what this will mean,* she thought, on a rising tide of excitement. *Photos of him holding my hand at the funeral . . . driving me away from the church . . .*

'Sorry about the vicar and all that,' Matt said, piloting the car through the messy tangle of Riseholme's streets with the aid of his satnav. 'Bringing up Maxie. Must have been upsetting for you.'

Deeley heaved a sigh. 'It's not like I wasn't thinking about her all the time anyway,' she said sadly. 'And the vicar was right – Maxie *should* have come to the funeral.'

Matt was concentrating on driving, but Deeley saw his mouth quirk in an ironic smile.

'Somehow,' he said dryly, 'I don't think your sister's that big on repentance.'

'No, she isn't.' Deeley sighed again. 'She only confessed because it was all on tape and her solicitor told her she couldn't hope to be acquitted. Particularly,' she said in a small voice, 'because Devon and I said we were prepared to testify against her.'

Matt shook his head in silent empathy for Devon and Deeley's situation.

'I was really glad to hear you weren't going to be charged,' he said. 'Devon told me a few days ago.'

'Yes, we've been lucky, I suppose,' Deeley said dully. Of course it was a huge relief that the police had decided not to press charges against them for their involvement in Bill's murder, or their part in concealing his body, but using the word 'lucky' in any context referring to the whole miserable situation seemed much too ironic.

She thought of the TV footage of Maxie being arrested; the media had been tipped off, probably by some police officer making some extra cash on the side by passing information to the tabloids. Word had got round, and by the time a furious Maxie was escorted out of the Bilberry offices, the press was clustered outside, ready to eat up this highly juicy story. Maxie, usually so perfect when dealing with the press, had been so angry that she'd been unable to control herself; her face had been twisted into a snarl, her shoulders hunching as she tried to shake off the hand a police officer had placed on her shoulder.

She'd looked guilty. Plain and simple.

Deeley closed her eyes, letting the events of the last couple of weeks wash over her. The interviews with the police, who at first had been almost unable to believe what they were hearing. Finding a solicitor to represent her and Devon. Hiding out from Olly's wrath, when he realized what Maxie's sisters had done, and from the media, who were doorstepping every McKenna and Stangroom they could find, relishing this story. It had everything: three beautiful sisters, rags to riches, English aristocracy, politics, glamour, fashion and a huge buried scandal.

But most of all, of course, it had pictures of beautiful women. All the McKenna sisters were very photogenic, and nowadays photos were what drove a story faster than anything, and kept it in the news. One picture of Deeley in her LA glamour days, of Devon smiling, spilling lusciously out of a Vivienne Westwood dress, or Maxie doing promotion for Bilberry, was worth a thousand words.

'She'll be going away for a while,' Matt commented, and Deeley knew who he meant. 'Even pleading guilty, and with all her connections – I mean, she killed someone, and covered it up for years. That isn't just a slap on the wrist.'

'It's a mandatory life sentence, our solicitor says,' Deeley said, still with her eyes closed. 'Usually it's a minimum of fourteen years. But the judge gives you a tariff, so you serve that and then apply for parole. And apparently Maxie's got some kind of thing with the chief whip of Olly's party, and he's got a lot of pull with a lot of judges. So she might get much less than fourteen years. She's going to try to argue that there are plenty of mitigating circumstances. Our mum, having to look after me and Devon, all that.'

'Yeah, well . . .' Matt turned the BMW onto the sliproad for the M1. 'I'm sure she'll know how to work the system,' he said cynically. 'Bet you she'll be running that prison in a couple of months. Everyone jumping to her tune.'

Deeley couldn't help smiling at that: he was absolutely right. Maxie would have warders and inmates alike under her thumb in no time.

'And what about Olly?' Matt asked. 'What's he going to do about all this?' He winced. 'Poor bloke. I never liked him, but no one deserves *this*.'

'I really don't know,' Deeley admitted. 'I don't know if Olly'll divorce her or not. He'll probably have to, just to save his career.'

'The sooner you get little Alice away from him the better,' Matt observed. 'He never wanted her in the first place.'

'I already have,' Deeley said proudly. 'We've been staying at a flat that belongs to some friends of Devon – they're travelling or something. I tracked down that nice Australian nanny who walked out on Maxie and Olly, and she's been helping me for a bit. She's looking after Alice today. I didn't want to bring her.' She grinned. 'Also, I don't imagine you can fit a baby car seat in a Lamborghini.'

'I was going to ask you about that,' Matt said, and Deeley opened her eyes, just a little, so she could look at him under her lashes. 'If you had any rush to get back to London, I mean.'

Her heart leaped up into her throat and started pounding at her windpipe.

'Not really. The nanny's got Alice all day – she said not to worry about it. I think she's taking her to the zoo this afternoon. She's staying in the flat, too, so I don't have a curfew or anything.'

'Great,' Matt said. 'Because I was wondering if you wanted to maybe make a day of it . . . you know, since we're out already. Go to the Cotswolds for an early dinner? I know this really nice little country house hotel that does great food . . .'

Deeley sank her fingernails into her thighs to stop herself yelping aloud. 'I'd love to!' she exclaimed, trying incredibly hard not to gush.

'Seems a bit mad,' he said, looking at her briefly. 'Driving all over the country. But there's bloody paparazzi at all our places, and this way we can have a nice day out without anyone shoving cameras at us.'

'Oh, absolutely,' Deeley agreed demurely. 'Really sensible.'

She was smiling now from ear to ear, a warm glow spreading across her entire body. The miracle had happened; the unbelievable happy ending was actually within her grasp. Matt glanced at her again, and she saw that her smile was mirrored on his face; he was attempting to be cool, but actually he was beaming like a madman. He reached out his left hand and put it on her leg; his palm was so big, it covered half her thigh. The contact made Deeley jump with shock and pleasure. All the memories she had been trying so hard to repress came flooding back in a tidal wave: that evening on the sofa, on Matt's lap, grinding against him, his hands on her skin, his body hard and eager beneath her. Excitement rushed through her, her lower body beginning to melt. She reached down and put her hand over his, pressing his palm deeper into her thigh.

'Jesus,' Matt muttered, the BMW swerving a little as his other hand trembled on the wheel.

'Or we could just stop at a Travelodge,' she suggested. 'There's bound to be one along the motorway, isn't there?'

'Deeley!' he said in frustration. 'I'm a romantic guy! I was going to take you to a country house hotel . . . this lovely stone manor house, they've got a suite with a four-poster bed and stunning views . . .' He went red. 'Not that I was taking anything for granted,' he added quickly, as the car swerved again, causing a lorry to honk. 'Jesus,' he muttered in parentheses, pulling into the slow lane. 'I was just thinking we could have a nice meal, get to know each other more, have a really good conversation . . . they've got gorgeous gardens, I thought we could take a walk there and then have a cocktail on the terrace . . .'

'*Or*,' Deeley said firmly, her entire body now burning with frustration, 'we could find a Holiday Inn Express, check in, and fuck each other's brains out.'

The BMW swerved yet again; a coach full of schoolchildren passed them, and some rowdies in the back, seeing Matt's hand on Deeley's leg very clearly in the open convertible, banged the windows and yelled encouragement.

'Deeley!' Matt said crossly. 'How do you expect me to drive safely when you say stuff like that? I'm only human!'

Deeley was too far gone to care now; she felt completely suffused with golden, sparkling joy, bathed in sunshine. She pulled his hand further up her leg. Matt groaned and dragged it away reluctantly.

'I haven't been able to think of anything else since that night,' she said happily. 'I've been trying so hard not to remember it, but all I can think of is sitting on your lap, kissing you, touching you—'

'Right! That's it!'

Matt wrenched at the wheel as an exit came up, shooting the car up the off-ramp. Deeley held onto the seat with both hands; he was speeding like a madman, whizzing round a roundabout, into a narrow, undistinguished country road, and down it, past side lanes and hedged fields, as the countryside sprawled out, becoming more sparse and unpopulated, finally squealing to a halt, rubber screeching on tarmac, shoving the car into reverse, backing up fifteen feet and stamping on the accelerator as he spun the wheel, sending the BMW bouncing down a narrow farm lane with a decrepit, clearly long-abandoned gate at the end of it.

He slammed the car to a stop and turned to look at Deeley, about to say something. But she had already kicked off her shoes, unsnapped her seat belt and was hitching up her skirt, climbing over the leather armrest to sit on his lap.

'Put your seat all the way back,' she said, straddling him, her knees on either side of his legs, wrapping herself deliciously around his wide torso. Bending over, she kissed him, her hands sliding around his neck, pulling him towards her.

'Deeley . . .' he started, but she bit his lip.

'Stop talking and put your seat back,' she whispered, reaching down to unbutton his jacket. She popped the buttons open, and then the shirt below, sliding her hands down his ripped abdominals to the waistband of his trousers, finding the buckle of his belt.

'Oh God – Deeley . . .'

Matt reached down, found the lever and slid the seat back, his legs stretching out and widening, giving Deeley more room to manoeuvre.

'I don't have anything . . .' he started to say.

But Deeley was on fire. She dragged his head to one side, kissing and licking down his neck, making him groan, his body surrendering to her as she unzipped his trousers and pulled him out, hard as a rock. His hands slid under her skirt, finding her knickers and pulling them and her tights down, the sensation of his palms on her bare skin making her gasp in delight; she writhed in pleasure, wriggling her skirt up to her waist.

'I don't care,' she said, almost cried, as she straddled him, her tights ripping. 'I don't care at all . . .'

She bore down, guiding him into her, biting her lip to stop herself screaming in rapture.

'Oh God,' Matt yelled, pulling her towards him, kissing her as deeply as he was bucking inside her. 'Oh God, Deeley, I don't care either, I don't care . . .'

Grinding against him, finding the exact place where she wanted him, Deeley realized that she was going to come almost immediately; she kissed Matt back with everything she had, riding him as hard as she could, wanting to make him come too, crazy and fast, to have them explode together here, in the open air, the sunshine, under a canopy of tree branches, Matt's hands digging into her bottom, his tongue in her mouth. She started to cry from sheer, unadulterated happiness, coming and sobbing at the same time, feeling Matt jerking wildly under her, coming too.

'Oh God,' he said, shuddering with pleasure, tasting her tears on her mouth. 'You're crying – oh God, Deeley, are you all right? Did I hurt you?'

'No,' she managed to say, collapsing against him, her face buried in his neck, her mascara running, blackening the collar of his shirt where she'd ripped off a button tearing it open: *We can't go to a country house hotel, looking like this!* she thought with huge amusement. *I doubt they'd even let us check into a Travelodge . . .*

'I'm OK,' she mumbled against his shirt. 'In fact, I'm fantastic.'

'You are.' Matt's arms closed tightly around her as he kissed the top of her head. 'Know something? This is the best first date I've ever had in my life.' He stroked Deeley's hair as she hiccuped out tears and laughter. 'And I bloody well hope that it's the last one I ever have.'

BOOKS AND THE **CITY**

Home of the sassiest fiction in town!

If you enjoyed this book, you'll love...

978-1-84983-437-7	Divas	Rebecca Chance	£6.99
978-1-84739-396-8	Bad Girls	Rebecca Chance	£7.99
978-1-84739-852-9	Daughters of Fortune	Tara Hyland	£6.99
978-1-84739-626-6	Girl on the Run	Jane Costello	£6.99
978-1-84983-126-0	Baby Be Mine	Paige Toon	£6.99
978-1-84983-400-1	Good In Bed	Jennifer Weiner	£7.99
978-1-84983-203-8	An Autumn Crush	Milly Johnson	£6.99

For exclusive author interviews, features and competitions log onto
www.booksandthecity.co.uk